The Matchmaker Meets Her Match

MATCHMAKING MISCHIEF MAKERS, BOOK 3

BEVERLEY OAKLEY

© Copyright 2026 by Beverley Oakley
Text by Beverley Oakley
Cover by The Swoonies – theswoonies.com

Dragonblade Publishing, Inc. is an imprint of Kathryn Le Veque Novels, Inc.
P.O. Box 23
Moreno Valley, CA 92556
ceo@dragonbladepublishing.com

Produced in the United States of America

First Edition February 2026
Trade Paperback Edition

Reproduction of any kind except where it pertains to short quotes in relation to advertising or promotion is strictly prohibited.

All Rights Reserved.

The characters and events portrayed in this book are fictitious. Any similarity to real persons, living or dead, is purely coincidental and not intended by the author.

AI Statement: No AI or ghostwriting was used in the creation of this story, or any story, published by Dragonblade Publishing. All text, structure, content, ideas, and concept are 100% human generated solely by the author whose name appears on the cover. It is prohibited to use this material, or any copyrighted material, for AI engine training.

ARE YOU SIGNED UP FOR DRAGONBLADE'S BLOG?

You'll get the latest news and information on exclusive giveaways, exclusive excerpts, coming releases, sales, free books, cover reveals and more.

Check out our complete list of authors, too!

No spam, no junk. That's a promise!

Sign Up Here
www.dragonbladepublishing.com

Dearest Reader;

Thank you for your support of a small press. At Dragonblade Publishing, we strive to bring you the highest quality Historical Romance from some of the best authors in the business. Without your support, there is no 'us', so we sincerely hope you adore these stories and find some new favorite authors along the way.

Happy Reading!

CEO, Dragonblade Publishing

ADDITIONAL DRAGONBLADE BOOKS BY
AUTHOR BEVERLEY OAKLEY

Matchmaking Mischief Makers
War of the Wedding Wagers (Book 1)
Fortune Favors the Frivolous (Book 2)
The Matchmaker Meets Her Match (Book 3)

Chapter One

LADY EUGENIA TOWNSEND tipped her face to Venice's clear winter light—so unlike London's gray murk at this time of year—and allowed herself the radical indulgence of being happy.

Freedom at last. After years of being comfortably independent yet thoroughly overmanaged by her formidable friend Lady Pendleton, she had let other people button up her life. (Lady Pendleton, thank heaven, was presently buttoning up someone else's.) Now, at last, she was mistress of her own destiny.

"Eugenia! Your parasol! Your nose is already turning crimson!"

Eugenia sighed and turned. Miss Catherine Bentley—her younger chaperone by a decade—lowered herself into the cane chair opposite with the unruffled elegance of a duchess (which she most definitely was not). Yes, Catherine was the price of these precious months in Venice with Lord Thornton: part companion, part social barometer, always pontificating precisely what Eugenia ought—or ought not—to be doing.

Steeling herself to respond with quiet restraint, Eugenia smiled and said, "Ah, Catherine, I fear the battle is lost. I am an old woman already."

An old woman definitely not in need of a chaperone, she added inwardly, irritation pricking as she spied Thornton, his tall frame silhouetted against the opulent interior of the rented palazzo that had been home to their assorted band of English travelers for some months.

As ever, her heart attempted a youthful somersault at the sight of him—salt-and-pepper hair, broad shouldered, and beautifully improved by the Italian light. At her age, somersaults ought to have been relegated to the distant past. Yet Thornton had the peculiar effect of making her feel as hopeful and agile as any schoolroom miss.

His physique, alas, continued to draw admiring glances from ladies far younger than Eugenia—a fact Catherine had taken to pointing out with increasing frequency. And it was Thornton who had insisted that Catherine—the sister of his late wife—should accompany them.

"I thought I might find you ladies with your easels and paints, closeted in the water salon," Lord Thornton remarked, taking a seat.

"The thought occurred to me, but I was too enraptured by the view to bestir myself," said Eugenia. She turned back to the sun glinting on the waterway, its elegant backdrop of weathered palazzos rising from the canal like ancient sentinels. "Perhaps it defies being captured. I daresay even Turner himself would struggle to paint that precise shade of blue where the canal meets the lagoon."

Catherine leaned in toward Thornton's elbow with a little rustle of disapproval. "Oh, you and all your talk of painters! Why don't we visit the casino instead?" Though she pretended impeccable respectability, Catherine was not one for scholarly pursuits, preferring the glittering social whirl of Venetian society.

"Or perhaps a ride on a gondola, given the magnificence of the weather," said Thornton, subtly shifting away from her. "In fact, I took the liberty of ordering a gondolier after Mr. Rothbury suggested it, as he was hurrying off to Count Morosini, who grows ever more demanding for his Italian translations."

Catherine craned her neck at a shout from the canal below.

"Perhaps that is the gondolier already? Goodness, Thornton, no warning? Of course, we ladies must change." Her tone suggested that Thornton ought to have consulted her first—as though she, rather than Eugenia, were the principal lady of their little Venetian party.

Eugenia twisted slightly to watch as a sleek black gondola with elegant gold trim approached the water entrance of their palazzo, the gondolier's calls echoing off the ancient facades that lined the canal.

"I didn't request a gondola until this evening," Thornton said, rising and joining Eugenia, who had gone to stand at the balustrade.

The boat glided to a stop at the water steps beneath their balcony, two figures now standing ready to disembark. One, dressed in the height of English fashion, tilted her parasol against the late afternoon sun, obscuring her face as the older woman beside her paid the gondolier.

And then, as the younger woman was helped onto dry land, first her golden hair, then her young familiar face came into view. Eugenia gasped, her gloved hand flying to her mouth. "Good heavens! If I'm not mistaken—"

"Indeed, you're not! That's Miss Playford," Thornton cut in, clearly as surprised as Eugenia. "But what on earth is she doing in Venice?"

"On her marriage tour, perhaps?" suggested Catherine, her tone sharpening with interest as she joined them.

"I believe I would have heard if that were the case," said Eugenia.

"As yes, she was betrothed to Lord Windermere, then came into money and had the sense God gives a sparrow to throw him over." Catherine's tone crackled with disapproval. "The sheets called her the Unexpected Heiress. Or Unlikely. I forget which adjective. Alone in Venice? Brave. Or reckless."

Eugenia glanced between Catherine and Thornton. He was holding his tongue, though Eugenia knew he'd held a soft spot for

Miss Playford when he'd first met her at Lady Pendleton's "Ghostly Gathering" a few years before. The girl had been a quiet, frightened thing then, straight out of the schoolroom and overshadowed by her domineering aunt.

So, Miss Playford, England's newest heiress, was here in Venice. Alone.

And Eugenia would offer her every kindness, for it was due to Eugenia's audacious wager regarding Miss Playford's marital conquests the year before that had led to Eugenia being in Italy in the first place.

Thank the Lord that the "good sense of a sparrow"—as Catherine put it—had prevailed and Miss Playford had escaped the clutches of that villainous fortune hunter—and kidnapper—Lord Windermere.

"So, Miss Playford has come to conquer Venice." It seemed that Catherine was determined to remain unimpressed by Miss Playford's good qualities: her bravery and her beauty.

To Eugenia's mind, the young woman's skin appeared even more luminescent than she remembered, and there was an almost ethereal cast to her features. The frightened and timid demeanor that had distinguished her while she had been under her Aunt Pike's guardianship back in London was no longer in evidence. In its place was a charming poise with a touch of vulnerability that tugged at Eugenia's soft heart.

"I would imagine Miss Playford is here to make up for her lack of freedom while in her aunt's care. Neither the aunt nor Lord Windermere was kind to her."

She cast a pointed glance at Thornton, silently urging him to speak up on the girl's behalf.

"She is a charming young lady. I'm sure you will like her very much, Catherine," Thornton finally said, catching Eugenia's meaning. "And her presence here will no doubt augment our enjoyment. She has likely heard that this is where the best of her English countrymen stay when in Venice."

This elicited no more than a raised eyebrow from Catherine.

Eugenia wondered if she knew the full story of Lord Windermere's disgraceful attempts at manipulation in trying to force Miss Playford to become his wife before, burned by the scandal—which had been exposed by their own dear Mr. Rothbury—he had quit England, no doubt to try to find himself another heiress given his own parlous finances.

Mr. Rothbury! With a start, Eugenia wondered if the young man knew that Miss Playford was in Venice.

Oblivious to the discussion of which she was front and center, Miss Playford now paused on the marble steps leading up to the palazzo entrance, closing her parasol with a delicate snap that carried across the water.

"She deserves every penny and more after what that scoundrel put her through," Eugenia said firmly. "Miss Playford is a woman of impeccable character and considerable intelligence," she went on, more forcefully for Catherine's benefit. "I've seldom met a young lady with such quiet dignity in the face of adversity."

A servant appeared at the balcony doorway, bowing, as he said, "My lord and ladies, a Miss Venetia Playford has arrived and inquires whether Lady Eugenia Townsend is at home."

"Please tell her I'd be delighted to receive her!" Eugenia exclaimed. "And have refreshments brought to the water salon."

Catherine's expression tightened as the servant withdrew. "What a remarkable coincidence that she should appear at the very palazzo where we are staying." She hesitated, adding, "I wonder if she wants something."

"Nonsense," Eugenia replied, sweeping past her toward the door with a rustle of silk skirts. "The girl couldn't possibly have known we were here. I wrote to precious few people about our specific accommodations."

The water salon—so named for its proximity to the canal and the way light reflected off the water to create shimmering patterns on its ceiling—was the palazzo's most extraordinary room. Tall windows offered uninterrupted views of the canal, while ornate mirrors on the opposite wall doubled the impression of light and space.

Within minutes, Venetia Playford stood by one of the windows, and Eugenia was struck once again by how much more beautiful she was than she remembered. Where many ladies might have appeared travel worn after navigating Venice's waterways, Venetia looked as fresh and composed as if she were attending an afternoon tea in Mayfair.

"Lady Townsend!" their young visitor exclaimed, her face lighting up with pleasure. "I can scarcely believe my good fortune in finding you still here."

"My dear Miss Playford," Eugenia replied warmly, crossing the room to take the younger woman's hands in hers. "What an unexpected delight! I had no forewarning that you were traveling to Venice."

"It was rather a sudden decision," Venetia admitted, her smile dimming slightly. "After everything that happened in London, there came a point where I suddenly found myself in desperate need of new surroundings. And I succumbed to impulsiveness."

Eugenia nodded. "Allow me to introduce Miss Catherine Bentley, Lord Thornton's sister-in-law, who has kindly agreed to act as our companion for this journey. And, of course, you remember Lord Thornton."

Once pleasantries were exchanged, Venetia's lady's maid, Mollie, dispatched, and they were seated with tea and delicate Venetian biscuits, Eugenia turned to their unexpected guest.

"You must tell us everything, my dear. How long have you been in Venice? Where are you staying? And are you traveling alone?" This last question carried a note of concern, for even a woman of independent means would find solo travel challenging, particularly in a foreign city where Italian customs differed so markedly from English.

"I arrived yesterday," Venetia replied, setting her teacup down. "I'm staying not far from the Piazza San Marco. And yes, I am alone, save for my lady's maid." She hesitated, her gaze dropping momentarily to her teacup. "I thought the events of last season would be forgotten more quickly than they have."

"Yet I am surprised you chose Venice," Thornton remarked. "Given its reputation as a playground for characters as disreputable as any in London."

Venetia's smile was tinged with irony. "Precisely why I chose it, my lord. In London, I am 'that poor Miss Playford' or, worse, 'the heiress who was entangled with Lord Windermere.' Here, I am simply another English traveler, anonymous among the crowds that fill the Piazza San Marco each day."

"Well, you're among friends now," Eugenia said brightly. "And you must join us for dinner this evening."

"That is very kind of you. I would be delighted." Venetia leaned back in her chair and closed her eyes briefly.

"Excuse me, ladies. Lord Thornton." Edward Rothbury appeared in the doorway, tall and ink smudged, but handsome in that earnest, appealing way, thought Eugenia as she watched the greeting between the pair.

It promised to be very illuminating.

"Miss Playford," he managed, with a bow that was a touch too low.

"Mr. Rothbury," she returned, with a smile a touch too bright.

They were, Eugenia decided happily, perfectly matched.

A biscuit chose that moment to shed a shower of sugar over Venetia's lap. She laughed—a small, delightful sound—as she brushed it away, and the air lightened.

Smiling, Eugenia surveyed the pair.

There was no doubt that Mr. Rothbury was a handsome man. His features were strong rather than classically handsome, with intelligent eyes that surveyed the room briefly before returning, with that same look of shocked wonder, to Venetia.

For a moment, all eyes were on the young couple, both of whom now, with the silence that followed, appeared unable to speak.

"Miss Playford," Mr. Rothbury finally said, his voice carefully controlled though Eugenia detected a slight tremor. "I... did not expect to see you in Venice." He glanced at Eugenia with a hint of accusation. "You made no mention of the fact we would be so honored." Then he flushed slightly, as if aware he had revealed too much.

"I did not tell anyone I was coming," Venetia said, her own voice steadier than her pallor would suggest. "In fact, I was quite sure Lady Townsend would no longer be in Venice." She swallowed visibly. "I certainly never expected to see you here, Mr. Rothbury. What an extraordinary coincidence!"

Eugenia reached across the settee to place a reassuring hand on Venetia's forearm, feeling the young woman's tension beneath the fine silk of her gown. She tried again to read the expressions on both young faces. The pair's last meeting had, after all, been fraught and dramatic.

It had been nearly ten months since Mr. Rothbury had plunged Eugenia's carefully orchestrated comet-viewing event into turmoil when he had arrived, travel-stained and breathless, with the news that penniless Venetia had been named the unexpected beneficiary of the richest man in Derbyshire. The timing could not have been more dramatic—or more fortuitous—for at the time, penniless Venetia had been on the verge of being all but forced to wed sly, demanding Lord Windermere.

Eugenia wondered if Miss Playford had shown sufficient gratitude toward Mr. Rothbury for his intervention. Had she even had time to do so before she'd been spirited away while her former fiancé, Henry Ashton, had ascended in the balloon in which he'd asked his childhood sweetheart, Caroline, to instead become his wife? Eugenia remembered that Caroline had been Venetia's best friend and wondered if the sudden switching of allegiances might have caused ill feeling between the young ladies.

With a sinking heart and a healthy dose of self-recrimination, Eugenia realized, as she observed the charged silence between the two young people, that there was still so much unresolved.

And that she was, perhaps, to blame for not following through on her matchmaking instincts sooner.

"We were still digesting Miss Playford's arrival, for she has been here barely five minutes, Mr. Rothbury," Eugenia said, breaking the silence.

She did not miss the way Venetia looked down at her slippers, a becoming blush spreading across her cheeks, nor the awkwardness Mr. Rothbury displayed when his usual unforced friendliness deserted him, leaving him uncharacteristically tongue-tied.

Eugenia felt a rush of compassion.

These two young people had coincidentally entered her orbit… or was it coincidence?

No, perhaps it was divine intervention, she thought, as she was visited by a delicious impulse. Twice, she had wagered Thornton, the coming together of seemingly impossible unions.

This would be just one more. Suddenly, Eugenia felt ten years younger.

"Mr. Rothbury, we'd be delighted if you'd join us for dinner this evening," she said, seizing the opportunity. She felt confident of success. Already the excitement of joining two such worthy individuals was seeping through her marrow like the warmth of a good brandy. "Miss Playford has just accepted our invitation, and we'd be delighted to include you as well for a dinner of famous Venice squid risotto, if you were so inclined."

She waited expectantly. She knew Mr. Rothbury well now, for he'd been a resident at the palazzo for many months, often joining them for meals when his translation work permitted. And it appeared he lacked society other than the staid, elderly group that, she admitted ruefully, included herself.

"You are kind, Lady Townsend, but Count Morosini is eager to have Chapter Four of *Ivanhoe* before week's end." He lifted ink-stained fingers in evidence. "If I dine with you, I shall translate until dawn; if I begin now, I may sleep by midnight. Venice has so many temptations—squid risotto among them—but sadly I cannot be drawn."

He looked at Venetia. "I am glad you are in Venice, Miss Playford."

His smile was genuine and kind. Then he bowed himself away.

Eugenia was disappointed. But when she saw that Miss Playford's disappointment clearly exceeded her own, she was filled with hope.

Yes, she thought with satisfaction, this matchmaking mission was going to be much easier than her previous ones.

HALF AN HOUR later, Eugenia was again gazing out at the Grand Canal in the water salon, seated opposite Thornton.

"I should dress for dinner," she said, making no attempt to rise. "Miss Playford will join us soon."

"But not Mr. Rothbury, and for that reason the excitement has drained from the evening," Thornton surmised, raising an eyebrow. He leaned back, regarding his old friend with knowing eyes. "You wish to unite our worthy couple, but have you considered that the divide between them is greater than it ever was?"

Eugenia had once orchestrated a whole comet viewing, only for Mr. Rothbury to turn up with last-minute intelligence that blew every plan sky-high—Lord Windermere's most of all. Clearly, the universe had found its favorite partner in mischief in her.

Miss Playford had been sent here by some divine intervention for one reason only: so that she, Eugenia, could orchestrate her happily ever after.

"Mr. Rothbury and Miss Playford were meant for each other," she said decidedly.

"My dear Eugenia, it matters not one jot how worthy Rothbury is; he is penniless—just as Miss Playford once was. But as Miss Playford is now an heiress, you must accept that they are as out of reach of one another as they ever were. No," he added, his tone decided, "Mr. Rothbury sees matters as they stand, and I applaud his good sense in choosing to withdraw gracefully before you begin meddling, trying to achieve an outcome that will never come to pass."

Eugenia pushed back her shoulders. "Do you think that hearts do not have their own way of triumphing above such pecuniary considerations? I believe Mr. Rothbury was on the point of offering for Miss Playford a year ago but was held back by honor when she suddenly became an heiress. But she holds his heart. I saw it on his face."

Thornton smiled indulgently. "It was not so long ago, Eugenia, that you were certain our penniless Miss Playford was the ideal marriage partner for young Henry Ashton. You helped push them together before their real feelings were made known, and Henry pledged his troth to Caroline. You had to concede you were wrong in that instance, and I believe you are wrong if you believe Miss Playford and Mr. Rothbury are suited."

"Well, in pushing for a match between Miss Playford and Henry, I've come to know the young lady's temperament much better as a result," Eugenia replied, trying not to sound defensive. "And she has changed greatly in that money has given her safety and confidence... but it has not changed the way her heart beats. Believe me, Thornton, I saw real hope and feeling in her eyes when she beheld Mr. Rothbury. He was like a haven to her. Besides, you can't forget that he was the one who rescued her from being whisked off unwillingly by Lord Windermere."

"Only by delivering—in a timely fashion—the unassailable fact that she had come into money. He was the messenger only," Thornton countered, his eyes twinkling with the familiar light of friendly debate.

Eugenia allowed herself an exasperated sigh. "You speak as if hearts do not hold sway over heads, and that is not true. No,

Thornton, you are wrong. The pair of them would make each other very happy—"

"I don't discount that. But at the very least, Rothbury's pride will stand in the way. To be considered a fortune hunter by offering for Miss Playford is more than his honor will bear."

"…and if you will humor me one more time, I will stake my *Persephone* on it," said Eugenia.

Thornton's eyes danced. "Madam, you have already won your magnificent painting—"

"And in truth, you won it back," Eugenia said serenely. "This is my opportunity to have it on my wall where it belongs."

He laughed. "Very well. If love triumphs, the painting will be hung where it belongs, even if temporarily."

"Nothing about love is temporary," Eugenia said, with an arch look.

Chapter Two

"Would miss like the blue silk or the cream muslin this evening?" asked Mollie, displaying both lovely creations.

Venetia hesitated. The blue suggested regal confidence. The cream was more girlish but charming and safe.

She ran a finger over the blue's embroidery. Imagine—such gowns in her wardrobe were now as commonplace as the browns and grays she'd once thought permanent.

"The sapphire would flatter you, miss," Mollie ventured, "and it won't show when a gondolier splashes."

Venetia smiled despite herself. "How practical of you."

"I'm practical and devoted to seeing you appear at your best, miss." Mollie smiled, then hesitated before adding, "You're very brave, miss."

Venetia swallowed, smiling her thanks as she recalled the reason she was here. Following her unexpected elevation to heiress, London had brought nothing but stress and anxiety.

The final straw had been the Marchioness of Hartley—audible for three rooms—who'd declared Venetia "too provincial to keep a fortune a twelvemonth." Venetia had thought herself heroic by not dropping her teacup. Then she'd slipped away on the next packet to try to find the only person who'd ever offered genuine kindness: Lady Townsend.

And within mere minutes of locating that good lady, she'd come face to face with the one man who set her heart racing with the most improper palpitations: Mr. Edward Rothbury.

What were the odds? Venice contained approximately 60,000 people, and she'd walked straight into the one person she most hoped—and most feared—to see.

But he'd made it abundantly clear that whatever regard he might once have held for her was now extinguished. At first, she'd imagined she'd glimpsed a flash of genuine delight illuminating his features when his eyes met hers across Lady Townsend's water salon.

He'd looked pleased—and then very determinedly he'd chosen not to join them for dinner. Since then, his manners had been scrupulous, his distance exemplary, and his timing—whenever she'd entered a room during the two days since she'd taken up residence there—remarkably educational.

"The blue, I think," Venetia said with sudden decisiveness. If Mr. Rothbury was determined to treat her with such cool detachment, she would at least present herself to her utmost advantage while enduring it. "And the sapphire pendant that matches. The one with the diamond surround."

Mollie lowered her voice. "Begging your pardon, miss, but after what befell the Countess Barbarigo's rubies… they say there's a thief about who fancies the English style of valuables."

"Then he shall be disappointed," Venetia said. "We won't let a rumor rearrange our wardrobe."

Mollie pursed her lips, failing to hide a spark of admiration. "Very good, miss. You don't let nothing scare you, do you?"

Smiling, she began to arrange her mistress's hair in the latest Parisian style while Venetia's thoughts returned to Mr. Rothbury. What occupation claimed his attention at this very moment? Working on his translations, no doubt, his brow furrowed in concentration as he bent over ancient texts in the flickering candlelight of his chamber.

She recalled with painful clarity his arrival on horseback a year ago, just as Lord Windermere was about to seal her fate by forcing her into Lady Townsend's hot-air balloon. For one breathless, heart-stopping moment, she'd thought he'd come for her—not as a messenger of news, but as a man staking his claim. Then he'd announced her inheritance, and everything had changed in an instant.

Was that why he maintained such distance now? Did he believe her character fundamentally altered by her newfound wealth? Or was it his own pride that erected an insurmountable barrier between them?

Pride. Honor. Noble restraint. Why must men make everything so unnecessarily complicated?

"There, miss," Mollie said, securing the final pin in Venetia's elaborate coiffure with a flourish. "You look a proper picture. Like one of them fine ladies in the paintings at the Doge's Palace."

Venetia studied her reflection in the ornate mirror, scarcely recognizing the elegant young woman who gazed back at her with uncertain eyes. How peculiar that outward transformation could occur with such rapidity, while inwardly she remained the same diffident girl who'd trembled beneath her aunt's dissatisfied scrutiny.

"Thank you, Mollie," she said softly. "That will be all for now."

She rose, smoothing the silk of her gown with gloved hands. Mr. Rothbury was merely one gentleman among many in this city of romance and intrigue.

Perhaps it was time to look forward rather than backward. To embrace the liberty her fortune had bestowed and seek happiness on her own terms, in this city where the very air seemed perfumed with possibility.

EDWARD DREW THE candelabra closer. The Conte Morosini's obsession with the novels of Sir Walter Scott seemed to have gathered steam since Edward's first few translated chapters had made it into his hands.

He tried to force himself to concentrate on his work, but the memory of Miss Playford's smile was too distracting.

With a sigh, Edward rested his head in his hands, the Italian text momentarily forgotten. He was fatigued, certainly, but even more keenly, he was famished. And it was, he knew from experience, exceedingly difficult to render accurate translations when one's stomach demanded satisfaction with such persistent insistence.

The memory of Miss Playford—not as she appeared today in all her finery, but as he'd first known her, a quiet child with serious eyes and a gentle smile—rose unbidden in his mind. He'd been but fourteen to her eight, already preparing for his naval career while she played quietly with her dolls in the corner of her father's study during his visits, with his father, to Mr. Playford's estate. Even then, there had been something singular about her—a thoughtfulness beyond her years.

He remembered gifting her a small volume of fairy tales, illustrated with colored plates depicting knights and princesses. The radiance of her smile had warmed him, and, not having siblings, he'd thought of her often during his years at sea—wondering what had become of the solemn child with the luminous smile.

When fate had brought them together last year, he'd scarcely recognized her—though some essential quality remained unchanged beneath the weight of her aunt's oppression. And now, transformed once more by the magic of unexpected fortune…

Was she still, at her core, the same Venetia? Or had wealth corroded what had been most precious in her nature?

Edward shook his head sharply, forcing his attention back to the work before him. Such ruminations were fruitless and, worse still, entirely inappropriate. Miss Playford was now one of the wealthiest heiresses in England.

And he, by contrast, was a scholar of modest means, dependent upon his own industry for advancement.

The gulf between them had grown too vast to bridge—that much was indisputable. And yet…

Chapter Three

TWO DAYS LATER, Venetia had decided that Mr. Rothbury's avoidance would not spoil her Venetian sojourn—any more than a spot of rain spoils a sprigged muslin. She smiled dutifully through luncheon and dinner and even survived Miss Catherine Bentley's dissertation on Venetian arches. (Miss Bentley knew a great many arches, each more magnificent than the last.)

Lady Townsend, meanwhile, was clearly determined to ensure that Venetia expand her social horizons.

At the Contessa Barbarigo's rout, she'd introduced her to six eligible gentlemen of varying charm and solvency. Venetia had danced until her toes ached and her tongue felt tied in knots as she conversed in her mediocre—but rapidly improving—Italian.

Oh, she'd been studying hard.

Now, with a night's reflection, she'd nearly convinced herself that Mr. Rothbury's indifference need not cast a shadow over her visit to Venice.

Nearly. Almost. Not quite. But nearly.

She would follow Lady Townsend's unspoken advice and cast her net wider—ideally somewhere with less dancing requiring her to be on display—and more books.

The endless social whirl was not the answer. If her visit to Venice was to help her look further afield for love, she'd obviously made a wrong side step. She wanted a husband and children.

Wealth bought carriages and emeralds, not true love. She still wanted the old-fashioned things: a husband who liked her before he tallied up her accounts. And she wanted a nursery filled with laughter.

But perhaps she was going about it the wrong way.

Ensconced at the water-salon escritoire, her quill hovered over a sheet of creamy vellum. A drop of ink plopped onto the margin and made up her mind for her: She would write cheerfully to Caroline and keep the dramatic references of her favorite novelist, Mrs. Radcliffe, to a minimum. Venetia had kept her temperament under control for so many years now, she couldn't afford to let her guard down and spiral into the sometimes-extreme responses to matters beyond her control that had led Aunt Pike to incarcerate her in a dark cupboard for days.

"Venetia, am I interrupting a masterpiece?" Lady Townsend appeared in the doorway, looking elegant in a pale-blue pelisse. "Come and tell me about last night. I saw you were popular with many of the contessa's gentlemen guests, yet I gather none of them took your fancy." Her eyes twinkled as she added, "I wonder if that is because there was someone special—who was not there."

Oh dear. She knows.

Setting aside her half-written letter, Venetia rose and crossed to the comfortable settee where Lady Townsend had seated herself. Lord Thornton and Miss Bentley were not around, a small mercy, for there was something about Miss Bentley that made Venetia feel perpetually measured and found wanting.

And although she had no intention of admitting her infatuation with Mr. Rothbury, it was entirely possible that Lady Townsend's keen understanding of the human heart had already made the deduction.

"I enjoyed myself to a degree," Venetia admitted. "Certainly, I was mesmerized by my surroundings. And by the light reflecting off the water as I danced," she added. "Venice feels like a different planet to England. The way the palazzo's chandeliers cast their glow through those enormous windows onto the canal below created the most enchanting spectacle."

Lady Townsend hesitated, her eyes kind but sharp. "I saw you when you made your entrance. Were you looking for someone in particular?"

Venetia winced. "Was I so obvious? I'd hoped merely to appear confident and self-contained."

"Both highly commendable," Lady Townsend said. "I imagine recent experience has rendered you justifiably cautious in matters of the heart."

How precisely Lady Townsend had divined the truth of her situation. Venetia clasped her hands tightly in her lap, then, unable to contain her nervous energy, plucked at the fine fabric of her gown. "I half expect to discover Lord Windermere materializing from behind every ornate Venetian column," she admitted, a shudder running through her. "His determination to possess my fortune has left its imprint."

"But surely he presents no immediate danger?" Lady Townsend said, her tone comforting. "His disgraceful scheme was thoroughly exposed, and he now stands revealed as the fortune-hunting charlatan he truly is. His reputation in English society is irredeemably tarnished. You've escaped his machinations, my dear, and it's high time you set aside such fears and directed your attention toward discovering what will bring you genuine happiness." She smiled warmly. "I admire your bravery in removing yourself from London—and, more importantly, from your aunt's malign influence."

"Do you find Venice agreeable, then?" Venetia asked, not wishing to speak of her aunt. "It seems so very... foreign to English sensibilities. Yet you've remained here these eight months." Her fingers worried the silk. Fine stuff. Half a year's rent, for those less fortunate than herself. "I'm learning to enjoy beauty without apologizing for it," she said, half to Eugenia, half to herself.

"I find the contrast with England most refreshing," Lady Townsend replied, her gaze drifting to the window where sunlight danced on the rippling surface of the canal. "The quality of light here possesses a clarity one never encounters in London's perpetual haze. The very air seems imbued with potential." A secretive smile played about her lips. "And I confess I've come to value greatly the companionship I've found here."

"Miss Bentley is a wonderful repository of facts," Venetia said, assuming Lady Townsend referred to her female companion. "She introduced me to the Conte di Valmarana and three of his ancestors—at least, I think they were his ancestors; they were certainly on the walls. She also seemed to possess an exhaustive mental catalogue of every nobleman and noblewoman in attendance." Boldly, she added, "I wonder if she is perhaps looking to alter her status."

That came out more tartly than intended.

But the way Miss Bentley had gripped Venetia's arm with barely concealed eagerness when introducing her to the Conte di Valmarana—whose estate, Venetia knew, because Lord Thornton had told her, was in a state of genteel decay despite his exquisitely tailored attire—had been rather discomfiting. Was she trying to foist Venetia on some Venetian nobleman? Or find one for herself?

"I was not referring to Catherine," Lady Townsend said with a twist of her lips. "No, I refer to other friendships I've discovered in Venice, so that I don't miss England at all."

A brief silence fell between them, during which Venetia wondered whether she'd been overly hasty in fleeing London. For she could think of no one in Italy who would allow her to simply be quietly herself. Every nobleman to whom she'd been introduced had been flamboyantly garrulous.

She sighed. "At times, I do wonder if I acted with excessive impetuosity in coming to Venice. Do you think I ought to return to England?"

Lady Townsend lifted a brow. "After crossing half of Europe? My dear, you didn't come to Venice merely to retreat at the first onset of the blue devils."

"You do know why I came to Venice, don't you?"

"Venice is the city of love," Lady Townsend said as if it were the last word.

She reached across to pat Venetia's restless hand. "Your substantial fortune grants you a liberty that few women can claim—the freedom to travel where you wish, to choose your own path without bowing to the dictates of family or financial necessity. Yet great wealth brings its own form of isolation, as I've discovered through long experience."

"You've felt isolated, too?" Venetia asked, startled. "But surely that cannot be so! You receive invitations to every significant social event, and you're perpetually surrounded by friends and admirers."

"You refer to the individuals who seek my company?" Lady Townsend's smile held a shadow of melancholy. "I've discovered over many years that those who most assiduously cultivate one's acquaintance are often those of whom one should be most wary." She cleared her throat delicately before adding, "Particularly when one possesses a substantial fortune."

Venetia leaned forward. "Yet despite your wealth offering you such choices, you never married," she observed.

"Independence, however precious, doesn't entirely satisfy the longings of the heart."

Venetia cast a quick glance around the salon to ensure they remained alone before leaning closer still. "I want love," she said simply. "And I want children—a family of my own, bound by affection rather than obligation or financial necessity."

Her gaze darted to the canal beyond the window, where a gondola filled with laughing children glided past, their joyful voices carrying clearly through the open casement.

"The Italians are unembarrassed by happiness," Lady Townsend observed. "And it's what we should all strive for." She squeezed Venetia's hand warmly. "I'm delighted beyond measure to hear you express such natural desires. You were never destined for spinsterhood, my dear. Unlike me, you possess extraordinary beauty, natural vivacity, and genuine charm. I have no doubt you could capture any heart you set your sights upon."

Venetia blushed. And when she attempted to protest, the older woman dismissed her objections with a wave of her hand.

"Let us not engage in false modesty. I never possessed the sort of beauty that inspired men's admiration, my dear girl. I was acutely conscious of my deficiencies in that regard, and I allowed that awareness to foster a deplorable timidity in matters of the heart." Her tone softened. "I constructed walls around myself as protection against rejection, never realizing that in doing so, I was condemning myself to precisely the loneliness I most feared."

"You mean to say that you... deliberately closed your heart against the possibility of love?" Venetia asked.

"The gentleman I loved married one of my dearest friends," Eugenia said, almost lightly—as if she were reciting words well-rehearsed. "I mistook kindness for interest. I learned to be wary—to my detriment."

Venetia blinked. "Truly?" She could scarcely contain her astonishment. She'd long assumed that Lady Townsend, with her considerable fortune and secure footing on society's ladder, could have had her choice of husbands, had she wished to marry. "But surely you must have been obliged to fend off numerous fortune hunters over the years?"

"Oh, fortune hunters... I could pick them a mile away!" the older woman declared lightly. "I could see them calculating the artwork before they even looked at me. No, thankfully, none pursued me with the ruthless determination that Lord Windermere displayed in his pursuit of you. As for that gentleman," Lady Townsend went on, brighter, "reliable intelligence has him posted to Constantinople as an attaché. I hear he left a fortnight ago and will be gone for at least two years."

Venetia exhaled. "An attaché? As long as he's not attaching

himself to me, then I'm happy."

"You wish to marry? Excellent. Let us talk about that!" Lady Townsend clapped her hands. "You have everything requisite—looks, kindness, and—" she hesitated "—an unpredictable streak. I've seen signs of it, yes. Well, that, together with your courage, is a good start."

Lady Townsend's gaze drifted meaningfully toward the doorway of the water salon, which was suddenly filled by a tall figure.

Venetia knew that particular breadth of shoulder before her heart had time to behave. Mr. Rothbury bowed—slightly too low—and, in rising, she saw the edge of his cuff was again streaked with ink. His gaze flicked to Venetia, warmed—just for a breath—and then he recollected himself.

There. That warmth. I didn't imagine it, did I?

"Forgive the intrusion," he murmured, and retreated with the speed of a man who'd remembered an appointment with a dictionary, Venetia thought with despair.

Eugenia's smile turned positively conspiratorial. "My dear Venetia," she said, "I told you I could spot a fortune hunter a mile away—" she gripped Venetia's wrist and gave it a squeeze "—as well as I can spot a man in love."

Oh.

Chapter Four

EDWARD HAD COME to Venice the previous year determined to throw himself into Italian translating in order to rid his mind of impossible thoughts.

Thoughts like the way Miss Playford had looked at him when he'd ridden his black stallion into the crowd at Lady Townsend's Comet Viewing. The news he had brought had not only saved her from a life sentence as the wife of odious Lord Windermere, it had given her unimaginable freedom.

Freedom to find a husband worthy of her elevated status.

Not a man like himself.

Yet again, he told himself—firmly—that he was here in Conte Morosini's library to translate, not to be distracted by its beautiful surroundings or—more aptly—to twist his mind in knots over Miss Playford. Then his stomach, perfectly unhelpful, reminded him that admiration and twisting his mind in knots stimulated appetite.

He gave himself a mental shake. Heart matters would have to wait; Count Morosini's commas could not. Edward was proud of his work—his Italian mother had gifted him the music of the language; the count supplied everything else.

As he immersed himself in *Ivanhoe* in a library designed to uplift the soul with a window view of a fountain performing for his own entertainment, he'd finally stilled his restless mind when a small, delicate cough interrupted his battle with a tricky sentence.

Not the count—too airy for that. Possibly a maid? Another cough followed, a touch theatrical, as if someone were practicing being discovered.

"Oh dear, you look positively fearsome when you frown so," a feminine voice floated down from the shadowed gallery—in perfect English with a lilting Italian music to it.

He drew back, shocked, as he searched for the speaker. A child?

"Please don't inform my grandfather I said so," the voice added cheerfully. "He would confine me to my chambers, and I've been exceptionally well-behaved for nearly eleven minutes."

"Your grandfather is Count Morosini?" Edward rose.

"My only relative," came the reply—and a girl of eighteen or nineteen stepped into a shaft of sun, golden curls artfully arranged, and a pair of sparkling brown eyes that regarded him above a smile full of mischief. For one disorienting heartbeat, she was the echo of another golden head. Edward tried to banish his imagination before it performed any more tricks.

"Your grandfather is Count Morosini?" Edward repeated, concern rising to the fore. "He has made no mention of a granddaughter, though I have been visiting this palazzo for the better part of eight months."

"My grandfather prefers not to acknowledge my existence to those beyond our immediate household," said the young woman with a hint of a smile. "He harbors the antiquated notion that young ladies should remain invisible until they are formally presented to society."

Edward offered a respectful bow, belatedly recalling his manners. "Edward Rothbury, at your service, signorina. I have the honor of serving as translator to your esteemed grandfather."

"And I am Signorina Sofia Morosini," she replied. "A pleasure to make your acquaintance, Signor Rothbury. You are a hard worker. I have observed you over many days."

Edward regarded her with consternation. The thought of having shared this space—unchaperoned—with a young lady of quality, mere feet away yet entirely undetected, was profoundly inappropriate. If discovered, Edward's lucrative commission might be forfeit, along with his professional reputation.

"You cannot possibly have been present in this room during my previous visits?" he said, unable to keep the note of alarm from his voice.

"Frequently," she said, pleased. "I'm very quiet. Philosophers keep my secrets," she added, pointing to the gallery above. "They bore Grandpapa and they're out of your line of sight. Giulia—my good maid—hides my sketchbook behind them. We have an understanding."

"Good heavens!" Edward exclaimed. "I have never once detected your presence. I cannot conceive that my powers of observation have grown so lamentably dull."

The young woman laughed. "Do not reproach yourself, signor. I have become exceedingly adept at moving silently through this palazzo. One develops such skills when living under my grandfather's restrictive regime."

"You are an artist, then?" Edward inquired, striving to maintain a tone of friendly interest rather than betraying his concern.

"I aspire to be," Sofia responded. "Would you care to examine my work? I should value the opinion of an educated Englishman."

Before Edward could respond, Sofia began to ascend the delicate spiral staircase that led to the gallery. "Allow me to retrieve my current project," she called over her shoulder.

Edward cast a nervous glance toward the library door, half expecting the count to materialize despite his granddaughter's assurances.

His concern was interrupted by Sofia's musical laugh. "Truly, signor, you need not concern yourself with surprise visitors. The servants have strict instructions not to disturb you when you are engaged in your scholarly pursuits."

She returned with a canvas. The Grand Canal at sunset painted with tender light, lengthening shadows—employing a technique beyond her years, and a feeling beyond most people's.

"You look delighted."

"Yes, I do."

"Another thing. I had hoped you might assist me in a strictly mercantile matter," she said. "Do you know anyone who buys pictures? Or perhaps you…"

Edward blinked. "I—"

"I should very much like to keep it," she confessed, "but I am determined upon *escape* even more."

"Escape?"

"Grandpapa intends me for a gentleman of 'mature years,' which is another way of saying *old*. This particular gentleman admires my portrait." She shuddered delicately. "I prefer my freedom."

Edward opened his mouth to offer a sensible objection.

"Before you say anything," she rushed on, "I should warn you that if you refuse me, I shall be forced to—" she pressed the back of her hand to her brow "—announce to Grandpapa that you have been alone with me in his library every Tuesday and Thursday since Epiphany."

Edward stared.

Sofia dropped the hand and laughed. "I am teasing you, Signor Rothbury. If I told him, he would make you offer for me at once, and that would ruin *both* our plans."

Despite his alarm, Edward felt a surge of sympathy for the young woman's plight. Arranged marriages were still commonplace among the Venetian aristocracy, with considerations of wealth and social connection frequently outweighing the personal inclinations of the parties involved. "Surely your grandfather would not force you into a union against your wishes?" he ventured. "Such practices are considered archaic in England."

"Perhaps in your country," Sofia replied, "but they remain

depressingly common in mine. My grandfather has already accepted a substantial gift from this gentleman as a token of his intentions."

Edward shook his head. "I am sorry, signorina. But I fail to see how the sale of your paintings—"

"I require sufficient funds to escape Venice with the man I truly love," she interrupted, her eyes suddenly alight with fervor. "I have already sold two canvases through the discreet assistance of my maid's brother, who deals in art among the foreign visitors. With the proceeds from perhaps five more sales, Paolo and I shall have enough to travel to Florence, where his uncle has promised to help us."

Edward felt as though he had inadvertently stepped into a scene from one of the very romances he was engaged in translating—complete with a spirited heroine, a controlling patriarch, and a secret love affair.

Dangerous! The rational part of his mind recognized the impropriety of becoming entangled in such a domestic drama.

"I understand your predicament," he said carefully, "but I fear I cannot—"

She extended the canvas toward him with an entreating gesture. "Would you not prefer to assist two young people in securing their happiness through an honest exchange of value? My art for your assistance?"

The logic of her argument, combined with the genuine talent evident in the painting and her obvious passion for this unseen Paolo, began to erode Edward's resistance. What harm could there be in helping this spirited young woman escape a loveless marriage to a man likely old enough to be her father?

Watching him, Sofia added with remarkable insight, "Perhaps you yourself have experienced the frustration of loving someone whom circumstances have placed beyond your reach? Or the pain of maintaining silence when every fiber of your being cries out to declare itself?"

The words struck uncomfortably close to Edward's own

situation with regard to Venetia Playford. Had his feelings been so transparent that even this young stranger could divine them? Or was it merely a fortunate conjecture based on his age and unmarried state?

Sofia pressed her advantage. "All I ask is that you take this painting and attempt to sell it on my behalf. I have several more completed works that might interest potential buyers. If you could secure prices similar to what my previous paintings fetched, Paolo and I would soon have sufficient resources to begin our life together."

Edward was torn. The painting was genuinely excellent—worth considerably more than whatever modest sum she had previously received. And the thought of facilitating a union based on genuine affection rather than financial calculation appealed to the romantic sensibility he typically kept carefully concealed beneath his natural reserve.

However, his position would be tenuous if the count discovered his collusion.

Nevertheless, he heard himself say, "Very well," though a voice of caution continued to sound faintly in the back of his mind.

Chapter Five

A FORTNIGHT HAD elapsed since Venetia's arrival in Venice, and during that interval, her encounters with Mr. Rothbury had been little more than fleeting exchanges in the palazzo's grand entrance hall. He was too engaged with translating the works of Sir Walter Scott into Italian to spare a thought for Venetia, it would appear.

But she would make him attend to her—given the chance.

"*Ivanhoe* is my particular favorite among Sir Walter's works," Venetia told her elderly English friends, during a rare occasion that Mr. Rothbury was in attendance.

But although she saw his eyes flash with interest, he remained silent.

A fact which might have accounted for the change of direction taken by Lady Townsend and Lord Thornton in their apparent matchmaking efforts.

Had they given Mr. Rothbury up as a lost cause? Did they no longer believe his regard for her was either sincere or lasting?

Indeed, their sudden enthusiasm for introducing her to the most eligible gentlemen of Venice came to border on the excessive, she decided a week later.

"The Conte di Valmarana possesses extensive vineyards in the Veneto region, with an ancestral palazzo that boasts no fewer than twenty-seven reception rooms," Miss Bentley had informed her only the previous evening, steering Venetia toward a tall, elegantly attired gentleman who seemed far more interested in her altered status as an English heiress than with anything above her neckline.

Venetia had dutifully admired his cravat while he catalogued his property holdings with the enthusiasm most men reserved for discussing their favorite horses. Property holdings no doubt greatly in need of an injection of English funds.

Lady Townsend, not to be outdone, had then maneuvered her into the path of the charming but positively Methuselah-like Marchese di San Pietro. This gentleman owned half a small island in the lagoon, Lady Townsend had whispered breathlessly, as if this might compensate for the fact that he appeared to have been present at the island's original formation.

Even Lord Thornton had joined the campaign, though his contributions—a parade of earnest English gentlemen who blushed at her slightest smile—suggested he'd mistaken "eligible" for "terrified of women."

By week's end, Venetia had seriously considered compiling a ledger: *Suitors Met, Reception Rooms Owned*, and *Apparent Interest in My Actual Personality* (this column remained depressingly blank).

The social whirl continued.

Several days later, she'd been momentarily charmed by the enthusiastic discourse of Signor Baretti (whose family, she had been informed, owned extensive shipping interests throughout the Mediterranean) and intrigued by the smoldering glances of the handsome Conte Grimani, Venetia still found Mr. Rothbury's measured responses and thoughtful observations vastly more to her taste.

Now, unexpectedly, Mr. Rothbury had joined their English friends for tea in the water salon, and was saying, "*Ivanhoe* is indeed a remarkable work. I've developed an even greater appreciation for its nuances while translating it for Count Morosini."

His voice sent an involuntary shiver down Venetia's spine. She wished he'd look at her.

"Curiously enough, it's also the count's granddaughter's favorite among all Sir Walter's novels."

How ungratifying.

"Which constitutes yet another point of similarity between you and that young lady," Mr. Rothbury continued, apparently oblivious to the sudden chill in the room that only Venetia seemed to feel. "For, like you, she has golden hair and a daintiness about her that quite brings you to mind."

Venetia's teacup paused halfway to her lips. Was he truly comparing her to another woman? At tea? Had the man learned nothing about self-preservation during his naval career?

"I wonder if you've had occasion to make her acquaintance since her recent introduction to society?" He leaned forward earnestly. "Though I understand her movements are rather strictly circumscribed by her grandfather's antiquated notions of propriety."

"How terribly unfortunate for her," Venetia replied through gritted teeth. "And what glorious weather we've been having, have we not?"

Mr. Rothbury, demonstrating either remarkable courage or remarkable obtuseness, sailed directly past this conversational lifeboat.

"Young ladies in this country aren't permitted the independence accorded to their English counterparts—or so Signorina Morosini informs me." His gaze met Venetia's with warmth that would have been delightful had he not just spent the last two minutes rhapsodizing about another woman's hair. "You, Miss Playford, being familiar with restrictive guardianship, might appreciate the comparison. Though your circumstances have happily altered."

Yes, thank you for that reminder, Venetia thought, her smile now requiring considerable muscular effort to maintain.

"I mention the signorina only because she bears such a striking resemblance to you in both appearance and spirit."

Venetia wondered if it would be terribly improper to dump her tea over his head. "Really?" She managed to turn the gritting of her teeth into a smile.

"As we are among trusted friends, I would request your discretion in this matter." Mr. Rothbury leaned forward even more, lowering his voice to a confidential murmur that necessitated Venetia inclining closer to hear him. "But past experience has demonstrated your sympathy toward young ladies subjected to oppressive authority, and I have, in fact, found myself in a position where I might be able to render assistance—if delicately managed."

Venetia only realized she'd been holding her breath when her lungs began to protest, compelling her to exhale discreetly. The attentiveness in Mr. Rothbury's manner, directed toward herself after days of apparent indifference, was as intoxicating as it was perplexing.

But was his interest centered on Venetia—or this Italian signorina who supposedly resembled her?

Nevertheless, unwilling to appear unsympathetic to the plight of another young woman, particularly one in circumstances reminiscent of her own former situation, Venetia adopted an expression of concerned interest. "Pray tell me, Mr. Rothbury, what assistance might be rendered to this Signorina Morosini since you seem so concerned about her?"

Mr. Rothbury reached into the capacious leather satchel he carried for his translation materials and withdrew a sheet of heavy vellum, which he carefully positioned in the center of the table, prompting exclamations of interest from the assembled company.

"Good heavens, I recognize the Campanile and Doge's Palace!" exclaimed Miss Bentley. "What an exquisitely rendered scene! Surely this is the work of a master. Did the count himself execute this piece?"

"His granddaughter, Signorina Sofia Morosini, is the artist," Mr. Rothbury declared, leaning back in his chair and regarding the painting with an expression of such proprietary pride that Venetia experienced another unwelcome pang of envy. "She seeks a patron or purchaser for her work."

Venetia could not deny the exceptional quality of the painting. The artist had captured not merely the architectural splendor of the Venetian landmarks but also the particular quality of light that suffused the city at sunset, lending the scene an almost ethereal beauty. The technical skill displayed was remarkable, particularly if the artist was, as Venetia surmised, not much beyond her own age.

"This demonstrates extraordinary talent," Lady Townsend observed, echoing Venetia's private assessment. "The command of perspective and the handling of light are quite remarkable. I should be delighted to purchase this piece if the young lady wishes to part with it. It would make a splendid addition to my collection." She smiled at Lord Thornton before adding, "Perhaps beside my beloved *Persephone*."

"It may be obliged to replace your *Persephone*, in fact," Lord Thornton rejoined with a cryptic half smile before returning his attention to Mr. Rothbury. "Have you assumed the role of art dealer for the young lady, or might there be a more... personal interest in her circumstances?"

Venetia tensed as she awaited Mr. Rothbury's response, noting the heightened color that suffused his features as he opened his mouth to reply.

Before Mr. Rothbury could respond, one of the palazzo's liveried servants appeared at the doorway. "Signoras and signors," the man announced with a bow, "Captain Teodoro Rizzi of the Venetian Guardia requests an audience on a matter of some urgency."

The small gathering exchanged puzzled glances as the servant stepped aside and Captain Rizzi swept into the room. His midnight-blue uniform gleamed with enough silver buttons and epaulettes to stock a small jewelry shop.

"I must beg your indulgence for this intrusion," he began in heavily accented English, executing a bow so low, Venetia feared he might not be able to straighten again. "I am investigating a matter wherein certain details, perhaps deemed inconsequential by those who observed them, might prove invaluable to the satisfactory furtherance and, potentially, resolution of my inquiry."

Venetia tried not to giggle at his pomposity before remembering that she was hardly one to judge another on his linguistic abilities.

"You have attended several social gatherings over the past three weeks," Captain Rizzi continued, his gaze moving from one face to another with unsettling intensity. "During these events, a series of unconscionable thefts have occurred."

"A thief!" Miss Bentley gasped, her hand flying to the modest pearl choker around her throat as if the criminal might materialize and snatch it that very moment. "How dreadful!"

"Indeed, signora. The situation is particularly distressing for the Contessa di Barbarigo." Captain Rizzi paused. "Two nights past, during her musicale, she was relieved of a pair of emerald earrings and matching emerald pendant. A wedding gift from her late husband."

With a flourish, he produced a small silver case from his uniform coat, extracting several calling cards embossed with the insignia of the guardia. "I would be most grateful if you would report any observations that might assist our investigation," he added, placing the cards on the center of the table.

Murmurs of concern filled the room.

"The perpetrator will face the full severity of Venetian justice when apprehended." His expression became one of grim determination. "I intend to see this individual consigned to our most inhospitable prison cell before the month concludes."

With a final bow, Captain Rizzi withdrew.

A moment of silence followed, broken by Miss Bentley launching into the sort of enthusiastic speculation usually reserved for the most scandalous gossip.

"The Marchese di Falconi's footman had a most furtive manner," Lady Townsend declared, warming to her new role as amateur investigator. "I observed him lingering near the ladies' withdrawing room."

"The Austrian diplomat's wife—the Baroness von something—mentioned her own concerns," Miss Bentley countered, clearly unwilling to let Lady Townsend claim all the sleuthing glory.

While the two ladies competed to identify the most suspicious characters they'd encountered—a contest that was growing more creative by the minute—Mr. Rothbury turned to Venetia, his expression softening as his gaze settled on the sapphire pendant at her throat.

"You should exercise particular caution, Miss Playford," he said quietly. "That pendant would tempt someone with larcenous intent." Then his voice warmed. "Though it pleases me greatly to see you in circumstances that permit such indulgences. I recall how, even as a child, you had discerning taste—adorning your dolls in miniature finery."

Venetia's irritation about the golden-haired signorina evaporated in an instant. "You truly remember such details? I was only eight years old."

"I remember more than that." His smile was gentle. "Your parents' fondness for each other. Their pride in you. My father, who served as your father's land steward, remarked upon it frequently."

The warmth of this unexpected gift—these preserved memories of her beloved parents—wrapped around Venetia's heart. She might have continued the conversation indefinitely if Miss Bentley hadn't interrupted with all the subtlety of Captain Rizzi making an entrance.

"Venetia, you should wear paste replicas instead of genuine gemstones," she announced. "Far safer, given what we've just learned."

"But considerably less satisfying." Venetia touched her pendant. "My aunt prohibited any adornment, deeming it 'unsuitable for a girl of my station'—by which she meant my dependence on her grudging charity. I won't apologize for enjoying my changed circumstances. I'll simply be vigilant."

"As indeed we all must," Lady Townsend said with a delicate shudder. "One cannot determine with certainty whom to trust."

"I have found that complete trust is a luxury one can ill afford," Miss Bentley pronounced.

"You maintain exceptionally exacting standards, Miss Bentley," Venetia replied sweetly—a phrase that could be taken as either compliment or gentle mockery.

The conversation drifted to safer topics, but Venetia remained acutely aware of Mr. Rothbury across the table. Occasionally their eyes met, and in those brief moments, something unspoken passed between them—she was sure of it.

When the gathering finally dispersed, Mr. Rothbury paused beside her chair. He seemed to have been working up courage, which Venetia couldn't decide if she found endearing or exhilarating.

"Perhaps we could meet tomorrow afternoon, Miss Playford? There's a matter I should like to discuss." He glanced at her ever-present companions. "Perhaps a walk along the canal? Perhaps a gondola ride? With your lady's maid, naturally."

Venetia's heart performed contortions that would have scandalized her former aunt. "I should be delighted, Mr. Rothbury."

His smile—warm and properly unguarded for the first time since their reunion—accompanied his bow. "Until tomorrow, then."

Tomorrow. How could she possibly wait until tomorrow? What did he wish to discuss? Her pulse quickened. Would he confess that the dramatic events of last year—events that had transformed her life so completely—had awakened feelings he could no longer deny?

Now wouldn't *that* be delicious?

Nearly a year had passed since then. A year of fears dissipating, of growing into her new identity, of finally feeling in control of her own destiny.

Now she was ready for the next stage: finding love with a man who'd love her for herself, not her fortune.

Mr. Rothbury, she felt increasingly certain, was that man.

Chapter Six

EDWARD SIGHED AS he flexed his right hand, the joints protesting after hours hunched over his translation work.

The light slanting through the library's tall windows had shifted considerably since he'd begun the morning's pages of *Ivanhoe*—Sir Walter's tale of a disinherited knight and his impossible love for the wealthy Rowena.

Rising from his chair, Edward paced the magnificent library, acknowledging ruefully that bodies required attention no matter how absorbed the mind became in scholarly pursuits.

Even more ruefully, he acknowledged that no matter how diligently he labored, he would never achieve the social standing necessary to honorably offer marriage to Miss Playford. The fact that she now resided in the very same palazzo—that he might encounter her daily if he wished—was nothing short of exquisite torture.

Before he'd ridden to the rescue at Lady Townsend's Comet Viewing extravaganza with the news that Miss Playford was now an heiress, he truly had still harbored hopes.

With a surge of despair, he ran his hand across his brow as he recalled what else he'd discovered amongst his father's papers—not pertaining to the happily elevated Miss Playford... but to himself.

What a mixed blessing it had been to have involved himself in the young woman's affairs.

In discovering the evidence to provide freedom to Miss Playford, he'd discovered evidence that showed how truly beneath her he was.

He knew the sensible course would be to banish her from his thoughts entirely.

His heart yearned for a loving partner. A wife and a family. And Miss Playford was the epitome of his greatest dreams.

But that could never be.

So, if he wished to marry, logic dictated he should involve himself more extensively in Venice's social circles, where he might encounter a worthy young woman whose modest expectations aligned with what his salary could provide.

The trouble was, his heart possessed no appetite whatsoever for rational arrangements.

"Did you speak to your kind, dear friend as you promised?"

Edward turned sharply at the lilting voice. "Signorina Sofia! You gave me your word you would not enter this library while I worked alone."

"Grandfather has gone to inspect his vineyards," Sofia replied, waving this minor detail away as she stepped into the sunlight streaming through the Gothic windows. "He won't return until tomorrow evening, and the servants have strict instructions not to disturb your scholarly endeavors. Besides, what harm is there in a brief conversation?"

Sofia glided through the dappled light, which caught the jeweled pins in her elaborate golden coiffure, sending tiny rainbows dancing across the mahogany shelves. There was no doubt she was supremely aware of the power of her beauty.

So different, he thought, from Miss Playford, whose looks were equally exquisite, and yet she carried herself as if she were completely unaware of the fact.

Sofia perched herself on the edge of Edward's desk with complete disregard for the scattered papers beneath her silk-clad form, her look calculating.

"If you can assure me you've spoken to her, I shall leave you in peace," she said, toying with an escaped curl.

Edward struggled to maintain an even tone. "I am to speak with her this very afternoon. You are exceedingly impatient."

Swinging her silk-slippered feet with the insouciance of a child, she smiled. "Your conversation with this kind lady is all that stands between me and blessed union with my Paolo. Of course I'm impatient."

"She may very well decline to assist you." While Edward had initially viewed Sofia's request as a wonderful excuse for seeking Venetia's company, he'd since developed second, third, and approximately seventeenth thoughts. How could he ask such an honorable young woman to participate in a deliberate deception? Why should her superficial resemblance to Sofia constitute grounds for involving her in romantic subterfuge?

What indeed had possessed him to consider such a scheme?

The answer was painfully evident: Love transformed even the most rational gentleman into a complete fool.

He flexed his wrist and winced. If Count Morosini ever discovered Edward's complicity in this affair, he would certainly forfeit his lucrative position. Possibly also his kneecaps.

"But you declared her the kindest young lady of your acquaintance," Sofia pressed, slipping down from the desk to move closer. Her perfume—jasmine and orange blossom—created an invisible cloud between them. "You said she possessed an instinctive sympathy for noble causes. Surely no cause could be more virtuous than uniting two hearts that beat as one?"

Edward angled himself backward. The girl was alarmingly adept at invading personal space. "Such an undertaking would pose considerable risk to her reputation, significant danger to my career, and—most critically—grave peril to your own future, signorina. I begin to think I was exceedingly foolish to entertain your proposal. You possess a remarkable talent for bending gentlemen to your will—just as you've obviously managed with your Paolo."

Sofia's lower lip trembled with theatrical skill. "But Signor Edward, you cannot comprehend the desperation of my circumstances! Grandfather is about to begin negotiations for my betrothal—to that detestable Conte Bembo, who is not only old enough to be my grandfather but has the breath of a Venetian fish market!" She dabbed at her eyes. "Paolo and I have mere weeks—perhaps only days—before Grandfather announces my engagement publicly. How do you think I enjoy being bartered like livestock?"

Despite his better judgment, Edward felt his resolve wavering. "Even so, I cannot in good conscience ask Miss Playford to—"

"You could frame it as Christian charity," Sofia interrupted, her tears miraculously ceasing as she seized upon his hesitation. "Inform her I'm desperately unhappy, that my heart will shatter without this single afternoon of stolen joy with my beloved. Surely a lady of such compassion wouldn't refuse a fellow woman in dire distress?"

"You're asking me to exploit her generous nature," Edward said, though he could hear his objection losing steam.

"I'm asking you to appeal to her better angels," Sofia countered with silken persuasion. "And consider this, signor—if you're artful, such a request could provide entirely legitimate grounds for spending an afternoon in her delightful company."

Edward stiffened. "That would play no role in my—"

"Naturally not," Sofia agreed with utterly false innocence, though her knowing smile suggested complete comprehension of his true motivations. "But surely the prospect of such agreeable companionship might render the small deception more... tolerable?"

Edward closed his eyes, immediately conjuring Venetia's gentle smile, her musical laugh. Would he not risk everything for the privilege of her company?

Yes, he would.

"You know," Sofia continued, moving to examine the manuscript pages scattered across Edward's desk, "I'm quite entranced by your translation. Poor Rowena—" She sighed, trailing her finger along the manuscript's edge. "Born to wealth and station, yet her heart belongs to a man society deems unworthy of her elevated position. And noble Ivanhoe—stripped of his inheritance, possessing nothing but his honor and his love, yet convinced that honor itself prevents him from declaring his feelings."

The parallels hit Edward with the subtlety of a Venetian gondola to the face.

"How tragic that pride and circumstance should keep two souls apart when their hearts beat in perfect harmony," she mused, glancing up at him. "Of course, in Sir Walter's tale, external forces eventually unite the lovers. But in life..." She shrugged delicately. "In life, sometimes one must create one's own opportunities for happiness, must one not?"

Edward remained silent, though his brain was shouting rather loudly. Was he not exactly like Scott's Ivanhoe—a man of honor but modest means, loving a woman whose fortune placed her beyond his reach? And was Venetia not like Rowena—wealthy, elevated, yet possessed of a heart that might, perhaps, beat for him if circumstances permitted?

"I've often wondered," Sofia continued with diabolical insight, "whether Ivanhoe's rigid adherence to the chivalric code was truly noble, or merely cowardice disguised as virtue. After all, by refusing to speak his heart, did he not risk losing Rowena forever to a more pragmatic suitor?"

The question hung in the air while Edward contemplated the devastating possibility that his own principles might be costing him the only happiness he'd ever desired.

Also, when had this eighteen-year-old girl become a philosopher? It was deeply unsettling.

"If you truly cannot bring yourself to assist me," Sofia said, her voice returning to its earlier whisper, "then I shall be obliged to find another method of being with my Paolo. Of course, when Grandfather discovers my absence and searches the city…"

Edward's attention snapped back to her. "You would not dare."

"What alternative would you leave me?" Sofia turned from the window, her expression one of tragic determination—though Edward was beginning to suspect she'd practiced it in front of a mirror. "At least with your plan, Grandfather would believe me safely engaged in musical instruction. He might not discover my absence at all. But if I simply vanish from the palazzo…" She allowed the sinister implication to resonate.

Edward sank into his chair. The girl was far more cunning than he'd initially credited. She'd maneuvered him into a position where refusing her assistance seemed almost cruel—and where helping her offered the one thing he desired most desperately in the world.

Moreover, her observations regarding Ivanhoe had struck with precision at his deepest fears. Was he not guilty of the same prideful cowardice that nearly cost Scott's hero his happiness? By maintaining rigid adherence to propriety, was he not risking the loss of Venetia's affections to some more audacious suitor—perhaps one of those Italian counts Lady Townsend seemed so eager to parade before her?

Could it be possible he was exaggerating his deficiencies?

"You are a most dangerous young woman, signorina," he said at last.

Sofia's smile blazed with triumphant satisfaction. "I'm merely a woman in love, signor. Surely you, of all gentlemen, understand such feelings?"

Edward stared at her for a long moment, recognizing when he'd been thoroughly outmaneuvered. "Very well. I will present your request to Miss Playford. But I make no promises regarding her response."

Sofia clapped her hands together delightedly. "Oh, Signor Edward! You are the kindest, most reasonable gentleman in all of

Venice!"

"I'm a fool," Edward muttered, already dreading the conversation ahead while simultaneously anticipating it with shameful—and, he had to admit, rather exciting—eagerness.

Chapter Seven

AT THREE O'CLOCK the following afternoon, Venetia stood at the elegant casement windows of the casa's principal drawing room, her gaze scanning the narrow canal below with the intensity of a naval officer watching for enemy ships.

Could this truly be *the moment*? An honest declaration of Mr. Rothbury's sentiments? The warmth in his tone yesterday had been unmistakable—or so she fervently hoped. Her tendency to misinterpret male attention was, admittedly, not well-documented, given her limited experience. But surely she couldn't be *that* wrong?

Her heart—and, she acknowledged with considerable discomfort, certain other parts of her anatomy—had responded to his proximity yesterday with embarrassing enthusiasm. The very thought of his hands touching hers with deliberate intent rather than mere courtesy caused a most improper flutter that she refused to examine too closely.

When Mr. Rothbury appeared from beneath the stone archway leading to the palazzo's water entrance several minutes later, Venetia released a breath she hadn't realized she'd been holding. She'd been half convinced he might lose courage and dispatch some hastily scrawled excuse about an urgent translation.

Telling her lady's maid she was ready, Venetia hurried from

the palazzo, her heart thrilling at the nervous smile he offered.

He *did* have feelings for her. He must.

After an initial exchange of somewhat awkward civilities, Venetia accepted his assistance into the waiting gondola, while her maid settled herself discreetly at the stern.

Rich burgundy velvet cushions lined the gondola's seats, while an ornate canopy of midnight-blue silk provided shelter from curious eyes in palazzo windows above. Someone—Mr. Rothbury?—had arranged small luxuries: a crystal decanter of what appeared to be chilled wine, delicate Venetian glass goblets that caught the dancing light, and white roses whose perfume mingled with the salt-tinged air.

Oh, this was very promising indeed.

By this point, Venetia's imagination had constructed approximately seventeen romantic scenarios. Perhaps Mr. Rothbury had determined to remain in Venice and wished ardently for a wife to share his scholarly pursuits. Perhaps he longed to return to England and desired a companion for that journey. She'd even entertained the possibility that his career required extensive travel, and he sought a hardy partner willing to accompany him to exotic Mediterranean postings.

All of these prospects, Venetia would embrace with rapturous—possibly unseemly—enthusiasm.

Yes, she was an heiress now, a woman of considerable fortune whose circumstances had been transformed beyond recognition. But wealth complicated romance in unforeseen ways. While she could never be entirely certain whether suitors were drawn to her person or her purse, a noble gentleman like Mr. Rothbury might not pursue an attachment for fear of being labeled a fortune hunter.

What a relief, then, that he'd apparently discarded those tiresome notions of honor!

Seated beside him in the gondola's intimate confines—with her maid positioned far enough away to preserve propriety but not so close as to actually hear anything—conversation turned to childhood, family tragedy, and the subsequent trials under Aunt Pike's guardianship. The gondola glided through narrow canals flanked by palazzos whose weathered marble facades rose directly from emerald-tinted water.

Venetia closed her eyes briefly, savoring the cooling breeze and distant church bells. "To speak freely of both the joys of my childhood and the challenges under Aunt Pike creates such a sense of... connection."

She'd chosen her words carefully, hoping he might interpret them as encouragement to take her hand. What remained eloquently unspoken was the crucial role *he'd* played in her liberation.

Mr. Rothbury's expression softened as she opened her eyes and sent him what she hoped was an encouraging look.

"You endured unconscionable treatment, Miss Playford. I am so happy to see you now flourishing." He reached across to briefly touch her forearm—a gesture of solidarity that sent such a jolt through Venetia that she barely suppressed the impulse to capture his hand and press it against her racing heart.

"Flourishing... because of your intervention," she managed, feeling warmth flood her cheeks at such boldness. When he didn't respond immediately, she pressed forward with reckless determination. "When you appeared at Lady Townsend's Comet Viewing Gala astride that magnificent stallion like some hero from ancient legend, bringing word of my inheritance just as Lord Windermere was preparing to whisk me into that balloon—" She lowered her voice. "You, Mr. Rothbury, are the very reason I'm able to flourish."

He shifted uncomfortably on the velvet cushions. "You attribute far more significance to my actions than they merit. I was merely fortune's instrument. Felicitous timing, nothing more. You would have inherited regardless."

Venetia wished he'd acknowledge greater personal investment in her welfare. With perhaps fifteen minutes before they must return, she needed to encourage him past his natural reserve.

Clearing her throat delicately and resting her hand on the cushion mere inches from his, she began with more audacity than she'd known she possessed: "Yesterday you indicated there was some matter you wished to discuss."

"Ah, yes. Indeed." He suddenly appeared profoundly uncomfortable. "I have a most delicate request."

Here it comes!

"Then pray make it, Mr. Rothbury," Venetia encouraged, her heart performing acrobatics. "I'm certain I shall be favorably disposed to hear whatever you wish to say." She placed her hand on his coat sleeve—well-tailored but showing age, perhaps not cut in the latest fashion.

She noted these details because newfound wealth had awakened an appreciation for luxury previously suppressed during years of privation. Not that Mr. Rothbury needed expensive tailoring—his keen intellect and fundamental kindness distinguished him far more effectively than sartorial splendor.

Nevertheless, she'd gladly outfit him in London's finest if he'd permit such generosity. *Would* his pride make her wealth an insurmountable barrier?

"With your permission, Miss Playford, I shall proceed," he said, looking like a man approaching the gallows rather than declaring devotion.

Nerves. Perfectly natural.

"Nothing you might ask could ever be an imposition!" Venetia gazed at his beautifully shaped mouth, imagining sensations his lips might evoke. There was nothing she desired more at this moment.

"You truly are the most generous-spirited young woman I've encountered," he said awkwardly.

"Generosity is hardly required for a proposition that's noble and well-intentioned," she assured him, pulse racing. "What do you wish to ask?"

Mr. Rothbury's fingers drummed nervously against the gondola's brass fitting. With a deep breath, he began: "The matter concerns Signorina Sofia—"

Venetia's sharp intake of breath might have given him pause, but he pressed forward with grim determination.

Oh no.

"She finds herself in trying circumstances, and I've given my word to assist."

The words struck like a physical blow. "You've promised to aid Signorina Sofia," she repeated slowly, voice scarcely audible above the gondolier's oar, "and *this* is why you requested this private meeting?"

Only iron discipline instilled by years enduring Aunt Pike's cruelties enabled her to maintain composure.

"And precisely how," she continued with barely controlled emotion, "do you propose I assist Signorina Sofia?"

Of course. Of course it's about her. The golden-haired, dainty paragon.

"As I mentioned, you bear a striking resemblance to the young lady," Mr. Rothbury continued, seemingly oblivious to her distress. "Your exquisite golden tresses and your—" His gaze traveled involuntarily to her décolletage, whereupon he colored violently and averted his eyes. "Your general... proportions are remarkably similar. Signorina Sofia hopes you might lend perhaps twenty minutes to effect a temporary substitution. Don her clothing, step into a gondola, depart toward her music master's residence while her grandfather observes—"

"So Signorina Sofia may slip away undetected to meet her lover?" Venetia concluded with savage clarity, eyes desperately seeking a nearby landing stage.

Her lover. Who was presumably the man currently blushing beside her in this ridiculously romantic gondola.

The full magnitude of her misinterpretation pressed upon her consciousness like a crushing weight.

Mortifying!

"I'd hoped you'd comprehend her predicament, given your

aunt's similar control," Mr. Rothbury said, clearly dismayed. "Though I attempted to dissuade her—she has a determined temperament." He pressed his lips together, then continued carefully. "I offer my sincerest apologies for suggesting something so contrary to your principles, Miss Playford. Clearly, I've committed a grave error. Perhaps we should consider this conversation as never having occurred."

The gondola had entered a wider canal where distant vendors provided a soundtrack to Venetia's crushing disappointment. Even Venice's beauty seemed to mock her romantic delusions.

She fought to sound charitable rather than churlish. "I can appreciate the lengths to which a desperate young woman might resort."

Mr. Rothbury's expression brightened. "Then you'll consider—"

"I didn't say I'd *participate* in this deception," Venetia interrupted. "Merely that I understand the motivations."

"Of course," he agreed hastily. "I'd never press for an immediate decision."

Uncomfortable silence settled between them, broken only by the rhythmic splash of the oar and distant seagulls.

Well, this has been a spectacular disaster.

"There's another matter," Mr. Rothbury said suddenly, tone shifting to forced lightness. "Count Morosini is hosting a masquerade ball next week—Byzantine style, in his palazzo's ballroom. He's extended invitations to all English residents, and I wondered..." He hesitated. "I hoped you might consider attending. It promises to be spectacular, with Venice's finest musical performers."

Venetia hoped her smile didn't reveal her emotional turmoil. Was he trying to change the subject? Did he desire her company?

Or would her attendance simply provide additional opportunities for Signorina Sofia's schemes?

She shrugged. "Another entertainment?"

"You'll consider it?" Mr. Rothbury pressed.

Venetia bowed her head, considering possible responses. "I shall give it due consideration, Mr. Rothbury. As with the *other* matter you've raised today."

The matter where you asked me to impersonate your beloved so she could run off with her secret lover. That matter.

The gondola approached the Casa Bonaldi's water entrance, where late afternoon shadows gathered in the narrow canal. Soon this uncomfortable interview would conclude, and Venetia could retreat to examine the ruins of her romantic hopes in private.

"Until we meet again," Mr. Rothbury said, preparing to assist her from the gondola.

"Indeed," Venetia replied, accepting his hand for the necessary moment. "Good afternoon, Mr. Rothbury."

And good riddance to romantic delusions.

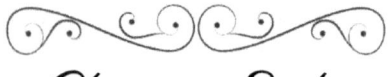

Chapter Eight

From the balcony of their palazzo, Eugenia lowered her opera glasses with a satisfied smile.

"How very interesting," she murmured to herself, noting the dejected slope of Mr. Rothbury's shoulders as he climbed back into the gondola, and the studied manner with which Venetia had avoided so much as a backward glance. "Very interesting indeed."

That had not gone well. Therefore, it was time to take another tack.

Twenty minutes later, Eugenia swept into Lord Thornton's private study where she found him at his mahogany writing desk, a letter half finished before him.

"My dear Eugenia," he said, rising with the resigned expression of a man who knew resistance was futile when he saw her expression. "What secret knowledge are you dying to divulge?" He narrowed his eyes. "Am I right in believing it concerns your supposedly worthy young couple?"

"Well, Thornton, I've just witnessed the most *satisfying* spectacle from my balcony," she said, settling into the comfortable chair opposite his desk. "Dear Miss Playford and Mr. Rothbury have concluded their gondola expedition, and I can report with absolute certainty that both parties are desperately, hopelessly, and quite obviously in love with one another."

Lord Thornton's eyebrows rose. "So your efforts to introduce

Miss Playford to Venice's unequal opposition have succeeded?" He looked doubtful. "From what I observed from *my* window, they looked rather like participants in a funeral procession. Miss Playford appeared particularly subdued."

"Precisely!" Eugenia clapped her hands together with delight. "Do you not see? Their very *misery* is proof positive of their attachment." She leaned forward conspiratorially. "Mark my words, Thornton, that young man asked her something of great import, and the manner of his asking—or perhaps her response—has left them both in exquisite torture. There's nothing quite so romantic as lovers convinced their affections are unrequited."

"Your theory is creative," Thornton conceded. "Though I confess I fail to see how mutual misunderstanding advances your cause. Generally speaking, understanding tends to be more conducive to romance than confusion."

"Because it creates perfect conditions for dramatic resolution!" Eugenia declared, waving away such pedantic concerns. "And fortune—or perhaps Providence—has provided the ideal opportunity. Count Morosini is hosting a grand masquerade ball in the Byzantine style within the fortnight. All the English residents are to be invited."

Thornton's smile held equal parts amusement and apprehension. "A masquerade, you say? And how will this further your agenda when the couple currently reside under the same roof and can speak whenever they wish? What mischief are you contemplating?"

"Not mischief! Romantic intervention of the most sophisticated kind!" Eugenia protested with wounded dignity. "A masquerade ball would provide an opportunity for… shall we say, strategic costume choices that might capture a certain gentleman's attention."

"Strategic costume choices," Thornton repeated slowly. "Why do I feel this will involve considerable expense and even more considerable drama?"

"I may have suggested," Eugenia continued, ignoring his

interjection, "that appearing as a Byzantine empress—all gold and jewels and imperial splendor—might serve to remind certain scholarly gentlemen that beauty and wealth, when combined with genuine affection, need not be obstacles to happiness but rather gifts to be gratefully received."

"In other words," Thornton translated dryly, "you intend to dress the girl so magnificently that our modest diplomatist will be overwhelmed by her sheer radiance." He frowned. "But such magnificence will only reinforce that she's too far above him in station—"

"Thornton!" Eugenia protested. "Have you no imagination whatsoever? First, I do not agree with you on this point, as you *very well know*. I'm persuaded Miss Playford would have him if he only asked. And the anonymity of a masquerade might provide the perfect opportunity for a lady to… take certain initiatives that strict propriety might otherwise prohibit."

She leaned back with satisfaction. "A masked lady, after all, might dance more than the usual conventions would allow, speak more freely, even—" she paused for dramatic effect, "—steal a private moment in a moonlit garden for purposes of clarifying unfortunate misunderstandings."

Lord Thornton shook his head with reluctant admiration. "I admire your determination in the face of what I see as clear defeat, Eugenia."

"I prefer *determined*," she replied serenely. "These two young people are clearly destined for one another, and if gentle manipulation of circumstances is required to overcome their mutual diffidence and his misguided sense of social inequality, then I consider such intervention a positive moral duty."

"Moral duty," Thornton muttered. "Is that what we're calling such blatant interference now?"

She smoothed her skirts with satisfaction, ignoring him. "Besides, think of the delicious irony—Mr. Rothbury, who's been so scrupulous about observing proper social boundaries, will find himself in an environment specifically designed to blur such distinctions. A masquerade is democracy in silk and satin, where a count might dance with a merchant's daughter and no one's the wiser."

"And what of your own interests in this entertainment?" Thornton inquired.

Eugenia studied her fingernails. "I confess the prospect of a romantic Venetian evening, complete with masks and moonlight, holds certain appeal. One is never too mature to appreciate beauty and atmosphere."

"Particularly when one has recently staked one's beloved *Persephone* on the outcome of romantic proceedings?"

"The wager was merely a gesture of confidence," Eugenia replied with dignity. "Though I admit, losing that painting to your smug satisfaction would be vexing. Intolerable, actually."

Thornton rose and moved to the window, gazing at the canal where evening light painted the water in shades of rose and gold. "You realize masquerades can be dangerous affairs? The very anonymity you see as advantageous also provides cover for less wholesome activities. Venice has a reputation for intrigue."

"All the more reason to ensure our young people find happiness quickly," Eugenia replied briskly. "Besides, what harm could possibly come to them in the palazzo of a respected Venetian nobleman, surrounded by the entire English community?"

"Famous last words," Thornton murmured as he turned away.

Eugenia joined him at the window, her heart suddenly beginning to beat very fast as she wondered whether to seize this opportunity for candor. "Do you truly think I'm overreaching, Thornton? Sometimes I wonder if my desire to see others happy is merely a substitute for... other concerns."

There. She'd said it. Sort of.

Thornton turned to her, his expression softening. "I think, dear Eugenia, that your gift for understanding the human heart is exceeded only by your generosity in wishing to share the happiness you've observed in others. If that isn't the finest motivation for matchmaking, I cannot imagine what would be."

She gave a satisfied smile, warmth flooding through her. "You always know precisely what to say to restore my confidence in my schemes."

"Not always," he replied quietly, his gaze lingering on her face with an intensity that made her pulse quicken in a thoroughly unseemly manner for a woman of her years. "But in this instance, I believe your instincts are sound. Those two young people are indeed perfectly suited, and if a Byzantine masquerade provides the stage for their romantic denouement, I can think of worse settings."

"Then you'll support my plans?"

"Your plans?" He smiled, and something in his expression made her breath catch. "I will support *you*, Eugenia. As I have for thirty years, and as I hope to for thirty more."

The moment hung between them, weighted with things unsaid.

"Well," Eugenia managed, suddenly finding the view of the canal extraordinarily fascinating. "That's settled then. I shall begin costume arrangements immediately. And perhaps consult Miss Bentley—though heaven knows she'll have opinions on everything under the sun that will need to be diplomatically circumvented if I am to achieve my aims."

"Heaven forbid anyone circumvent Miss Bentley's opinions," Thornton said, the moment passing as his tone returned to its usual dry humor. "The woman's sense of propriety would, I am sure, put Captain Rizzi to shame."

Eugenia laughed, relief and something else—something she wasn't quite ready to examine—mingling in her chest. "Indeed. The captain could learn much from Miss Bentley's powers of observation. Though thankfully, her detection skills don't extend to matters of the heart."

"A mercy for us all," Thornton agreed.

"For us all," Eugenia echoed, wondering if he heard the question she wasn't quite brave enough to ask.

Chapter Nine

MISERABLY, EDWARD DESCENDED the worn marble steps of the palazzo, his footsteps echoing in the grand entrance hall with all the cheerfulness of a funeral dirge.

The palazzo's ornate lobby, with its soaring ceiling adorned with frescoes depicting Venice's maritime glories, had once impressed him. Now it seemed to mock his dejected spirits as he made his way toward the heavy, brass-studded double doors.

Whereas previously he'd deliberately timed his departure to coincide with Miss Playford's morning constitutional—hoping for even the briefest glimpse of her—he now orchestrated his movements to ensure their paths would *not* cross. The shame of having offended her with his unconscionable request weighed upon his conscience. He couldn't bear witnessing reproach in those expressive eyes that had once regarded him with such warmth.

So, it came as a considerable shock to hear her voice calling his name as he reached for the ornate bronze door handle.

"Mr. Rothbury, I've reflected upon what you asked yesterday. I'm prepared to give you my answer now, so you may convey it to Signorina Sofia."

Edward turned, his heart pounding uncomfortably within his chest. Miss Playford—with her maid several steps behind—stood framed by one of the graceful arches, her white muslin morning dress making her appear almost ethereal in the diffused light.

But the stress he observed on her features made him realize his error. He'd leaped at any excuse to spend time in her company, so blinded by his own desires that he'd failed to consider the moral quandary this would pose.

Idiot. Complete and utter idiot.

"Miss Playford, please give the matter no further consideration," he said hastily. "I release you entirely from any involvement in what I now recognize as a rash and thoroughly ill-conceived scheme. Signorina Sofia will understand completely."

Would she? Doubtful.

"No, Mr. Rothbury," Venetia interrupted. "What you said yesterday was perfectly reasonable, and it was I who responded with unconscionable selfishness." She appeared genuinely distressed, her fingers pleating the fine fabric of her skirts. "I've spent the night examining my conscience, trying to understand my initial reaction. I thought only of myself, didn't I? I dismissed entirely the notion of assisting another young woman in precisely the same desperate circumstances I once faced—and for what reason?"

Oh no. She was being noble. That was worse than reproach.

"Perhaps my sudden elevation in fortune has rendered me inward looking. Self-absorbed." Her voice dropped to a whisper. "I'm thoroughly ashamed of myself, Mr. Rothbury. Please convey to Signorina Sofia that whenever she requires it, I'm entirely at her service. I'm more than willing to provide whatever deception is necessary so she might escape an oppressive guardian's scrutiny and find peace—even briefly—with someone who shows her genuine kindness."

She swallowed hard, her composure threatening to crumble. "Kindness is so essential to human happiness, and Heaven knows I wouldn't deny her that precious gift."

Edward felt two inches tall. Here was this remarkable woman—who had every right to refuse such an outrageous request—

blaming *herself* for hesitation that was entirely justified.

"You have demonstrated the greatest magnanimity, Miss Playford," he said, wishing desperately that he possessed the Continental ease that would permit him to lift her gloved hand to his lips in gratitude. But he remained a properly restrained Englishman, so he contented himself with a stiff nod. "Signorina Sofia will be grateful beyond measure for your extraordinary kindness."

Though frankly, Sofia didn't deserve such kindness.

"Well, it is agreed then," Miss Playford said, lingering awkwardly, as if she expected him to say more. Indeed, he was desperately trying to think of something to say; only, just as he opened his mouth to say it, she apparently gave up and, with a short nod, concluded the conversation with, "Good day to you, Mr. Rothbury."

Forlorn and mentally kicking himself, Edward watched Venetia depart with a rustle of muslin skirts. Only when she was entirely out of sight did he turn toward the canal where his gondola waited to transport him to his meeting with Sofia.

A meeting he was dreading with increasing intensity.

"About time she finally decided to do what was the only right and proper thing!"

So much for Sofia's gratitude.

This was Signorina Sofia's response to Edward's carefully delivered news—a reaction quite different from what he'd anticipated. He'd expected perhaps some expressions of relief, maybe even a tear or two of feminine appreciation.

Instead, he got this.

Sofia had positioned herself beside an ornate marble table where her drawing materials lay scattered, ostensibly engaged in sketching the panoramic view. Edward suspected the artistic endeavor was merely a pretext for their clandestine meeting.

Her maidservant, a sharp-eyed woman of middle years, hovered at a respectful distance near the terrace entrance, looking like she'd seen this particular performance before.

Sofia tossed her golden head, her voice carrying a hard edge that jarred with her angelic appearance. "We women must look after one another, though she required some time to see the light of duty, didn't she, Mr. Rothbury?" She raised one perfectly arched eyebrow, her speculative gaze so knowing that Edward felt heat flood his cheeks. "Or perhaps you employed some gentlemanly persuasion to encourage her change of heart?"

"I am not so ungentlemanly as to employ persuasion of any sort," Edward objected, though he was beginning to wonder if "gentlemanly" was code for "spectacularly foolish."

"You describe Miss Playford as possessing such maidenly sensibilities that she could hardly have reached such a decision independently, without benefit of your... persuasive influence." Sofia's laughter held a mocking quality that made Edward's skin crawl. "So you must thank me, Mr. Rothbury. My desires may well prove the key to discovering your own."

Edward was thoroughly unaccustomed to such bold discourse. The casual mention of desire—his own unrequited longing, and Sofia's brazen appetites—caused uncomfortable warmth to flood through him.

When had this conversation taken such an alarming turn?

"Miss Playford could marry any gentleman of her choosing," he said carefully, trying to steer them back to safer waters. "Yet her elevation hasn't caused her to forget the trials she endured when she was penniless and subject to others' whims. I consider it an act of extraordinary generosity that she chooses to donate her time to your cause."

"So you insinuate I'm an ungrateful wretch?" Sofia shrugged with magnificent indifference. "Ah well, let us not quarrel over such trifles. I am what circumstances have made me—a young woman whose love won't be sanctioned by the grandfather who controls my life, my fortune, and my future." Her expression hardened momentarily before resuming its mask of youthful petulance. "I'm grateful to Miss Playford for condescending to assist my cause, considering her elevated status as one of

England's wealthiest heiresses. You may convey my appreciation using whatever flowery phrases you deem appropriate."

Flowery phrases. Right. "Dear Miss Playford, Sofia says thanks but also sort of implied you're a self-absorbed heiress who took too long to see reason."

She turned back to her sketching, adding, "And you may also inform her that my next music lesson is scheduled for noon the day after tomorrow. Provided she hasn't experienced another attack of maidenly scruples, I'd be greatly obliged if she'd meet me at the San Tomà landing stage at noon. I shall provide an appropriate costume for our little masquerade."

Edward studied Sofia's profile as she bent over her drawing, noting the calculating set of her features that seemed distinctly at odds with her professed romantic desperation. Something in her manner—a certain coldness beneath the surface charm—stirred unease.

How had he not noticed this before? Well, he had, but he'd been too busy mooning over Venetia to pay proper attention to the increasingly suspicious young woman he was helping.

"Signorina," he said slowly, "I hope you understand the considerable risk Miss Playford is assuming on your behalf. Should this deception be discovered—"

"Oh, Mr. Rothbury," Sofia interrupted with a tinkling laugh that now sounded distinctly artificial, "you worry unnecessarily. What could possibly go wrong with such a simple substitution? I shall slip away for a few precious hours with my Paolo, and Miss Playford will enjoy a pleasant gondola ride through Venice's most picturesque canals. With you, if you choose." She smiled brightly. "Really, when you consider it properly, I'm offering you both a delightful afternoon's entertainment."

Her casual dismissal of potential consequences troubled Edward deeply. Either Sofia was far more naïve than he'd credited, or she was far more calculating.

Neither possibility offered much comfort as he contemplated the web of deception he'd helped weave around the woman he loved.

"Very well," he said at last, though doubt gnawed at his conscience like a particularly persistent rodent. "I shall convey your arrangements to Miss Playford. But I must insist that should any complication arise—"

"Nothing will arise, dear Mr. Rothbury," Sofia said, not bothering to look up from her sketch. "Nothing that cannot be easily managed, I assure you."

Edward had the distinct impression that Sofia's definition of "easily managed" and his own might differ considerably.

He was also beginning to suspect that he'd made a terrible mistake.

Several terrible mistakes, actually.

But it was too late to back out now.

Chapter Ten

EARLY THE FOLLOWING morning, Eugenia found Venetia taking tea while staring disconsolately through the window like a heroine in a tragic opera.

She hesitated, trying to frame the right response. "The Grand Canal has so many moods, Miss Playford, that I don't wonder you're mesmerized. And I'm astonished at how well the talented Signorina Sofia has captured it in her painting." She paused, studying the girl's dejected posture. "But I observe you look in poor spirits this morning. Perhaps they'll be cheered if I show you the canvas Mr. Rothbury delivered last night."

"I have no wish to see it, thank you, Lady Townsend," said her young protégé with downcast eyes that would have done credit to a gothic novel. "Mr. Rothbury has asked me to assist this young lady in a romantic adventure, and his eager insistence is quite at odds with my reservations."

Romantic adventure? Eugenia was taken aback. "What exactly has he asked you to do?"

Even her agile imagination—which was considerable—couldn't conceive what such a romantic adventure might constitute. Or how Mr. Rothbury, Signorina Sofia, and Miss Playford might all be involved.

Miss Playford sighed and put down her teacup with a gentle

clatter. Wiping her eyes with the back of her hand—she'd clearly been crying—Eugenia's heart gave a little leap with a mixture of hope and distress.

Could Miss Playford feel such disappointment—jealousy, perhaps—at Mr. Rothbury's request? But then, with a surge of alarm, she wondered if Mr. Rothbury had turned his attention toward courting Signorina Sofia, believing Miss Playford's fortune put her out of contention.

That would be spectacularly disappointing. But then, Signorina Sofia's status placed her just as above the young man as Miss Playford. No, Signorina Sofia did not pose a threat, she finally reassured herself.

"He wishes me to dress as the signorina—as we apparently resemble one another—and float away in a gondola to satisfy her father or jailers, or whomever keeps this young woman so dreadfully imprisoned." Venetia's voice dripped with sarcasm. "Meanwhile, Signorina Sofia can waltz off to be with her sweetheart."

"And you think that might be Mr. Rothbury?" Eugenia asked, though privately she thought it unlikely. The man was clearly besotted with Venetia, not Sofia.

Miss Playford gave a little gasp, reddened, then said evasively, "I had thought Mr. Rothbury a man of such nobility, but now I don't know what to think."

"Perhaps he considers it noble to assist a young woman who has no other recourse," Eugenia suggested gently, placing a hand on her forearm. "Just as he assisted you when you had none. Have you considered you're attributing to him motives that may not be his real motives? Perhaps this has given him an opportunity to speak to you. To be involved in a plan with you that will bring happiness to someone else."

And possibly spend more time in your company, which is clearly his primary objective in life.

"Why would he need an excuse to talk to me?" Miss Playford asked, as if she genuinely couldn't imagine any good reason.

Oh, sweet girl. So clever about everything except this.

Eugenia shrugged, deciding not to answer. Some lessons were better learned through observation. "And have you decided whether you'll accede to Mr. Rothbury's request?"

Venetia nodded miserably. "I've already agreed. It would have been churlish to refuse."

"Churlish to refuse to help a young lady who was as powerless as you once were?" Eugenia kept her tone gentle.

Venetia reddened, pressing her lips together. Then she sighed. "I admit that it was more Mr. Rothbury's *interest* that I found difficult to reconcile."

"Perhaps it would serve you best to find out what kind of young lady Signorina Sofia really is," Eugenia suggested. "And how matters lie between her and Mr. Rothbury. You might discover the situation is quite different from what you imagine."

Miss Playford gave a rueful smile. "I shall take your wise counsel, Lady Townsend. And I shall bury my jealousy and concentrate on my supposedly charitable nature, which I confess has been in limited supply since Mr. Rothbury invited me to accompany him in a gondola for what I had imagined was quite a different reason."

"No need to give up hope." Eugenia squeezed her hand briefly. The girl had all but confessed deep feelings for Mr. Rothbury. And since Mr. Rothbury wore his heart on his sleeve—practically embroidered there in large letters reading "I LOVE MISS VENETIA PLAYFORD"—Eugenia believed she could happily predict that within an even shorter time than she'd imagined, the pair would be united.

Assuming, of course, that this ridiculous substitution scheme didn't blow up spectacularly in everyone's faces.

But what were the odds of that?

Everything would work out perfectly at the masquerade ball.

It always did in novels, anyway.

Chapter Eleven

AFTER A MORNING of tortured self-recrimination, Edward had to admit that pleasure rather than guilt was at the forefront of his feelings as he made his way to the casa's water entrance.

Which probably said terrible things about his character. But he'd worry about that later.

To his surprise, he observed Miss Playford seated on the stone steps leading down to the canal, a leather-bound volume open in her lap, her maid a short distance away. She appeared absorbed in her reading, one gloved hand shielding her eyes from the afternoon glare while the other held her place on the page. The scene struck him as so naturally graceful, so perfectly in harmony with Venice's timeless beauty, that he hesitated to intrude upon her solitude.

"Mr. Rothbury!" she called, having noticed his approach despite her apparent concentration on her book. "How fortuitous. I was just thinking I should seek you out to discuss… the matter we spoke of yesterday."

Edward's chest tightened. "Miss Playford," he said, executing a formal bow as he approached the landing stage. "Are you on your way somewhere?"

"Just enjoying the sunshine and needing a little respite from the possibility of being waylaid by my lovely—but somewhat overbearing, at times—English friends," she replied, with a nod toward the casa.

Edward chose not to comment, though he understood her feelings perfectly. Lady Townsend's enthusiasm for orchestrating social encounters bordered on military campaign planning.

"I've spoken with Signorina Sofia," he began carefully, settling himself on the stone step a respectful distance from where she sat. "She was... most grateful for your generous offer of assistance."

"Most grateful" was perhaps stretching it. "Minimally appreciative" was more accurate.

"I'm glad to hear it," Venetia replied, though Edward detected a note of constraint in her voice. "And the arrangements? When does she require this... service?"

Edward noted her careful choice of words—*service* rather than *deception*—and admired her attempt to frame their conspiracy in terms that preserved her moral equilibrium. "Tomorrow at noon. She wishes to meet you at the San Tomà landing stage at half past eleven, after her maid, Caterina, provides you with an appropriate costume to ensure the... substitution is convincing."

Venetia nodded. "And the duration of this masquerade?"

"Perhaps two hours," Edward replied, hating himself for the hope that colored his voice. "Enough time for her to visit her... friend... while her grandfather believes her safely engaged with her music instructor."

A moment of silence stretched between them, broken only by the distant cry of a fruit vendor navigating the canal in his laden gondola.

"Mr. Rothbury," she said at last, turning to meet his gaze directly, "may I speak frankly?"

"Of course," he replied, though her serious tone filled him with apprehension.

Nothing good ever followed "may I speak frankly." It was practically a law of nature.

"Yesterday, when you first presented this request, I reacted with what I now recognize as selfish concern for my own reputation. But upon reflection, I find myself troubled by different considerations altogether." She paused, clearly choosing her words with care. "You know Signorina Sofia better than I. In your estimation, is she... that is, do you believe her motivations are entirely what they appear?"

Edward felt as though she'd struck directly at the heart of his own mounting concerns. "What makes you ask such a thing?" he replied carefully, unwilling to voice his own doubts but curious about the source of hers.

Venetia hesitated, her gaze drifting to where a pair of gondoliers were engaged in animated conversation as their boats passed. "Perhaps it's merely that I've learned to be wary of situations that seem... too convenient. Two years ago, I was nearly destroyed by someone who presented themselves as no threat while harboring entirely different intentions." She returned her attention to Edward, her expression earnest. "I suppose I've developed an unfortunate tendency to question motives that once I would have accepted at face value."

Edward felt a chill that had nothing to do with the palazzo's shadow above them. Venetia's past experience with Lord Windermere's deception had obviously left her with sharper instincts for detecting duplicity—instincts now alerting her to potential danger in Sofia's seemingly straightforward request.

Instincts that were, unfortunately, probably correct.

"Your caution is entirely understandable," he said slowly. "And I confess that I, too, have found myself... questioning certain aspects of the situation."

"Then why do you continue to assist her?" Venetia asked, and Edward heard genuine curiosity rather than accusation in her voice.

The question pierced to the core of his moral dilemma, and Edward found himself trapped between honesty and the protection of his own dignity.

"I suppose," he said carefully, "that I'm not entirely immune to appeals to my... sympathetic nature. And once I'd given my word to assist her, I found it difficult to withdraw that support without compelling evidence of actual wrongdoing. That is, having satisfied myself that you, yourself, would be in no danger."

Venetia studied his face with an intensity that made him distinctly uncomfortable. He had the unsettling sensation she was reading far more in his expression than he intended to reveal.

"There's another consideration," she said quietly. "During Signorina Sofia's masquerade, where will I go? I assume there are potential spies who'll want to be satisfied she's going where expected—to her music master."

"That's correct. You'll be accompanied by Signorina Sofia's maid, Caterina."

"And you, Mr. Rothbury? Surely you have a responsibility to also accompany me in case of unforeseen circumstances?"

Was she aware of the undercurrent of attraction that seemed to complicate every interaction between them? That made it difficult to speak candidly?

"If you wish me to accompany you, I would gladly do so."

Gladly. Enthusiastically. With unseemly eagerness, actually.

Venetia's smile held a quality he couldn't quite decipher—was it disappointment? Relief? Amusement at his obvious discomfort?

Probably the latter.

"Very well then," she said, rising from the stone steps with the grace of someone who'd just won a subtle negotiation. "I shall meet Signorina Sofia tomorrow as arranged, and I will depart with her maid, giving the impression she's going to her music lesson. And then, Mr. Rothbury..." She paused, looking down at him with a smile tugging at her lips. "I will look forward to you bearing me company during the time Signorina Sofia is otherwise occupied."

His heart lurched unexpectedly. Two hours at the very minimum in this angel's company? It was more of a bargain than he'd realized.

A bargain that involved deception, potential scandal, and probably about seventeen different ways this could go catastrophically wrong. But two hours with Venetia!

His priorities were clearly in shambles. He'd address that later.

"If that is what you wish, Miss Playford," he said carefully.

She nodded. "It is."

Chapter Twelve

"THE MASQUERADE BALL. What will you wear?"

Venetia had barely given this a thought, due to her preoccupation with her promise to Signorina Sofia the following morning.

But now she found herself seated opposite Lady Townsend, who was examining a collection of fashion plates spread across the rosewood table between them in the water salon. The older woman's eyes sparkled with an enthusiasm that made Venetia immediately suspicious.

Was Lady Townsend orchestrating another of her elaborate romantic stratagems? Had Mr. Rothbury indicated disinterest?

Her heart clenched with disappointment at the thought—and with the worry that Lady Townsend might have lined up yet another wealthy, chinless peer for the masquerade.

"My dear girl," Lady Townsend began, "on the off chance you haven't yet turned your attention to the matter, I've been giving considerable thought to your costume for Count Morosini's masquerade ball. The event presents such extraordinary opportunities for... shall we say, meaningful encounters... that we must ensure you're attired to maximum advantage."

Venetia shifted uncomfortably in her chair. "To be truthful, Lady Townsend, I'm not entirely certain I shall attend. Such elaborate entertainments seem rather..." She searched for a diplomatic phrase. "Rather beyond my current inclinations."

Although it was Mr. Rothbury who'd first told her of the ball, she'd subsequently heard that with Count Morosini's feverish desire for *Ivanhoe* to be at the halfway point of translation, Mr. Rothbury therefore might have to slave away at his work, and Venetia most certainly did not want to be matched with someone else Lady Townsend deemed suitable.

"Nonsense!" Lady Townsend declared. "You absolutely must attend. I have it on excellent authority that certain gentlemen"—here she fixed Venetia with a meaningful look—"are particularly anticipating your presence."

She couldn't be referring to Mr. Rothbury, though the thought of him caused a familiar flutter in Venetia's chest, especially as she thought of tomorrow's masquerade with Signorina Sofia. The whole overwhelm of it loomed in her thoughts like a gathering storm cloud.

"Now, a Byzantine empress would answer your needs, I think," Lady Townsend continued, apparently oblivious to Venetia's reservations. "All cloth of gold and precious jewels, with a magnificent headdress that will make you appear absolutely regal. No gentleman of sense could fail to be impressed by such a vision."

"But, Lady Townsend, I really am not in the mood for making a match—"

"Nonsense!" Lady Townsend leaned back with a frown. "I made that mistake, and I'm not about to see you squander your opportunities when you're in the prime of your life."

Venetia didn't know what to say. Misery tugged at her heartstrings. Would Mr. Rothbury ever find the courage to speak his mind when she saw him tomorrow? Or had Venetia completely misinterpreted his feelings?

Initially, she'd thought his enthusiasm for helping Signorina Sofia was because he'd formed a romantic attachment to the young woman, but now Venetia strongly suspected he was using his promise to her as a means to spend time with Venetia herself.

Yet was it a good idea for Venetia to risk her heart if he ultimately never came good with a marriage proposal? He really might prove too morally upstanding for his own good—and hers.

Lady Townsend leaned forward conspiratorially. "What could be more fitting than for the gentleman of your dreams—your future husband—to encounter his very own empress at a masquerade ball?"

Heat crept up Venetia's neck at Lady Townsend's transparent machinations. Who did she have in mind? If she knew Mr. Rothbury wasn't attending—and surely she did?—who else could she be thinking of?

"Lady Townsend, I am very content as I am."

A complete lie.

Before Venetia was forced to back this up with more robust evidence, the sound of approaching footsteps in the marble corridor announced the arrival of another participant in their impromptu consultation.

"My dear ladies!" Miss Bentley appeared in the doorway, her expression even more self-satisfied than usual—which was saying something. "Forgive the interruption, but I have the most delightful news to share." She advanced into the room with the air of someone bearing treasure. "I've just had the extraordinary good fortune to encounter the most charming gentleman in the palazzo's entrance hall—a Count Theodore di Montefiore, recently arrived from Naples. When I learned he was seeking an introduction to English society, I naturally took it upon myself to extend our hospitality."

Lady Townsend rose with polite interest that didn't quite reach her eyes. "I confess I'm not familiar with the name, Catherine. Is he Venetian nobility?"

"Neapolitan, actually," Miss Bentley corrected with evident pleasure in her superior knowledge. "The family holds extensive properties in the south, and the count has been touring northern Italy to indulge his cultural interests. He expressed particular fascination with English customs and society. Such a refined gentleman, and so elegantly outfitted!"

Venetia noted with some amusement Miss Bentley's almost vulgar enthusiasm, which was obviously calculated to impress. Perhaps Miss Bentley's own romantic prospects had been so thoroughly exhausted that she now sought vicarious satisfaction in arranging introductions for others.

Or perhaps she, herself, was interested in this Continental paragon.

"I hope you haven't committed us to entertaining this stranger without proper references," Lady Townsend said mildly. "Venice attracts all manner of adventurers, and one must be cautious about extending intimacy to unknown quantities."

Miss Bentley's expression darkened. "I am hardly naïve in such matters, Eugenia. The count carries letters of introduction from several prominent English families currently residing in Naples. I would hardly invite a person of questionable character into our circle."

"Of course not," Lady Townsend replied smoothly, though Venetia detected a note of skepticism beneath her diplomatic response. "Well then, if his credentials are satisfactory, I see no reason why we shouldn't extend the courtesy due to a fellow traveler in foreign lands."

Venetia studied the two women and realized, for the first time and with a slight start, that they really weren't the friends she'd supposed, despite the veneer of apparent sisterhood.

"The count has expressed particular interest in meeting English residents," Miss Bentley continued, her enthusiasm undimmed by Lady Townsend's reservations. "I've taken the liberty of inviting him to join us for tea this afternoon, if that arrangement meets with your approval."

"This afternoon?" Lady Townsend repeated, clearly caught off guard by the immediacy of the invitation. "*This* afternoon?"

"I thought it best not to delay the introduction unnecessarily," Miss Bentley explained with a slightly aggrieved and defensive air.

Translation: I didn't want to give you time to object.

Venetia glanced between the two older women, more aware than ever of the subtle tension crackling between them like sparks before a storm.

"Very well," Lady Townsend said at last, upon a note of resignation. "Though I do hope, Catherine, that you haven't given this gentleman any reason to expect more than polite hospitality."

It wasn't long before the sound of the majordomo's measured footsteps in the corridor suggested that their mysterious visitor had indeed arrived with remarkable promptness.

"Ah," Miss Bentley said with satisfaction as the servant appeared in the doorway, "here is our guest now."

The majordomo stepped aside with a formal bow, and Venetia looked up expectantly as a tall, elegantly dressed figure entered the water salon. His dark hair was fashionably styled, his clothing impeccably tailored in the Continental manner. A neatly trimmed beard adorned his lower face, while his overall bearing suggested he was quite accustomed to being warmly welcomed wherever he presented himself.

Possibly too accustomed.

"Ladies," Miss Bentley said with obvious pleasure, practically preening, "may I present Count Theodore di Montefiore. Count, I have the honor of introducing Lady Eugenia Townsend and Miss Venetia Playford."

The count executed a bow, his dark eyes settling on each lady in turn with flattering attention. When his gaze reached Venetia, she noticed a momentary intensification of interest that sent an inexplicable chill down her spine, though his expression remained one of polished courtesy.

Why did that feel... calculating?

"The pleasure is entirely mine, ladies," he said in accented English that somehow managed to make even commonplace phrases sound sophisticated. "Miss Bentley's gracious invitation has transformed what might have been a solitary afternoon into an occasion of unexpected delight."

Venetia smiled politely, though something about the count's overly smooth manner made her instinctively wary.

Chapter Thirteen

AT LAST CAME the moment that Venetia had both feared and looked forward to in equal measure.

Mostly looked forward to, if she was being honest. The fear was more of a nod to what she really ought *to be feeling.*

Having conquered her resistance to Mr. Rothbury's request to help Signorina Sofia, she'd entered into the subterfuge with more than a thrill at her own daring, arriving with her maid Mollie at the agreed location—a dim antechamber in a palazzo near the departure point—for her transformation.

Sofia's lady's maid, a sharp-eyed woman named Caterina, had pinned Venetia's golden hair into an elaborate arrangement that apparently mimicked her mistress's preferred style, complete with jeweled combs. Now Venetia stood at the weathered stone steps of the San Tomà landing stage, plucking nervously at the unfamiliar folds of Sofia's emerald silk gown.

The borrowed garment felt strange against her skin—the bodice cut in a more daring Continental style than her own modest English fashions.

But the transformation had been remarkable. When Venetia had glimpsed herself in the looking glass at the secluded dressing chamber Sofia had arranged, she'd been startled by her own reflection. She no longer looked English. Whether she looked sufficiently like a Continental signorina to trick a distant observer, time would tell.

Now that she was prepared, her impatience over Mr. Rothbury's arrival was growing. The plan was that Venetia would leave in a gondola with Caterina—disguised as Signorina Sofia—while Mr. Rothbury would be waiting at another location with Mollie to meet Venetia for the duration of Sofia's assignation.

The arrangement, decided quickly the previous evening, thrilled her, though the questionable morality nevertheless weighed upon her conscience. She was, after all, actively participating in a deliberate deception that could compromise not only her own reputation but also Count Morosini's trust in his granddaughter.

However, she couldn't deny that beneath this righteous discomfort ran a current of anticipation so strong it left her breathless.

Two hours alone with Mr. Rothbury. Well, not alone—Mollie would be there. But still.

By the time Caterina had stepped back with a nod of satisfaction at her handiwork, Venetia had banished her reservations. The prospect of spending time in Mr. Rothbury's company was far more thrilling than it was morally concerning.

As further justification, she had to admit sympathy for a young woman being forced into marriage. If Sofia's young man was worthy, why shouldn't she have the opportunity to follow her heart? Venetia knew the horrors of being pushed into marriage against one's will.

"Ah, Miss Playford, you came," came a lilting accented voice from the shadows before the young Italian woman emerged.

Venetia raised her eyebrows at the imperious tone and was taken aback by the girl's breathtaking beauty.

And her vanity, it would appear, for the beetling look she received was more impatient than either grateful or admiring. "I daresay you'll pass as myself as far as my father's minions are concerned, watching from the tower as the gondola leaves the landing stage. But do carry yourself with a little more grace, or the game will be up, as I believe you English are wont to phrase it."

You're welcome for risking my reputation, by the way, Venetia thought with a surge of irritation.

"Now, the gondola is here. You must go with Caterina while I wait for a separate conveyance."

The plan, as Sofia had outlined it, called for the gondola containing Venetia to follow a circuitous route through Venice's quieter canals before depositing her at a predetermined location where Mr. Rothbury would be waiting. This elaborate choreography was designed to ensure that any observers—particularly Count Morosini—would witness what appeared to be Sofia's routine journey to her music lesson.

Naturally, there was nothing to do but obey. With a nod, Venetia allowed herself to be assisted into the graceful watercraft, settling herself against the velvet-tasseled cushions while keeping her head bowed to minimize the risk of exposure.

The gondola's route took them through some of Venice's most enchanting backwaters, where narrow canals wound between palazzos whose foundations had been laid centuries before England's Norman conquest. Laundry hung like colorful banners from wrought iron balconies, while the calls of street vendors echoed off ancient stone walls.

If Venetia's heart hadn't been beating so erratically, she might have enjoyed it more.

After some minutes navigating through this aquatic maze, the gondola approached the small, secluded landing stage Mr. Rothbury had designated, nestled between two crumbling palazzos that appeared to have been abandoned for decades. Tall weeds sprouted from cracks in the marble steps, while iron mooring posts bore the green patina of age and neglect.

It was precisely the sort of location her favorite author, Mrs. Radcliffe, might choose for clandestine meetings—sufficiently isolated to ensure privacy, yet accessible enough to serve as a rendezvous point.

Or the sort of place where one might be murdered and never found.

Venetia's heart beat even harder as she waited in the gondola. Was Mr. Rothbury more of a romantic than she'd believed? Might he have something to say to her that went beyond mere pleasantries?

Mollie and Mr. Rothbury soon appeared, the latter stepping forward to help Venetia onto the landing stage. "Miss Playford," he said, his eyes wide with shock as his hand gripped hers, "your transformation is extraordinary."

Venetia blushed. "I hope the resemblance was sufficient to serve Signorina Sofia's purpose."

"I'm sure it was." The intensity of his gaze made her skin warm beneath the borrowed silk. For a moment, something flickered in his eyes—an expression she couldn't quite decipher but which sent a delicious shiver down her spine.

Please say something romantic. Please.

"Though the resemblance is remarkable," he said, "you remain entirely yourself, naturally, but the effect is quite…" He trailed off, clearly struggling with some internal conflict before saying more decisively, "Caterina will wait here with the gondola while we ensure sufficient time passes for Sofia's purposes."

With barely a glance in their direction, Caterina settled herself comfortably in the gondola's shade, producing needlework from her reticule with the air of one who'd performed this duty many times before.

"Would you care to walk?" asked Mr. Rothbury, and at her nod, he led Venetia along a narrow walkway that skirted the edge of a particularly quiet canal, Mollie a few yards behind.

"I confess that I've been wrestling with considerable guilt regarding this entire enterprise," Mr. Rothbury said, his words halting as they walked. "The more I consider the potential consequences—to you, to Sofia, to my own professional standing—the more concerned I become that I've exercised—" He stopped and turned to look at her. "Unconscionably poor judgment."

Venetia stopped, too. "Yet you proceeded nonetheless."

Because you wanted to spend time with me. Please say it's because you wanted to spend time with me.

Even if they were exposed, she thought, she could think of far worse fates than being required by propriety to marry Mr. Rothbury.

For surely that's what he was hinting at? Again, her heart performed another little lurch. Was this the moment?

"I suppose," he said slowly, "that I'm not as immune to selfish desires as I'd believed myself to be. The prospect of spending these hours in your company proved more compelling than my better judgment could withstand."

Venetia held her breath.

Oh. Oh, that was nearly a declaration.

The honesty in his admission hung between them like a bridge neither quite dared to cross. What could she say in response that would encourage him yet not appear overly eager?

"I feel exactly the same" seemed too forward. *"How interesting"* seemed too cold. *Why was conversation so difficult?*

Before Venetia could formulate a response, their moment of intimate conversation was interrupted by an unexpected commotion from the direction they'd come. Raised voices, speaking rapid Italian, echoed off the canal walls, accompanied by the sound of hurried footsteps on stone.

Of course. Because nothing can ever be simple.

"What is this—" Mr. Rothbury began, but his words were cut short as a figure burst around the corner of the walkway, running at full speed directly toward them.

The man—a gondolier judging by his costume—appeared to be fleeing from some pursuit, his face flushed with panic. Behind him, additional voices suggested he was indeed being chased.

"*Scusi, scusi!*" the man gasped as he approached, his eyes wide with terror. Without ceremony, he grasped Edward's arm. "You help, signor? *Per favore?* Bad men come, want money, I have nothing!"

Well, that's what Venetia's rudimentary Italian translated.

Smoothly, Mr. Rothbury positioned himself between Venetia and the agitated stranger, asking in Italian, "What's happened?"

Before the gondolier could respond, the sound of pursuing footsteps grew louder, and three rough-looking men rounded the corner. Their clothing marked them as laborers from the Venetian docks. The cudgels they carried suggested their intentions were far from peaceful.

"There he is!" one of them shouted. "The thief who took our week's wages!"

Venetia was sufficiently well versed in the Italian language to catch the gist. She saw Mr. Rothbury's hand move instinctively to where a gentleman might carry a sword, though of course he bore no weapon on what was supposed to be a simple afternoon's outing.

The narrow walkway offered little room for maneuvering, while the canal on one side and the palazzo's sheer wall on the other provided no avenue for escape.

"Venetia," he said quietly, using her given name without conscious thought, "stay behind me. Whatever happens, do not—"

He called me Venetia. In the middle of what might be our imminent demise, that's oddly thrilling.

But his words were interrupted as the fleeing gondolier, apparently realizing the narrow walkway offered no further escape route, made a desperate decision. With a muttered prayer to what sounded like several different saints, he leaped directly into the canal, disappearing beneath the murky water with a splash that sent ripples racing toward both banks.

The pursuing men reached their position seconds later, their faces dark with anger and frustration as the man they pursued began to swim away. The leader, a burly man whose arms were scarred and knotted with muscle, fixed Edward with a suspicious glare.

"*Inglese?*" he demanded, apparently recognizing Mr. Rothbury's nationality from his clothing.

Mr. Rothbury nodded carefully. "Is there some assistance we might provide?"

The man's expression remained hostile as his gaze shifted to take in Venetia's elaborate costume. Something in his eyes suggested he was reassessing the situation, perhaps wondering whether these well-dressed foreigners might represent a more profitable target than the vanished gondolier.

Oh no. Oh, this is bad.

"Pretty lady," he said in broken English, taking a step toward Venetia which Mr. Rothbury blocked. "Nice jewels. Maybe she share with poor working men?"

Sofia's jewels.

"We're merely tourists," said Mr. Rothbury, consolidating his position in front of Venetia, "with no involvement in whatever dispute you had with that fellow."

The leader's smile held no warmth whatsoever. "Tourists with money, yes? Rich English, always have money. You give some, we let you walk away. Is good bargain, no?"

Venetia saw Mr. Rothbury stiffen. He was outnumbered and at a disadvantage, with the canal on one side and no means of escape except past the three ruffians.

Her throat closed up, and she could utter no sound.

This is not how I imagined this afternoon going. Not at all.

Would she feel the grasping of calloused hands about her neck as they tried to prize Sofia's necklace from her person? And how would she explain its loss?

That's if they got out of this situation at all.

Chapter Fourteen

"Gentlemen."

Mr. Rothbury's tone was smooth and unruffled as he addressed them in polite, respectful Italian.

Venetia could scarcely believe his composure. Instinctively, she pressed closer against his side, and it was then she became more conscious of the effort it took him to appear unfazed—she could feel the strong beat of his heart.

At least one of us is maintaining dignity. I'm fairly certain I've stopped breathing.

"Please let us pass. This young lady is under the protection of Count Morosini, whose palazzo you see there"—he gestured toward a distant building whose upper windows were just visible above the canal walls—"and she is his honored guest, expected for music lessons within the hour while I bear her escort. Your interference with our passage will not be kindly regarded by the count, whose guards are observing your every move and will arrive at a signal from me."

That's... actually quite impressive bluffing.

The leader of the three men hesitated. Venetia could see him reassessing the situation, weighing the potential value of their purses against the risk of offending Venetian nobility. For a moment, she dared to hope that brave Mr. Rothbury's bold gambit had succeeded.

But then the ruffian's expression hardened, and she realized with a sinking heart that desperation had made him reckless.

"Count or no count," he snarled, "we see no servants, no guards. Just rich English with full purses and nowhere to run."

Venetia's first instinct was to flee, but it was Mr. Rothbury who moved first, pushing her behind him as the three men advanced. "Run, Venetia!" he commanded, but there was nowhere to flee when two of the men moved to block her. The narrow walkway stretched behind them, while ahead lay only the canal and the stone wall of an abandoned palazzo.

What followed happened with the terrible swiftness of a nightmare. Mr. Rothbury, with the reflexes of a man who'd once served His Majesty's Navy, managed to land a solid blow on the first attacker before the second man's cudgel caught him across the shoulder with sickening force. Venetia watched in horror as he staggered, his feet slipping on the moss-covered stones, before a third blow sent him sprawling onto the ancient cobblestones with a sound that made her stomach lurch.

No. No, no, no—

"Mr. Rothbury!" The cry tore from her throat as she dropped to her knees beside his motionless form, her skirts pooling around them. The men loomed over them, reaching for Edward's fallen purse, when the sound of approaching voices echoed from the direction of the main canal.

"Someone comes!" one of the attackers hissed, and with muttered curses they snatched what coins had scattered from Mr. Rothbury's purse before disappearing into the maze of narrow passages that honeycombed this section of Venice.

Alone with Mr. Rothbury's motionless form, Venetia's hands trembled as she touched his face. A thin line of blood trickled from a cut above his left temple, and his coat was ripped at the shoulder beneath the cudgel's impact.

But his chest rose and fell with reassuring regularity, and when she whispered his name, his eyelids fluttered in response.

Thank God.

"Edward," she breathed, cradling his head in her lap with complete disregard for the damage to Sofia's borrowed finery. "Oh, my dearest Edward, please open your eyes. Please be well."

His dark lashes lifted slowly, revealing eyes that were unfocused but blessedly conscious. "Venetia?" he murmured, his voice hoarse with pain. "Are you... did they harm you?"

"No," she assured him, smoothing his hair away from the bleeding cut. "No, they took nothing but a few coins. You saved me... You could have been killed!"

"Venetia," he said again, seeming to forget he was using her Christian name as he raised his hand to cover hers where it rested against his cheek. "I could not bear it if anything had happened to you. When I saw those men threatening you, I thought... I've never been so frightened in my life."

He's saying all the right things. Oh yes, just keep saying them...

"Nor I," she whispered, abandoning all pretense of reserve as the words poured from her heart. "When you fell, when I thought you might be seriously injured, I realized that nothing else in this world matters to me as much as your safety, your happiness. Oh, Edward, I would rather be poor again with a man I love than rich and miserable with someone chosen for his bloodline or bank account."

"You must not say such things," he interrupted, though his thumb traced gentle circles across her knuckles in contradiction of his words. "You're wealthy, titled, sought after by gentlemen of fortune and standing. While I... I'm nothing more than a poor translator with modest prospects and no family name to recommend me."

"Do you truly believe I care about that?" Venetia demanded. "Have you learned nothing of my character in all these months? The fortune I inherited is nothing compared to finding a companion whose mind and heart call to my own."

Edward's eyes closed briefly. "Venetia, you speak from emotion, from the shock of what just occurred. But think of what you would be sacrificing—"

"The only thing I would sacrifice," she said with quiet intensity, "is the chance for true happiness, if I allow false pride and social conventions to stand between us."

He smiled suddenly, and for a moment Venetia glimpsed the depth of longing he'd been struggling to conceal. His hand tightened on hers, and she was certain he was about to speak the words that would change everything between them.

Finally. FINALLY.

"*Madonna mia!* What has happened here?"

Oh, for the love of—

The exclamation, delivered in rapid Italian, shattered their moment of intimacy like a stone thrown against glass. Venetia looked up to see a well-dressed Venetian gentleman hurrying toward them, his face creased with concern.

Of course. Because we're in apparently the most populated deserted corner of Venice.

"Signor," Edward said, struggling to sit upright despite Venetia's attempts to keep him still. "We encountered some... difficulties... with local brigands."

"I saw the scoundrels fleeing as I approached," the gentleman replied, introducing himself as Signor Benedetti as he produced a clean handkerchief from his coat. "You are fortunate, my friend. The blow to your head appears superficial, though you'll have a considerable bruise on that shoulder. Can you stand?"

With Signor Benedetti's assistance, Edward rose to his feet, and amidst a volley of questions, was escorted toward his gondola moored nearby.

"You're a translator for Count Morosini? Yet an English gentleman?" Signor Benedetti's curiosity was clearly growing as he helped steady Edward. "The accent in your Italian—it's flawless. You are, in truth, a local?"

"My mother was Italian." Edward winced as Signor Benedetti touched his wounded shoulder. "From these parts."

"Your mother? What was her name? I am from these parts,

too. Perhaps I knew her?"

Edward frowned with the effort of movement, muttering, "Isabella—" before pressing his lips together, though he added, his breath labored, "She was a singer."

A singer? This was the first Venetia had heard about Edward's mother. She resolved to question him later.

"*Madonna santissima!*" Benedetti stopped so abruptly as he stared fiercely into Edward's eyes that they both stumbled. "Not La Monteverdi? The nightingale of La Fenice? But she was... she was magnificent! I heard her sing Desdemona when I was but a youth—never has such beauty graced our stages since!" His eyes shone with reverence. "Why, now you mention it, I can see your resemblance to the incomparable La Monteverdi. And you are her son?"

"I never said that," Edward ground out.

"Ah, but what a scandal it was!" Benedetti continued, as if Edward hadn't spoken. "The whole city spoke of nothing else for months! She was at the very pinnacle of her art—contracts from Milan, from Naples, even whispers of Vienna calling for her services. And Marchese Alessandro Valenti, from one of our most distinguished families, had declared his great love!" His voice dropped to a conspiratorial whisper that somehow managed to carry even more clearly. "But then tragedy!" He shook his head sorrowfully. "And afterwards came this English signore, and puff!—" he snapped his fingers dramatically, "—she abandoned everything! The stage, the count, her career, all of Venice mourning the loss of such a voice, as she sailed away to become a mere wife in some English countryside we had never heard of!"

Oh. Oh dear.

Venetia's limited Italian caught enough of the rapid words—*scandalo, abbandonato.*

All about a story that Edward was denying.

But if it *was* true that his mother gave up everything for love, did he think Venetia wouldn't do the same?

"Of course," Benedetti added hastily, perhaps sensing the

sudden chill in his audience, "nothing can stand in the way of true love, eh? I'm certain she found great happiness and rewards in her new life in England. A woman of such spirit—she would have made any home a palace with her presence! Now, let me assist your companion and her maid into the gondola, monsieur. What a pleasure it has been to know you." He bowed deeply, his pleasure unabated as the gondolier pushed off from the bank.

They were several minutes into their journey before Venetia was able to break through the awkwardness. "Edward. Mr. Rothbury—" she amended quickly, for it seemed their earlier intimacy had been eroded by Signor Benedetti's enthusiastic admiration. "You must see to your cut for it's deep. We should return to our palazzo rather than Count Morosini's."

He shook his head. "We'll go to Count Morosini's because Caterina will be waiting for you." His voice was dull. "It's more important that Sofia's soiled gown be attended to than my cuts and bruises."

Sofia's gown. SOFIA'S GOWN? I just confessed my feelings and he's worried about SOFIA'S GOWN.

"Of course," Venetia said quietly, gathering the soiled folds of Sofia's skirts around her with as much dignity as she could muster.

When they reached the landing stage where Caterina stood with her hands on her hips, clearly irritated by their tardiness and having obviously dispatched Sofia, the maid took in the state of her mistress's borrowed clothing with sharp eyes but no visible surprise.

Perhaps Sofia's adventures not infrequently resulted in such disasters.

But her eyes widened at the cut above Mr. Rothbury's eye.

"Footpads," he explained shortly. "No harm done other than to Signorina Sofia's lovely gown. I shall, of course, pay the dressmaker's bill."

He barely looked at Venetia as he helped her out of the gondola, followed by Mollie, before bowing and saying, "I must return to my translation duties for the count. Pray excuse me, and please, Miss Playford, forgive me for the dark turn this afternoon has taken."

Miss Playford. We're back to Miss Playford. Wonderful.

Venetia felt something squeeze her heart as if it really were putty in the hands of some unknown force.

"It wasn't your fault," she whispered. "You were so brave."

But he merely nodded, not making eye contact as he said to Mollie, "Look after your mistress. She had something of a fright this afternoon, and the shock may be delayed. Perhaps a soothing posset would be in order."

A posset. He's prescribing a soothing posset?

And then he was gone, and Venetia was back in the gondola, heading toward the palazzo where she knew she'd be received with eager excitement by Lady Townsend, who'd quiz her on every word spoken and meaningful glance shared.

But what could she tell her?

That her heart belonged more than ever to brave, handsome, gallant Mr. Rothbury.

But that he was further away than ever?

Chapter Fifteen

EDWARD ENDURED A fitful sleep that night. His precious time yesterday with Venetia had been on the cusp of promising something deeper than the genial friendship they'd hitherto enjoyed. She'd tried to speak to him of what was in her heart and, indeed, he was about to let her.

For why should his misplaced honor stand in the way of their happiness? If she believed he was worthy of her, he'd be a fool to persuade her otherwise.

A fool. Which, frankly, he'd been acting like for months now.

The violent encounter with the footpads had truncated talk of love and affection—a conversation just resurrected before the well-meaning Signor Benedetti had ruined everything with his recognition of Edward's true identity.

Yet, on reflection, he realized this had been his unexpected salvation.

For, as Miss Playford had uttered those heartfelt words indicating the depth of her feeling, his susceptible heart had answered.

Dangerous!

What would he have answered had his response not been cut short by the arrival of the ruffians but, more importantly, by Signor Benedetti? The gentleman's recollections of Edward's mother had been a salient reminder that memories were long, and his mother was far from forgotten in these parts.

Which only bore up how long some memories would prove to be if he were to announce to English society—much less Italian—that he, Signor Edward Rothbury, was to wed one of England's most substantial heiresses.

Not only would this set tongues wagging, it would not be long before the truth was laid bare for all to judge. Was Mr. Edward Rothbury, with such a stain upon his reputation—the illegitimate son of an Italian opera singer—worthy to be the husband of one so untainted and elevated as Miss Playford?

With a groan, he pressed his fingertips against his temples, willing away the persistent ache that had plagued him since yesterday's encounter with Venice's less savory elements.

The bruising along his shoulder had deepened overnight to an impressive palette of purple and yellow, though that was nothing compared with the vulnerability and dangerous territory his heart had led him into.

Returning to Scott's prose, he tried to rid his mind of Venetia's lovely image, but the passage describing Ivanhoe's internal conflict between duty and desire only led Edward back to those precious moments when Venetia had cradled his head in her lap, her voice breaking as she spoke words that had shattered every careful barrier he'd constructed around his heart.

"I would rather be poor again with a man I love than rich and miserable with someone chosen for his bloodline or bank account."

She'd spoken with such passionate sincerity, such complete disregard for the conventions that governed their world, that for a brief, shining moment he'd almost believed their love might indeed conquer all obstacles.

Almost. Before reality and common sense reasserted themselves with its usual impeccable timing.

Edward stared down at the manuscript before him, seeing not Scott's carefully crafted sentences but the image of Venetia's face transformed by borrowed finery. Even disguised as Sofia, the essence of her goodness had shone through.

Her goodness and her naivete.

How could he have been so foolish as to imagine, even for a moment, that such a woman could find lasting happiness with a man whose greatest achievement was his facility with foreign languages? Venetia might speak of preferring love over luxury, but she'd never truly experienced poverty's grinding humiliations.

Unlike his mother, who'd chosen love and—according to Benedetti's rapturous account—abandoned everything. Which had worked out... he paused... actually, it had worked out reasonably well until the fever that had taken her life when he'd been a boy. But that wasn't the point.

At the sound of approaching footsteps in the marble corridor outside the library, Edward straightened in his chair, hastily arranging his features into an expression of scholarly concentration. Count Morosini rarely visited the library during Edward's working hours, preferring to review completed translations in the comfort of his private study. The elderly nobleman's unexpected appearance this morning was therefore both surprising and somewhat concerning.

"Ah, my dear Rothbury," the count said as he entered the magnificent room. "I hope I'm not disturbing your scholarly endeavors?"

"Not at all, Count Morosini," Edward replied, rising and bowing. "I'm always honored by your presence."

Also terrified.

The count advanced through the library, his fingers trailing along the leather spines with apparent affection. Despite his age, he was an imposing figure—tall and elegantly garbed, with silver hair that gleamed in the afternoon light, and keen dark eyes that missed absolutely nothing.

"I trust you're recovering from yesterday's... unpleasantness?" the count inquired, his gaze settling on the faint bruising visible at Edward's temple. "Signor Benedetti was greatly concerned when he related the circumstances of your unfortunate encounter."

Edward felt a chill of apprehension at the realization that news of the attack had reached the count's ears.

Oh dear Lord, might Benedetti also have mentioned the presence of a young woman with golden hair?

What Benedetti knew about Edward was damaging enough—though Edward hadn't actually endorsed his suppositions—but what might he have revealed about the golden-haired beauty in his company?

"I'm quite recovered, thank you," Edward replied carefully. "I should have known that such incidents are not uncommon in Venice's more isolated quarters."

"Indeed," the count agreed, settling himself in one of the leather chairs positioned near the tall windows. "Venice is a hotbed of individuals of questionable moral character, and one must exercise considerable caution when venturing beyond the more civilized districts." He paused, his dark eyes fixed on Edward with uncomfortable intensity. "Particularly when one travels in the company of... valued companions."

There it is.

The subtle emphasis on his final words confirmed Edward's worst fears.

"I was indeed fortunate that Signor Benedetti arrived when he did," Edward said, barely able to look his patron in the eye. "His assistance was most timely."

Count Morosini smiled—an expression that managed to convey both warmth and warning in equal measure. "Benedetti is a man of considerable discretion as well as generosity. He understands that certain... arrangements... require careful handling to avoid unfortunate complications."

The count rose from his chair and moved to examine one of the completed manuscript pages spread across Edward's desk, his expression thoughtful as he read the elegant Italian prose that had emerged from Scott's English original.

"Your work continues to exceed even my high expectations,"

he said. "It has heightened the eagerness of my dear friend and fellow Scott enthusiast, the marchese, to have *Ivanhoe* translated before the month is out. The manner in which you capture not merely the literal meaning but the essential spirit of these romantic tales is truly remarkable. Scott's *Ivanhoe*, in particular, seems to have inspired your most eloquent translations."

"The story possesses considerable emotional resonance," Edward admitted, unable to keep a note of personal feeling from coloring his voice.

"Indeed, it does," the count agreed, settling back into his chair with the air of one preparing for a longer conversation. "The tale of a disinherited knight who loves a lady far above his station—such themes have appealed to romantics throughout the ages. Though one must acknowledge that Scott was wise to provide his hero with restored lands and noble title before permitting him to claim his lady's hand."

And then, with these words, Edward... knew.

Oh no.

Benedetti had indeed told Count Morosini that Edward had been with a young blonde beauty, clearly an aristocrat given her dress.

Yet while the older man's words carried no obvious criticism, their implication was devastatingly clear: Even in fiction, love required the support of compatible social positions to achieve lasting happiness.

"Sir Walter understood the practical considerations that govern such matters," the count continued with deceptive casualness. "A gentleman of modest means who attempts to court a lady of great fortune courts not romance but tragedy. The world is harsh in its judgment of such presumption, and the lady herself, however sincere her initial feelings, must eventually confront the reality of what such a union would cost her in terms of social standing and material comfort."

Edward frowned as fear skittered up his spine. Could Benedetti have overheard Venetia's declaration of... love? A declaration which the merchant might have misconstrued as having been uttered by Sofia?

Please, God, no.

The count paused, his gaze drifting to the canal visible through the library's tall windows, and in the drawn-out silence, Edward heard the beating of his heart and knew some response was expected.

"*Ivanhoe*'s tale is as relevant today as it ever was," Edward murmured. "It would be wise to remember that."

The count turned his keen gaze on Edward. "Indeed, it would. Temptation comes in many guises, and while Ivanhoe won his heart's desire, the return of his title and estates made him worthy. But a penniless youth, however talented, who pursues the precious granddaughter of his patron, risks tragedy for both himself and the object of his affections."

So, he truly refers to his granddaughter?

Edward sucked in a shocked breath.

He thinks I was with Sofia? He thinks I'm pursuing Sofia?

"One would hope common sense would assert itself when he realizes he runs the risk not only of ensuring her social ostracism but his own financial ruin," the count continued. "Sometimes true love requires the courage to step aside rather than the boldness to press forward."

For a moment Edward was blinded by panic. If Benedetti had mistaken Miss Playford for Sofia—as he would have, given Sofia's elaborate dress—and revealed to Count Morosini that the pair were alone together when the footpads attacked, would there be further consequences beyond this warning? This veiled threat?

I'm going to be dismissed. Or worse. What are the dungeons like in Venice?

Briefly he closed his eyes. What could he say without compromising either Sofia by disclosing her duplicity, or his own involvement in it?

"But of course common sense would prevail," Edward said numbly, taking the gamble that a tacit acceptance of guilt was better than protests the count was unlikely to believe.

Brilliant. Confess to something you didn't do to avoid confessing to something you actually did.

"I'm glad you think that," the count said softly, rising but not moving toward Edward. He hesitated, clearly pondering his next words. "Now, I've interrupted you longer than I'd intended. I do not believe a more skilled translator exists for the exacting nature of my work. My impatience for *Ivanhoe* to be completed has tempered other emotions now that I feel I've been reassured."

Reassured that I'm not pursuing your granddaughter. Which I'm not. But I am helping her deceive you. Wonderful.

"My granddaughter finds power in breaking hearts, and there has been more than one young man who has suffered my ire. I had thought you different, Mr. Rothbury. I certainly would be loath to lose you. But if you're a wise man intent on proving his loyalty to his patron, then I shall be glad to know that once *Ivanhoe* is translated, you will move on to the translation of further volumes by the unequaled Sir Walter Scott."

Edward bowed. "I understand completely, Count Morosini."

"Excellent," the count said, moving toward the door. "I knew I could rely on your good sense."

Chapter Sixteen

EUGENIA SETTLED HERSELF comfortably in a silk-upholstered chair that commanded the best view of the Palazzo Contarini's elegant drawing room while she waited for Thornton to join her.

The English residents who'd assembled for afternoon refreshments were all pleasant enough acquaintances, some of whom had made Venice their home on a semipermanent basis.

But none sparked the depth of feeling that Thornton did. After thirty years, he was more than a true friend.

Whether he felt the same was something that—she'd admit to no one but her personal diary—kept her awake at night.

Well, that and Catherine's snoring from the adjacent room.

So, perhaps it was for this very reason that she'd taken such a personal interest in dear Miss Playford, whom she now observed picking distractedly at a macaron on her fine bone china plate while pretending to attend to Catherine.

Eugenia could tell the girl was barely listening. She prided herself on her social acuity. Being an heiress was a lonely business—to that she could attest.

As for being a heartbroken one, well, Eugenia could see the signs as clear as daylight even from across the room.

The girl looked like she was attending a funeral. For her own happiness.

Of Mr. Rothbury there was no sign, and while it would have been a relief to put Miss Playford's dismal spirits down to his simple absence, Eugenia knew it was far more serious than that.

The previous day, she'd observed the stilted interactions between the pair as they'd passed one another in the corridor and, with sinking heart, had known that something of import had occurred between them. And that it did not augur well for a bright and happy future together.

They'd practically fled from each other. Like pigeons scattering from cannon fire.

She took a sustaining breath as she brought her teacup to her lips. Ever the pragmatist—she had to remind herself—there was always hope while both remained unattached.

And tomorrow evening's masquerade ball promised a plethora of opportunities for Miss Playford and Mr. Rothbury to discover a side of each other that perhaps could only be revealed when in disguise, since both of them were clearly such hostages to convention.

And to their own spectacular inability to simply talk to each other like rational adults.

Where was Thornton? Impatient, Eugenia put down her teacup with a rattle and scanned the room more thoroughly, her eyes alighting on Catherine's latest acquisition, Count di Montefiore.

There was something about the gentleman she couldn't quite place. His appearance was certainly striking: tall and elegantly proportioned, with dark hair fashionably styled and a neatly trimmed beard that lent him an air of distinguished maturity.

Yet something in his manner troubled her.

Rather like a snake might trouble one. If the snake wore expensive tailoring.

Perhaps it was the way his dark eyes seemed to catalog and assess every detail of their surroundings, or the calculated manner with which he deployed his considerable charm. Eugenia had met many Continental gentlemen during her travels, and while they were often more demonstrative than their English counterparts, this count's attention felt somehow predatory rather than merely appreciative.

"My dear count," she heard Catherine say, "how discerning of you. Indeed, I would say it is perfectly correct to say that Miss Playford's extraordinary elevation is a romantic tale of unexpected fortune!"

Had Catherine been twenty years younger, she'd no doubt have been trying to ingratiate herself into the count's good graces for her own purposes.

But now Eugenia observed with growing alarm the alacrity with which Catherine responded to the count's interest with more than necessary detail regarding Miss Playford's finances.

"You see," Catherine continued, moving forward to speak to him as he reclined in the seat opposite, "dear Venetia was quite penniless until last year—living under the guardianship of a most disagreeable aunt who treated her little better than an unpaid companion. But then, in the most dramatic fashion imaginable, she inherited the entire fortune of her great-uncle, Mr. Leonard Harrington, who was reportedly one of the wealthiest men in Derbyshire."

Catherine. CATHERINE. Stop talking.

Count di Montefiore's expression remained politely interested, though Eugenia noticed his posture had subtly shifted, as though Catherine's words had captured his attention in a distinctly unsettling way.

And little wonder. Catherine was preparing their dear young friend on a platter, as if she were an heiress in need of a husband—or a fortune hunter in need of a target.

This was not edifying talk. But what could Eugenia do beyond clear her throat very loudly, try to interject and—when that failed—observe, very closely, how such information was received?

No, she really did not like or trust Count di Montefiore. Not one bit.

"How fascinating," the count now murmured in his beautifully accented English. "Such sudden elevation must have been quite overwhelming for a young lady of modest background."

"Oh, that's only the beginning of the tale," Catherine replied.

"Catherine!" Eugenia tried to catch Catherine's eye, but the woman went on, "The inheritance came with the most unusual conditions—you see, Mr. Harrington had originally designated his nephew as heir, but apparently grew concerned about the young man's moral character. The old gentleman was obsessed with preserving the family's reputation, and he included the most extraordinary clauses in his final will."

Eugenia's chill of apprehension increased as she observed the count's reaction to this revelation. His fingers, which had been casually drumming against the arm of his chair, suddenly stilled, while something flickered in his dark eyes that looked suspiciously like hunger.

"What manner of conditions?" the count inquired, his tone remaining neutral despite the intensity of his focus.

Catherine visibly preened at his attention. "The most dramatic provisions imaginable! The entire inheritance—every penny, every property, every investment—was left to dear Venetia on one very particular understanding. Mr. Harrington stipulated that if, within three years of his death, his chosen heir should be reported to the trustees as having engaged in 'persistent moral turpitude'—that is, any pattern of public scandal, notorious impropriety, or conduct unbecoming a lady of honor—then her interest would immediately cease and the whole of the estate would pass instead to the nephew—this Mr. Greene."

The count's brows lifted a fraction.

Catherine leaned forward, delighted by his interest. "It is all spelled out in the most meticulous fashion. There is to be no quibbling. The trustees are empowered—indeed obliged—to treat any formal report from the proper authorities, here or in England, as sufficient proof that Mr. Harrington's misgivings were justified. If they receive such a report describing a pattern of dishonorable conduct, they must consider the conditions of the will breached and hand everything over to Mr. Greene. Mr. Harrington was absolutely determined that his fortune should never rest with anyone whose name might be linked to public disgrace."

"What a... comprehensive set of conditions," the count observed.

"But here's the most remarkable part," Catherine continued, oblivious to any undercurrents in the conversation. "Mr. Harrington became so concerned about his original heir's character that he secretly changed his will just weeks—if not days—before his death. The nephew—a Mr. Greene, I believe—knew nothing of this alteration until after the old gentleman's death. Can you imagine the shock? One day expecting to inherit a fortune, the next discovering it had all gone to a penniless niece he'd probably never even considered! And yet, should she be convicted of any such offense before those three years are up, all would fall back to him. It is like one of those horrid melodramas one only reads about."

The count inclined his head. "How unfortunate for the nephew," he said quietly. "Such a dramatic reversal of fortune must have been... devastating."

"Oh, I'm sure it was," Catherine agreed with cheerful callousness. "Though from what I understand, Mr. Greene's subsequent behavior rather vindicated the old gentleman's change of heart. There was some sort of scandal involving an attempted elopement and considerable debts. Really, Mr. Harrington showed remarkable prescience in recognizing his nephew's unsuitability."

Lord Thornton, who had arrived for the last of this exchange and had been listening with apparently growing discomfort, cleared his throat diplomatically. "Perhaps we shouldn't dwell overmuch on the misfortunes of absent parties. Such matters are surely private to the families involved."

Thank you, Thornton. Voice of reason as always.

"Nonsense!" Catherine declared with a dismissive wave of her jeweled hand. "It's hardly gossip when the story was reported in all the London papers. Besides, it only serves to emphasize dear Venetia's remarkable transformation. From penniless ward to one of England's wealthiest heiresses! And the dear girl has handled her elevation with such grace."

Eugenia glanced toward Venetia, out of earshot near the supper table, her fingers worrying nervously at the intricate gold bracelet that adorned her wrist—a piece that Eugenia recognized as part of the spectacular jewelry collection that had been part of Venetia's inheritance.

Wearing a fortune on her wrist while Catherine advertises her vulnerabilities. Marvelous.

Where was Mr. Rothbury? she wondered. Or, more to the point, why was he not bearing her company when she clearly needed protection from Catherine's enthusiastic indiscretion?

The count smiled. Perfectly polite. Utterly chilling. "How remarkably... thorough of this... Mr. Harrington. One can only admire such attention to preserving family honor."

The look of savage satisfaction was gone so quickly Eugenia might have imagined it. But every instinct she possessed was now screaming warnings about this allegedly charming nobleman.

Right. Intervention time.

Eugenia swept over to interject herself into the conversation. "Count di Montefiore," she said sweetly, "I've no doubt Italian families employ similar protective measures? Tell me more about yours."

The count's attention shifted to her with the fluid grace of a serpent focusing on potential prey. "Mediterranean families have always understood the importance of protecting their interests from unsuitable influences. One cannot be too careful when substantial fortunes are at stake."

"Quite so," Eugenia agreed, holding his gaze steadily. "And I realize how little I know of yours." She hesitated. "Your family, I mean."

Catherine remained oblivious to the menace crackling through the afternoon air as Count di Montefiore regarded Eugenia.

Then, making a sound like a sigh of regret, the count rose. "It is late and I risk overstaying my welcome," he said. "I am sure you ladies have much to prepare for tomorrow's masquerade ball."

Eugenia inclined her head.

Well, tomorrow's masquerade would provide the perfect stage for matters to unfold in just the direction she wanted them to go.

Venetia would be in no danger from Count di Montefiore because whatever villainy he might be concocting would be rendered null and void by the real hero of Miss Playford's worthy heart—Mr. Rothbury—finally presenting himself as her knight in shining armor.

In fact, she thought, straightening as a sudden inspiration sharpened her resolve, perhaps Count di Montefiore was precisely the catalyst needed to galvanize Mr. Rothbury into action.

Nothing motivated a hesitant hero quite like a genuine villain.

Perhaps if that noble young man were made aware of the danger the count posed to the woman he seemed only prepared to love from afar, he would be prompted to declare himself.

Chapter Seventeen

EDWARD STARED AT the Foreign Office seal attached to the official correspondence spread across his writing desk.

The letter from Lord Pemberton had arrived that morning, offering him a prestigious posting to Constantinople with a salary that had the potential to transform his circumstances from genteel poverty to genuine prosperity.

"His Majesty's Government recognizes your exceptional linguistic abilities and diplomatic acumen," the letter stated. "The position of Senior Translator at the Embassy in Constantinople carries considerable responsibility and commensurate reward. Your acceptance of this appointment would represent a significant advancement in your career prospects, with opportunities for further promotion within the diplomatic hierarchy."

His throat felt dry. With Count Morosini's recent warning about how easily he could be dismissed—despite his desire for Scott translations—he wondered if his benefactor had a hand in this.

Perhaps Count Morosini had decided that Edward's valuable contribution to his library was outweighed by the supposed danger he posed to his beautiful granddaughter.

A granddaughter Edward wasn't even pursuing.

He reread the letter.

The practical advantages were undeniable. The salary alone would elevate him from his current status as a modestly compensated translator to that of a gentleman of independent means. Within three years, he could return to England with sufficient resources to establish himself in society, perhaps even to purchase a small estate befitting his enhanced position. It was everything he could dream of—recognition, financial security, and the prospect of genuine advancement.

Yet the thought of accepting the posting filled him with a desolation so profound he could barely contemplate it.

Three years in the Ottoman capital. Three years of not seeing Venetia. Three years during which she would certainly find someone else.

By the time he returned to England, she'd likely be married to some worthy gentleman of appropriate fortune and standing, perhaps already the mother of children who would never know how desperately their mother had once been loved by a man too proud to pursue his heart's desire.

He stilled. Wasn't this going to happen regardless? He'd already accepted Miss Playford was beyond his reach, and the reasons were quite simply insurmountable. Even if Miss Playford declared she could never love another, he could never subject her to the consequences of what marriage between them would entail once the sordid truth regarding his parentage came out.

He had to stifle something close to a sob. The irony. Had he never been so assiduous in going through his father's correspondence with Venetia's father, and all those other documents, he might never have learned that he was not, in truth, a Rothbury.

What that did in fact make him, he had no idea...

Perhaps Signore Benedetti might hazard a guess if asked about Isabella Monteverdi's famous lovers.

But, he supposed, he had Signor Benedetti to thank for making him realize that pledging his troth to Venetia would open a Pandora's box promising eternal misery.

Edward rubbed his temples, where the persistent ache from his recent injuries seemed to throb in rhythm with his troubled thoughts, before approaching footsteps in the palazzo's marble corridor interrupted his brooding, followed by the soft knock he'd come to recognize as Sofia's distinctive demand for attention.

Edward sighed, hastily folding the Foreign Office letter and securing it in his desk drawer.

"*Entrate*," he called, and Sofia swept into his chamber with her usual graceful confidence, wearing an afternoon dress of rose silk, her golden curls arranged in an elaborate coiffure.

"Signor Edward!" she exclaimed with warmth. "I hope I'm not disturbing your scholarly pursuits, but I simply had to express my gratitude for your assistance yesterday. Everything proceeded exactly as planned, thanks to your dear Miss Playford's extraordinary kindness."

Edward's jaw tightened at her casual reference to Venetia, particularly given the emotional upheaval that had resulted from their supposedly simple masquerade. "I'm pleased the deception served your purposes, signorina, but I must tell you—"

"Oh, it was more than satisfactory!" Sofia replied with a tinkling laugh that struck Edward as distinctly artificial. "Paolo and I had the most wonderful afternoon together. We walked through the Giardini della Biennale and spoke of our future plans. He's so impatient for us to begin our new life together, far from Grandfather's interference."

Wonderful. So glad your romantic afternoon went well while mine ended in violence and heartbreak.

She settled herself gracefully in the chair opposite his desk, carefully arranging her skirts while her chocolate-brown eyes studied his face with uncomfortable intensity.

"Tell me, I'm just dying to learn more of tomorrow evening's entertainment," she continued. "I understand from the servants' gossip that your Miss Playford will be attending Grandfather's masquerade ball. How delightful!"

Edward stiffened at her assumption regarding his relationship with Venetia. "Miss Playford is not 'my' anything, signorina. She's simply a fellow English resident who was kind enough to assist in your romantic schemes."

At considerable personal cost, I might add.

Sofia's smile held a knowing quality that made Edward distinctly uncomfortable. "Of course, signor. Though I confess I find it curious that a gentleman would take such a personal interest in arranging assistance for a lady who was nothing more to him than a casual acquaintance."

Before Edward could formulate a response to this uncomfortably perceptive observation, Sofia leaned forward conspiratorially. "I happened to encounter Miss Bentley this morning at the Mercato di Rialto," she said. "Such a charming woman, though rather… talkative."

Edward nodded.

"She was most enthusiastic about tomorrow evening's entertainment and particularly about Miss Playford's costume—"

"I cannot imagine why Miss Playford's costume would be of interest to you." Edward felt a prickle of unease at Sofia's interest in Venetia's plans.

"Oh, but it is of the greatest interest!" Sofia exclaimed. "You see, Miss Bentley mentioned that your dear friend plans to appear as a Byzantine empress, complete with a magnificent headdress and cloth-of-gold gown. She described some of the jewelry Miss Playford intends to wear—apparently Lady Townsend has been advising her on creating the most spectacular effect possible."

There was a calculating gleam in Sofia's eyes that suggested an interest beyond mere feminine curiosity about fashion.

Why do I feel like I'm watching someone plan a military campaign?

"Apparently, Miss Playford plans to wear her sapphire parure—the necklace, earrings, and bracelet that belonged to her uncle's wife. The pieces are quite magnificent, with stones of exceptional quality and historical significance, according to Miss Bentley."

And Miss Bentley apparently provides inventory lists to anyone who asks?

"You seem remarkably well-informed about Miss Playford's

jewelry collection," Edward observed with growing suspicion.

Sofia laughed lightly. "Oh, you know how ladies are about such matters! Miss Bentley said the sapphire ensemble was valued at several thousand pounds...so of course Miss Playford must be very careful in view of this...scoundrel thief who is terrorizing all of Venice."

Edward felt increasingly uncomfortable. Sofia's interest in the specific value of Venetia's jewelry struck him as strange and mercenary. "I have seen you adorned with jewels to equal hers, signorina," he said mildly.

"Yes, but they are not mine. Otherwise Paolo and I would have eloped long before now," she said with a shrug. "Grandpapa has charged Caterina with keeping a careful inventory. However," she went on with renewed animation, "here is where I hoped to contribute to the evening's success! I happen to possess a particularly exquisite gold and sapphire tiara that would complement Miss Playford's planned ensemble perfectly. It was my grandmother's—a piece of considerable antiquity and beauty that has been in our family for generations."

Edward blinked.

This is a trap. This is definitely a trap.

She reached into her reticule and withdrew a small velvet jeweler's box, which she placed on Edward's desk. "I would be honored if Miss Playford would consent to wear it tomorrow evening as a token of my gratitude for her assistance yesterday."

Edward stared at the box, his mind racing through the implications of Sofia's unexpected generosity. The offer seemed both extravagant and suspicious. Why would a young woman lend an heirloom of significant value to someone she'd met only once? And why the intense interest in ensuring that Venetia wore specific pieces of jewelry to a crowded social event?

"That is... very generous of you, signorina," he said carefully, his pulse quickening. "Though I wonder if Miss Playford might feel such a loan places her under too great an obligation. Surely her own jewelry collection is sufficient for the occasion?"

Sofia smiled. "Oh, but you see, this particular piece would merely complement what Miss Bentley says she is wearing. She said Miss Playford was missing only a tiara of sapphires to look the part. And what I would like to offer her on loan was worn by the doge's daughter at her wedding to a Byzantine prince in the fourteenth century. What could be more appropriate for a lady appearing as a Byzantine empress?"

Her enthusiasm seemed forced now, and Edward's unease crystallized into active suspicion—and then, with horrifying clarity, into certainty.

Sofia is the thief. Or working with the thief. And she's setting up Venetia.

"I will convey your generous offer to Miss Playford," said Edward, making no move to accept the jeweler's box and keeping his voice carefully neutral. "Though of course the decision must be entirely hers."

The decision being "absolutely not under any circumstances."

"Naturally," Sofia agreed. "Though I do hope she'll consider it favorably. After all, such opportunities to wear truly historic pieces are quite rare, and the masquerade would provide the perfect setting for displaying such magnificence."

She rose from her chair and picked up the jeweler's box—then, to Edward's horror, slipped it into his leather satchel before he could object.

No. No, take it back. I don't want it anywhere near me.

"Tell her I shall be so disappointed if she declines," she said with a smile that no longer looked charming at all. "I shall have Caterina speak to her maid to persuade her."

Over my dead body.

Edward stared at his satchel as if it contained a viper while Sofia glided out of the room.

He realized he'd been very wrong in his assessment about Sofia.

She wasn't a desperate romantic. She was a calculating criminal who'd used him—used *Venetia*—as pawns in the scheme she was orchestrating.

And now he had approximately twenty-four hours to work out how to protect Venetia from whatever trap Sofia was setting at tomorrow's masquerade.

Constantinople was starting to look rather appealing.

Chapter Eighteen

VENETIA GAZED WITH awe at the grand salon that had been transformed into Byzantium. Silk banners in purple and gold fell from the vaults; a thousand candles flickered across inlaid marble. Masked guests—saints, sinners, emperors—glided to a melody played by troubadours in blue and gold silk.

"My dear Venetia, the gold and sapphire tiara is the crowning glory." Smiling, Lady Townsend stood at her side, her excitement palpable.

"You look magnificent, too," responded Venetia. And she did. In cloth-of-gold set off by an emerald diadem, Lady Townsend looked every inch the equal of the grandest empress.

"But it is your jewelry that will have heads turning," Lady Townsend went on. "I'm sure that Thornton was quite right to insist you wear Signorina Sofia's family tiara when she wished so much to show her friendship."

Venetia's heart clutched.

Friendship? From someone who'd barely thanked her for risking her reputation.

Oh, why had Mr. Rothbury brought the dreadful thing back to the palazzo, and why had Lord Thornton—upon seeing it on the table when Mr. Rothbury had briefly pulled it out of his briefcase—said it would be a snub to the great family if she refused to wear it?

It was supposedly a mark of gratitude for her deception of a few days ago. But Venetia did not want the young woman's gratitude.

Nor did she want her jewels to be the focus of tonight. Yet Miss Bentley had insisted she "wear them all."

The clear admiration on so many faces should have buoyed her. Instead, it rankled. Gallant speeches itemized her jewels. Fans fluttered, and the words "the English heiress" drifted from lip to lip like gossip served on a tray.

Not "the lovely young lady" or "that charming Miss Playford." Just "the English heiress."

Surrounded, she felt oddly, thoroughly alone.

Yes, she had Lady Townsend's friendship. And Lord Thornton was an ally. She had mixed feelings about Miss Bentley.

Mixed being generous. Miss Bentley was exhausting.

But it was Mr. Rothbury, alone, who had the power to make her heart feel... connected to another being.

She looked for a scholar's black among the costumes. Was Mr. Rothbury going to attend? He'd been vague.

Embarrassed?

He was behind with his work, he said. Count Morosini's friend, the reclusive marchese who, she'd learned, was the main instigator of the ambitious project to translate all of Sir Walter Scott's Waverley novels was getting impatient and Edward was feeling the pinch.

Or, perhaps he was too busy contemplating the foreign posting he'd apparently received and which Miss Bentley had described with such relish.

Three years in Constantinople. Three years of not seeing Edward. Three years of dying inside.

The music washed over her while the floor seemed to tilt.

She felt a touch at her wrist—too familiar—and turned to find a tall Renaissance prince in black velvet and a gold mask. Not Edward. The stranger's eyes lingered where eyes should not: at her throat, her tiara, her bracelet—as if tallying.

Oh, how tired she was of it all.

"You are melancholy, *bella imperatrice*," he said in smooth English. "How can that be, when dressed in such magnificence?"

"Thank you for your concern, signor," Venetia returned, barely considering the words as she stepped back to reclaim proper distance. "I fear I'm not much in the mood for festivities this evening."

"Then you require the right companion." He closed the distance by a fraction. "Do you not recognize me? I am Count di Montefiore." He paused. "And you are far from alone. Miss Bentley admires you excessively, and Signorina Sofia speaks glowingly of your generosity."

At Sofia's name, a thread of cold pulled tight.

Sofia. Sofia knows this man? Why does that feel ominous?

"You know a great many people despite being so recently a stranger here," Venetia said, not caring that her words sounded slighting.

"My letters of introduction were well received by Count Morosini. Subsequently, I've learned from the signorina herself of her desire to find a market for her talents."

Her talents. What talents? Being vain and ungrateful? Oh yes… her painting.

Venetia inclined her head. "Then the signorina is fortunate." What else could she say? She simply wanted to be gone.

"As am I to be enjoying these precious moments with one of the most beautiful women here tonight." His gaze flicked again to the tiara. "So exquisitely fitting the role you play."

"I beg you'll excuse me." Venetia took a step toward the canal-facing windows and the balcony beyond. She needed air.

And an escape route. Preferably one involving a gondola and immediate departure from Venice.

"But of course," he said with exaggerated courtesy, though his dark eyes continued to study her when she glanced over her shoulder to ensure he wasn't following.

Hunter's eyes.

With relief, she slipped through a side entrance onto the marble balcony that overlooked the palazzo's private garden.

And there she gave into her distress, alone with the sobs that wracked her. Would Edward really leave her for a lucrative posting in Constantinople?

"Forgive me."

The voice made her spine straighten. English. Familiar. She turned slowly, her heart fluttering like a caged bird attempting escape.

Edward.

A figure in scholar's black stood at the balcony entrance—simple robes, plain mask, but the voice that had just apologized was unmistakably Edward's. He stepped forward, clearly wrestling with propriety.

"I saw you in distress, madam." He swallowed visibly. "If you wish, I can find a friend. Lady Townsend is wonderfully kind." He trailed off, the ethical puzzle of addressing a masked stranger warring with basic kindness.

"You don't know me?" Venetia managed.

"No, but—" He moved closer. "No one should suffer alone."

The words broke something in her chest. Here he was, offering comfort to a stranger because he couldn't bear to see pain. This was why she loved him. Not because he was handsome and clever. But because he was the kind of man who couldn't walk past suffering.

Even when it was inappropriate. Even when it might compromise him.

Oh, Edward.

"Edward."

His name slipped out and she heard the longing in her tone.

Just as she saw recognition hit—his body going rigid, his breath catching.

"Venetia?" It was barely a whisper.

"I thought you wouldn't come—" She swallowed, then added, "But you're going away, aren't you?" she whispered. "Miss Bentley told me."

He didn't refute it.

Miss Bentley had eagerly supplied the details. Three years in Constantinople stretched between them. Three years of him buried in diplomatic translations while she was parceled off to some suitable husband. The thought made her reckless.

Well, if propriety had already fled, why not honesty?

"Edward, if you leave—"

"Don't." But his protest died as she stepped close enough to touch, her gloved hands framing his face through the mask. The wool of his scholar's hood rasped softly beneath her fingertips; his skin was warm where lips accidentally brushed his jaw below the edge of the satin.

His breath hitched. So did hers. The cool night air smelled of orange blossom and candle smoke, but beneath it was the quieter, steadier scent that was uniquely Edward—clean linen, ink, a whisper of some bitter shaving soap. It grounded her. Made everything else—gold tiaras, Venetian gossip, Count di Serpentine—fade into irrelevance.

"I love you," she said, the words pouring out before courage failed. "I've loved you since I was eight years old. If that means nothing, tell me now."

There. I've said it. I can't take it back. Mortification or happiness—one of those is coming.

His eyes closed as if her confession caused physical pain. "Venetia, I have nothing. A salary. No prospects beyond what my own work—"

"I don't care."

"Your fortune, your position—"

"Mean nothing without you."

Why was this so difficult for him to understand?

She could feel the war inside him, see it in the tension in his shoulders, the way his hands opened and closed at his sides as if fighting the urge to seize her and push her away at once.

He stood so close now she could count the rise and fall of his chest. The fabric of his robe brushed her skirts; a single movement would have them flush together. Heat seeped across the small space between them, awareness prickling over her skin like sparks from a fire.

"We cannot—" he began hoarsely.

"We already have," she whispered. "You said you'd rather see me safe and happy than have anything for yourself. This is what makes me happy, Edward. You."

His gaze dropped helplessly to her mouth, then jerked away, as if even looking were an indulgence he had no right to.

She watched the moment his resolve shattered, the exact heartbeat when duty loosened its grip and love tightened its own. The line of his jaw eased; something raw and unguarded flared in his eyes. He stopped fighting what they both wanted. His hands rose and covered hers where they cupped his face, his fingers dwarfing her gloved ones.

"God help me, I love you beyond reason," he whispered. "You are my heart."

Finally. FINALLY.

Her pulse thundered in her ears. Slowly, almost reverently, she slid one hand upwards and pushed his mask aside. The silk ribbon snagged briefly against his hair before giving way; the mask dropped, dangling from her fingers. For a moment she simply looked at him—at the beloved planes of his face freed from disguise, the vulnerable softness at the corners of his mouth, the crease between his brows that she'd wanted to smooth away for months.

Then she rose onto her toes and kissed him.

The first brush was almost nothing—a question, a trembling press of lips against lips. For one suspended instant he stayed utterly still, as if the slightest movement would shatter them both. She could feel his breath, warm and uneven against her cheek, could taste the faint sweetness of wine and something indefinably Edward.

Then his restraint snapped.

He made a sound—half groan, half prayer—and his arms came around her, pulling her against him with a desperation that stole what little breath she had left. The world narrowed to the strength of his hold and the sure, searching warmth of his mouth as he answered her kiss and deepened it.

Her hands slid from his face to his shoulders, feeling the solid muscle beneath the scholar's robe. He was always so controlled, so careful; she had never quite allowed herself to imagine how it would feel to be held by him with no carefulness at all. Now she knew. It felt like safety and ruin and home, all at once.

The marble balustrade pressed cool against her back as he angled them, but she barely felt it. All her senses were consumed: the rough edge of his jaw grazing her gloved knuckles as he cupped her face; the faint tremor in his fingers as though he, too, could scarcely believe this was allowed; the way his thumb brushed the sensitive skin just beneath her ear and sent a shiver racing down her spine.

She parted her lips on a sigh and his breath caught, his hand tightening in the small of her back as he deepened the kiss in earnest. Heat unfurled low in her belly, a slow, dangerous bloom of wanting that had nothing whatever to do with prospects or fortune. There was only this: the slide of his mouth over hers, the unsteady exhale when she answered him with all the feeling she'd hoarded for years.

He whispered her name against her lips, the syllables breaking slightly, as if it cost him something to say it and yet he could not stop.

"Venetia."

Her heart clenched. She had heard him say her name so many times—courteously, wryly, diffidently—but never like this. Never like a vow.

She dared to slip one hand up into his hair, feeling the thick, slightly unruly strands give beneath her fingers. He shuddered, a small, helpless reaction that thrilled her more than any compliment in the candlelit ballroom ever could. His lips gentled, then claimed hers again, slower now, exploring.

This was what she had imagined in lonely moments and fierce, foolish daydreams: the weight of his body anchoring hers, the solid warmth of his chest beneath her palms, the sense of...rightness. As if some misaligned piece inside her had finally slid into place.

If this was what sin felt like, she thought wildly, she could quite see why people risked eternal damnation for it.

One of his hands lifted to her cheek, his bare palm warm against the cool satin of her mask's ribbon where it had slipped to her neck. Gently, he tugged the mask free and let it fall, his gaze roaming over her face as if he, too, wanted to see clearly the person he'd been trying not to love.

"You should not have done that," he murmured, sounding entirely unconvinced by his own rebuke. His thumb traced the curve of her lower lip, slightly swollen from his kisses. "You should not have kissed me."

"You kissed me back," she managed, a little breathless.

His mouth curved. "I know. I am a very poor example of moral restraint."

"Thank goodness for that," she whispered, and leaned in again.

This time, when their lips met, there was no hesitation at all. They both knew exactly what they were doing and did it anyway. His hand splayed over her ribs, careful and yet claiming, feeling the race of her heart beneath silk and tight lacing. She pressed closer, fitting herself along the length of him, memorizing the feel of the hard line of his thigh, the way his chest rose sharply when she dared to taste him a little more boldly.

She had never been kissed like this. Oh, there had been the odd stolen salute in the past, clumsy and hurried in shadowed gardens, but those had been mere gestures. This was...real. Every lingering stroke, every soft, startled gasp answered by a gentler caress. Weeks and months of wanting dammed up and finally allowed to spill over.

If this were all they ever had, she thought, she would still be grateful. She would spend the rest of her life knowing, at least once, what it was to be truly, wholly wanted by the man she loved.

The taste of him, the way he whispered her name against her mouth—this was what she'd been missing. This rightness, this completion.

This was perfect. Absolutely perfect and nothing could possibly—

Then voices erupted from the ballroom.

Oh, for the love of—

"The contessa's emerald earrings! They're gone!"

"Search everyone!"

"No one leaves until the thief is found!"

No. No, no, no. Not now. Not when we've JUST—

Footsteps rang upon the stone floors and Captain Rizzi appeared, florid-faced and looking victorious, pointing an accusing finger.

At her.

"An English lady in a Byzantine diadem," he said briskly. "You match the account I was given."

His gaze went straight to the tiara she wore, not her face. He hadn't glanced around to search or question. He came straight for her, as if he'd already been told exactly whom to find.

Someone described me?

Her stomach flipped. Not only was she alone with Edward—ruin enough—but someone had marked her out in advance, as neatly as a hunter setting snares.

Sofia's tiara burned against her scalp.

Oh God. The tiara. Sofia loaned me the tiara. And now there's a theft and Captain Rizzi came straight to me.

This was a trap. This had been a trap all along.

And I walked right into it wearing several thousand pounds of jewelry and kissing the man I love on a semi-public balcony.

Chapter Nineteen

"Captain Rizzi." Venetia's hands shook as she looked at the captain, a dozen gawping guests behind him. "Of what do I stand accused?"

"Signorina Playford," he began, emphasizing her maiden state as he glanced accusingly between her and Mr. Rothbury. "Your description matches that of the… thief seen making off with a pair of emerald earrings."

Theft?

"I've done nothing other than seek solitude after the dancing."

"Solitude?" The captain raised an eyebrow, then said with sarcasm, "You were far from seeking solitude when I found you."

Edward stepped closer. "Captain, I protest any suggestion about Miss Playford's character—" Against her ear, he murmured, his horror palpable, "Sofia's tiara. I never intended you to accept her offer. How did you—?"

"Mr. Rothbury." Count Morosini appeared from behind the captain. His voice was cold. "You've said enough."

Oh God. Count Morosini? What does he have to do with this?

"Captain Rizzi, if you'd let me explain—"

"Explain? I do not need you to explain what was reported by several of my guests. Miss Bentley!"

Venetia turned, surprised to see Miss Bentley emerge from the crowd.

"Count di Montefiore asked you to keep an eye on several of Count Morosini's guests. Firstly, what explanation could excuse such behavior?" Captain Rizzi's arm encompassed the balcony.

Miss Bentley shook her head sorrowfully. "I should have known a man of modest means would compromise dear Venetia to force an advantageous marriage."

Compromise? We had ONE kiss and suddenly I'm a fallen woman?

The accusation hit Venetia like a slap. In Miss Bentley's version, Edward was a calculating fortune hunter rather than the honorable man she knew. The suggestion was so vile she could barely process it.

"That's not—"

Captain Rizzi raised a hand. "Miss Playford, perhaps you'll explain how you came to wear Signorina Morosini's family tiara tonight?"

The question made her stomach drop as her hand flew to the elaborate piece Sofia had insisted she borrow—the crowning touch of her costume that now felt like a crown of thorns.

Mr. Rothbury stepped forward. "Signorina Sofia offered it. She said it would complement Miss Playford's costume."

"Perhaps she did. But it's not the tiara itself that's of interest. Not its outward appearance, at any rate." Captain Rizzi took a step forward and indicated that Venetia was to hand it over.

With trembling hands, she gave it to him.

"You didn't notice anything unusual about your tiara's construction?"

She whipped her head up to face him. He was talking about the tiara? "Construction? I don't understand."

But within seconds of the captain inserting a tiny pin into what was suddenly revealed as a hinge, a section of the tiara sprang open, revealing two emerald earrings set off with tiny diamonds.

A secret compartment. The tiara had a secret compartment?

"These gems," Captain Rizzi announced with the theatrical flourish of a man who'd been waiting all evening for this moment, "which you had hidden in the tiara you wore tonight, match the Contessa di Barbarigo's missing pendant."

A collective gasp rang out. There were more guests witnessing her humiliation than Venetia had realized.

She stared at the emeralds, her mind reeling. Sofia's loan was simply part of an elaborate deception. The insistence on the tiara, the knowledge of Venetia's costume, the careful timing—all calculated to make her the perfect scapegoat.

"That's impossible." But even as she spoke, she grasped the trap's perfection.

"The evidence is clear," Captain Rizzi declared. "Stolen gems, concealed in jewelry you wore all evening."

She felt Edward's warmth as he moved closer against her side. "Captain, surely you can't believe Miss Playford would wear stolen goods openly? She was lent the tiara by Signorina Sofia Morosini. In fact, the signorina gave it to me stating her desire that it complement Miss Playford's costume. As she says herself, she's been made a scapegoat. Look elsewhere for your criminal."

Thank you, Edward. At least someone believes me.

Captain Rizzi glanced about him. "Several guests observed Miss Playford showing unusual interest in the contessa's jewelry earlier." His gaze alighted on Miss Bentley. "We merely followed up on certain... concerns."

Venetia heard Edward's intake of breath.

Concerns. MISS BENTLEY had concerns? Miss Bentley, who told everyone about my inheritance conditions?

So even her innocent admiration had been twisted into evidence. Every glance, every comment she'd made about the beautiful pieces around her now looked like criminal calculation.

I complimented someone's necklace and now I'm a jewel thief?

"This is absurd," Edward said, his anger clearly building. "Miss Playford is a young woman of the utmost integrity. I would be far from the only one to vouch for her."

"And yet, what else would account for the discovery of jewels stolen from the contessa two weeks ago in the tiara worn by this young lady?" Captain Rizzi repeated coldly. He glanced once more at Miss Bentley, and the flare of self-righteousness that crossed that woman's face made Venetia flame with hurt and shock.

No. Surely not. Miss Bentley couldn't be part of this. Could she?

Edward turned in her direction, demanding quickly, "You've known Miss Playford for some time, Miss Bentley. You surely would pledge your support for her strong moral character."

Captain Rizzi raked Miss Bentley with a somewhat ambiguous look before Venetia caught the flash of collusion, confirming her suspicions.

Oh God. She IS part of this. Miss Bentley is actually part of this.

When she remained silent, the captain asked, "You revealed your concerns, madame, when we communicated with you. I don't think you would now vouch for the young lady."

Trembling—though whether from genuine emotion or theatrical effect, Venetia could no longer tell—Miss Bentley thrust out her chin. "Miss Playford is, indeed, charming but... perhaps the transition from penniless ward to heiress came as too great a shock and challenged her moral foundations."

Challenged my moral foundations? I kissed someone! Once! After months of agonizing restraint!

There was a collective gasp, Edward's louder than anyone's, before he said with deadly quiet, "Captain Rizzi, Miss Playford's character isn't subject to anyone's assessment when it's quite clear the real jewel thief is at large."

"Indeed. But what of your own character, Mr. Rothbury? What should we make of a gentleman who compromises a lady as you did tonight?"

One kiss. ONE KISS. And suddenly we're scandalizing all of Venice.

There was silence, broken by Venetia who said, "Mr. Rothbury heard me weeping and came to offer comfort, Captain Rizzi. That is all. I give my word as a gentlewoman that I had no knowledge of theft, no awareness of emeralds in the tiara, no criminal intent."

"Your word as a gentlewoman?" Miss Bentley laughed suddenly—a sound that made Venetia's skin crawl. "When your behavior tonight shows such disregard for proper conduct."

Is she DRUNK? Has she lost her mind? What is happening?

Venetia stared. This was not the Miss Bentley she knew. Or thought she knew.

Edward's hands clenched. "Madam, I won't tolerate your implications about Miss Playford's character."

"What action do you propose, Mr. Rothbury?" Captain Rizzi inquired. "The facts speak for themselves. I applaud your efforts to play the gentleman at so late a stage, but if you're so ready to champion Miss Playford on the basis of refuting aspersions upon her character, might I suggest your efforts would be better spent discovering the identity of whom you believe is the real thief."

The real thief being Sofia. And possibly Miss Bentley. And possibly half of Venice, apparently.

Venetia saw the moment Edward realized her position was hopeless. His face went ashen. Any protest would deepen suspicion. The kiss that had been their moment of perfect connection had damned them both.

We finally confessed our feelings and immediately everything went to hell.

"Miss Playford," Captain Rizzi said, clearly enjoying this far too much, "you must accompany me for questioning."

Guards moved to flank her. Her composure cracked.

She was trapped in circumstantial evidence and social prejudice, her greatest happiness transformed into destruction.

Edward reached out, then stopped. Even comfort would look like conspiracy. The anguish in his eyes reflected her own devastation.

"Venetia," he said quietly, her name carrying love and desperation and everything they couldn't say.

"I know," she whispered, understanding his unspoken apology—for failing to protect her, for their stolen moment becoming her condemnation, for everything going so spectacularly wrong.

I know you love me. I know you tried. I know this is all Sofia's fault and possibly Miss Bentley's and definitely not yours.

As Captain Rizzi escorted her from the balcony, she caught one last glimpse of Edward frozen among his accusers, his face a mask of controlled anguish. The man she loved was as trapped as she was.

The masquerade continued below—music and laughter a cruel counterpoint to the drama above. But for Venetia, the evening had become a nightmare with no visible dawn.

From first kiss to arrest in under half an hour.

Chapter Twenty

Eugenia hesitated in the marble corridor, hands trembling with fury.

Deep breaths, she counseled herself.

The sight of dear Venetia being led away like a common criminal had stirred every protective instinct she possessed. But it was Catherine Bentley's venomous performance that truly ignited her rage.

To witness such calculated cruelty from a woman she'd known for twenty years, to see Catherine's obvious satisfaction at Venetia's downfall, shook Eugenia's faith in her own judgment. The Catherine she remembered had been sharp-tongued, certainly, but this display of malicious pleasure suggested depths of spite she'd never suspected.

Or Catherine has been compromised? By someone?

Lord Thornton emerged from the drawing room where he'd been speaking with agitated guests. His expression was grim as he took in Eugenia's distress.

"My dear," he said quietly, "you look ready to commit murder."

"Not murder, though the thought occurred." Eugenia took a steadying breath. "Thornton, you must speak with Catherine immediately. What she did to that poor child was unconscionable."

"I witnessed the exchange. Catherine was…" he frowned as if he couldn't reconcile his sister-in-law's actions before settling upon, "extraordinarily harsh."

"Harsh?" Eugenia's voice rose. "She systematically destroyed Venetia's character with lies that would shame a fishwife! That girl is innocent, and Catherine knows it. Her behavior wasn't justice—it was revenge."

Or something worse. Something orchestrated.

Thornton's expression grew troubled. "Revenge? Against what injury, do you suppose?"

"She raised concerns with Captain Rizzi, then pointed him toward Venetia at the very moment she and Mr. Rothbury were finally embracing. The very moment for which you and I were colluding!" She frowned. "Catherine twisted those circumstances into a criminal conspiracy because it suited her purposes."

But whose purposes? Catherine's? Or someone else's?

"Eugenia, your loyalty does you credit, but I'm sure the situation can be resolved. We can all attest that Signorina Sofia loaned Miss Playford her tiara—"

"But can we attest that it already contained the stolen gems?" Eugenia's voice rose. "No, and Catherine's meddling made everything far worse. She's been circling that poor girl like a vulture since we arrived, waiting for an opportunity to strike. Tonight she found it."

Or tonight she was given it. By someone who knew exactly how to manipulate her.

Thornton seemed at a loss. "What possible motivation could Catherine have for incriminating Venetia?" His chest rose and fell as he tried to control his breathing, warring between decency and duty. "Catherine is family, and I've no doubt she believes she acted appropriately, though she occasionally speaks thoughtlessly."

"She's either a fool or being used as someone else's tool." Eugenia met his gaze. "Please—speak with her. Tell her to reconsider her statements. Publicly."

Thornton nodded. "Of course. Though I fear Catherine's opinion of Miss Playford was formed long before tonight."

Eugenia swung round. "You've never said so before! What do you mean?"

"Nothing specific," Thornton replied evasively. "Merely that Catherine has, in the past, expressed reservations about Miss Playford's circumstances. About... unfairness in the entirety of such a fortune going to Miss Playford."

Reservations that emerged when? After meeting the count?

Before Eugenia could press further, approaching footsteps announced Catherine's arrival. She swept toward them with triumphant bearing, her mask of concern replaced by unmistakable satisfaction.

That's not the look of someone acting on conscience. That's victory.

"Eugenia, Thornton," she said with false warmth, "what a dreadful evening. Though I confess I'm not entirely surprised."

"Not surprised?" Eugenia had trouble controlling her voice. "A young woman we've known for months stands accused of theft, and you're not surprised?"

Catherine's smile was regretful. "Surely you can't be so naïve as to believe sudden wealth guarantees virtue? Some people remain essentially common, regardless of circumstances."

Common. She's never used that word about Venetia before. Never.

"Common?" Thornton interjected with warning.

"Should I pretend Miss Playford's behavior was anything other than what one might expect from someone of her background?"

Eugenia's temper snapped. "Her background? What are you implying?"

"I'm stating plainly that Miss Playford has shown her true nature. The grasping creature who would steal jewelry and compromise herself with fortune hunters."

"That's a vile lie!" Eugenia's voice was strangled. "Venetia Playford is one of the most genuinely kind young women I've encountered. You've always treated her as a friend. You've shown no indication you bore her ill will. If you had concerns, why not speak to us? Why tell Captain Rizzi—"

"How dare I speak truth?" Catherine's laugh held no warmth. "Your charitable nature blinds you to what should be obvious."

"And what should be obvious?" Thornton asked, his tone carrying a warning.

"That Miss Playford has been performing since inheriting her fortune. The grateful innocent overwhelmed by good fortune? The sweet girl needing guidance? Performance designed to make us overlook her inadequacies."

Inadequacies. Since when does Catherine use such language?

Eugenia stared in growing horror. "Catherine, what's possessed you to speak so cruelly of someone who's shown you nothing but sweet deference?"

Catherine's expression shifted, revealing something raw beneath her polish. "Sweet deference? When someone flaunts undeserved fortune while others who've earned their positions through sacrifice watch from the sidelines?"

"Others?" Eugenia's instincts sharpened. "What others?"

Here it comes.

"Do you think it escaped notice how Count di Montefiore attended to her every word tonight? How he sought her company exclusively while dismissing the rest of us as provincial?" Catherine's voice grew bitter. "A distinguished Continental gentleman, wealthy, titled, sophisticated—and he had eyes only for the golden heiress who stumbled into fortune."

There it is. The count.

Eugenia saw it now—Catherine's particular attention to the count since his arrival, her eagerness to impress him, her satisfaction when introducing him to their circle. Her increasingly detailed discussions of Venetia's wealth and circumstances.

And lately, Catherine had begun repeating, almost word for word, the count's little maxims about money and character—how "sudden wealth bred temptation," how "men of honor had a duty to protect families from unsuitable heirs." Eugenia had dismissed them at the time as mere Continental philosophy. Now they sounded more like instructions.

Oh, Catherine. What has that man done to you?

She recalled now the way the count had bent his dark head toward Catherine two nights ago, his voice low and earnest as he praised her "rare discernment" and "English integrity," while his gaze never quite reached his smile. Catherine had glowed for hours afterwards.

"You had hopes there?" Eugenia surmised, watching Catherine's face carefully.

"Hopes?" Catherine laughed bitterly. "A mature woman of breeding and accomplishment should naturally interest a cultured gentleman more than some provincial child whose only recommendation is inherited wealth. But no—one smile from our golden girl, and he was utterly captivated."

Captivated. Or pretending to be. To feed your jealousy.

"Catherine," Thornton said gently, though Eugenia caught the sharp intelligence in his eyes—he'd seen it too. "Surely you can't blame Miss Playford for the count's attentions—"

"Can't I? She arrives with her fortune and her youth and her wide-eyed innocence, and suddenly every gentleman in Venice is competing for her attention. What chance does any other woman have against such overwhelming advantages?"

The naked envy in Catherine's voice revealed everything. Not ancient grievances, but present humiliation—the pain of being overlooked for someone younger, richer, more beautiful. Pain that someone had clearly cultivated and weaponized.

"You speak of Miss Playford's worthiness," Eugenia said carefully, "yet the count seems to have taken remarkable interest in the details of Miss Playford's circumstances. Almost as if he had particular reasons beyond mere attraction."

Catherine flushed. "He's a gentleman of culture! Naturally he's curious about how English law differs from Continental customs. I was simply providing information—" Catherine hesitated, something flickering in her expression. A realization that she'd said too much?

Thornton raised an eyebrow. "You provided very clear details of her inheritance. The unusual conditions of the will. The nephew who was disinherited. How vulnerable Miss Playford—and keeping her inheritance—was to scandal—"

"I said nothing that wasn't true!"

"A gentleman of noble birth would not pursue such a discussion," said Thornton. "He would find it rather vulgar...unless he had specific interest in exploiting such information."

Catherine's face went white, then red. "The count is a true gentleman—"

"With no hand in tonight's devilry?" asked Eugenia. "For I would stake my life on the fact that Miss Playford had nothing to do with the theft of the Contessa's emeralds."

"Yet you all but handed her over to Captain Rizzi."

At last, Thornton. You needed to be the one to say it so plainly.

Catherine drew herself up. "Captain Rizzi specifically asked me to keep an eye on Miss Playford," Catherine said sharply. "He spoke of...certain rumors regarding English visitors and missing trinkets. She was already under suspicion. I only reported what I observed. He said there had been...small discrepancies...with other guests," she added defensively. "He suggested that, as someone of unimpeachable discretion, I might notice what others overlooked."

Eugenia glanced at Thornton, who said, "And did your Count di Montefiore plumb you for more information than that which you were so eager to impart to him in our hearing not so long ago? Did you not wonder that a younger, handsome man paying marked attention to a mature woman of 'breeding and accomplishment' might have ulterior motives beyond admiration. Particularly if that man then encouraged loose talk of a wealthy young heiress."

"That's absurd!" But Catherine's voice wavered. "The count is genuinely interested in—"

"In what, precisely?" Thornton asked. "Your company? Or your knowledge of Miss Playford's vulnerabilities?"

The moment of truth.

Catherine's expression grew calculating. "The count has been nothing but attentive and respectful—"

Eugenia cut her off. "Do you not find it odd that a mysterious Continental nobleman appears from nowhere with letters of introduction no one has verified. He cultivates your company. He asks detailed questions about a wealthy young woman's legal vulnerabilities. He encourages your resentment. And then, conveniently, that young woman is accused of theft using evidence planted by someone with intimate knowledge of her movements."

Catherine's face worked through several emotions. "The count is a gentleman of honor—"

"Is he?" Eugenia asked softly. "Or is he precisely what he appears to be—someone with specific interest in destroying Miss Playford's reputation and claim to her fortune?"

Someone who knew exactly which vulnerable woman to target with flattery.

The silence stretched. Catherine's triumph had curdled into something approaching panic.

"I am sure that if I spoke to him, he'd be able to prove himself entirely above your slurs," Catherine declared. "Miss Playford stole those gems. They were found in her tiara. She nearly got away with it, but she is guilty. And if she is not guilty, she will be exonerated."

"And what motive might Miss Playford have for stealing two emeralds, supposedly around the very night she arrived in Venice?" Eugenia asked. "Do you not think that odd, Catherine? That a young heiress who has all the wealth in the world would commit a crime that would put that wealth in jeopardy?" She paused. "I do not think you have told us everything about the count's interest in our Miss Playford. And I don't think you have even begun to consider the horrors that she is now undergoing as she is being questioned by Captain Rizzi, whose information was supplied, in large part, by you."

Chapter Twenty-One

EDWARD, WHO HAD just left Venetia in the company of Captain Rizzi—who'd been adamant she needed no chaperone other than Mollie while he interviewed the supposed jewel thief—found Lord Thornton and Lady Townsend in the marble corridor, their faces reflecting the same shock and outrage churning in his chest.

He'd passed Miss Bentley's retreating figure moments earlier, disappearing around a corner ramrod straight with self-righteous indignation.

The ghastly woman had all but delivered his beloved Venetia into the hands of the authorities.

"Lord Thornton," Edward said, "surely you understand this is nothing but a plot to discredit Miss Playford." He closed his eyes briefly, pressing his fingers to his still-bruised temple. "A very elaborate, very calculated plot—for reasons as yet unknown."

"Of course it is," Thornton acknowledged. "Though the evidence appears damaging, I naturally share Lady Townsend's conviction that Miss Playford is entirely innocent—"

"Miss Playford is the most virtuous person I've ever known!" Edward burst out.

Lady Townsend made a sympathetic sound. "Indeed, she is. She wore a tiara loaned to her by Signorina Sofia. That is, of course, where Captain Rizzi should begin his investigations."

"And I've no doubt Miss Playford will be released within the hour when this is made clear," Thornton added. "I tried to intervene on her behalf, but Captain Rizzi was adamant that any interference was unnecessary."

Lady Townsend shook her head. "The captain is a very decided gentleman, but I am sure it will soon be made clear to him that she is but a hapless victim."

"Of whom?" Edward demanded. "And for what reason? Why would Signorina Sofia wish to harm Miss Playford? There can be no other explanation for this… travesty of justice."

"Justice is the outcome of Captain Rizzi's investigations," Thornton said, in that maddeningly reasonable tone of his. "And I've no doubt that justice will be delivered appropriately. We can do nothing but wait patiently for Italian justice to take its course."

Lady Townsend looked enquiringly at Edward. "Do you have any suspicions? Miss Bentley appears a dupe, but claims not to know—or will not say—who planted the emeralds."

Edward steadied himself on the back of a velvet sofa. "Signorina Sofia isn't the romantic innocent she appears. It was she who wished Miss Playford to wear the family tiara—though I counseled against it."

Thornton's expression tightened. "It was I who insisted Venetia accept Signorina Sofia's loan."

"Which she eventually agreed to because the signorina's plight so echoed her own situation until a year ago," Edward muttered. "Do you truly think the signorina did not know the gold tiara contained stolen gems?"

Of course she knew, thought Edward. She probably loaded the compartment herself while humming a cheerful tune.

"You really think Sofia Morosini is the only one involved in orchestrating this?" Thornton shook his head. "She did not even attend tonight's masquerade. Besides, the jewels were stolen weeks ago. Surely a young woman who enjoys the trappings of wealth would not need—"

"It's not about need," Edward cut in, the words spilling out with bitter self-recrimination. "And I've been a spectacular fool. I should have been more alert to inconsistencies in her story, seen through the calculated nature of her appeals to my sympathy. Instead, I allowed myself to be manipulated because..." He stopped, the admission sticking in his throat.

Because I'm an idiot. A lovesick idiot.

"Because?" Lady Townsend prompted gently.

"Because she offered me exactly what I most desired," Edward said, the truth scraping out of him. "An excuse to spend time with Miss Playford. A reason to be alone with her, to speak with her, to..." His voice broke. "God help me, I love her. And that love has made me a fool—and a danger to the very person I most wish to protect."

"My dear boy," Lady Townsend said softly, "love is hardly a crime, nor does it make you responsible for others' machinations."

"Doesn't it?" Edward turned to them. "Every step of this conspiracy depended on my willingness to involve Miss Playford in Sofia's schemes. Without my participation, Venetia would never have been positioned to take blame for tonight's theft. I'm as responsible for her destruction as if I'd placed that cursed tiara on her head myself."

"You're being too harsh," Thornton replied. "Miss Playford is clearly innocent and she will be vindicated. If Signorina Morosini orchestrated this, then you were as much her victim as Miss Playford. Self-recrimination will not undo what's been done."

Edward laughed, a short, rough sound. "Won't it? Then what will, Lord Thornton? What action can possibly restore Miss Playford's reputation, clear her name, prove her innocence when evidence has been so carefully arranged to suggest guilt?"

He began pacing, unable to contain the agitation coiling in his limbs. "And there's more. Something that makes this situation even more impossible."

Might as well confess everything, he thought. It can't get

much worse.

"More?" Lady Townsend asked, anxiety sharpening her tone.

"Count Morosini believes I'm pursuing Sofia," Edward said flatly. "After the attack by the footpads—you remember, Lady Townsend, the incident I mentioned?—a well-meaning merchant named Benedetti saw me with a young, well-bred, golden-haired woman in elegant dress. He naturally assumed it was Sofia, given the clothing. He told Count Morosini."

Oh, what a fool I've been. A lovesick, credulous fool.

"The count summoned me to his library," Edward continued, his voice tight. "He gave me the most exquisitely civil warning I've ever received. All couched in discussions of *Ivanhoe* and how even in fiction, love requires compatible social positions. The message was clear: step away from my granddaughter or lose your position."

Thornton's expression sharpened. "But you weren't with Sofia. You were with—"

"With Venetia," Edward finished. "Wearing Sofia's dress. As part of Sofia's scheme. But I can't tell Count Morosini that without revealing his granddaughter's deception and making everything infinitely worse."

Also, he'd probably have me thrown into whatever dungeons Venice still maintains.

"So you see," Edward said, desperation rising, "I can't appeal to Count Morosini for help. He already thinks I'm a fortune hunter pursuing his granddaughter. If I now suggest Sofia framed Venetia—a wealthy English heiress—to protect herself—what will he think?"

"That you're deflecting blame," Lady Townsend said slowly, understanding dawning.

"Exactly." Edward stopped pacing, his hands clenched. "To him, it would look as though I seduced both young women, conspired with one to rob the other, and am now trying to save my own skin by implicating his beloved granddaughter."

Who is actually guilty. But try explaining that to her grandfather.

"Moreover," Edward went on, "I'm the one who delivered the tiara to Venetia. I'm the one who encouraged her to help Sofia. I'm the one found alone with her on that balcony. Every piece of circumstantial evidence points to me as either conspirator or mastermind."

"Which is precisely what Sofia intended," Thornton said grimly.

"Yes, but knowing that doesn't help Venetia!" Edward's voice cracked. The more he teased at the difficulties, the tighter the knot became. "She is sitting in some room now, being interrogated, her reputation in tatters, while I stand here explaining why I can't do anything to help her."

He faced them again. "I am the root of all this. Sofia used my feelings for Venetia to manipulate me. Count Morosini suspects me of pursuing his granddaughter. Captain Rizzi caught me compromising Venetia on a balcony. Every thread of this conspiracy leads back to me."

"I hope you're not about to propose what I—?" Lady Townsend began warily.

"I propose that I confess," Edward said, cutting across her. "To everything. I'll tell Captain Rizzi I manipulated Miss Playford into wearing the tiara, that I used her innocence and trust as cover for my own criminal activities. The evidence supports it."

"Absolutely not," Thornton said at once.

"Why not?" Edward demanded. "It would free Venetia. It would explain everything without implicating Sofia—which means Count Morosini might show mercy. He values my translations. He might petition for clemency if he believes I acted alone."

"You're proposing to confess to a crime you didn't commit," Lady Townsend said slowly, "to save a woman you love, while relying on the mercy of a man who has already warned you away from his granddaughter?"

"When you put it like that, it sounds terrible," Edward admitted.

It IS terrible. But what choice do I have?

"It sounds like madness because it is madness," Thornton said bluntly. "Rothbury, you're not thinking clearly. Desperation has overwhelmed your judgment."

"Perhaps," Edward conceded. "But what's the alternative? Wait while Venetia suffers? Try to investigate Sofia while her grandfather shields her? Hope that somehow evidence emerges that clears Venetia without implicating me or Sofia?"

"Yes," Thornton said firmly. "Precisely that."

"Lord Thornton, you don't understand the position we're in—"

"I understand perfectly," Thornton interrupted. "You love Miss Playford. You feel responsible for her predicament. You're desperate to help her, regardless of the cost to yourself. These are admirable sentiments, Rothbury. They are also a wretched basis for strategy."

"But time is working against us," Edward protested. "Every moment Venetia spends under suspicion, her reputation deteriorates further, which further imperils her fortune. It only takes a letter from Captain Rizzi—" He broke off. "And I can't approach Count Morosini for help without—"

"Without revealing truths that would make everything worse," Lady Townsend finished. "Yes, we understand."

"Then you see why confession might be the only option?" Edward pressed.

"We see why *you* think it is the only option," Thornton corrected. "We do not agree."

Edward sank into a chair, his energy draining away. "Then what would you have me do? Stand by helplessly while the woman I love is destroyed by enemies who used my own feelings as weapons against her?"

Because that's worked so well thus far.

"I would have you use the rational, analytical mind that has served you so well," Thornton replied with patient firmness. "Channel your passion into investigation. Discover the true extent of this conspiracy, identify all participants, and gather evidence that will not merely clear Miss Playford but expose the real criminals."

"Investigation takes time," Edward said dully.

"Yes," Lady Townsend agreed. "But confession takes only moments and, once made, cannot be undone. If you confess falsely now, you eliminate any chance of uncovering the truth later."

Edward stared at his feet. "So you're advising me to wait. While Venetia suffers."

"We're advising you to think," Thornton said. "To use your intellect rather than your guilt, your strategic abilities rather than your despair."

"There is more to this than Sofia's individual malice," Edward said slowly, his mind, despite himself, beginning to work again. "Tonight's scheme required planning and resources beyond what a young woman might accomplish alone."

"Precisely," Thornton said. "Someone with knowledge of English society, access to valuable information about Miss Playford's circumstances, and the ability to position multiple elements exactly where they needed to be."

"Someone like Count di Montefiore," Lady Townsend added quietly. "A man who appeared at precisely the right moment, with exactly the right credentials, showing exactly the right interest in Venetia's affairs. And who seems to have manipulated Miss Bentley into providing damaging testimony."

Count di Montefiore. Another piece of this nightmare puzzle.

"Then we have multiple conspirators," Edward said, rubbing at his temples. "Sofia, possibly the count, perhaps others. A web of deception rather than a single villain."

"Which makes your confession even more foolish," Thornton pointed out. "If you take the blame for a crime committed by multiple conspirators, you do not save Venetia. You simply give the real criminals freedom to continue their schemes while eliminating the one person who might expose them."

"So, what do we do?" Edward asked, hearing the defeat in his own voice.

"We investigate," Lady Townsend said firmly. "We gather evidence. We expose the truth. And we do it together, using our combined resources and intelligence rather than relying on grand romantic gestures that accomplish nothing."

"Even if that means Venetia suffers in the interim?" Edward asked quietly.

"Even then," Thornton said gently. "Because the alternative—your false confession—would make her suffer even more, for even longer, with no hope of eventual vindication."

Edward nodded slowly. "Very well. Investigation. Evidence. Truth. Though every instinct I possess is screaming to act immediately."

"Those instincts do you credit as a lover," Lady Townsend said with a sad smile. "But they would disqualify you as Venetia's savior. She needs your mind, Edward. Not your martyrdom."

Back in his chambers later, Edward stared at the Foreign Office letter still tucked in his desk drawer. Constantinople beckoned—a prestigious posting, financial security, an escape from this nightmare.

Run away to Constantinople? Let someone else save Venetia?

Dear Lord, regardless of how tempting Constantinople once seemed, it was now out of reach. While Venetia remained in danger, he would remain in Venice.

He could almost hear Thornton's voice: *Use your rational mind.*

The trouble was, his rational mind kept circling back to the same conclusion: Venetia was in danger, he'd helped put her there, and confession might be the fastest way to extract her.

Even if it destroys me in the process.

Even if Thornton is right that it won't actually work.

Even if it's the stupidest plan imaginable.

Truth and investigation would take time—time during which Venetia would endure daily humiliation as an accused criminal.

Chapter Twenty-Two

THE CELL SMELLED of damp stone and old river water. Venetia sat on the narrow bench, arms wrapped around herself, and tried not to shiver. Her gown—embroidered silk that had seemed so splendid a few hours ago—was utterly inadequate against the creeping chill. The cold seemed to seep up from the flagstones, through the thin soles of her slippers, into her bones.

She could still taste Edward.

That was the absurd thing. Her lips tingled faintly, as if his mouth had only just left hers, as if she were still pressed against him on the balcony with the night air on her neck and his fingers trembling at her waist. The echo of that kiss warmed her far more than the coarse blanket someone had tossed in her direction when they'd shut the door.

She swallowed a hysterical laugh. It caught in her throat and turned into something rougher. She pressed her knuckles to her teeth until the impulse passed.

Outside, somewhere above, bells tolled the hour. She'd lost count. Time down here was a gray, unmeasured thing: the drip of water in a distant corridor, the occasional clank of keys, the muffled voices of guards. No music, no light but the faintest smear seeping under the door and through a high, barred opening that gave onto blackness.

She stared up at that narrow window. A slice of sky, dull and starless. The lagoon lay beyond the walls, she supposed. Gondolas gliding like shadows. People laughing, drinking, dancing. Life.

Meanwhile, the English heiress sat in a cell, trying not to think about emeralds she had never seen and a will clause she had tried very hard, until now, not to dwell on.

The solicitor's voice came back to her with painful clarity, as if he were reading in the next room:

"Within three years of my decease, should my chosen heir be convicted in any court of law of theft, fraud, or any crime of public dishonor, her interest shall cease and the whole of my estate shall pass to my nephew, Mr. Greene."

Her stomach cramped. She curled forward slightly, hands gripping the coarse wool of the blanket.

Three years. It had seemed a remote threat at the time, a gloomy old man's attempt to keep his fortune unsullied. She'd signed documents while her aunt sniffed and the solicitor droned on.

And now, a year later, here she was. Accused of theft. In another country, yes—but surely that wouldn't matter. The condition didn't specify *English* courts, did it? Just "any court of law."

Any court, anywhere. Any verdict, however unjust, and it would all vanish.

Leonard Harrington's careful provisions, the old house in Derbyshire, the London townhouse, the investments—gone. Back to Greene. Back to the man whose own behavior included attempted seduction and elopement with an heiress.

And if you lost it all, a traitorous voice whispered, then Edward would no longer have to fear being branded a fortune hunter.

The thought slid through her like a knife. Cold. Precise. She squeezed her eyes shut, furious at herself.

Yes, of course. That would be one way to solve his ethical

quandary. Strip her of everything but a stained reputation, and he might finally feel virtuous enough to love her openly.

She couldn't decide whether to laugh or sob.

"I don't want to be an object of pity," she murmured into the darkness. Her voice sounded small in the stone space. "I don't want him to marry me because I've fallen."

She wanted him to marry her because he loved her. Because tonight, when she'd put her hands to his face and said the words at last—*I love you*—she'd seen the answering agony in his eyes, heard his own confession tremble on his lips.

God help me, I love you beyond reason. You are my heart.

Her heart twisted. She could almost feel his hands again, warm against her cheeks, his hair rough beneath her fingers, the solid strength of his body anchoring hers. The way he'd kissed her—first wary, then with a hunger that had made the world fall away.

She pressed her fingertips to her mouth as if she might recapture some trace of that warmth. Her lips were dry and chapped from the cold.

Of all the settings for that long-dreamed-of kiss, she had not imagined a balcony that would, minutes later, become a crime scene.

Captain Rizzi's voice intruded on the memory, brisk and satisfied: *"An English lady in a gold diadem. You match the account I was given."*

An account. Someone had described her. Not *a* lady in a tiara, but *the* English lady in a very particular one. The realization had sliced through the glow of Edward's embrace like ice.

Miss Bentley's words echoed next, sharp and cruel. *Common. Performing. Undeserved fortune. Grasping creature.*

Venetia stared at the opposite wall, tracing the damp streaks with her eyes. She tried to picture Miss Bentley's face as she'd spoken to Captain Rizzi, pointing, insisting. Had she looked triumphant? Righteous? Genuinely convinced?

Had the count been standing just behind her, murmuring

encouragement? Or had he merely planted the ideas in the days before, with those soft, poisoned phrases about sudden wealth and hidden vice, then left Miss Bentley to carry them out alone?

It hurt more that Miss Bentley might have believed it. That a woman who had praised her embroidery and her "sweet nature" could, in the space of an evening, recast her as a scheming little thief.

And then there was Count Morosini.

Would he lift a finger on her behalf? Or would he see only an awkward complication under his roof? An English scandal imported into his palazzo. A young woman whose very existence had upset his granddaughter's expectations and whose affection threatened to distract his prize translator.

If he truly believed Edward was pursuing Sofia, then tonight's scene on the balcony must have looked like confirmation of the worst kind of entanglement. A translator, a foreign heiress, disgrace, stolen jewels.

Perhaps he would do nothing. Perhaps he would simply step back and let Italian justice take its course, wash his hands of her and Edward both.

No. Edward. She forced herself to sit a little straighter.

Surely Edward would not abandon her. He'd been there when Captain Rizzi arrived, his expression thunderous, his body instinctively shifting between her and the officer. She had felt, for one dizzy instant, that he might actually fight the captain, grapple for her like some knight in a story.

Then he had remembered his reason, his position, his own precarious standing with Count Morosini. She had seen the calculation in his eyes. The fury. The hatred of his own helplessness.

He won't let this stand, she told herself. He can't. He'll go to Lady Townsend. To Lord Thornton. Between them, they'll—

What? Charm the emeralds back to their owner? Magically erase the fact that they'd been found in her tiara while she was kissing a man on a balcony?

She buried her face in her hands for a moment. The stone beneath her feet felt very solid. Unyielding.

A key grated in a distant lock; footsteps approached, then receded again. Somewhere down the passage, a man laughed coarsely. Someone coughed. The sounds of other lives, other miseries.

Her teeth began to chatter. She clenched her jaw, annoyed with her own weakness. If she must sit in a cell, she should at least do it with some shred of dignity. She would not give Captain Rizzi—or Miss Bentley, or Count di Montefiore, or whoever else was relishing this—the satisfaction of imagining her collapsed in hysterics.

"Miss Playford?"

The voice came through the little grille in the door, tentative, accented. Not Rizzi. Younger.

She looked up. "Yes?"

The hatch scraped open. A pair of brown eyes peered in, wary and curious. "You are cold, signorina?"

"I have been warmer," she said, because if she started to list all the indignities of the evening, she wasn't sure she'd stop.

He hesitated, then pushed something through the gap: another blanket, rough but thicker than the first. He glanced over his shoulder as if expecting rebuke, then added in a rush, "My sister, she says English ladies are very proud. But you"—he looked almost shy—"you do not shout. Or cry. You say 'thank you' when Rizzi is... not kind."

She blinked. "You were there when he ordered me here?"

His mouth twisted. "The *capitano*, he likes when people are afraid. I think if you had shown you were afraid you might not have been sent here. He was angry that you were so... proud."

"Thank you," she said quietly. "For the blanket. And for the compliment, undeserved though it is. I assure you, I am quite terrified."

He gave a quick, sympathetic smile. "Maybe you are. But you do not look it. That is... brave." He seemed to grope for the right

English word. "Dignified."

Dignified. That was something, at least.

"Will they keep me here long?" she asked, hating the thread of hope in her own voice.

He shifted his weight. "There is talk." He lowered his voice. "The Count Morosini, he speaks with the capitano. Important men do not like trouble in their houses. Sometimes trouble... disappears." He realized how that sounded and flapped a hand. "Not like that. I mean—they make a problem go away. Quiet."

So Morosini *was* involved. Relief and unease tangled in her chest.

"Thank you," she said again.

He nodded, and for a moment looked as if he might say more. Then someone shouted his name down the corridor, and he straightened. "I must go. Wrap your feet, signorina. The floor is worst."

The hatch closed with a soft scrape. She spread the new blanket beneath her, tucked the other around her legs as best she could, and curled her toes into the rough wool. Her fingers had finally stopped shaking.

Count Morosini was negotiating. That could mean her release. It could also mean conditions and complications she could not yet imagine.

And Edward—would he have any say in whatever bargain was being struck? Or would decisions be made over his head, neatly severing the one bond that made any of this bearable?

Metal rasped again, closer this time. The turning of the key in her own lock.

Venetia drew in a breath and straightened her spine, forcing herself to stand as the door swung inward. Whatever waited beyond—freedom, further questioning, some new humiliation— she would meet it with what dignity she could muster.

She had survived Aunt Pike. She could survive Captain Rizzi. She would survive this night.

And when she saw Edward again—if she saw Edward again—

she would do it on her own two feet, not as some object of pity, but as the woman who had kissed him on a balcony and refused, even in a prison cell, to let go of that single, blazing truth.

She loved him. And he loved her. Her fortune—or the lack of it—changed nothing.

Chapter Twenty-Three

THE JOY THAT had once infused his work was gone. Words that had previously flowed as easily as the water in the Grand Canal now lay flat and lifeless on the page. Edward could think of nothing other than clearing Venetia's name.

Protecting her. Holding onto that one blazing, impossible moment on the balcony when everything had finally made sense.

Her mouth beneath his. Her hands on his face. The sound she'd made when he'd finally stopped fighting his feelings and kissed her as he'd dreamed of kissing her for years. For the first time since his mother's death, he had felt truly connected to another human being—not out of duty, not out of obligation, but out of a wild, mutual, chosen love.

That kiss had been his proof. Proof that whatever else the world thought of him, whatever titles or fortunes separated them, this was real. And nothing on earth mattered more to him than protecting that precious woman.

If necessary, he'd die doing it. The thought did not even startle him; it settled with cold, steady certainty.

Which was why he now sought an audience with his patron—a man who held both Edward's livelihood and Venetia's safety in his elegant, ink-stained hands.

The request was granted the following morning. Edward was

ushered into the stately room the count favored for its morning light.

And probably for its intimidation factor.

The elderly nobleman stood with his back to the door, gazing out at the canal where gondolas drifted past like black mourning boats.

"Ah, Mr. Rothbury," the count said without turning. "Punctual as always. Though I confess, after last evening's festivities, I wondered if you might be indisposed this morning."

Festivities. Yes, let's call the nightmare that was last night *festivities*.

Edward's stomach tightened. "Count Morosini, of course it is about the... injustice at the masquerade that I wish to speak to you—"

"Injustice?" The count turned slowly, his dark eyes holding a glint that made Edward's insides churn. "Is that what you're calling it? Your compromising position with a thief wearing stolen jewels on my balcony?"

"Sir, I must protest. Miss Playford is entirely innocent of any wrongdoing, and my presence there was—"

"Was what, precisely?" Count Morosini moved to his desk and settled himself in his chair. "I have ears and eyes who report upon everything, Signor Rothbury."

Of course you do.

"Was the fact that stolen emeralds were found on Signorina Playford's person an accident? You are quick to defend her, despite the irrefutable evidence. I am prepared to exonerate you of the charge of offering a somewhat... scandalous... degree of... solace to a thief. After all, how were you to know of her crimes before Captain Rizzi unmasked her? But I will not be persuaded that your... dear friend... Signorina Playford is innocent. No, she is a grand manipulator."

Like your granddaughter, Sofia.

Heat rose in Edward's cheeks. "Count, I assure you that my conduct has always been of the highest—"

"Has it?" The count's tone carried silky menace. "Because according to Signor Benedetti's account of your unfortunate encounter with street ruffians, you were accompanied by a young woman bearing a remarkable resemblance to my granddaughter. A young woman wearing Sofia's jewelry and costume."

"With the greatest respect, signor, Miss Playford was wearing a tiara loaned to her by your granddaughter," Edward burst out.

"Oh, so now you insinuate that my Sofia is complicit in some outrageous plot to discredit this other young woman with whom you were found in a compromising situation. Signor Rothbury, I thought I was employing a man of almost stultifying dedication to his work. Not a lothario."

Lothario. Edward had been called many things, but *lothario* was new.

"Sir, that is not what I was insinuating. Allow me to explain—"

"Can you?" The count steepled his fingers. "Very well, enlighten me. Explain how you came to be alone with a young woman described as Sofia. Certainly, she wore Sofia's clothes and jewelry, according to Signor Benedetti. Furthermore, she was put in grave peril and required rescue from footpads." The count leaned back. "Explain how, two days later, you are with a blonde beauty—another blonde beauty, or the same?—at my masquerade ball, again wearing Sofia's jewelry, again in your company, again in compromising circumstances."

Well, when the count put it like that, it did look suspicious.

Edward's mind raced through possible responses, but every explanation would either expose Sofia's deception or confirm the count's suspicions about his relationship with Venetia—in which case his desire to save her would be construed as the ravings of a man undone by passion.

The memory of the balcony flickered—Venetia's fingers in his hair, the small, shaky breath she'd taken when he'd whispered that he loved her. That single, searing moment in which he had known—more certainly than he knew his own name—that he would stand between her and the world, sword in hand like any of Scott's doomed knights, if it came to that.

"I see your difficulty," Count Morosini continued with false sympathy. "The truth would implicate you in behavior most unsuitable for a gentleman in my employ. A man who has been translating in my library while conducting secret assignations with my granddaughter."

If only you knew how little I want to conduct assignations with your granddaughter, thought Edward.

"That is not what happened—"

"Is it not?" The count's voice sharpened. "Then what did happen, Mr. Rothbury? And please, spare me any gallant attempts to protect the lady's reputation. I am her grandfather. Her welfare is my primary concern."

Edward stood trapped between impossible choices. To reveal Sofia's true activities would expose her romantic schemes and potentially destroy her chance of happiness with her Paolo. To deny the count's interpretation would require explanations that might endanger Venetia further. And to confess the truth about his feelings for Venetia would confirm suspicions of fortune hunting that could ruin them both.

Essentially, every option was terrible.

He thought, absurdly, of *Ivanhoe*—of knights hemmed in by oaths and loyalties, forced to choose which duty to betray. He had always admired Wilfred's stubborn honor from a safe distance. It was quite another thing to feel the vise of conflicting loyalties closing around one's own throat.

"I thought not," the count said after Edward's prolonged silence. "Your discretion does you credit, though it hardly absolves you of responsibility for last evening's scandal."

Discretion? So he was calling his paralyzed inability to speak *discretion*.

Edward straightened his shoulders. "Clearly the young woman with whom I was… conversing… on the balcony was—as you put it—a blonde beauty who bears a similarity to your granddaughter. She was, in fact, Miss Playford. And she was wearing a tiara loaned to her by your granddaughter. What else would you have me say, Count Morosini?"

"Nothing, at present. The question is what you will do." The count rose and moved back to the window. "Miss Playford was released this morning on my personal recognizance. Captain Rizzi was most accommodating when I explained that the young lady was my guest, that her character was known to me, and that I would personally guarantee her appearance for any future proceedings."

Edward's heart leaped. "She's been released?"

Thank God. Thank God, thank God, thank God.

"She has. Though naturally, the charges remain pending. The investigation continues. And Captain Rizzi has made it clear that any new evidence of criminal behavior would result in immediate re-arrest." The count spoke carefully. "Such evidence might include, for instance, testimony about previous suspicious activities. Or witness accounts of her association with unsavory characters."

Oh, how easily such charges could be manufactured.

The threat hung in the air like poison.

"I see you understand my position," the count continued. "Miss Playford's freedom rests upon my continued goodwill and influence with the authorities. Should that goodwill be... compromised... I fear I would find myself unable to intercede on her behalf in future."

"What do you want?" Edward asked quietly.

"I want my granddaughter protected from scandal. I want my household to remain free from gossip and speculation. And I want my translator to remain precisely where he is—not dashing off to accept some lucrative offer in Constantinople—dedicated to his scholarly work without distraction from romantic entanglements that could prove... problematic."

So Count Morosini knows about Constantinople, thought Edward. And it was not he who orchestrated the offer to be rid of him.

"I want *Ivanhoe* finished by the end of the month so that you can begin on Sir Walter Scott's next."

The end of the month? He wants eight weeks of work done in two weeks?

Edward stared at him. "You actually want me to stay."

"Yes, did I not speak plainly enough? I want you to decline that Constantinople posting. And I want you to maintain appropriate distance from both my granddaughter and Miss Playford. For clearly you are much too invested in this Miss Playford to attend properly to your work."

Too invested. That was one way of putting *desperately in love*.

"And if I refuse?" Edward asked boldly.

Count Morosini's smile held no warmth. "Then I fear Miss Playford's situation may become considerably more precarious."

Edward felt something constrict around his heart. The count was offering him a devil's bargain—his obedience in exchange for Venetia's safety. His silence and distance in return for her freedom.

In *Ivanhoe*, knights boasted of their willingness to die for their ladies. Dying suddenly seemed the easier part. Living at arm's length from Venetia while she believed he had abandoned her—that was the real martyrdom.

"I see you appreciate the delicacy of the situation," the count said. "Naturally, Miss Playford need not know of our arrangement. Such knowledge would only distress her unnecessarily. Better that she believe your withdrawal stems from natural discretion rather than... external pressures."

"You want me to let her think I'm abandoning her?" Edward's voice came out hoarse.

"I want you to protect her from further scandal by maintaining proper distance. What she thinks of your motives is between you and your conscience."

My conscience. Which is already screaming in protest.

He thought of Venetia in some cold little cell, her gown crumpled, her hair disordered, her brave chin lifted. He thought of the way she had said *I love you* on the balcony.

She had given him truth; he was now being asked to meet it with a lie.

To agree would mean watching her suffer the pain of his apparent rejection, doubting his love, perhaps even despising him. To refuse would mean exposing her to dangers he could neither foresee nor prevent.

This, then, was his own trial by ordeal. Not fire, not steel, but the slow torture of enforced distance—of being close enough to breathe the same air, yet forbidden to reach out a hand.

"Do I have your word that she will remain safe?" he asked at last.

"You have my word that my influence will continue to protect her, provided you honor our agreement. Cross me, Signor Rothbury, and I fear my ability to shield her from Venice's harsher realities may prove... limited."

Limited. Another polite Italian way of saying *I'll destroy her.*

Edward opened his eyes to find the count watching him with a small, satisfied smile. The old man knew exactly what he was asking—and exactly why Edward would have no choice but to accept.

He thought of walking away. Of resigning, of going to Venetia, of telling her everything and facing the consequences together as equals. But what then? Rizzi's renewed zeal; Morosini's retracted protection; Greene waiting in the shadows for the slightest chance to seize the Harrington fortune through a convenient conviction.

If he defied Morosini, Venetia paid the price. If he obeyed, he paid it. There was no version of this story in which both of them came away unscathed.

In Scott's tale, Ivanhoe had sacrificed land and honor and comfort, trusting that the woman he loved would understand his devotion even when appearances were against him. Edward could not even claim that comfort. Venetia would never know. From her perspective, he would simply vanish when the scandal broke, leaving her to bear it alone.

And yet, what choice did he have, if her safety truly depended on his compliance?

"Very well," Edward said, the words tasting like ashes in his mouth. "I agree to your terms."

"Excellent." Count Morosini returned to his desk, already reaching for the manuscript pages of *Ivanhoe*. "Now then, there is still some way to go and my dear friend, Marchese Valenti, is even more impatient than I that it should be finished. Go now to the library and return to Sir Walter's tale of impossible love. I believe we left our hero facing insurmountable obstacles to his heart's desire."

The irony was not subtle. At all.

Edward left, taking the seat at his desk in the library, staring at the pages before him. The ink blurred slightly. He blinked hard.

"Sir Wilfred," he muttered under his breath, "you have no monopoly on insurmountable obstacles."

Like Scott's knight, he was now bound by honor to sacrifice his own happiness for the woman he loved. But unlike the fictional hero, he saw no prospect of a neatly tied conclusion in which virtue triumphed and love was rewarded.

Also, Ivanhoe got his lands and title back. Edward had had neither lands nor title to be returned.

He set his pen to the paper. The words he rendered into Italian were full of chivalry and noble suffering—men risking death in the lists to prove a maiden's innocence. He, meanwhile, sat in a sunlit Venetian study, condemning himself to a quieter kind of death: the slow extinguishing of hope.

He had traded his freedom for Venetia's safety, his happiness for her protection. And the terrible part was that she would never know the price he had paid—or the love that had driven him to pay it.

She'll think I abandoned her. She'll think I didn't care. She'll think last night's kiss meant nothing.

And I can't tell her otherwise without putting her in danger.

Outside the window, Venice glittered in the morning sun, beautiful and treacherous as ever. Gondolas slid along the canal, black and elegant as funeral barges. Voices drifted up from the water, bright and careless.

For Edward, the city had become a prison whose bars were forged from love itself.

Chapter Twenty-Four

VENETIA SAT ON the bed, staring at the letter that had secured her release.

From accused jewel thief to free woman in under twelve hours.

Yet she'd been unable to leave her room for two days following her release.

No ordeal had sapped her of strength as spending the night in a dank, chilly cell, accused of something she had not done.

This was not the dark cupboard at her Aunt Pike's that she knew was a temporary confinement.

This could have been forever.

And she'd been like an invalid, pretending to be asleep when Lady Townsend had knocked. Unable to face her English friends over meals.

The letter's official seal bore Count Morosini's coat of arms, and the elegant script promised his personal guarantee that she would remain free "pending no further charges."

No further charges.

As if charges could not be conjured out of thin air by the right malicious tongue.

She folded the letter along its already-tired creases and set it aside. Freedom, such as it was, allowed her to sit here instead of in a cold stone cell. It allowed her to walk Venice's labyrinthine streets, to return to Casa Bonaldi, to endure the whispered conversations that faltered when she entered a room.

And it allowed her, dangerously, to hope.

If this were *Ivanhoe*, she told herself, last night's ordeal would be the trial before the triumph, the test of endurance that proved the lovers' worth. Edward would emerge more clearly than ever as her knight—her Wilfred—ready to break every injunction of class and prudence to vindicate her. Their kiss on the balcony had felt like the beginning of that story: his mouth on hers, his hands trembling as if he knew there was no turning back.

That moment had been the most real thing she had ever experienced.

"Miss, you've no appetite at all," Mollie fretted from the small table, where the bread and fruit sat untouched. "You must try something."

"I'm not hungry," Venetia said absently.

Her gaze drifted to the second letter on the coverlet. Not Morosini's this time. The familiar, neat hand on the outside had made her heart leap when the errand boy delivered it.

Edward.

She picked it up again, though she could have recited it from memory.

Dear Miss Playford,

I was relieved to learn of your release and trust you are regaining your strength after the unfortunate events of last evening.

The circumstances now surrounding your name are, as you know, delicate, and will require some time and care to be untangled. In such a climate, any appearance of undue intimacy between us can only serve to draw unwelcome attention and increase the risk of further misunderstanding.

I therefore believe it would be wisest for the present that our acquaintance be conducted at a proper distance. You may be assured that I shall follow your situation with the greatest interest and will rejoice to hear of your complete vindication.

I remain,
Your most obedient servant,
E. Rothbury

No endearment. No reference to the balcony, to the kiss, to whispered declarations that had changed her entire world. Only "delicate circumstances" and "proper distance" and "most obedient."

The sort of letter any honorable gentleman might write to any young lady in a scandal.

So he was withdrawing.

Her knight, her Ivanhoe, was lowering his lance and stepping back from the lists before the tournament had even begun.

"Bad news, miss?" Mollie asked carefully.

Venetia folded the paper very precisely, trying to hide her trembling hands.

"Mr. Rothbury believes it would be... imprudent to be seen with me," she said. "Given the delicacy of my circumstances."

Saying it out loud hurt less than she'd expected. Or perhaps she was simply numb.

"He can't mean that in his heart," Mollie burst out.

"I know what his heart felt like on that balcony," Venetia said quietly. "But hearts are apparently no match for Venetian gossip and elderly counts."

She pressed the folded letter briefly against her sternum, as if she could force some hidden meaning out of the ink. Was there a hesitation in the line where he spoke of distance? A pressure of the pen where he wrote "follow your situation with the greatest interest"?

If there were, it was too subtle for her shaking nerves to read.

He thinks this protects me, she realized. He genuinely believes vanishing is an act of chivalry.

DESPITE HER FLAGGING spirits, she took Mollie with her to Madame Bertolini's cramped little dressmaker's shop off a narrow *calle* near San Polo, ostensibly to have her gown mended after its adventure in the cells.

In truth, she had needed to *do* something. Anything.

Madame Bertolini clucked over the crushed pleats and soiled hem, murmuring her sympathy and outrage.

"Such a scandal, signorina," she said, pins between her lips. "In *my* gown, too. The whole quarter is talking."

"I imagine they are discussing the emeralds," Venetia said coolly.

"There is talk, you know, of a certain gentleman who came to Venice not long ago with letters of introduction and an accent too contrived to be true, who calls himself Count di Montefiore." Madame rolled the name in her mouth and her eyes gleamed. "Some say he also had a particular interest in emeralds. And in you."

Venetia's pulse had jumped. "Oh?"

"He appeared from nowhere, yet everyone is suddenly eager to please him. He spends a great deal of time at La Serafina's *salon*." Madame's tone transformed the word into something between admiration and disapproval. "When a gentleman wishes his secrets to be kept, he should not speak of them in a courtesan's drawing room. But they always do."

"La Serafina," Venetia repeated. "The singer?"

Madame smiled thinly. "Once a singer. Now—more. She knows everyone's business. Men forget themselves when they are flattered and comfortable. They speak of fortunes and quarrels and nephews cheated of their inheritance. They speak of English wills." Her gaze sharpened. "If anyone knows the true history of Count di Montefiore, it is La Serafina."

Nephews cheated of their inheritance.

Mr. Greene's furious face rose in Venetia's memory: the man who had believed Leonard Harrington's fortune his by right; the man whose shock at its loss had been the talk of Derbyshire. The man who had tried to lure Caroline into a scandalous elopement when he'd still been in funds.

He has every reason to hate me.

If Greene had somehow encountered this so-called Count di Montefiore, if he had told his grievances to a man already skilled in deception...

"And the count?" Venetia had asked, striving for casual interest. "You say he visits La Serafina often?"

"Very often," Madame said. "He has other names in other cities, I am told. A man of many masks. La Serafina entertains him because he pays well and is amusing, but my cousin's husband"—she spread her hands—"he swears he heard him called by another name in Paris. A French name, not Italian at all. These gentlemen," she concluded, making a neat little stitch, "they think changing their coat and title changes who they are."

A man of many masks. A French name. A courtesan who collected secrets.

If anyone could discover whether Count di Montefiore had ever received letters from an embittered Englishman named Greene, perhaps it would be La Serafina.

And if what he knows could convict *me*, Venetia thought, then what *she* knows might save me.

Time, however, was not on her side. Captain Rizzi had not cleared her; he had merely let her out on a leash tied firmly to Count Morosini's belt. The more time passed, the more opportunities her enemies had to arrange "new evidence," to twist any bold step she took into proof of her depravity.

She could almost feel that three-year clause in Leonard Harrington's will ticking in the background, like a bomb no one else could hear.

She could not wait for Edward. Not now. Not when he was muzzled and leashed by the very man who currently shielded her.

If this were *Ivanhoe*, the knight would defy his overlord and rescue her in a blaze of glory. But Edward had been ordered to stand down, and Edward obeyed orders.

So the maiden would have to find the courage and audacity to sneak her way into the enemy camp herself.

Chapter Twenty-Five

NOT SO LONG ago, Edward had actively thrilled at the thought that he was fulfilling his life's dream, translating the works of a writer as celebrated as Sir Walter Scott.

The irony wasn't lost on him that he spent his days rendering tales of noble knights and impossible love while living his own version of such torment.

But today he would have done anything to quit his position and return to England, had it not meant literally sacrificing Venetia to house arrest—or worse. The count had made his terms crystal clear: Edward's continued service in exchange for his protection of Venetia.

Cross that agreement, and the young woman he loved would find herself facing the full weight of Venetian justice with no one to intercede on her behalf.

Inquiries were taking place, but Count Morosini had made it clear that his willingness to vouch for Miss Playford's character—and guarantee she wouldn't abscond—depended entirely upon Edward remaining in his employ.

The arrangement was as elegant as it was diabolical.

Head down, Edward set his steps toward the grand expanse of the Piazza San Marco, where ancient stones had witnessed centuries of intrigue and the basilica's golden domes caught what little light filtered through the oppressive clouds. Tourists and locals moved about their business, the usual morning commerce of a city that had perfected the art of beautiful corruption.

He raised his head in time to catch a glimpse of golden hair and a Pomona green gown with which he was familiar. Sofia.

He knew it was her with the certainty of someone who'd spent too many hours translating in her vicinity, memorizing details he'd had no business noticing. Why? Because she reminded him of Venetia. Or rather, Miss Playford to him.

Beside her walked her maid Caterina, the woman who'd assisted in positioning Venetia for destruction.

Edward knew the penalties for engaging Sofia in conversation. Count Morosini's warnings had been specific and unmistakable.

"Stay away from my granddaughter." Very clear. Very emphatic.

But what other opportunity would he have for challenging her directly about the events of that cursed evening? Conversation between them was impossible in the count's home, where every word was potentially observed and reported.

But surely a few moments in the anonymous crowd of the piazza would be unlikely to be witnessed by the count's spies.

Hurrying forward, he pulled his cloak about him and waited for his opportunity. Sofia and her maid were examining silk scarves at a merchant's stall, their attention focused on the vendor's persuasive patter about the exceptional quality of his wares.

The crowd provided excellent camouflage—pilgrims and merchants, nobles and commoners, all mixing in the democratic chaos of commerce.

Edward approached with the casual air of someone happening upon an acquaintance by chance. "Signorina Sofia," he said quietly, positioning himself so that Caterina could not easily hear. "How pleasant to encounter you here."

Sofia turned, and for just an instant, he saw something flicker across her features—guilt, perhaps, or calculation. Then her practiced smile slipped into place, though it didn't quite reach her eyes.

"Signor Edward!" Her voice carried its usual musical quality, but underneath he detected a note of nervous energy. "What a surprise. I thought you were always at your scholarly work at this hour."

"Even scholars require occasional air," he replied, studying her face for telltale signs of deception. "I hoped I might encounter you. There are matters we should discuss."

Matters like framing innocent women for theft.

Her smile faltered. "Matters? I cannot imagine what—"

"Can you not?" Edward's voice dropped to a whisper. "The events of the masquerade ball, perhaps? The curious circumstance of Miss Playford wearing jewelry provided by you that contained stolen gems? Strange that this doesn't appear to feature in the current investigation."

Sofia's color heightened, but her gaze remained steady. "I'm sure I don't know what you mean. I lent her my tiara for her costume—such a generous gesture on my part—but certainly not with the emerald earrings. If I'd known they were there, I'd have absconded with Paolo by now."

Wait. What?

"Your generous gesture was an effort to compromise an innocent woman—though I'm still trying to understand why."

Sofia's laugh held a brittle quality that made Edward's skin crawl. "Signor Edward, surely you cannot be so naive as to believe I would simply lend her a tiara already containing stolen gems—"

I... actually yes. That's exactly what I believed.

"I believe Miss Playford is guilty of nothing more than trusting someone who betrayed that trust for personal gain." Edward stepped closer, noting how Caterina had moved to provide a subtle shield from prying eyes. "The question is why. What could you possibly gain from destroying someone who showed you nothing but kindness?"

For a moment, Sofia's mask slipped, and Edward glimpsed something raw and desperate beneath the calculated charm.

When she spoke again, her voice carried a note of genuine anguish that surprised him.

"You think I planned for things to unfold as they did?"

"Didn't you?"

Sofia glanced around nervously, then moved closer to the merchant's stall, using the hanging silks to create a pocket of privacy. "You don't understand the pressures I face, the impossible choices. My grandfather forges ahead with his ideas of marrying me to Conte Bembo, which could happen any day—"

"And that justifies destroying Miss Playford?"

"It justifies doing whatever is necessary to secure my freedom!" Sophie burst out, glancing around to ensure they hadn't been overheard. "Paolo and I have so little time before my grandfather's plans become irreversible. We need money to disappear, to start a new life where his influence cannot reach us."

"So you decided to steal."

Sofia's eyes blazed. "I did what I had to in order to survive. I wasn't permitted to attend the masquerade but the emeralds had been...secured. I'm watched every second so I made an arrangement with my—"

"Accomplice?" Edward frowned, trying to make sense of her hurried explanation.

Wait. She's saying she didn't *put the emeralds in the tiara?*

"If you like. Someone who, during an unguarded moment, would assist Signorina Venetia with her dress, hold her tiara while she attended to her hair, and, when she wasn't looking, place the emeralds inside." Sofia's words tumbled out faster now. "Miss Playford was supposed to return the tiara to me *with* the emeralds. I don't know whose diabolical machinations were behind the exposure and quite frankly, I don't care. All I know is that I've been cheated of the emeralds that were supposed to provide a future for Paolo."

Edward stared. This was more complicated than he'd expected.

"Do you know what my life will be like married to Conte Bembo? An old man whose previous wives died young, worn out by his demands and his temper? I would rather die than submit to such a fate—"

Several wives?

But no sympathetic entreaties could excuse the magnitude of her betrayal—*if* she spoke the truth?

"There were other ways—"

"Were there? Easy for you to say, when you have the freedom to choose your own path." Sofia's voice turned bitter. "You could leave Venice tomorrow if you wished, pursue your career wherever opportunities present themselves. I'm trapped by birth, by gender, by family obligation. The only escape I have is the one I create for myself."

"By destroying others?"

"By doing what I must." Sofia straightened, and Edward saw the moment when vulnerability gave way to cold calculation. "Miss Playford will survive this scandal. She has wealth, connections, the protection of powerful friends. She'll find some gentleman willing to overlook her tarnished reputation in exchange for her fortune."

"You truly believe that?"

"I believe she has options I will never possess." Sofia's tone had grown arctic. "She can buy her way out of disgrace. I have no such luxury."

Edward stared. Sofia spoke of necessity and survival, but underneath her justifications lay a ruthlessness that chilled him.

She merely had to tell the authorities—tell her grandfather— what she'd told him, and Venetia would be entirely exonerated.

But she'd weighed Venetia's destruction against her own freedom and found the calculation acceptable.

Before Edward could respond, Caterina stepped closer with urgent whispers in rapid Italian. They'd been observed. Someone was taking too much interest in their conversation.

"I must go," Sofia said quickly, her mask of composure slipping back into place. "Perhaps you should remember, Signor Edward, that everyone has secrets. Even you. But mine is that I'm in love with a man of whom my grandfather disapproves. Not that I'm a jewel thief."

Technically you ARE a jewel thief. Just not the jewel thief who framed Venetia.

Sofia and her maid melted back into the crowd, leaving Edward frozen by the merchant's stall.

Sofia's desperation was genuine—of that he was certain. Her love for Paolo, her fear of forced marriage, her willingness to do whatever necessary to escape—all of it rang true.

She declared she'd not been responsible for planting the jewels in the tiara Venetia was wearing.

Which meant someone else did. Someone who knew about Sofia's theft scheme and used it to frame Venetia.

If so, who had helped her? And then betrayed her?

Someone with resources and knowledge beyond what a desperate young woman could command alone.

Someone with an agenda against Venetia specifically.

Count di Montefiore? It had to be.

Edward started walking toward the count's palazzo, his mind racing.

Sofia had stolen the emeralds. Someone else—probably the count—used her theft to frame Venetia. Sofia was too self-interested to confess. And Edward couldn't tell anyone what he'd learned without admitting he'd approached Sofia.

Which means Venetia is still in danger, I'm still trapped, and now I know the conspiracy is even more complicated than I thought.

He clutched his satchel tighter. It was time to translate *Ivanhoe*... where, in fiction, the hero always won.

Chapter Twenty-Six

So, EDWARD HAD withdrawn to protect her. Venetia was not a fool. She understood this.

Which meant, who else would fight to clear her name? Who else would undertake the risks needed to ascertain the role played by the man she now suspected of being at the root of her downfall.

Count di Montefiore.

And Greene.

By the time evening fell, Venetia had dressed for battle.

She stood at the top of the Casa Bonaldi's grand staircase, fingers smoothing the silver lutestring over her hips, checking the fall of the daring neckline in the reflection of a polished silver vase.

Not bad.

If people were determined to stare at her, they might as well stare at something other than the specter of stolen jewels.

The gown—Madame Bertolini's latest triumph—skimmed her figure more closely than any truly decorous lady would approve, and pearls threaded through her hair gleamed in the light of the beeswax candles.

She looked, she thought with grim satisfaction, exactly like the sort of woman Venetia Playford was now rumored to be.

Wicked. Bold. Untrustworthy.

"You look beautiful, miss," Mollie muttered from behind her, torn between pride and horror. "And like you might get into a great deal of trouble."

"Good." Venetia adjusted her mask, the black satin obscuring enough of her face to give the illusion of anonymity. "Trouble is what I need if I'm going to find answers."

"Are you sure about this?" Mollie whispered. "Just because Madame Bertolini says—"

"Madame Bertolini's instincts for fashion cannot be faulted," Venetia said lightly. "Perhaps she has equal talent in gossip."

Low laughter and the clink of glasses drifted from the blue salon at the end of the corridor. Venetia drew a breath, braced herself, and walked in.

Conversation faltered. She felt the weight of glances skim over the silver gown, the pearls, the mask.

"Venetia, my dear, you are not staying in this evening?" Lady Townsend's voice held a careful brightness that suggested she was alarmed.

"She looks very fetching," Lord Thornton said, rising. "Come and make up a hand of whist, Miss Playford."

"You are very kind," Venetia replied. "But I have other plans." She moved fully into the room, acutely aware of Miss Bentley's speculative gaze. "I've been invited to La Serafina's salon this evening."

The silence that followed was almost comical.

Lady Townsend's teacup rattled in its saucer. Lord Thornton's eyebrows vanished into his hairline. Several lesser guests pretended to find the carpet pattern fascinating.

"Venetia," Lady Townsend said carefully, as if addressing someone balancing on a balcony rail, "surely you cannot mean the opera singer's establishment? My dear girl, such gatherings are hardly—"

"Respectable?" Venetia raised her eyebrows. "I care less about respectability with each passing day. Especially when it appears most of society considers I no longer have any more respectability to lose."

"All the more reason to show ladylike restraint until they recover their senses," Lady Townsend urged.

"And how did you *receive* such an invitation?" Miss Bentley demanded.

"It came through my dressmaker, if you must know," Venetia went on. "Madame Bertolini also dresses La Serafina and apparently could not resist recounting my recent adventures. La Serafina expressed a desire to meet me."

A murmur rippled through the room.

Lord Thornton cleared his throat. "Miss Playford, La Serafina's salons are known to attract a… mixed company. Artists, adventurers, men whose reputation is… not always savory."

"Precisely why I wish to attend." Venetia took a chair with deliberate composure. "Where better to observe those who move at the edges of respectability? Where better to learn who might have profited from doing what was done to me?"

Lady Townsend stared at her. "You cannot possibly believe that going to La Serafina's will help clear your name, my dear? Why, it will make things much, much worse."

"I believe the proper authorities are more interested in confirming their neat little story than in finding the truth," Venetia said crisply. "My name is already tarnished; my reputation, for all practical purposes, is gone. So tell me, Lady Townsend—what does your ladylike restraint propose I do? Sit quietly and hope my enemies grow bored?"

"Venetia, we are doing all we can," she said softly. "Thornton and I—Edward—"

"Edward," Venetia repeated, and the single word seemed to pull the air out of the room.

She drew the letter from her reticule, tapped it against her palm. "Mr. Rothbury has decided," she said, managing a smile that felt like it might crack her face, "that it would be 'wisest' our acquaintance be conducted at a proper distance while things are... untangled."

Lady Townsend's eyes filled with quick understanding. "My dear, I am sure there are reasons—"

"Oh, I'm sure there are," Venetia cut in. "He is an honorable man working under the patronage of a powerful one. I do not doubt that chains have been wrapped around him from every direction. But the result is the same, is it not? I stand accused. And he is not able to help me."

There was silence.

Thornton set his glass down carefully. "What do you *hope* to find at La Serafina's?" he asked. "This is not a rhetorical question."

"Information," Venetia said simply. "Madame Bertolini tells me that Count di Montefiore is often seen there. That he is not what he claims to be. That he likes to pay court to older women—"

She speared Miss Bentley with a look, causing the older woman's cheeks to flame though she said nothing.

A flicker of interest crossed Thornton's features. "Count di Montefiore?"

"Yes." Venetia leaned forward, energy thrumming in her veins. "A man who appears in our circle just as my inheritance becomes the talk of Venetian society. A man who pumps Miss Bentley for every detail of the will's conditions. A man who stares at my jewels as if assessing their value for someone else. A man of 'many names' who visits a courtesan known for her knowledge of other people's private business." She drew breath. "Does that not strike you as... convenient?"

Lady Townsend, who had been listening with tightening lips, said slowly, "Madame Bertolini told you this?"

"And more." Venetia's fingers twisted the letter unconsciously. "According to her cousin, he was called by another name in Paris. A French name. We know of at least one Englishman with reason to hate me who speaks French and considers himself cosmopolitan."

"Mr. Greene," Lady Thornton whispered.

"Mr. Greene," Venetia agreed. "Disinherited in my favor, in debt, in need of funds and revenge. What if he met this so-called Count di Montefiore somewhere on the Continent? What if he spoke of a foolish old man's will and a clause about scandal? Would that not present a tempting opportunity to a man who specializes in other men's misfortunes?"

"And Sofia?" Thornton asked quietly.

Venetia's jaw tightened. "Sofia is vain and easily swayed. If a charming, worldly count whispered to her that her romantic dreams could come true if only she helped him with a little scheme... Do you really think she would resist?"

Lady Townsend closed her eyes briefly. "Oh, child."

"I am not a child any longer," Venetia said, more steadily than she felt. "I may be foolish in many things, but I am starting to see the pattern resolving itself."

"Even if your theory is correct," Thornton said, "La Serafina's drawing room is hardly a safe place for investigation. Deliberately placing yourself in disreputable company will hand your enemies more ammunition."

"Or it may hand me the proof I need before they can finish ruining me." Venetia rose, smoothing her skirts. "If I do nothing, Captain Rizzi builds his case. If I wait politely, Greene—if it *is* Greene—and his pet count tighten their net. If I sit in this respectable salon playing whist, I will wake one morning to find I have lost not only my reputation but my fortune as well."

She lifted her chin. "My inheritance can be taken with a stroke of a pen if Captain Rizzi were to write a scathing letter about my conduct to my trustees. My freedom can be taken with a word from the wrong man. My reputation, practically speaking, is already gone. What I have left is the ability to act."

"Venetia," Lady Townsend said desperately, "if you must do something, let us at least help you. We can make inquiries. There are more discreet means—"

"I know," Venetia said more gently. "And I am grateful. But

discreet means take time. I do not have time. Men like Count di Montefiore do not linger once their work is done. If he is planning to vanish, it will be soon."

She drew in another breath. "I will go masked. Mollie will be with me. I will not drink anything I haven't seen poured. I will sit at the edge of the room and listen. And if La Serafina is half as perceptive as people say, she will know my questions before I ask them."

Mollie made a faint squeaking noise that suggested she had not entirely agreed to this plan, but Venetia pressed on.

"Please," she said to Eugenia and Thornton, and her voice broke on the word. "You have both been so kind to me. I know this seems reckless. It *is* reckless. But I cannot bear another night waiting while other people decide my fate. If I am to be ruined, let it at least be in the attempt to save myself."

"She's going to go whether we approve or not," Thornton murmured.

"Yes," Lady Townsend said. "I can see that."

"Then the question," he said, "is whether we leave her to it—or arrange to be close enough to catch her if she falls."

Lady Townsend straightened. "Very well, Venetia. Go. But do not think for a moment I intend to let you flounce into a courtesan's salon without some measure of protection. Thornton, we know at least three men who would be welcome in such a place and discreet enough to keep their mouths shut."

"Four," Thornton corrected. "I'm one of them."

Venetia's lips twitched. "Lady Townsend, Lord Thornton, you cannot possibly—"

"Oh, we absolutely can," Lady Townsend said briskly. "You may insist on throwing yourself into danger, my dear, but you shall not go alone into the lion's den. Neither Thornton nor I would ever agree to that."

Chapter Twenty-Seven

THE ENTRANCE TO La Serafina's palazzo was marked only by a discreet brass plaque and a doorman whose knowing smile suggested he'd admitted far more scandalous guests than one English heiress with questionable judgment.

Venetia stepped over the threshold with her heart in her throat and Mollie close at her side. Somewhere behind them, in the shadows of the *calle*, Lord Thornton had murmured a last reassurance.

"I'll be inside," he'd said quietly. "But I shan't hover. You'll have room to speak as you need. If anything feels wrong, you look for me."

Now, as they crossed a marble-floored vestibule where classical statues posed in attitudes that would have made Aunt Pike reach for the vinegar bottle, Venetia was acutely conscious of Thornton's silent promise at her back. Not a knight in shining armor—not tonight—but a sober English peer in plain evening black, blending into the crowd, eyes everywhere.

The salon itself defied her expectations. Rather than the tawdry, smoky den she'd half imagined, the room rivaled any noble drawing room in elegance. Silk wallpaper in deep claret glowed in the candlelight, a rich foil for paintings: misty landscapes and mythological scenes rendered with disturbing frankness.

Crystal chandeliers cast a warm light over clusters of guests. Here, a countess in diamonds talked earnestly with a young man whose paint-stained fingers proclaimed his trade. There, a gentleman in sober evening dress leaned in to listen to a woman whose rouge and laugh would have scandalized a London drawing room. Italian, French, and English flowed together, rising and falling like the tide against the foundations.

"Signorina Playford." The voice was low and melodious, carrying easily over the hum of conversation.

Venetia turned to find herself face to face with their hostess.

La Serafina was perhaps fifty, silver threads glinting through dark hair artfully arranged. Her gown of midnight-blue silk was cut with Continental daring, yet worn with such confidence it seemed the height of sophistication rather than impropriety. Diamonds sparkled at her throat, but it was her eyes that held Venetia—the eyes of a woman who had seen much more than Venetia certainly had, yet remained amused by the world.

"Madame," Venetia said, dipping an instinctive curtsy that felt hopelessly provincial.

La Serafina caught her hands and drew her up. "No, *cara*. We do not kneel to one another here. We meet as equals." Her smile deepened. "You are even more interesting than Madame Bertolini described. Such courage, to walk into the lion's den with your head high when others would hide under their beds."

"Courage," Venetia said lightly. "Or recklessness."

"In Venice," La Serafina replied, "they are often the same thing." Her gaze flicked over Venetia's gown, her mask, the set of her shoulders. "You have a protector with you."

Venetia's heart jerked. "A protector?"

"The English milord by the door." A tiny tilt of La Serafina's head directed Venetia's eyes toward Thornton, half concealed behind a column, apparently engrossed in discussion with a Venetian gentleman. "He watches you without watching you. Very correct. Very English. Now." Instantly she changed tack. "What is it you hope to find here?"

Venetia gripped her glass. "You know the man who calls himself Count di Montefiore."

A flicker crossed La Serafina's face. "Many men call themselves many things in this room," she said lightly. "But yes. I know the gentleman you mean."

"I've heard rumors that he is not who he claims to be," Venetia whispered, her heart hammering. "That... he is involved in... this scheme against me."

La Serafina glanced briefly across the room; Venetia followed her gaze and saw Thornton, outwardly relaxed, in conversation with a Venetian merchant and a thin, fox-faced Frenchman.

"It is good to have friends who hold your interests close." La Serafina stepped closer, her voice dropping. "And you are wise to be wary of Montefiore, whatever name he wears. He has been a Polish count in Vienna, a Spanish marquis in Paris, and a French vicomte in Milan. His accents are very good. His papers are always in good order. But his soul, *cara*—that remains the same."

A chill slid down Venetia's spine. "And what is that?"

"A man who lives by trading in other people's misfortunes. Debts. Lawsuits. Lost inheritances." La Serafina's expression grew grave. "He was at my salon months ago in company with an Englishman. They spoke in French, but anger sounds the same in any tongue. The Englishman complained of a legacy that should have been his, stolen by a girl in his country and by a meddling lawyer. He spoke of a clause in a will. Of scandal. Of how easily a reputation might be stained."

Venetia could barely breathe. "An Englishman. Do you know his name?"

"He gave one," La Serafina said, "but I doubt it was the right one. He called himself Monsieur Vert, amusingly. Green." Her eyes narrowed. "It made me think he was not very subtle. Montefiore is more careful."

Green. *Greene*.

Of course.

The room seemed to tilt for a moment. So, Mr. Greene had

been colluding with di Montefiore. Greene, who'd been disinherited in her favor; Greene, who had once tried to lure Caroline into ruin. And now Greene, drunk and angry in a Venetian salon, pouring his grievances into the ear of a man who specialized in exploiting such things.

"And do you have any information," Venetia managed, "that this count—whatever his real name—has made some arrangement with him?"

"I think a man like Montefiore does nothing without expecting profit." La Serafina touched her arm briefly. "And I think you, signorina, are profit. Your disgrace, properly arranged, would be worth a great deal to an Englishman who believes you stole his future."

"How can this be conveyed to Captain Rizzi to investigate?" Venetia asked, the words tumbling out. "Is it possible you could—"

La Serafina's smile thinned. "The good captain has visited me before. He prefers gossip that confirms his prejudices. He has already decided what kind of woman you are. My word against a respectable 'count' and a disinherited English gentleman? No, *cara*. The law will not save you. Only proof will. And proof is difficult when dealing with ghosts."

Venetia felt the excitement drain from her. "Then what do you advise?" she whispered.

"Patience," La Serafina tapped Venetia on the wrist with her fan, before her gaze rose to the large portrait on the wall beside them.

The woman in the painting was caught in the full glory of youth—a dark-haired beauty with luminous eyes and a sensuous mouth curved in an enigmatic smile. Her gown was simple white silk, leaving the drama to her expression. There was something vulnerable about her, despite the proud tilt of her chin.

"Behold *La vera Serafina*," her hostess said, encompassing the painting with a sweep of her arm. "If only *she* had had patience to wait the three years for her marchese to return—alive—from the shipwreck all Venice believed had taken his life."

"La vera Sarafina?" Venetia repeated with a puzzled frown.

"That's right. The true Seraphim they called her, because her voice, they said, came from heaven."

Venetia felt a shiver run down her spine.

"Isabella Monteverdi was her real name though no one remembers that. They remember only the voice from heaven. *La Serafina.*"

"And you—" Venetia hesitated, not wanting to presume.

"I took my name in homage after she left Venice, brokenhearted after waiting two years in the hope that her protector would return," her hostess continued. "But I was a pale echo of a great light. When I was a girl, I queued in the alley behind La Fenice just to hear her rehearsing. Her Desdemona could reduce men to sobbing wrecks. Her Violetta made women question every sensible choice they had ever made."

"She was an opera singer?" Venetia asked, though the answer was obvious.

"The opera singer." Pride and regret threaded La Serafina's tone. "She had the city at her feet. Contracts in Paris and Vienna. The marchese who worshipped her. And then—" She snapped her fingers. "Gone."

"Gone?" Venetia echoed.

"An Englishman came to Venice. A staid, boring gentleman. But he must have offered her what she wanted, for she stole away one night with her son—not a word to anyone—never to be heard of again." La Serafina's lip curled faintly.

"La Serafina." Thornton appeared then, bowing over their hostess's hand. "I hope you will forgive an Englishman for intruding upon your guest. Miss Playford's friends are perhaps overanxious."

"On the contrary, milord," La Serafina said smoothly. "Your anxiety does you credit. You English are so very good at pretending not to feel anything at all; it is refreshing to see one of you admit to concern."

Thornton's mouth quirked. "My concern is entirely selfish. I should be quite crushed if anything happened to Miss Playford while under my protection."

"Then you have chosen an interesting city for your guardianship." La Serafina's gaze flickered past them. "And an interesting evening."

Venetia turned—to find Count di Montefiore bearing down upon them.

Even masked, he was unmistakable: the height, the smooth carriage. His eyes gleamed behind his domino.

"Miss Playford," he said warmly, as if greeting a cherished acquaintance in the park. "What a delight to find you here. La Serafina's taste is as exquisite as ever."

"Count," Venetia said, every nerve on edge.

"And Lord Thornton." The brief inclination of his head held just enough respect to avoid insult. "We are very honored by your presence as well. Venice is truly favored when English respectability graces her less... orthodox salons."

"There is nothing inherently disreputable about art, music, or conversation, sir," Thornton returned pleasantly.

"Ah, but context is everything, is it not?" Montefiore smiled. He turned back to Venetia. "Signorina, you have been much talked of. I had hoped we might share a dance. La Serafina's musicians are tuning up now."

"La Serafina's musicians are indeed excellent," Venetia said. "But I am not dancing this evening."

"Come, come." His tone turned coaxing. "Surely you would not refuse when your reputation is already—how do you English say?—'beyond saving'?"

"That will do," Thornton said, his voice mild but edged with steel. He stepped a fraction closer to Venetia, his presence suddenly very solid.

For the first time, something like genuine interest sparked in Montefiore's gaze. "Your *particular* friend," he repeated. "How very gallant of you, milord. But gallantry can be dangerous in

Venice. A man may find himself swept along by currents he did not intend to enter."

"Fortunately," Thornton said, "I swim well."

Montefiore's smile sharpened. "Even the strongest swimmers tire." His gaze slid once more to Venetia. "Do not be too sure, Miss Playford, that everyone will be as willing to hazard themselves for your sake."

There. A threat. Veiled, polite, but unmistakable.

La Serafina shifted, subtly interposing herself between Venetia and the count. "I must borrow my guest," she said lightly. "There is a poet who wishes to recite something dreadful and needs an appreciative audience. Lord Thornton, you will remain? I should hate to think our English contingent fled so early."

"For a little while longer," Thornton said. His eyes met Venetia's, steady and reassuring. "Miss Playford, perhaps it is time we thought of returning. It grows late."

"Yes," Venetia said quickly. "I believe it does."

Montefiore inclined his head. "Of course. One should never keep a lady out too late, milord. People talk. And you in particular would not wish more talk."

Thornton's jaw tightened by the smallest degree. "Good evening, count."

They moved away. Venetia could feel Montefiore's gaze on her back like cold fingers.

"Do you see?" she whispered once they had crossed to the far side of the room. "He as much as admitted—"

"I saw enough," Thornton said grimly. "And heard enough to be more certain than ever that he is dangerous. I think we should leave," he continued. "Let me arrange a gondola. Stay where the footmen can see you. And do not," he added, meeting her eyes, "speak to the count again."

"I promise," Venetia said.

He gave her hand a brief, hard squeeze and then he was gone into the little crush near the cloakroom, swallowed by silk and black coats.

Mollie materialized at her side as if conjured, cheeks pink, eyes wide. "Miss?"

"We're leaving," Venetia said. "Lord Thornton's arranging a gondola. We'll wait by the door."

They did. For a minute. Two.

The vestibule grew more crowded as guests arrived and left, the doorman's discreet cough and the rustle of cloaks filling the space. Venetia craned her neck, searching for Thornton's fair head above the shorter Venetians.

Nothing.

Behind her, laughter flared in the salon—Montefiore's, unmistakable. A glance over her shoulder revealed him watching her, one elbow propped on the mantel, conversing with a thin, fox-faced man Venetia did not recognize.

The fox-faced man followed Montefiore's gaze. His eyes narrowed when they found her. Something in that look—assessing, cold, interested—made every hair at the back of her neck stand up.

"Miss," Mollie whispered, "I don't like this. I can't see his lordship. And that man—"

"I know," Venetia said. Her voice came out thin. The vestibule suddenly seemed too small, the walls too close, the doorman too far away.

"Perhaps Lord Thornton went out of the side door?" Mollie suggested. "To speak to the gondolier?"

Or perhaps he's been delayed, or cornered, or deliberately distracted. By whom?

Montefiore lifted his glass in an almost-toasting gesture, the smile on his lips friendly, the message in his eyes anything but.

"Come on," Venetia said abruptly. "Perhaps something has delayed him and he can't make his way back. Perhaps we should go after him."

She turned to the doorman. "The water-gate?" she asked in Italian. "Is it that way?"

"Sì, signorina." He gestured down a side corridor. "The gondolas wait directly outside. Should I have yours called?"

Venetia hesitated then shook her head. Lord Thornton was probably in a tussle trying to secure them transport at this very moment. They'd probably step right out of the door and find him.

They hurried down the corridor. The muffled music fell away, replaced by the soft slap of water and the muffled creak of mooring ropes. A glass-paneled door opened onto the water-gate: a small stone landing directly onto the dark canal, lantern-light gilding the ripples gold.

Several gondolas bobbed gently. A couple emerged from the nearest boat, laughing, the woman adjusting her shawl as they disappeared into the house.

No sign of Lord Thornton.

"What do we do?" Mollie whispered.

"We must go home," Venetia said.

The nearest gondolier turned at the sound of their voices. He was middle-aged, with a lined face and wary eyes.

"Casa Bonaldi?" Venetia asked in halting Italian, stepping toward him. "Can you take us there?"

He shrugged, raking his eyes the length of her. A proper lady did not go about alone at night. Not even with a servant. "If you pay, I row."

Good enough.

"Miss, shouldn't we wait for Lord Thornton—" Mollie began.

"I don't know where he is. So we must just go home," Venetia said, already stepping down.

She felt the boat dip under her weight, the sudden, unsettling give of wood on water. Mollie clutched her skirts and followed, almost tumbling into Venetia's lap in her haste.

The gondolier pushed off, and the landing fell away; the lights of La Serafina's palazzo slid swiftly backwards, shrinking to a smear of gold against the dark stone.

"Did you find what you were looking for, miss?" Mollie whispered.

Venetia gave a half nod as she said, haltingly, "I found the confirmation I needed."

Her maid clapped her hands.

Venetia sighed. "Alas, it's answers I really need, Mollie. Not confirmation of my fears."

Chapter Twenty-Eight

IT WAS NEARLY midnight by the time Edward returned to the casa, climbing the marble steps with leaden feet, his leather satchel digging into his shoulder. The day's translation work had been pure torment. Every line of Scott's prose about impossible love and noble sacrifice had been like salt rubbed into an open wound.

Ivanhoe gets to be noble and get the girl. I just get to be noble and miserable.

Count Morosini had been particularly exacting, demanding faster translations and refinements that seemed designed more to keep Edward chained to the desk than to improve the text. His stomach growled; he'd barely touched the simple meal sent up to the library. Food had no taste when every bite reminded him of the price he was paying for Venetia's safety—his silence, his distance, his apparent abandonment.

"Rothbury!" Lord Thornton's voice rang across the main drawing room the moment Edward appeared in the doorway. Relief and something very like panic sharpened his tone. "Thank God you're here."

All the air seemed to leave Edward's lungs. "What's happened?"

"It's Venetia," Lady Townsend said, rising from her chair, her usually composed face drawn tight with anxiety. "We don't know where she is."

The words hit him like a physical blow. "What?"

Thornton dragged a hand through his thick gray hair. "I left her at La Serafina's while I organized a gondola," he said. "When I returned, she was gone."

"La Serafina's?" Edward repeated stupidly.

"The singer's salon," Thornton clarified grimly. "Artists, adventurers, half of Venice's more *interesting* element attend."

"Yes, I know the place." He fought for control. "What was she doing there?"

"Her dressmaker hinted she would find answers there," Lady Townsend said helplessly. "Venetia would not be dissuaded from going, though Thornton accompanied her—"

"I cannot believe Miss Playford was so bold as to attend La Serafina's!" Edward scarcely recognized his own voice. Panic burst in his chest. "But now she's somewhere in Venice, and no one knows exactly where?"

"I could only assume she'd come straight back here," Thornton said. "La Serafina said Venetia had left minutes before I returned. I came back by the most direct route, praying she'd arrived safe and sound." He spread his hands. "She has not."

"I have to find her," Edward said, already turning.

"Edward, wait." Thornton caught his arm. "I understand that Count Morosini will take a dim view of it if you're seen publicly associated with her again. I was just on my way back—"

"This is Venice," Edward said, shaking free. "I will go. Half the city is masked after dark. They'll hardly notice another Englishman on the water."

And if they do, let Morosini rage.

Venetia's safety was worth every promise he shattered.

THE NIGHT WRAPPED Venice in velvet and shadow. Lanterns

bobbed on iron brackets, their reflections shivering in the black water. Laughter and distant music drifted from palazzi; the splash of oars and the occasional shout bounced off stone.

Edward strode down to the casa's landing. "A gondola," he barked, his fears for Venetia nearly crippling.

Within moments he was settled in the prow of a narrow black boat, the gondolier balanced at the stern, a dark silhouette against the stars.

"La Serafina's palazzo," Edward ordered.

As they cut through the water, Edward's mind flayed him with images: Venetia's pale face behind prison bars; Venetia's mouth beneath his on the balcony.

He had promised Morosini to stay away. Promised to bury himself in *Ivanhoe* as the price for Venetia's protection.

But Venetia needed protection now like never before.

They reached La Serafina's palazzo in minutes. Light and laughter spilled from the tall windows and the water-gate lanterns cast pools of gold on the stone steps. Edward bounded up, and was halfway into the vestibule before La Serafina herself appeared, fan in hand.

"Signor Rothbury," she said. "You English are like weeds here in my establishment—"

Edward interrupted. "I need to know—Miss Playford. Is she here?"

"She left ten, perhaps twelve minutes ago," La Serafina replied. Her look sharpened. "The man who calls himself Count di Montefiore left shortly after. He did not take the same route." A pause. "But Venice has only so many paths home by water, *caro*. If he wishes to intercept a boat, he knows where it must pass."

Cold slid into Edward's bones. "He's following her?"

"I did not say that," La Serafina replied. "But knowing what I know, I gave you that information for good reason."

"Thank you," Edward said tightly. He turned and hurtled back down to the water-gate.

"Signor Rothbury," she called after him.

He glanced back.

Her gaze softened, unexpectedly. "Be careful of this Count di Montefiore. Both of you."

He nodded once and flung himself into the waiting gondola. "We're going back toward the Rialto," he told the gondolier. "Fast. Watch for a boat with two women—an English signorina in silver and her maid. And another gondola shadowing them. I need to find them."

The gondolier grunted, set his shoulders, and drove the oar hard. The boat leapt forward.

They shot down a side canal, under a low bridge that scraped Edward's hair. Shadows loomed and fell away and Edward craned his head. Every curve of stone, every flicker of light might conceal Venetia's beautiful silhouette—or Montefiore's.

"Too many boats," the gondolier muttered. "Everyone going home."

"Keeping looking!" Edward said urgently. "A young woman—"

As if the city heard him, a tight sound reached his ears—half-laugh, half-protest—carried strangely on the damp night air. He strained to listen.

"...reputation already in shreds... what difference another tear makes..."

Montefiore.

"Over there," Edward snapped, pointing toward a narrower branch of canal. "Quickly."

They swung sharply, the gondola tilting alarmingly. Ahead, two dark shapes moved close together in the water—two gondolas, prow to prow, rocked sideways as if bumping.

As they drew nearer, the scene resolved: one boat bearing a single man, his cloak thrown back, one hand gripping the rail of the other gondola. In the second, two women: Mollie huddled small and pale at the stern, Venetia rigid in the middle, her arm caught in the man's hand.

Count di Montefiore.

"...be sensible, *mia cara*," he was saying, his voice silken with cruelty. "Your reputation is in ruins. You have just been released from prison, you have just attended a notorious courtesan's salon, and you were just discovered in a compromising position with Count Morosini's pet Englishman. The world already thinks the worst. You might as well profit from it."

"I would rather drown than go with you," Venetia said through her teeth, trying to wrench free.

Her gondola rocked; Mollie squeaked, clinging to the seat.

Edward could hear it. He could see it. But he was too far away to stop it.

Nor did he want to cry out and alert Montefiore, though it took all his willpower not to when Montefiore tightened his grip on Venetia's arm and leaned closer. "Dramatic, but unnecessary. You give me what I want, and I can help you. I know which strings to pull, which testimonies to silence. I can persuade certain English gentlemen to be... generous. Your inheritance could be safe. Or I can let events take their course and watch as you lose everything—to a man who has waited very patiently to see you fall."

"Mr. Greene," Venetia whispered, horror in her eyes.

"Ah, so you are not as naive as you pretend." His mouth curved. "Do you really think your troubles fell from a clear blue sky? Who told Rizzi where to look? Who described to him an heiress with a penchant for the wrong sort of company?"

"Let her go!" Mollie burst out, lunging forward.

Montefiore backhanded her away, not hard but contemptuous. Mollie cried out and sprawled on the seat.

That was as far as he got.

"Pull alongside," Edward said, and the two boats came together with a hollow thud.

Edward leapt.

He landed awkwardly in Venetia's gondola, grabbing the rail to steady himself. Venetia's eyes flew to his; a raw, incredulous joy flashed there, swiftly followed by terror.

"Edward—"

"Release her," Edward said to Montefiore, his voice calm.

The count's brows rose behind his mask. "Signor Rothbury. How very predictable of you."

He did not let go.

"I said," Edward repeated, "release her."

"Or what?" Montefiore asked softly. "You will challenge me? Here? In this pretty little gutter?" He smirked. "You English are always so romantic about heroics. It rarely ends well."

Edward didn't answer. He drove his fist straight into the man's jaw.

Montefiore staggered, grip loosening. Venetia wrenched free, stumbling back into the seat. Mollie scrambled to her side.

The count recovered quickly, eyes alight. "Ah. *Enfin.*"

He lunged.

They crashed against the rail, boots slipping on wet planks. The gondola swayed dangerously; the gondolier swore in rapid Italian, fighting to keep them from tipping.

Montefiore was taller, heavier, and had undoubtedly been in more tavern brawls than Edward ever had. But Edward had rage and desperation on his side. Months of restrained feeling exploded in one blazing purpose.

Montefiore swung; Edward ducked, felt the fist graze his ear, and drove his shoulder into the other man's chest. They slammed into the side of the gondola, the impact ringing up through Edward's bones. Another blow; a grunt of pain; spots flared at the edge of his vision. He clung on, tasting blood.

Somewhere, Venetia cried his name.

It spurred him on.

He feinted, then hammered his fist up into Montefiore's exposed ribs. The count wheezed. Edward followed with a sharp punch to the stomach, then an elbow to the chin when Montefiore bent forward with a curse.

The man's boot slipped on water; for an instant he tottered, arms windmilling. Edward shoved.

Montefiore toppled backwards into his own gondola, landing heavily. The boat rocked wildly; his gondolier yelped.

"That's enough," Edward said through his teeth, chest heaving. "If I see you again anywhere near her, I won't be so gentle."

Montefiore lay where he had fallen, teeth bared in a rictus that wasn't quite a smile. "You think you've won something here?" he rasped. "You've merely made my work easier."

"Row," Edward snapped to his own gondolier. "Now."

He turned to Venetia and held out his arms. "Come."

She didn't hesitate. She flung herself at him, fingers digging into his shoulders as if she'd never let go.

He lifted her—light and trembling—and stepped back into his own gondola, Mollie clambering after them with the agility of the terrified. The oar bit into water, the gap widened. And Montefiore's curse echoed after them and was swallowed by the dark.

Only then did Edward feel his hands shaking.

"Are you hurt?" he managed, searching Venetia's face in the dimness. "Did he—"

"No." Her voice broke. "No, not—not in any way that matters. Edward, you came."

"As if I could do anything else," he said hoarsely.

And then she was in his arms again, not clinging in fear but surging up, pressing her mouth to his with a desperation that matched his own.

The world fell away.

For a wild, endless moment there was nothing but the taste of her—salt from tears, the faint ghost of La Serafina's champagne, the sweetness that was uniquely Venetia. His hands framed her face, slid into her hair, memorizing every line, every silken strand. She made a small sound against his lips that undid him utterly.

This. This was right. This was what every line of *Ivanhoe* had made him ache for without knowing it—two souls who had circled and denied and tormented themselves finally colliding into this perfection.

He kissed her as if he could pour every unsaid word into her:

I love you. I will fight for you. I will burn every bargain I made if it keeps you safe.

She answered with a fervor that banished every doubt: hands in his hair, fingers curling into his coat, mouth moving under his with glorious, unpracticed ardor. There was nothing restrained, nothing decorous about her. She gave herself to the moment with the same wholehearted courage she gave to everything she did.

Finally, they broke apart. Foreheads pressed together, they laughed shakily into the small space between them.

"I thought—" she began, then stopped, swallowing. "I thought you'd decided it was wiser to stay away."

"I had," he said honestly. "And then you vanished into Venice. Thornton told me. Do you think I'd leave you to find your own way back?"

She gave a watery laugh. "In the cell to which Captain Rizzi marched me, I believed I'd never see freedom again. I was so frightened that when I was released, I couldn't just hide in my room. Not for long, anyway. So I marched off to find the truth, and I ended up nearly being manhandled into a villain's gondola and ruining everything."

"You *were* so brave," Edward said fiercely. He kissed the corner of her mouth, the damp track of a tear. "Venetia, I—"

"Don't," she whispered. "Not yet. If you tell me you love me in a gondola on a Venetian canal, I might actually expire from romance on the spot."

"In *Ivanhoe*," he said helplessly, "the hero—"

"Gets the girl," she finished for him. "You will not bribe me with Scott, Edward Rothbury. No matter how much I've always wanted to be Rowena."

"You're more Rebecca," he said quietly. "Braver. Clearer eyed."

She drew back enough to really look at him then, her expression softening, deepening. "And you? Which are you?"

He thought of Morosini and his library. Of Montefiore's threats, Greene's hatred, Rizzi's suspicions. Of his life, built from duty and caution and compromise.

For the first time, he didn't care.

"I'm the man who will fight for you," he said simply. "Even if it ruins me."

Something in her eyes went molten. "Edward…"

The gondola slid on, rocking gently, the night folding around them.

She told him, in gasps and snatches, of La Serafina and a famed opera singer named Isabella Monteverdi, of an angry French "Monsieur Vert" with a suspiciously familiar name. He stilled in momentary horror at her mention the famous Monteverdi before he returned his attention toward piecing together Montefiore's agenda: Greene's grievance, the will's clause, the elaborate staging of Venetia's disgrace.

He told her—finally—about Morosini's bargain. About the library, the veiled threats, the conditions tied to her freedom. Her hand clenched in his when she realized just how tight the net around them had been.

"And you came anyway," she whispered.

"How could I not?"

For half an hour—or perhaps a lifetime—they existed only on that strip of water between stone and sky as they opened up their hearts to one another.

He knew he would pay for it. He knew this night would have consequences that would ripple outward like circles on the canal. But he did not care.

If this was his ruin, he would go to it with his eyes open and her hand in his.

"Almost there, signore," the gondolier called softly at last.

The casa's landing materialized ahead, lanterns flaring golden against the night. Edward straightened, reluctantly loosening his hold as the gondola glided toward the steps.

"Whatever happens next," Venetia said, fingers tightening on his sleeve, "you know I feel the same as I ever did. Do you understand?"

What could he say? He nodded, and they shared one last, swift kiss and then the prow bumped gently against stone.

The gondolier steadied the boat. Edward rose, intending to step out first and then lift Venetia to the safety of the casa's private jetty.

He looked up.

And the world crashed down.

Captain Rizzi stood at the top of the steps, boots planted wide, hands clasped behind his back. The lantern light threw the angles of his face into harsh relief, his expression a blend of victory and long-awaited satisfaction.

Beside him, immaculate in dry evening clothes despite their recent encounter, stood Count di Montefiore.

Of course he'd recovered quickly. Of course he'd gone straight to Rizzi. Of course.

"Signor Rothbury," Rizzi said, his voice carrying coolly over the water. "And Signorina Playford. How fortunate. We were just discussing you."

Venetia's hand jerked in Edward's. He stepped instinctively in front of her, useless gesture though it was.

"Captain," he said, forcing his voice to steady. "It is late. Miss Playford has had a trying evening. Whatever business you have can surely wait until—"

"Until you have finished compromising her yet further?" Montefiore drawled. "But, my dear Rothbury, surely the damage is done. Look at you. Returning together from some nocturnal adventure, disheveled, alone. Imagine how that will sound in the proper ears."

Rizzi's gaze swept over them: Venetia's loosened hair, her flushed cheeks; Edward's bruised knuckles and cravat askew.

"If you thought yourself ruined before, signorina," Montefiore went on pleasantly, "you have outdone yourself tonight."

Venetia's chin lifted.

"I know," he said softly, "that I offered you a way out. A chance to ally yourself with someone who could protect you from what is coming. You spurned it." His eyes glinted. "Now you have placed yourself, and your very noble English translator, entirely in my hands."

Rizzi nodded once, as if confirming a report. "The count came to me as soon as he left La Serafina's. He told me of his concern for you, Signorina Playford. How he feared an English gentleman had enticed you into dangerous circles. How he worried you might be further compromised." His mouth thinned. "Then I hear that you leave La Serafina without your agreed escort, returning at midnight, alone…with a man." He hesitated. "Something I do not think your trustees will take kindly to learning."

Edward felt Venetia flinch.

"Let me be absolutely clear," Montefiore said, every word a poisoned drop. "My Englishman will hear of this."

He smiled at Edward. "You should have left her to me, Rothbury. I might have been kind. Now, when the story is told, it will be of the heiress and her lover, the theft and the tryst, the jewels and the kiss by night."

"And whose story will that be?" Edward demanded. "Yours? No chance for Miss Playford to put her side?"

"Mine," Montefiore agreed. "Captain Rizzi's. Mr. Greene's. The notaries'." He spread his hands. "The only people who will dispute it are the ones already under suspicion. You, and the signorina."

Rizzi stepped forward. "Miss Playford, you are still at liberty only through the Count Morosini's intercession. Tonight's excursion will be noted in my report. I suggest you consider carefully how you spend the remainder of your grace."

"And you, Signor Rothbury," Montefiore added softly, "might wish to consider how easily certain tales about a foreign clerk seducing his patron's guest could find their way to the right ears. In Venice. In London. At the Foreign Office."

"If you had accepted my hand when it was offered," Montefiore went on to Venetia, almost regretful, "I might have chosen to pull you out instead of push you under. But you are a proud little thing. Proud—and, it seems, not very clever. You have destroyed yourself, and you are dragging your English hero down with you."

Venetia's fingers dug into Edward's coat. He reached back, covering her hand with his.

"This is not over," he said to Montefiore, low and fierce.

"Oh, I sincerely hope not," the count replied. "I am enjoying it far too much."

Chapter Twenty-Nine

"THORNTON!" Eugenia beckoned him to the window, her fingers tapping sharply against the glass. "Do you see?" She pointed to the dark water below. "It's Captain Rizzi. And Count di Montefiore."

"Together?" Thornton came to stand beside her, so close she felt the warmth of him through the fine wool of his coat. His sleeve brushed the inside of her bare wrist and the contact sent a ridiculous little shiver up her arm. "But no sign of Venetia?"

"Oh—there she is. And, good Lord, alone with Mr. Rothbury." Catherine's voice cut across the room, bright with barely veiled censure. "How unfortunate to be found in such a compromising situation by the captain of all people. It seems Miss Playford does not understand how fragile her position already is."

"Something has happened. A trap has been laid," Thornton muttered. "I accompanied Miss Playford this evening, Catherine, and then sent Rothbury after her when we were separated. There is nothing compromising in their being together." His mouth tightened. "Unless Captain Rizzi chooses to interpret it so. Please find a servant and have the blue salon prepared for possible guests."

Dismissed, Catherine flounced away.

When the door closed behind her, Thornton's hand came to rest, warm and steady, on Eugenia's shoulder.

"I did the very best I could for her tonight, my dear," he said quietly. "You must be disappointed in me."

"Oh, Thornton, I could never be disappointed in you."

The words came from somewhere deep in her chest, where her heart seemed to unfold like a flower pressed flat for too many years. "You behaved with honor and kindness. You always do. It is why Elizabeth loved you. You were the husband of her dreams."

His mouth curved, the old, familiar smile lighting his features.

"I once thought you held similar feelings, a very long time ago, my dear Eugenia," he said gently. "After that fleeting kiss we shared at Lady Scarborough's ball—when I encountered you in the corridor on your return from the ladies' mending room."

Eugenia's mouth went dry.

That kiss. A brief, breathless brush of lips in a candlelit passageway; the smell of beeswax and spilled champagne; the roughness of his jaw against her cheek. She had been eighteen, absurdly hopeful, and the world had tilted on its axis. For one precarious heartbeat she had believed every foolish, romantic notion she had ever read in a novel.

And then she had seen him later—laughing with Elizabeth, dancing with her pretty friend, his dark head bent so tenderly—and shame had rushed in like cold water.

How could she have imagined herself the heroine of the story when her friend was so much prettier, so much more charming, and almost as well-dowered? Of course that brief, stolen kiss had meant nothing to a man like Thornton. Handsome, well-born, admired by every debutante in the room.

He could have had anyone. Why on earth would he have chosen me?

So she had done what sensible girls did when they realized they had badly misread their own importance: She had pretended indifference. She had laughed too loudly with Lord Flexley at Lady Ridgeway's soirée; had turned her head just as Thornton's gaze sought hers; had built a careful shell of composure over the raw, humiliated ache.

The memories pricked now like pins beneath the skin.

"I see you blush, my dear friend." His smile was fond, not mocking. "So you *do* remember it. I always wondered if it meant anything to you, for you barely looked at me the following day when we met at Almack's. And then, at Lady Ridgeway's soirée, you cut me dead and danced the evening away with Lord Flexley. I had thought you must have some understanding with the gentleman." He gave a rueful huff. "I was cut to the quick, I assure you. But Elizabeth clearly had feelings for me...and I developed a great tenderness for her."

His look softened. "I am very happy for your friendship after all these years."

Eugenia's heart gave a curious, painful twist.

All these years, and she had never once considered that he might have been wounded by *her* behavior. She had been so certain she was the one making a noble sacrifice—stepping aside for beautiful Elizabeth, burying an unrequited girlish infatuation, reinventing herself as the sensible friend, the amused observer. She had told herself she had imagined that brief flare of interest in his eyes; that a single stolen kiss could not possibly have unsettled *him*.

And now, to hear that he had gone home from those glittering evenings nursing his own bruised pride because of *her*...

What a waste. What a foolish tangle of youth and fear and misread glances.

She swallowed. Painfully. What good were regrets? She could not change any of it. Elizabeth had loved him, and he had loved her in return, and their marriage had been happy in its way. Eugenia would never begrudge her friend that. Indeed, in lonely hours she had taken comfort in knowing that someone she loved had been so cherished.

But to know, now, that she had not been entirely ridiculous at eighteen—that he *had* seen her, had *wanted* her, if only for a moment—sent a quiet warmth spreading through all the cold, locked rooms of her heart.

His hand was still on her shoulder, solid and reassuring. For thirty years that hand—offered in friendship, in support, in partnership over charitable ventures and matchmaking schemes—had anchored her. Whatever storms had shaken her life, Thornton had been the steady point by which she steered.

Perhaps, she thought, with the clear-eyed wisdom age sometimes granted, *it does not matter that we missed our moment. What has grown in its place has been no small thing.*

She covered his hand with her own, the gesture small but deliberate. "Then we have both been very foolish, haven't we?" she said softly. "Once, when we were young... and ever since, in not speaking of it."

His eyes searched hers, some new awareness flickering there.

Before either of them could say more, Catherine appeared in the doorway, cheeks flushed, eyes bright with importance.

"Thornton! Eugenia! Everyone is waiting for you in the blue salon," she announced, beckoning with imperious urgency.

Eugenia stepped back, allowing her hand to fall from his. The moment folded itself away. But the acknowledgment was still there, still newly precious, even as duty called them back into the brightly lit world.

"Then we must not keep them waiting," she said, though her pulse was still thudding from an entirely different urgency.

Thornton offered his arm. "Shall we?"

She took it, feeling once more that quiet, astonishing bloom of warmth in her chest.

THE BLUE SALON had never felt so small.

Venetia stepped over the threshold with Captain Rizzi at her back and Edward at her side, and the room seemed to shrink around her. Candlelight gilded the pale-blue silk on the walls; the air smelled of beeswax, wilting roses, and the lagoon.

Lady Townsend and Lord Thornton rose so quickly their chairs scraped over the carpet. Catherine hovered near the mantelpiece, her expression a careful mix of concern and *I told you so* that made Venetia want to throw something heavy.

"Mollie," Lord Thornton said gently, "go and sit by the fire, my dear. You look as if you might turn to ice."

Mollie bobbed and crept to the hearth, white faced, twisting her hands. Venetia longed to go with her, to hide in the shadow of the great marble chimneypiece like a scolded child and pretend none of this was happening.

Instead, she stood in the middle of the room with Edward's arm a firm, steadying line against hers.

She clung to that as Captain Rizzi marched past to plant himself on the far side of the central table, boots squeaking on polished boards. Behind him, Count di Montefiore sauntered in with slightly less than his usual grace, one hand dabbing theatrically at the bloodied handkerchief held to his nose.

Well. That was at least one pleasing sight.

"Signori," Rizzi said, bowing with perfunctory politeness to the assembled company. "We are here on account of a *disturbance* on the canal. A formal complaint has been made."

His gaze slid to Montefiore, who let the handkerchief fall for a moment to display his swollen, reddened nose like a trophy.

"Signor Rothbury assaulted me without provocation," the count announced, every syllable dripping injured dignity. "In an attempt, I suspect, to conceal his own misconduct with the signorina."

"Misconduct?" Venetia burst out. "He—"

"Miss Playford," Edward murmured, a quiet warning.

Venetia bit the inside of her cheek.

Rizzi lifted a hand for silence. "Please. I will hear all sides in due course. For now, understand that I have a complaint from a respected member of Venetian society alleging a violent attack."

Respected. She almost snorted.

"I shall naturally be speaking to Count Morosini," Rizzi went on. "Signor Rothbury is in his employ. The count may wish to recommend a course of action."

At that, she felt Edward go very still beside her, like a man bracing for a blow he saw coming.

Shame rose in her throat like bile.

Lady Townsend stepped forward, color high. "Captain Rizzi, you must understand—"

"Lady Townsend," he said, and though his tone remained courteous, there was steel underneath, "my duty is to the law. Not to English sensibilities." He shifted his gaze back to Venetia, and she felt as if someone had turned a lantern directly on her.

"As for you, Signorina Playford," he said, "I remind you that you remain under active investigation for the matter of the missing emeralds."

The words landed like cold drops down her spine. Under active investigation. Of course she was. Freedom had never been more than a thin shell.

"You have been released on the personal recognizance of Count Morosini," Rizzi continued. "This is a privilege, not an acquittal. In such circumstances, your conduct must be beyond reproach."

His eyes flicked briefly to Edward, then back to her. "Tonight, it was not."

Her skin burned. She had the sudden, absurd desire to fan herself with Catherine's ostrich plume, simply to have something to do with her hands.

"I saw you," Rizzi went on. "Alone at midnight in a gondola, in the arms of the very man my investigation has already flagged as... *interesting*."

Interesting. That was one way of saying "possibly involved in a jewel theft and definitely punching counts on the Grand Canal."

"You were returning from the establishment of La Serafina," he added. "A place of... varied reputation. Without a proper chaperone and in the company of an Englishman who had just engaged in a brawl upon the water."

Venetia's cheeks flamed. "Captain Rizzi, Count di Montefiore tried to drag—"

"I did not see it," he said sharply, cutting across her. "The law sees facts. Your feeble explanations hold no weight."

Her tongue went dry.

Rizzi folded his hands behind his back. "Therefore, until this matter is concluded, the following conditions will apply."

Conditions. Her stomach knotted.

"You will present yourself at the magistrate's office twice a week," he said, "to sign the register. You will not leave the city without permission. You will not attend establishments such as La Serafina's—or any other gathering I deem dubious. You will not be alone with a man not your relation or established guardian."

He paused, letting that sink in.

So: no freedom, no investigation of her own, no stolen minutes with Edward.

"And understand this," he added, voice dropping. "The English will of your late great-uncle was explained to me. The provisions about 'moral turpitude' are particularly pertinent."

The phrase sounded even uglier in his accented English. Moral turpitude. As if she'd been caught kicking orphans and stealing from the poor box.

"If I submit a report suggesting a pattern of dishonorable conduct," Rizzi said calmly, "your trustees in England may be obliged to consider you in breach of those conditions. Perhaps even without the inconvenience of a formal conviction."

The floor seemed to tilt under her feet.

Without conviction. They could strip her of everything because she had been seen in the wrong place with the wrong man. Not because she had done anything wicked, but because men like Montefiore had arranged the scene and men like Rizzi chose to see what they expected.

"You cannot mean—" she whispered.

"I mean," he said, "that the difference between a misguided young lady and a criminal in the eyes of the law is often a matter of how much trouble she causes. If I conclude that you are wayward but... *misled*"—his gaze brushed Edward again—"I may be inclined to recommend leniency in my report."

"And if you do not?" Lady Townsend asked.

"Then I will record what I saw," he replied simply, still looking at Venetia. "An heiress under suspicion, frequenting a courtesan's salon, in illicit company on the canal, involved—by choice or coercion—with a man who assaults my informant."

Montefiore dabbed delicately at his nose again, eyes glittering over the linen.

Informant. So that's what we're calling "blackmailing snake" now.

"So," Rizzi concluded, "I suggest you consider your future conduct very carefully, Signorina Playford. One more misstep, one more appearance that confirms rather than contradicts my suspicions, and the consequences may be... permanent."

Permanent. Like losing her fortune. Like Edward forever believing he had ruined her.

She swallowed, the room swimming slightly. The blue silk walls, the polished furniture, Miss Bentley's watchful eyes—all of it seemed suddenly distant, as though she were looking at the scene through water.

Mollie sniffed by the fire. Lady Townsend's fan trembled in her hand. Lord Thornton looked as if he might stride across the room and shake Rizzi until sense rattled into his skull.

But none of them could alter what had just been said.

"I understand," Venetia said, forcing the words out past the tightness in her throat.

"Good." Rizzi inclined his head, satisfied. "For now, I leave you in the care of your friends. I will contact Count Morosini in the morning."

He turned sharply on his heel. Montefiore followed, pausing

only to give Venetia a little bow and a look that said, quite clearly, *Who do you think won that round?*

She met his gaze and held it, refusing to flinch.

The door closed behind them.

For a moment, no one spoke.

Then Edward's hand closed more firmly around hers.

"I'm so sorry," she whispered, turning to him. "If you're ruined, it's because of me."

"No," he said, low but fierce. "If I'm ruined, it's because I chose to hit a man who deserved it. I would do it again."

Some part of her, buried under terror and shame, wanted to laugh. *Of course*, that would be his view.

But over his shoulder she saw the stricken worry in Lady Townsend's eyes, the grim set of Thornton's jaw, and the weight of what Rizzi had threatened pressed down again.

One more misstep. One more scandal. And everything—her fortune, Edward's future—could vanish like mist over the canal.

She had never felt less like a thief.

And never more aware that someone was trying very hard to steal her life out from under her.

Chapter Thirty

THE INVITATION ARRIVED with the chocolate.

Venetia had not slept. She'd dozed and jolted awake and stared at the ceiling while the words *pattern of dishonorable conduct* chased themselves round and round her brain. When Mollie brought her down to the breakfast room, she felt as if someone had stuffed her skull with wet wool.

Lady Townsend and Lord Thornton were already at the table. Miss Bentley sat straight-backed, attacking a bread roll, not looking up as Venetia took a seat opposite. The silver chocolate pot steamed gently; the scent, usually so comforting, made Venetia's stomach turn.

She had just managed a cautious sip when the footman appeared in the doorway with a silver salver and a heavy, cream-laid envelope sealed with a great blob of red wax.

"From Palazzo Morosini, my lady," he announced.

Palazzo Morosini? The public announcement of Edward's ultimate humiliation…to be laid at my door.

"You open it," Venetia whispered as she pushed aside the plate of fish that had been laid in front of her. How could she ever eat again?

Poor Edward. What would become of him?

Lady Townsend took the envelope, her fingers lingering on

the imprint of the Morosini crest. Her eyes flicked to Venetia with a look that said *brace yourself, dear child* better than words could.

She slit the seal with the fruit knife, unfolded the thick paper, and as her gaze skimmed down the page, her eyebrows climbed until they nearly vanished into her curls.

"Well," she said at last, "this was not what I expected."

Thornton lowered his newspaper. "What is the old spider saying about Mr. Rothbury?" he muttered.

"Nothing. He's planning a fête," Eugenia replied.

Venetia gave a mirthless laugh. "If that is another invitation for his English friends to attend, I can assure you that Count Morosini's Grand Masquerade Ball was all the entertainment I need in Venice."

Lady Townsend shook her head. "Count Morosini is to host a celebration in honor of his granddaughter Sofia's betrothal to—oh dear—Count Bembo."

"The one who smells of fish?" Venetia heard herself say faintly, for she'd heard the girl mutter the words to her maid, Caterina, during the brief time they'd been together.

Miss Bentley's fork clattered onto her plate. "Miss Playford!"

"Well, I'm just telling you what Signorina Sofia said," Venetia muttered into her chocolate. "She says that even his *handkerchief* smells of fish."

Thornton coughed into his napkin, suspiciously like a man disguising a laugh.

Lady Townsend cleared her throat. "Be that as it may, he is evidently considered a suitable match for Count Morosini's granddaughter. And apparently, he has chosen to combine the betrothal celebration with a display of modern science. He has engaged a French aeronaut to perform a balloon ascent over the lagoon. A 'Festival of Air and Nuptials'"—she consulted the letter again, gave a small laugh, then added, "Oh my! I did not think he was so intrigued by my descriptions of my own comet-viewing gala last year that he would want to do something similar."

"A balloon ride?" Venetia's indignation turned to horror as

she recalled Lady Townsend's similar extravaganza.

For a moment the breakfast room blurred: candlelit lawns in England, the shadow of a silk canopy against the stars, Lord Windermere's eager hand on her arm as he urged her toward the basket, Edward thundering across the grass like a hero in a gothic novel—

And now, here she was again. A balloon, a scandal, and a city eager for a show.

"I have a healthy aversion to balloons, with all due respect, Lady Townsend," Venetia said under her breath. "Your Comet Viewing Gala was well conceived but if there is a balloon within a mile of Signorina Sofia's betrothal, then I will decline the invitation."

Miss Bentley sniffed. "It would be a great snub to Count Morosini who has been so kind as to show he harbors no ill toward those who would touch his household with disgrace."

Touched by disgrace?

"And we," Lady Townsend said, "have the honor of being invited as his English guests. The entire party." Her gaze came to rest on Venetia with something like apology as she handed her the letter. "He is most particular, it seems, that you attend, my dear. To show that peace reigns in his circle."

"I do think it unwise to slight your host," Thornton said kindly. "The man who used his influence to secure your release. And whose goodwill you continue to rely upon."

Miss Playford set the letter down with a sigh. "I confess the thought of another balloon makes me feel quite faint. Especially as last year's comet fête very nearly ended in tragedy. I swore I'd never go within twenty yards of one of those contraptions again."

"I'll confess something," Thornton said dryly. "I rather enjoyed watching Windermere look like a plucked hen when his grand dramatic exit was foiled."

A small, unwilling smile tugged at Venetia's mouth.

"Still," he continued, "the contraption is dangerous. And not merely because hot air and silk should never be within hailing distance of one another. In the wrong hands, it's an excellent opportunity for mischief. Or worse."

"Does the invitation say who will ascend?" Venetia asked.

Lady Townsend picked up the letter again. "It mentions Signor Duval, the aeronaut, and speaks of 'a privileged passenger of noble blood who will cast favors to the crowd.' One assumes it must be Sofia."

"Not necessarily," Miss Bentley sniffed. "Count Morosini might wish to flatter his English guests. He showed particular regard to me at the masquerade."

"Or perhaps he will choose to shower Venetia with similar regard. To show Venice that he is above ill will," suggested Lady Townsend.

Venetia's stomach flipped. "Surely not. I could hardly be a more inappropriate choice." The thought of being suspended above the lagoon, every eye on her, while Count di Montefiore watched from the crowd made her palms damp. One tug at the wrong rope, one conveniently cut tether, and she could vanish into the water as quickly as any inconvenient piece of evidence.

Count di Montefiore was collaborating with Greene. She knew that now. And, clearly, Greene would stop at nothing to regain the fortune to which he was next in line.

"I won't go up in the balloon," she said, more fiercely than she'd intended. "I don't care if he asks me or not. I won't do it."

"Quite right, my dear," Lady Townsend said quickly.

Miss Bentley opened her mouth to add something but Thornton forestalled her.

"Whatever else happens," he said, "we shall not allow you to be used as a performing monkey in a Frenchman's air bubble, Miss Playford. You'll attend the betrothal fête because to refuse would be folly, but we shall keep you planted firmly on solid ground."

His words calmed her—slightly. Solid ground.

And Sofia. Betrothed to Count Bembo with the fish breath. She deserved him. The girl had been reckless and cruel, and her actions had put Venetia in this position.

"When is Signorina Sofia's betrothal?" Venetia asked, a sudden thought occurring to her.

"In exactly two weeks," Lady Townsend replied.

Venetia nodded. Two weeks?

Two weeks to possibly make a bargain. Two weeks in which to persuade Sofia to tell the truth about the emeralds—if Venetia could perhaps arrange some way to help Sofia avoid a lifetime of sharing a breakfast table with a man she despised.

She wrapped her hands around her chocolate cup, letting the heat seep into her fingers.

Rizzi's warning still rang in her ears. One more misstep. One more appearance in the wrong company, the wrong place, and her fortune would vanish.

But somewhere between now and Count Morosini's "Festival of Air and Nuptials," she might find a way to turn the spectacle to her advantage. To make the stage he'd built become a trap for the *real* villains instead of a noose for her.

She lifted her chin.

"One thing is certain," she said. "If Count Morosini means this fête to prove that scandal is over and order restored, someone had better tell the truth before the balloon leaves the ground."

And if Sofia Morosini knew that truth, then Venetia intended—very calmly, very carefully, with all the discretion Captain Rizzi could possibly desire—to pry it out of her.

Chapter Thirty-One

THE SMELL OF hot chocolate drifting from the casa's breakfast room had never been more enticing.

Edward caught it as he passed by on his way to take his gondola to perform another day of translation.

He imagined Venetia at the table in her morning gown, cheeks still pale from last night, fingers wrapped around a porcelain cup.

What he would have given to have had the opportunity to sit opposite her, reading the newspaper, reveling in a scene of cozy domesticity.

Instead, he tightened his grip on his leather satchel and stepped into the waiting gondola.

Work. Duty. Distance. Instead of drinking hot chocolate with his darling, he would observe the three pillars of his current purgatory.

The sky over Venice was a washed-out pearl, the early light turning the water to bruised silver. Oars creaked, pigeons wheeled above the terracotta roofs, and the faint smell of fish and smoke rode the breeze as the gondola threaded through narrow canals toward Palazzo Morosini.

Edward's days were long and started early, and he, Signor Rothbury, translator to a Venetian count, did not lie abed.

He only lay awake.

He wondered, not for the first time, if this would ever change. Or if he was destined to translate other men's romances while his own slowly strangled itself in the coils of honor and obligation.

By the time he reached the palazzo, his stomach was a tight knot of hunger and dread.

His footsteps echoed as he crossed the checkered marble to the familiar door of the library.

He had just set his satchel on the big walnut desk when a soft cough sounded behind him.

"Signor Rothbury."

It was the majordomo, grave and impassive. "His Excellency requests the pleasure of your company. At once."

Of course he does.

Edward followed him through a succession of high, chilly rooms until they reached Morosini's private study. The shutters here were half open, a blade of pale light cut across the carpet and picked out the gilt on the frames of somber ancestors glaring down from the walls.

Count Morosini stood by the window, hands clasped behind his back, watching a barge drift past below. He did not turn immediately—never a good sign.

"At times, Mr. Rothbury," he said at last, "I cannot decide whether you are a brave man or a very foolish one."

When he did face Edward, his expression held curiosity rather than outright censure. Somehow, that was worse.

Edward bowed his head. At present he felt almost entirely the latter.

"Or," the count went on, coming forward a few paces, "perhaps you are simply a man in love. Such dramatic violence suggests the actions of a gentleman who is consumed by passion."

He sighed, as if the whole notion were faintly tedious. "Did I not explicitly tell you I wished you to have nothing to do with Miss Playford? And yet you spent the evening alone in a gondola with her... after coming to blows with yet another gentleman who apparently wished to do the same."

Edward's jaw tightened. "I intervened to preserve the lady's honor when Count di Montefiore tried to force his attentions upon her."

Morosini's eyebrows rose. "Captain Rizzi neglected to mention the name of the gentleman whose nose you redecorated. di Montefiore, you say?" A faint curl of disdain touched his mouth. "Indeed, he is not a man I hold in particularly high regard."

He gave a small, almost reluctant nod. "I could almost commend you for it."

The words hung in the air, offering a sliver of hope.

Then, the shutters slammed shut.

"However," Morosini continued, "the fact remains that I specifically instructed you to stay away from Miss Playford. You are in my employ to translate the works of Sir Walter Scott, not to act as a knight-errant on the Grand Canal. The signorina is under suspicion for a crime that has not yet been solved. She is also clearly a... distracting influence."

Edward opened his mouth, then shut it again. Every reply that came to mind would make matters worse.

"Consider this a final warning," Morosini said, voice softening not at all. "Miss Playford enjoys my protection only so long as you put my work above all other considerations."

Edward knew he should bow and accept this. Knew that prudence insisted he murmur something about gratitude and redoubled efforts.

Instead, the words burst out of him before he could stop them.

"Then you accept that she was an unwitting pawn, sir? That she is not the jewel thief Captain Rizzi seeks?"

Idiot. Spectacular idiot.

The count studied him for a long moment, dark eyes narrowed.

At length he inclined his head, very slightly. "I accept that matters are... less clear-cut than certain witnesses would have them," he said. "Captain Rizzi has testimony that she was seen placing the emeralds in the tiara. Yet the descriptions of this supposed act do not entirely agree. I grant you that."

He shrugged one bony shoulder. "If it had suited my purposes better that she be detained, I would have had no compunction in accepting the version that achieved that end. But my paramount desire is for you to complete the translations of the entire body of Sir Walter Scott's works. There is, I think, no translator finer than you."

The faint compliment landed like a stone in Edward's stomach.

"And I suspect," Morosini went on, "that you are more... malleable... if Miss Playford is merely under suspicion and not incarcerated. For now."

There it was. The chain around his neck, politely described.

"That, however," the count finished, "depends entirely upon you."

The room felt suddenly airless. From the canal below came the distant cry of a gondolier; somewhere in the house a clock chimed the half-hour.

Edward swallowed. "I understand, sir."

"I am sure you do." Morosini's tone lightened with almost jarring swiftness. "Now. To more agreeable matters. You have heard, I assume, of my granddaughter Sofia's betrothal?"

"I have heard whispers in the household," Edward said cautiously. "A fête... and a balloon ascent?"

"Ah!" The count's eyes gleamed. "Then my secretary has done his work. Yes. We shall have a spectacle that will make Venice talk of nothing else for weeks. A French aeronaut—Duval, an eccentric genius—will ascend in his balloon from a barge anchored in the Bacino. The whole city will gather along the Riva to watch."

He moved to his desk and unfurled a large sheet of paper, beckoning Edward closer. It proved to be a sketch: the white dome of the balloon like a rising moon over a forest of masts, the Doge's Palace a lacework backdrop.

"We will have musicians on additional barges," Morosini said, tapping the drawing. "Fireworks from the Lido when the balloon reaches its greatest height. Sofia and her intended seated beneath a canopy on the main platform—very visible, very respectable. No one will remember a few missing jewels when they have seen such wonders."

"Indeed," Edward murmured, still staring at the sketch. The balloon's silk envelope bulged ominously, reminding him of the scene into which he'd ridden a year ago. Venetia about to be swept away, a prisoner of evil Lord Windermere.

"You, of course, will attend," Morosini went on. "Duval speaks little Italian. I require you to translate his scientific discourse on the principles of flight into something my guests can understand. We will also prepare a printed program in both Italian and English to distribute to the crowd. You will supervise that as well."

"Of course, sir."

Morosini's mouth thinned. "Captain Rizzi and I agree that it will be... advantageous... for Miss Playford to be present, as well. As a sign that my household remains united and that I harbor no ill will toward my English guests."

Edward's heart lurched. "Miss Playford?"

"Under appropriate supervision," the count added. "You are not that supervision. You will keep your distance, Mr. Rothbury. If Rizzi or anyone else sees you whispering together, I will be... displeased."

That seemed an understatement of heroic proportions.

"As for who will ascend with Duval," Morosini went on, returning to the sketch, "Sofia, naturally, is the obvious choice. A young, noble bride rising into the heavens—it is a pleasing image. But she is... nervous." His lips pressed together briefly. "English courage might be a useful corrective."

English... oh no.

"You are considering Miss Playford, sir?" Edward forced the question out calmly, though his blood had turned to ice.

"Perhaps." Morosini's gaze sharpened. "An English heiress placed in my care, displayed safely and triumphantly before the eyes of Venice? It would be a powerful statement. My guests would see that I am confident of her innocence. The gossips would choke on their own tongues."

Edward did not know what to say.

"I would not place her in danger," Morosini added, almost as an afterthought. "Duval assures me his contraption is perfectly safe."

Edward thought of Venetia in that fragile basket, silk and rope between her and the cold green water, while a city's worth of eyes watched. While her enemies watched.

"No contraption is perfectly safe, sir," he said before he could stop himself.

Morosini regarded him for a moment, then smiled thinly. "Nor is love, Mr. Rothbury. Yet people continue to risk it."

He rolled up the sketch. "You will begin work on the program this afternoon. And you will remember what I have said. The translation of *Ivanhoe* is your chief duty. At great speed. The marchese was enthralled by your last few chapters. Keep your distance from Miss Playford. Smile at the fête. If you behave, you may yet see your fair lady lifted above suspicion along with that balloon."

And if I do not behave, Edward thought grimly, I shall watch her fall without being able to move a finger to save her.

"Yes, sir," he said aloud, inclining his head.

Outside, the faint clang of ship's bells drifted in through the shutters, mingling with the slap of water against stone. He turned back toward the library, feeling as if he were navigating his way through a suffocating fog.

Ivanhoe, he thought bitterly, had no idea how easy he'd had it.

Chapter Thirty-Two

Back in the library, where he was expected to devote his full attention to Sir Walter Scott, Edward settled at the great walnut desk and stared unseeingly at the pages.

Did Count Morosini truly not perceive the irony?

Of course he did. The old man understood very well that the Ivanhoe whose trials Edward translated on the page had more freedom than the man bending over the manuscript. For a man who wielded such power, consideration for other people's inner lives was of very little account. Morosini craved the entertainment Edward's translations provided, and the obedience of others was as natural to him as breathing.

He might experience the emotional highs and lows of chivalric romance from his armchair; the emotional highs and lows of the people who served him mattered only insofar as they could be usefully arranged upon his chessboard.

The library was cool despite the late-morning sun. Dust motes drifted in shafts of light that broke through the high windows. Outside, somewhere far below, water slapped rhythmically against stone, the pulse of the city that was slowly becoming his prison.

He dipped his pen. *"Ivanhoe, though oppressed by fetters, felt his spirit as free as ever..."*

Lucky Ivanhoe.

A soft sound from the upper gallery—a muffled sniff, followed by a strangled gulp—jerked his head up.

For a heartbeat he hesitated. The Morosini library possessed a thousand small noises: settling wood, turning pages, the distant clatter of servants. But this sound carried unmistakable human misery.

"Signorina Sofia!" he burst out, rising quickly. "How many times have I told you that you should not be here?"

Her small figure was half hidden at the top of the ladder. At the sound of his voice she stilled, then peered over the carved railing, eyes red rimmed and enormous in her pale face.

"My position is tenuous enough as it is," he went on, the anger that had been simmering since the gondola incident finding a convenient target. "Your grandfather already harbors... misconceptions... regarding my feelings toward you. Your deceptions have caused both Miss Playford and myself a great deal of grief."

Yes, this young woman had used them both—played upon his scruples and Venetia's compassion—and he saw no reason to waste sympathy on crocodile tears.

"Oh, Signor Rothbury!" she wailed, pressing a crumpled handkerchief to her mouth as she began to descend. She missed the last rung and half stumbled onto the floor.

When she lifted her face to him, tear-stained cheeks and tragic eyes, she looked less like the glittering, spoiled conspirator he'd known and more like a frightened girl.

"You have heard about my betrothal?" she demanded. "And yet there is no feeling in your heart for what I am suffering? I am to marry Count Bembo. Count Bembo, with the breath of a fishmonger!"

The last word broke on a half sob that sounded painfully genuine. Against his will, a corner of Edward's heart softened.

"Yes," he said, more quietly. "Lady Townsend received the announcement. I am... sorry, signorina."

"You are *sorry*." She gave a short, bitter laugh. "You, who know what it is to love?" Her gaze searched his face. "I thought you, at least, would understand. Instead, you scold me as if I were a naughty child."

He drew a breath, counting to three before replying. "You surely knew that you could not marry your Paolo," he said, trying for kindness and not entirely sure he achieved it. "I do feel for you. Like you, I must accept that the one person in the world I love above all others is… out of reach."

Her lips curled. "Pah. That is because Miss Playford is an heiress and you are penniless." There was no malice in it, merely brutal, youthful clarity. "My Paolo is the second son of a grand family. His elder brother is unmarried. There is every possibility that in several years circumstances might change. *Then* my grandfather would be more amenable to a match. But he has no patience." Her shoulders slumped. "None."

Edward acknowledged this with a grim nod. "He certainly wants his Sir Walter Scott novels completed before he will allow me any latitude to follow my heart. Like you, I am a prisoner here. I am forbidden even to converse with Miss Playford; my work keeps me at this desk from dawn to dusk. And it is only due to your grandfather's goodwill—no, his desire to keep me a prisoner to his translations—that he continues to protect her from prosecution, though both you and I know she is guilty of no wrongdoing."

The bitterness leaked through despite his efforts, and he added, "You realize that it is you who relies on my goodwill? I could report the truth of your involvement to your grandfather."

He realized belatedly that he was glaring at Sofia. She had the grace to look down at her clasped hands.

"It was not I who stole the jewels," she said quietly. "I have already told you that. Of course, I would not have, had I feared that you telling my grandfather would put me in jeopardy. He would be angry with you for daring to tarnish his precious granddaughter's name."

"Yes," Edward replied, tightly.

"Besides, it was not my intention to cause harm to Miss Playford." Her fingers tightened around the handkerchief. "And, in any case, I did not steal the emeralds."

"So you have said. However, you will forgive me," he said dryly, "if I do not accept that on faith."

"You do not believe me, Signor Rothbury?" she asked, looking up through damp lashes. "Why, it is the truth. The thief was the maid of the contessa who took the emerald earrings some weeks ago, when her mistress visited the palazzo of Signor Albrizzi."

"The contessa's maid? So, you made this arrangement with her?"

Sofia shook her head. "Paulo did. You forget that I am even more of a prisoner of my grandfather than you are. I was not permitted to attend the masquerade just as I am accompanied wherever I go. It was Paulo who sought out Griselda. *He* paid her. He promised her protection and restitution. In three years he comes into an inheritance when he reaches five-and-twenty; he swore he would repay the contessa twice over and protect Griselda. But in the meantime our situation was desperate. Grandpapa was already hinting that he'd decided to arrange my marriage to Bembo. We had to act before he succeeded in tying me to this... decrepit fish." She looked up at him. "Would you not act with similar desperation if you were about to lose your one chance at happiness?"

Edward shifted uncomfortably. What *was* he doing to prevent happiness from slipping away? Protecting Venetia was an act that enabled them both to be close, practically, but separated in any other way. And his attempts to prove her innocence would simply result her in freedom to...

Leave Venice.

And leave him... forever.

Briefly he closed his eyes. What choice did he have? He was not so much a prisoner of a Morosini as he was a prisoner of his poverty and—he swallowed—his lowly birth. Bitter shame washed over him once more. What could he do to help Venetia? The illegitimate son of an opera singer? He'd been taken in as charity after his adoptive father—the staid, but kindly bailiff, Rothbury—married her.

Why had he never been brave enough to have confessed to Venetia that, in truth, it was the fact he was a bastard rather than penniless, that accounted for the reason he could never honorably offer her marriage?

"This maid, Griselda," he said, forcing himself to return to the topic. "Where is she now? Have you considered the risks she took on your behalf. Have you even thought she might be dismissed—languishing in a dungeon—if her part is discovered?"

Sofia's chin jerked up. "As long as Miss Playford is under suspicion, Griselda is safe. Besides, you speak as if *I* arranged this. I merely… agreed." She faltered. "And we never meant harm to Miss Playford. That was not part of it."

He let out a slow breath. "Yet it is Miss Playford who stands accused. You've admitted so much already. You might as well tell me the rest."

Color rose in her cheeks. She twisted the handkerchief between her fingers. "The tiara," she admitted, "was my idea. We needed a place to hide the earrings. Griselda could not keep them in the contessa's apartments—it would have been far too obvious. So I told Paolo that I could find a better way."

"There it is," Edward said softly. "The part you do not wish to look at too closely."

She flinched as if he had struck her.

"She was in the ladies' mending room at my grandfather's masquerade," Sofia hurried on. "Miss Bentley was there, fussing with her gown. Griselda came in with a box of pins and thread. She saw the tiara in Miss Playford's hands and exclaimed about its beauty. She told Miss Bentley that a lock of Miss Playford's hair was caught, and Miss Bentley—foolish woman—took the tiara to examine it and handed it to Griselda."

Sofia drew a shaky breath. "That is when she slipped the emeralds into the hidden compartment. She was quick. No one noticed. I swear to you, there was no intention to ruin Miss Playford. The plan was merely that I would reclaim the tiara later, containing the earrings. That would have given us enough to flee. But everything... went wrong."

She looked genuinely stricken now, her usual dramatic flair stripped away, leaving only raw misery.

Edward rubbed a hand over his face. He had no proof she spoke truth, no way to confirm details without drawing the attention of the very man most invested in keeping his granddaughter unsullied. Even repeating this story to Morosini would mean explaining how and why he and Sofia had shared such confidences.

The count would not thank him for that.

"Perhaps," Sofia said quietly, watching his struggle, "my words give you at least this comfort: that you may be entirely certain your beloved is not guilty of the crime for which everyone insists on suspecting her."

"As if I ever thought her guilty for a single moment," Edward retorted, more sharply than he intended.

Her mouth twitched. "No. You thought *I* was."

"You *are* guilty," he said, holding her gaze. "If not of theft, then of recklessness. Of vanity. Of playing with other people's lives because you could not bear to be thwarted in love."

She flinched again, but did not look away. "Yes," she said at last, the word very small. "Of that, I am guilty."

She straightened, drawing herself up to her full, unimpressive height. "But not of the crime for which Miss Playford stands accused. That is Griselda's doing, at Paolo's request. And now it is too late to change anything. I will marry Count Bembo, and you will molder here until you have translated Grandpapa's entire library." A bleak little smile touched her lips. "We are both his prisoners, Signor Rothbury. Miserable and helpless. And there is nothing to be done about it."

Chapter Thirty-Three

"So," Eugenia said across the breakfast table, breaking her roll rather more fiercely than necessary, "we know now that Mr. Greene is pulling strings from England in collaboration with that odious Count di Montefiore, for the express purpose of blackening Miss Playford's character so that he may inherit her fortune."

Thornton set down his cup with a soft chink, his brows drawn together. "That does appear to be the case," he conceded. "But the situation is not simple to remedy." He leaned back. "We are in a foreign country. Di Montefiore may merely be acting on Greene's instructions. And Captain Rizzi—" his mouth tightened "—may be in their employ, or at the very least deaf to any interpretation that does not end with Venetia in chains."

He lifted his hands in a rare gesture of helplessness. "Truly, my dear Eugenia, I do not yet know how we begin to mitigate the dire situation in which our dear girl finds herself."

He paused, his gaze meeting hers, and his voice gentled. "But of course we will."

"Both our dear friends," Eugenia corrected, her heart squeezing. "Do not forget Mr. Rothbury."

"Indeed not," Thornton said.

She pushed aside her plate, appetite gone. "You do realize

that Count Morosini has made his continued protection of Miss Playford entirely conditional upon Edward remaining his faithful drudge, translating Sir Walter Scott to the last full stop? Sir Walter Scott has three published books released this year. Why, poor Mr. Rothbury will be here another seven years at least before he can hope to be released—and that's only if the great author slows down."

Thornton gave a faint snort. "He could be gone long before then if he so chooses—"

"Could he?" Eugenia sent him a beetling look over the rim of her teacup. "Perhaps you underestimate the capacity of a young man in love. We know—without a shadow of doubt—that Mr. Rothbury is desperately in love with dear Venetia, and while she is under suspicion of an as-yet unsolved crime, for the emerald pendant is still missing, she cannot leave Venice. Nor will he. He will die in chains in that count's service, if need be, rather than risk abandoning the woman he loves but cannot wed."

The words hurt as she said them; they were too close to old wounds of her own. She softened her tone. "I hope, at least, you will concede that the hearts of Miss Playford and Mr. Rothbury beat as one."

Thornton's stern face eased. The morning light caught the silver in his hair, and for an instant she saw the younger man he had been—the one who'd once stolen a kiss in a corridor and set her poor eighteen-year-old heart aflame.

"I concede it," he said quietly. "And I will confess that their plight troubles me greatly. You are not the only one invested in the happiness of our dear Miss Playford, my dear."

Eugenia felt a warmth spread through her chest quite unrelated to the coffee. *Our* dear Miss Playford.

"I would see them happily united as much as you," he went on, fiddling with his spoon. "I merely wish I knew where to begin in unmasking the true perpetrators of the contessa's emerald thefts. Until we can prove Venetia's innocence and expose di Montefiore and Greene, Rizzi and Morosini hold all the cards."

Outside, a gondola glided past the window, the splash of the oar a soft, rhythmic counterpoint to her racing thoughts. Eugenia put down her cup with a small rattle and rose.

"Then we must begin where information is thickest," she declared. "I propose we pay a visit to La Serafina this very morning."

Thornton looked up sharply. "La Serafina? Again?"

"Yes, again," Eugenia said. "Miss Playford will come with us—in disguise—and we will speak to the most knowledgeable woman in all Venice. On a busy evening, whilst surrounded by admirers, La Serafina had too little time to impart what she knows. But in the quiet of the day—" She lifted her chin. "When it is made clear to her that the happiness of two young hearts rests on the quality of intelligence, I have no doubt she will be more forthcoming."

Thornton's mouth curved, the expression half rueful, half fond. "You are determined to play Fate, are you not, my dear? Matchmaker, strategist, and avenging angel all in one?"

"Someone must," she said briskly, though his teasing warmed her. "Heaven knows Edward and Venetia are making a muddle of it by themselves. If left to their own devices they will sacrifice themselves into early graves, their virtue entirely intact and their happiness entirely absent."

He chuckled. "You do them an injustice. Rothbury is not entirely without sense, and Miss Playford has developed a positively alarming streak of courage."

"Courage without guidance is merely recklessness," Eugenia retorted. "They need allies. They have us."

Thornton's eyes met hers and held. For a moment, the distant calls on the canal faded.

"Yes," he said softly. "They have us."

He rose, pushing back his chair. "Very well," he said. "Let us go and corner La Serafina in her den. For Venetia. For Rothbury." His smile deepened. "And perhaps, for the satisfaction of proving that two English relics may yet outwit a nest of Venetian intriguers."

Eugenia laughed. "Relics indeed. Speak for yourself, my lord. I fully intend to prove that I am as formidable now as I was at eighteen."

He offered his arm with exaggerated gallantry. "My dear Eugenia, I have never doubted it."

Chapter Thirty-Four

THE VISIT TO La Serafina would, Venetia told herself, be exactly what she needed. Her thoughts were in tatters, her body too restless to sit meekly in a drawing room and sip chocolate.

She would go with them, she said.

First, however, there was the small matter of a torn sleeve.

Her silver-gray evening gown—embroidered at the hem— had caught on a nail in the casa's narrow stairwell. The rip at the wrist gaped accusingly every time she moved her hand. Madame Bertolini could fix it in minutes, so with a promise to Lady Townsend and Lord Thornton that she would be back in time to accompany them to La Serafina in the early afternoon, Venetia set out with Mollie.

The market near the Rialto was already in glorious chaos. Fishmongers shouted their wares over the slap of gutted fish on marble slabs; baskets of lemons glowed like small suns; bolts of striped cotton hung from stalls like the sails of ships. The air smelled of brine, crushed herbs, and humanity.

Venetia drew in the chilly morning air, hoping it would clear her head. Instead, every turn of the narrow lanes seemed to knot her thoughts further.

"Why, there is Mr. Rothbury!" Mollie exclaimed suddenly,

clutching her arm as a barrow piled with cabbages lurched past them. "A handsome man he is, miss, though always so serious—" She gave a beatific sigh, adding, "except when he's defending your honor, miss."

Venetia's heart gave a violent leap against her stays.

Edward.

She saw him at once: tall, hat brim low, leather satchel couched under his arm, moving with that purposeful stride she knew so well. A lock of hair had fallen over his brow. He looked tired. And beautiful. And entirely out of reach.

You should keep walking, a sensible voice in her head said. *You are under orders. So is he. Be a good girl, Venetia, and go and have your sleeve mended.*

Another voice—louder, wilder—cut in. *This may be the only chance you have for days. Take it.*

Count Morosini wanted to own Edward—body, mind, and time. Any association with Venetia threatened that ownership. To run to him, to draw attention to them both in the middle of the market, would not be kind.

But she could contrive a chance meeting.

She drifted toward a stall heaped with glass beads and cheap trinkets, leaning over as if examining them. If she turned at exactly the right moment, the press of bodies would hide the briefest of conversations.

That was all she wanted. Just a greeting. Just to be near him. She had not seen him since the stolen, glorious, disastrous kiss in the gondola.

Since Captain Rizzi's outraged interruption.

For he made sure to leave before she was up, and to return after she had dined.

"Mr. Rothbury," she said softly, turning with a smile that she tried—quite unsuccessfully—to temper. She felt it burst across her face, pure and unguarded.

"Miss Playford!" He stopped short. For an instant he did nothing but look at her, as if she were something he'd conjured from longing. Then he cast a quick, furtive glance around and, shielded by the crowd, reached for her hands.

The warmth of his fingers closed around her gloved ones, solid and sure. Venetia stepped closer, as though the tide of Venetians had pushed her there, and let herself lean into him for a heartbeat—just long enough to feel the steady rise and fall of his chest—before she straightened and gave his hands a quick, answering squeeze.

"I have missed you so dreadfully," she said under her breath. "Why do I never see you anymore?"

Color flared along his throat and up into his cheeks. Guilt, pain, and longing chased across his face in quick succession.

"You know," he said quietly, "how much it costs me to leave before you are awake and return when you have retired." His voice roughened. "But you also know I have no choice."

"Because your first obligation is to your employer?" she asked, trying—and failing—to keep the hurt from her tone.

"My first obligation," he murmured, his grip tightening fractionally, "is to you, my dearest Venetia. That is precisely the difficulty. You know we are both in an impossible position. Count Morosini will guarantee your protection only so long as I remain his perfectly obedient translator. I am in service to a demanding taskmaster. He wishes to read the ending of *Ivanhoe* in his own tongue faster than I can reasonably provide it."

A rueful smile twisted his mouth. "It is a curious irony to work for a man whose sole delight appears to be the exaltation of high romance on the page, while he has not the slightest regard for the real romance unfolding under his nose."

"Do you refer to his granddaughter Sofia..." Venetia asked, boldness pricking at her, "or to us?"

His eyes softened. "He can only truly dictate the romantic direction of his granddaughter," he said. "It is your very liberty he controls."

Liberty. Not heart. The distinction stung.

"Do you care only for my liberty, then—and not my heart?"

she asked. The flash of pain that crossed his features made her instantly sorry and fiercely glad both at once.

"What is in your heart—or mine—my darling Venetia," he said, voice low with feeling, "cannot be allowed to govern how I act. You are so far above me in station. I will not drag you down—"

"You confuse the matter entirely." Her laugh came out shaky. "If there's any dragging to be done, I assure you I would be the one doing it, Edward."

He stared at her, torn between amusement and anguish. She wished she could reach inside his head, shake sense into all those noble principles and line them up behind her instead of against her.

With another quick glance to make sure Mollie was momentarily occupied haggling over oranges and that no one seemed to be paying them particular attention, Venetia freed one hand and brushed her knuckles lightly along his cheek.

"Were you, perhaps, concussed," she whispered, "when I told you I would give up my fortune for happiness with you?"

His eyes closed for a moment, as if the touch hurt. "You would give it up in vain," he said roughly. "You are in danger initially—and only my continued good standing with Count Morosini will keep his protection on you—" He swallowed, "—and your fortune safe. If I defy him, I cannot keep you—or your fortune—safe."

He hesitated, then pressed his lips together as if deciding something. "This morning, Signorina Sofia told me who was responsible for stealing the emeralds."

Venetia drew in a shocked breath. "She actually confessed?" The thought was at once shocking and vindicating. "That is dangerous... but very gratifying. At least you can be assured of my innocence."

"Assured?" His mouth curved. "I have never," he said gently, "doubted your innocence for a single instant. Not in this matter, nor in any other." He drew a breath. "As to why she told me...

reality has at last impressed itself upon her. She is to marry Count Bembo, not her Paolo. She was half wild with misery. In that state, she told me it was Griselda—the contessa's maid—whom Paolo approached."

He spoke quickly, giving her the essentials in low, urgent tones: Paolo's pressure, and promises, the moment in the ladies' mending room when Griselda had admired the tiara, taken it from Miss Bentley who'd held it while Venetia attended to an errant curl, and slipped the earrings into the hidden compartment.

"To be perfectly honest," he finished, "I think there was little for Griselda to gain and much to lose if she refused. Paolo was obviously very persuasive."

She pressed her lips together, thinking. "How does this work, then? If this is, indeed, the truth, how am I to be vindicated? Of course we can't go to Captain Rizzi and tell him until we have irrefutable proof," she said. But her body thrilled with hope. The truth was now known. By Edward. Not that his faith and belief in her needed any bolstering. She knew that, but still—

"Rizzi," Edward said grimly, "is almost certainly in the pay of Count di Montefiore and Mr. Greene. If we go to him now and repeat what Sofia told me this morning, he will twist it to suit his employers, and we will be worse off than before. We must find the right moment, the right avenue. We need proof."

"Perhaps," Venetia said suddenly, "I should simply confess."

His head jerked. "Good God, Venetia, what are you saying?"

"That I might be better off confessing to the crime and being stripped of my inheritance," she said, hearing the wildness in her own voice and not caring. "Then my situation would be more equal to yours. If I were penniless, you might at last be inclined to give me my heart's desire."

"It might also see you locked in a dungeon—or worse," he replied hoarsely.

But there was no mistaking the way her words shook him. His hands tightened around hers, his eyes dark with terror and longing, and for an instant Venetia felt a fierce, reckless satisfaction.

Well, she thought, *if reason cannot move him, perhaps the prospect of me cheerfully ruining myself in order to marry him will.*

Chapter Thirty-Five

VENETIA WELCOMED THE reassuring squeeze of Lady Townsend's arm as the young servant bowed them into La Serafina's salon an hour later.

In daylight the rooms looked quite respectable. The crimson silk on the walls appeared elegant, the gilt chairs and carved tables seemed luxurious rather than decadent. A bowl of hothouse roses perfumed the air, not incense and wine as on the previous visit.

Of course, the last time she'd been here she had been one frayed nerve away from collapse—shaken from the cells, half mad with fear that she might spend the rest of her life in some Venetian prison for a crime she had not committed. In that state, the laughter and masks and candlelight had taken on monstrous proportions.

Mostly, though, it had been Count di Montefiore. His threats. His hand closing on her wrist.

Lady Townsend's quiet, undemonstrative kindness since then had been balm to her disordered state. With her parents gone so early, Venetia had grown used to making do with neglect, to telling herself she needed no one. Having someone fuss over whether she had eaten, whether she slept, whether she was warm enough, had awakened an ache she had not known was there.

Perhaps that is why I love Edward so hopelessly, she thought wryly. *If one is starved of care, one is always vulnerable to the first perfectly decent man who offers it.*

Not that Edward was merely decent. He was so much more than that. If ever a woman could feel blessed by friends and a husband both, it would be she, with Lady Townsend, Lord Thornton... and him.

"How kind of you to receive us at such an unfashionable hour," Lady Townsend said as their hostess swept toward them.

La Serafina looked as if she had just risen from a couch in a Tiepolo painting. Her dark hair, threaded with silver, was coiled high and fastened with pearl-tipped pins. Her gown was of deep-green silk that clung rather more closely than any English modiste would permit, its lace sleeves falling back from elegant wrists heavy with bracelets. Her perfume—amber and orange blossom—greeted them as she stepped forward.

"It is always an honor to receive English friends," she said, with a graceful inclination of her head.

"And it is an honor to receive Venetian hospitality," Lady Townsend returned. "Have you ever experienced our English ways?"

"Venice is everything to me. I have never been tempted." La Serafina's smile deepened. "I do not think I would thrive beneath your gray skies."

"As a renowned opera singer, I had thought you might have performed on our shores," Lord Thornton said, bowing over her hand.

She gave a little theatrical shiver. "I should shrivel up entirely. It is what I fear happened to my eminent mentor, the great Isabella Monteverdi." Her gaze drifted toward the large portrait that dominated one wall. "She allowed herself to be lured there by a good man, yes... but she never sang again."

"Your art was more important?" Lady Townsend asked. "I recall hearing of Isabella Monteverdi, but I do not believe she ever graced our stages."

"La povera Isabella." La Serafina's mouth tightened with

something that was not quite disdain and not quite grief. "She became a little housewife. Her husband was kind but not a man of great culture. He rescued her and her child, perhaps—when she believed her first husband lost at sea. But this…" She flicked dismissive fingers, as if brushing away memories. "We are not here to talk of old tragedies. You come, I understand, to ask about a certain Count di Montefiore."

Venetia's heart picked up its pace.

"And I am very happy to tell you everything that I know of this gentleman," La Serafina added, a glint in her eye, "whom I do not hold in the greatest regard. Several of my girls have furnished me with unsavory reports about his conduct."

"What have they said?" Venetia asked before she could stop herself—and blushed when all three turned looks upon her.

La Serafina gave a mirthless laugh. "He is a relative newcomer to this city but the reports are beginning to gather. We are asked to believe him French-Italian, with a title that smells as false as his cologne."

"So the Italian title and accent are fabricated?" Thornton asked.

"The title is fabricated. The…breeding…is fabricated, I am convinced of it. He first came to my salons last winter with a gentleman I know to be English—a Mr. G—" She paused delicately. "Greene, he called himself that evening. They spoke in low voices near the musicians' screen. They forgot I, too, have English friends."

"What did they say?" Lord Thornton leaned forward.

La Serafina tilted her head, remembering. "I quizzed my friends when I heard of your…difficulties." She speared Venetia with a look. "They told me he spoke of 'trustees' and 'conditions in the will.' Of a young lady who had inherited 'what ought never to have left the line.' They said Mr. Greene was angry; he drank too much and called your English lawyers 'pious fools.' Your Count di Montefiore"—her voice dripped scorn on the title—"laughed and told him that reputations were fragile things. That with the right… arrangements, a fortune could be *redirected* without any need to go near a court."

Venetia's hands tightened around the reticule in her lap until the beaded silk cut into her palms.

"There was talk of debts. A maid who would be easy to sway; willing to do anything, for she had a brother who needed money. I did not then know of any emeralds, but when the theft was whispered occurred, and later when Miss Playford was arrested, I began to join the pieces."

"There were more pieces to join?" asked Venetia breathlessly.

La Serafina glanced about to ensure they were quite alone. "The maid," she whispered. "I heard her name was Griselda and that she was paid to take the emerald ensemble. I presume the contessa was her mistress. It makes sense. But now Griselda is in hiding, afraid for her life because of what this man Paolo required of her."

"Paolo? Do you know more."

La Serafina shook her head. "But I will tell you if I do."

For several minutes Thornton quizzed La Serafina, and she answered candidly, her gaze occasionally resting on Venetia with sympathy. Finally, after exchanging a grim look with Lady Townsend, he said, "Just as we suspected. It appears there is ample evidence to prove our di Montefiore is as much a nobleman as my valet, and that he is in the pay of Greene, the man who would profit should a poor report of Venetia sway her trustees."

"We are deeply appreciative of your time," Lady Townsend said after a few more questions, rising with a rustle of mauve silk. "We must not keep you from your rest."

"If you learn anything more that might confirm our suspicions," Thornton added, "we would be grateful if you would send word."

"But of course," La Serafina replied, spreading her hands with a gracious little flourish. She led them back across the salon, past a pair of velvet settees and a marble-topped table where a fan of tarot cards lay abandoned, their painted eyes staring up at the ceiling.

She paused, as Venetia had half hoped she would, before the enormous oil painting in the center of the wall.

"Behold the woman of whom I spoke," she said softly. "The great Isabella Monteverdi."

The portrait seized the light. Isabella stood slightly turned, as if about to move off the canvas. Her simple white gown was a contrast to her proud magnificence, her dark hair arranged in glossy coils, her eyes bold and knowing, her mouth ripe and sensuous. The painter had captured the proud line of her throat, the vulnerable slant of her shoulders, the strength in her mouth and eyes. Her hands were clasped loosely at her waist—elegant hands, long-fingered, capable.

Venetia stepped closer, the hush of the salon falling away for a moment. She heard only her own heartbeat and the faint crackle of the fire.

La Serafina's voice floated over her shoulder. "It was rumored she married a great Italian nobleman in secret, though never confirmed," she said. "Marchese Alessandro Valenti. Their time together was brief. His ship was lost, or so everyone believed. It was rumored she had a small child; that she was alone, desperate. I was telling Miss Playford the sad story of my inspiration…though she never inspired me to make a poor bargain when it came to love."

"And she did?" Lady Townsend asked.

La Serafina nodded. "When an Englishman offered marriage and safety, she took it. Ah, but if she had only been patient. Some months later, the marchese returned to find his wife gone, his son across the sea." She sighed. "A grand opera, no? Only without the music."

Venetia swallowed, her throat suddenly tight. She could almost feel the tragedy pressing from the paint—the sense of something unfinished, of words unsung.

"Forgive me, I repeat myself, Miss Playford," she said. "It is an old story, and I am an old woman who loves to tell it."

"I do not mind at all," Venetia said, eyes still on the portrait. "It is a pleasure to gaze more closely at such a magnificent painting."

Her gaze dropped to Isabella's clasped hands.

A signet ring gleamed there. The painting was large, and the ring's intricate detail was rendered with care. Heavy gold, the surface worn smooth in places, engraved with a crest: a phoenix, wings spread, and two tiny stars.

A jolt went through Venetia so sharp she had to lock her knees.

I know that ring.

Not merely the design, but the way it sat on the finger. The way the worn edge caught the light.

She had seen it a hundred times as Edward turned pages, as he rubbed his temple in thought, as his hand tightened around hers.

"I believe I have seen that ring before," she said slowly, her brow furrowing as if she could think the connection away.

La Serafina nodded. "It is the crest of the Marchese Valenti. Only the head of the line wears it." Her tone held reverence. "It denotes the lawful bearer of an ancient name. It was Alessandro's ring—which he placed upon Isabella's finger the day they married in secret. For I believe the marriage took place, even if it was never confirmed by the marchese who, heartbroken, disappeared onto his lonely island and was barely seen again."

The room seemed to tilt.

Conversation rustled faintly behind her—Lady Townsend murmuring something about Italian customs, Thornton asking a cautious question about the marchese's present whereabouts—but their words came to Venetia as though through water.

She worried at her lower lip, staring at the painted ring until it blurred. The chatter washed around her like the lapping of the canal.

"Have you not seen that ring yourselves?" she asked at last, turning to Lady Townsend and Lord Thornton.

They both looked at the portrait, then at her, and in that taut, suspended heartbeat she saw the moment recognition dawned in their eyes too.

Because there was only one other hand they had all watched wearing that very ring.

Edward's.

Chapter Thirty-Six

VENETIA COULD SCARCELY feel the stones beneath her slippers as they stepped out from La Serafina's cool vestibule into the dazzle of the street. Sunlight ricocheted off the green water of the side canal. Linen flapped from upper windows, a gondolier's song drifted round the corner, and somewhere close by someone was roasting chestnuts—the smoky sweetness making her eyes water.

She could not hold it in a moment longer.

"This is truly wondrous—"

"It is indeed excellent news to have the name of the woman directly responsible for the theft of the contessa's emerald earrings," Thornton said, misreading her, though he smiled at the brightness in her eyes. "A visit to this Griselda—for I'm sure we can discover her whereabouts—securing a confession, may—"

"No, no, I mean the ring Isabella Monteverdi was wearing!" Venetia burst out, barely preventing herself from hopping from foot to foot like a schoolgirl. Her hands were trembling so much she had to hide them in the folds of her skirt.

"I noticed it at the same moment you did, my dear." Lady Townsend was equally excited, her own eyes alight. "I could swear it's the very same signet Mr. Rothbury wears."

Thornton's brows drew together. He shifted automatically to

the outer edge of the alley to shield them as three young apprentices barreled past with a basket of fish.

"Ring? What ring?" he demanded. "We are talking about the stolen emeralds and how to provide proof of Miss Playford's innocence."

"Yes, of course—that is why we came," Lady Townsend agreed. "And learning the truth about the contessa's maid is a marvelous discovery." She touched Venetia's arm in quick, shared excitement. "But the portrait of Italy's most famous opera singer shows her quite plainly wearing the same signet that our young Edward wears on his right little finger."

Venetia drew in a breath, the memory of the painting flashing vividly before her: Isabella's graceful hands folded, the oval of dark gold, the phoenix and the two tiny stars. She could see just as clearly Edward's hand closing around her own on the gondola rail, that same ring and seal glinting in the lantern light.

It cannot be a coincidence. It *cannot*.

Thornton looked from one eager face to the other, then shook his head slowly, a rueful smile tugging at his mouth. "My dear ladies, one cannot place so much significance upon a detail in a painting. You are both steeped in the sort of romantic notions Mr. Rothbury spends his days translating from Sir Walter Scott."

He turned the full weight of his gentle regard onto Venetia. "And you, my child, are in more danger than most of seeing destiny in every shadow. It is no secret—indeed, I will confess it plainly—that Mr. Rothbury's heart belongs to you, and that your affection is entirely equal. But the disparity in your circumstances is what prevents a union. I perfectly understand why you would seize upon anything that hints at a change in that balance."

Venetia bit the inside of her cheek. His words were reasonable, sensible. And utterly lacking in magic or inspiration.

"But," Thornton continued, "we must not allow ourselves to be carried away by wishful thinking when we have other known matters to attend to. It is *excellent* news to have confirmation that Greene and di Montefiore are, in all likelihood, acting in concert against your interests, Venetia. And that we have this maid—Griselda—who has, I suspect, been more victim than villain. We must find her. That is the first thing we must do."

"Yes, of course, Lord Thornton," Venetia said obediently. Then the words burst out of their own accord. "But do you not *see* how the ring changes everything?"

Lady Townsend made an encouraging little sound. "It does seem rather more than chance, Thornton."

"The ring, the English bailiff, the lost Italian husband—surely it is all connected!" Venetia pressed on, heart hammering. She had put the pieces together in an instant. "If Edward is Isabella Monteverdi's son by her first marriage to this marchese, then he is not merely some obscure translator. He is—" Her throat closed around the enormity of it. "He is of a great Venetian house. He would not be beneath me at all."

He would be my equal, she thought.

"Of course you are excited, my dear," Thornton said kindly, though his expression remained skeptical. "But a tiny painter's flourish is hardly proof of a grand, life-altering inheritance—much as I know you would wish it so. We must verify calmly and cautiously before we build castles out of air."

Venetia pressed her gloved hands together until the seams bit into her fingers. Calmly and cautiously. While Edward toiled like a prisoner and Greene and di Montefiore plotted her ruin.

She lifted her chin. "Then we shall verify it. What is there to lose? If I am wrong, there will only be my...disappointment." She swallowed, feeling the wild leap of hope that refused to be quelled. "But if I am right..."

If I am right, everything changes. For Edward. For me. For us.

The bells of a nearby church began to toll the hour, the sound rolling out over the rooftops like a summons. Venetia glanced back the way they had come, toward La Serafina's palazzo, and then ahead, to where the narrow alley opened onto a sun-washed bridge.

Somewhere in this glittering, treacherous city, a reclusive

marchese wore a certain signet ring while he refused to disclose the secrets of his past.

Venetia walked silently beside Lord Thornton and Lady Townsend. Perhaps they were planning how they might discover the whereabouts of Griselda.

And of course, that was important.

But more important to Venetia was that this Marchese Valenti not carry his secrets to the grave.

Chapter Thirty-Seven

SHE HAD TO have time alone, she told the others. Time to think, reflect, and pray—or at least to pretend she was doing something so sensible.

The church was cool as a cellar after the heat of the *fondamenta*.

Venetia slipped inside and let the heavy door thud shut behind her, cutting off the shimmer of the canal and the cries of gondoliers. The scent of beeswax and old incense wrapped around her while colored light slanted through narrow stained glass windows.

Exactly the place for her wild hopes either to settle… or to be exposed as fantasies.

Quietly, she made her way along the side aisle. In her mind, the portrait at La Serafina's rose again with unnerving clarity: Isabella Monteverdi's graceful hands folded at her waist. The gleam of the signet ring on her middle finger.

The same design Edward wore. The same.

It could be wishful thinking, of course. Any number of noblemen might share a crest that included a phoenix.

But…

She drew in a breath that tasted of damp stone and candle smoke and turned into a side chapel, intending to sit and think.

Instead, she stopped short.

Someone was already kneeling before the small Madonna, shoulders shaking, a lace veil quivering with each ragged breath. The faint sound she'd heard on entering—the muffled, desperate sobbing—resolved into words in Italian, half prayer, half wail.

Sofia.

Venetia's first instinct was to turn on her heel and retreat. The girl had used her.

You've some nerve, Signorina Morosini.

She took a careful step back, knocking against a pew, and the kneeling figure jerked round.

"Miss Playford!"

So much for a graceful exit.

Venetia lifted her chin. "Signorina Morosini."

Sofia scrambled to her feet, clutching her rosary. She looked smaller in a plain dark gown, her hair scraped back under the veil, which she raised to look at Venetia.

"So, you do not wish to speak to me? All of Venice must be sneering," Sofia said with a brittle little laugh. Her face was blotchy and shiny with tears. "Have you come to gloat, Miss Playford? To tell me that you and your translator have triumphed, while I am to be sold to Count Bembo and his breath of old fish?"

"No," Venetia said quietly. "I came to think. I didn't know you were here."

Sofia's mouth trembled. "Then go. I have nothing to say to you."

Was there shame and contrition in addition to the misery? She could see no sign.

Venetia hesitated, then moved a little closer. The candle flames threw gold across the painted Madonna and caught the wet tracks on Sofia's cheeks. "Edward told me what you confessed."

Sofia's fingers froze on the rosary. Then she shrugged. "Did he? I wondered if he would, but what does it matter? There is no proof—Besides, what does it matter to me since happiness is beyond my reach now?"

"But what about the rest of us? There is the maid, Griselda," Venetia cut in, her own anger flaring at last. "You and your Paolo enlisted Griselda to steal the contessa's emeralds. You had her slip them into my tiara in the mending room. You set in motion everything that followed. You may not have *meant* for me to be accused... but that's what happened, and now I am a prisoner in Venice and might, quite possibly, lose my inheritance as a result of what *you* have done. Does that not trouble your conscience?"

The words rang more sharply than she'd intended in the small chapel, and she lowered her voice. "So, while you weep at being forced to marry a man you do not love, I am branded a thief in the eyes of the world and the man *I* love. A man I, too, may never have because of... you."

Sofia flinched. Then she recovered her spirit. "You have your English friends. And a man who is fighting for your reputation. You say you are in mortal peril, but you have money. Another country to flee to. I have only here. Only Grandpapa. Only the marriage he chooses."

"And Paolo," Venetia said, not unkindly. "You have Paolo. And because of what you both have done, I stand to lose everything."

Sofia sank back onto the narrow prayer bench with a sigh. "I decided," she said dully, "that if I did not seize happiness now, I would never have it at all. I was willing to try anything."

She twisted the rosary around her fingers, then sent a curious glance up at Venetia. "You despise me, but I think I am braver than you and the man you love. Signor Rothbury? He returns your love, so what is there standing between you? You have free choice. A privilege I will never have. I think you are the most fortunate—most stupid—pair of lovers I have ever heard of. No, I do not regret what I did for love. At least I tried." Her voice softened as she added, "And I would die trying."

Her words found their mark, but Venetia was not going to

take the bait. Edward would see matters the same way as Venetia did. Wouldn't he?

"If you don't care about me, what about Griselda, whom you say Paolo approached? What's become of her?" Venetia asked angrily. "And your grandfather? What will he say when your crime is revealed?"

Sofia's shoulders slumped, and she wiped her tear-stained cheek.

"All right! I am sorry for it all! If I am to marry Bembo, I will confess to Grandfather. And Bembo." A thoughtful smile curved her lips. "Perhaps the scandal will be such that Count Bembo will no longer wish for this betrothal."

Venetia nodded. "That is true," she conceded.

There was silence for a long moment. Perhaps the same kernel of thought was making its way through Sofia's mind. After all, it was she who'd said it.

But now it was Venetia who said, "Your betrothal to Bembo is to be announced in five days' time at the *grand ascension* your grandfather is organizing?"

Sofia nodded. "Grandpapa and the marchese are planning it as if I were some heroine from one of their Waverley romances. A magnificent balloon is to rise from the *piazzetta* and float over the lagoon while fireworks blaze and everyone cheers the happy couple." Her mouth twisted. "I am to wave like a prize hen in a basket while Bembo wheezes beside me."

Sofia waited. For sympathy from Venetia? Or something else?

Again, the silence lengthened. Venetia held her breath. What to say? She had to pick her words carefully. But suddenly her body was thrumming with excitement.

Were not both of them helplessly at the mercy of powerful men?

Were not both of them hopelessly in love with a man for whom their love could not be sanctioned?

Well! Sofia had the power to exonerate Venetia and thus ensure she was not branded a thief and therefore lose her fortune.

Granted, Sofia's confession would not remove *all* the obstacles between marriage between her and Edward.

But if Sofia used her knowledge of Venetian society and some artful means of helping Venetia see—even secretly—the marchese, might that not be enough to help Venetia orchestrate a reunion between Edward and—

His father?

She felt herself shaking. Of course, she might be wrong about all of it, but the more she thought about the signet ring adorning Isabella Monteverdi's left hand, and the signet ring she'd seen Edward wear, plus countless other clues, the more she felt the pieces of the puzzle begin to make up the glorious whole.

"Signorina Sofia," she said softly, glancing about to ensure they were not being overheard. She had to be careful. The wrong approach could throw Sofia offside even more. "There is more than just your happiness riding on this grand event in five days' time. That is also the day that Captain Rizzi must give his report to his superior regarding his belief in my testimony that I am innocent and his opinion regarding my character."

Sofia's expression was inscrutable.

Venetia waited for her to speak while Rizzi's grim voice returned to her: *One more impropriety, signorina, and my report to your English trustees will be very unfavorable indeed.*

One misstep, one ill-judged meeting, and she could lose everything. Except ironically, her heart—Edward already held that beyond recall.

Slowly, Sofia said, "You have already made that clear, Miss Playford. I wondered—" she hesitated "—if you are choosing your words carefully to make a case for some kind of... bargain between us?"

Oh, how sharp the girl was. But perhaps it was simply that when one had nothing to lose, and no bargaining power, one learned to be creative.

Venetia inclined her head slowly.

"I think we can both help each other," she said. The church

suddenly felt intensely cold before sudden warmth flowed through her body, and excitement fizzed in her blood as she added softly, "And I think you will consider the bargain more than adequate."

Chapter Thirty-Eight

STRANGELY, IT WAS Ivanhoe's grand internal struggles that steadied Edward's mind.

All morning the words had seemed to blaze on the page: honor, sacrifice, impossible love. The quill flew in his hand, scratching steadily across the paper while beyond the library windows, Venice shimmered in pale sunlight, but Edward scarcely noticed. For the first time in days, hope had edged out despair.

Sofia's confession—however self-pitying—had given him something solid: a name, a method, a chain of events that could, with care, be used to vindicate Venetia. Griselda. A stolen pair of emerald earrings. A desperate bargain made in a mending room.

It wasn't much, but it was more than the blind panic he'd been floundering in.

If Ivanhoe could endure chains and wounds and still ride to his lady's rescue, surely a mere translator could outwit a handful of conspirators.

I am not riding anywhere. I am sitting at a desk translating adjectives. But still.

He dipped his pen again, fighting the urge to race to Venetia with the news. Timing, he knew, was everything. Sofia's story was a double-edged weapon. Wielded clumsily, it could cut

Venetia as much as it sliced at Captain Rizzi's assumptions. He would have to find the precise moment—after the right allies had been prepared, after Griselda was put somewhere safe—to let the truth seep into the open.

And all the while, the clock ticked.

Morosini had not yet said as much, but Edward felt it in every tight line of the old man's face: The scandal must be neatly contained before the end of the great balloon extravaganza that would celebrate Sofia's betrothal to Count Bembo. Venice would be watching that day. So, no doubt, would Rizzi. And Greene. And di Montefiore.

Three days. Perhaps four. A handful of dawns and dusks in which to untangle a web that had taken weeks—no, months—to spin.

His pen slowed as that thought settled. Then, deliberately, he bent again to the work. Ivanhoe on the page, Venetia in his mind, a plan unfurling somewhere between.

He was so deep in it—half in England, half in Palestine—that the first murmur of voices above barely registered. The upper gallery was where Sofia hid when she was painting. Servants did not linger there. A deeper tone answered, roughened by age.

The voices grew clearer as the speakers descended the iron spiral stair. Edward hunched instinctively over his pages, letting the tall ranks of books shield him. It was not eavesdropping, he told himself piously, if the conversation insisted on walking directly into his hearing.

"...say what you like, Moriso, *Udolpho* has the finest atmosphere of dread ever penned," the stranger was saying in accented Italian. "Mr. Scott writes nobly of chivalry, but Mrs. Radcliffe—ah! She understands the secrets of the human heart. And her villains are true villains, not merely testy Normans."

Morosini snorted. "You sentimentalize corridors and moonlight, Alessandro. Scott gives us history. Nationhood. The clash of races, the making of a people. You speak of hearts—yet is not love of country the noblest passion?"

They emerged between the shelves—a stooped, gray-haired gentleman with a long beard that reached the worn velvet lapels of his coat. The stranger's garments were rich but a decade out of fashion, as if he'd stepped out of a portrait and forgotten to change.

Edward dropped his gaze to his manuscript, pretending absorption.

"You demand much of your authors," the marchese was saying, "but they cannot work fast enough."

Morosini laughed. "You were a skeptic when you tasted the first chapters of Scott. Now you devour it like a glutton. Do not pretend otherwise. Whose idea was it to commission translations beyond Waverley and Guy Mannering? Mine? No. It was 'the recluse of Valenti' who cannot sleep unless he has a new romance by his bed."

The marchese harrumphed, but without much heat. "A man must find consolation somewhere when condemned to exile on a damp rock with only gulls for company."

"Exile you chose," Morosini shot back. "Venice did not banish you."

"I banished myself because there was nothing left to me when I thought the preservation of my life had been a blessed gift from God," the marchese corrected. "Without my Isabella, it was a curse."

Their steps slowed near Edward's table. He felt Morosini's glance slide over him—the momentary assessing pause. Edward glanced up to see the faint flicker of satisfaction in his employer's eyes at seeing his translator bent dutifully over his task.

"Signor Rothbury," the count said. "You are acquainted with the work of Mrs. Radcliffe as well as Mr. Scott, are you not?"

Edward rose, bowing. "I have read *The Mysteries of Udolpho* and *The Italian* in the original English, Excellency. On your order."

"Just so." Morosini turned to his guest. "Here is the magician who turns your beloved romances into Italian, Alessandro. At such speed that even your voracious appetite may be satisfied."

The marchese's eyes—dark, deeply set—rested on Edward for a fleeting moment before he turned away, muttering, "How young you are to bear such responsibility." Then, turning back, he said from the doorway, "Tell me, do you find Scott equal to Radcliffe?"

Edward shrugged. "How does one compare two such masters? Scott has the broader canvas," he answered honestly. "Adventure. Romance. High stakes. But Mrs. Radcliffe has the keener eye for... fear. For what it is to be helpless and brave at once."

Something flickered across Alessandro's face—approval, or simply amusement. "A good answer."

"A romantic answer," Morosini said, half teasing. "Do you see? He infects even translators with his sentimentality. No doubt he will side with you over whether love should topple fortresses."

"If love does not topple fortresses, what is the point of fortresses?" the marchese retorted. "You grow old, Morosini."

"I am old," Morosini said dryly. "And with age comes the knowledge that fortresses cost money to rebuild. Which brings us to the subject I wished to raise."

Edward lowered his eyes again, but his ears sharpened as the two men turned and began to walk away, discussing the costs of Sofia's betrothal event. Barely a farewell to the lowly translator?

"Was it necessary to conjure up a balloon?" Alessandro asked.

"The whole city expects a spectacle from me. Sofia's betrothal must be celebrated with sufficient splendor that gossip about jewels and English heiresses will be flushed away like yesterday's tide." Morosini's tone held both pride and irritation. "We will have music in the Marciana gardens, fireworks from a barge, and a balloon ascent from the Piazzetta." His voice swelled with pride. "And all created within weeks, out of nothing, employing the energy of hundreds. Nothing has been done to rival it. I have made sure of that. I have secured a French aeronaut, very reputable, who assures me it can be done with safety."

"I've no doubt French aeronauts always assure one of that," Alessandro murmured dryly. "Until they land in a chicken yard and break both legs. Who is to ascend? The fish-merchant groom?"

"Bembo?" Morosini gave a bark of laughter. "You disrespect him. He bargained hard to get my Sofia, and I was reluctant at first. But he has a fat purse that will grant my granddaughter her most outlandish wish. She is that kind of young woman. She rails against the marriage, but she does not realize that the kind of love she dreams about appears only in sentimental novels like *Ivanhoe*. It is fleeting and will not last."

The marchese made a growl of objection. "You mistake the very reason I am sustained by my Sir Walter Scott and his tales of love and chivalry. I think you never enjoyed the love I had with my Isabella, my angel, my muse. She still sings to me every night, you know. Sings me to sleep and in my dreams. Bah! I pity your granddaughter, who will never win her heart's desire, even for a fleeting moment. You are a cold man, Morosini, for all that we are united in a common love."

"And you are a lonely, bitter one divorced from reality," Morosini said with equanimity as, halting by the door, he returned to his favorite topic. "Ah, but the balloon was an inspiration visited on me by an Englishwoman. If she can do it, anyone can! The spectacle is the thing—the silken globe rising over the domes, the people cheering, Sofia applauding prettily from the basket beside Bembo. All Venice will look up, and cheer as they feast their eyes on the balloon, floating up above them all, festooned in the colors of the House of Morosini. I will be lauded and feted until my dying day."

While poor Sofia chafes against the shackles of a marriage she does not want until her dying day, Edward thought grimly.

"The magistrate insists the city must see order restored before such an event," Morosini continued. "Rizzi wants a clean report for his files with the superintendent of the city returning the day after. If he cannot lay formal charges, he will settle for a confession and the requisite repentance. By the night of the balloon ascent, the matter of the contessa's emeralds will be quietly resolved."

Three days. Edward shivered.

The marchese snorted. "You think spectacle will change what people whisper in private? You have always believed in the theater of politics, Morosini. I prefer my dramas on the page."

"And yet," Morosini said smoothly, "you will refuse an invitation to watch? Surely even hermits are not immune to wonder? Will you come? Or will you sulk on your island with your books while the rest of us look to the heavens?"

There was a pause. Edward could almost hear the old man's reluctance.

"I will… consider it," the marchese said at last. "Bembo's presence offends me. Your granddaughter's plight offends me more. You trade her like a parcel of land."

"Do not quote romances at me again," Morosini snapped. "You of all men know why I do as I must for my family. Leave me to my calculations, and I will leave you to your ghosts."

From over his shoulder, Morosini sent a last glance at the pages on Edward's desk. "Work quickly, Rothbury. A city waits on Mr. Scott. By the time my balloon touches the sky, I would have both *Ivanhoe* concluded and Miss Playford's affairs… settled."

"Yes, signore," Edward said quietly.

Chapter Thirty-Nine

VENETIA HURRIED BACK to the casa, her mind racing faster than her feet. The bells were chiming the hour over the glittering canal, but all she could hear was Sofia's urgent whisper in the cool dimness of the church and her own wild answer.

Lady Townsend. She must find Lady Townsend at once.

If anyone would listen to a plan so daring, outrageous, and perilous that even Venetia could scarcely believe she'd agreed to it, it would be Lady Townsend. In that shadowed chapel, Venetia and Sofia had suddenly seen one another clearly—as two young women with their futures being bartered away by men who talked of honor while disregarding human hearts. Lady Townsend would understand that. She would not dismiss their idea out of hand.

Unfortunately, Lady Townsend was not alone.

Venetia found her in the water salon, framed against the long windows where late afternoon light bounced off the canal and dappled the painted ceiling. Catherine Bentley sat opposite her, her beady eyes darting toward Venetia over the rim of her teacup.

"Tsk, tsk, my dear girl," said the older woman the moment Venetia crossed the threshold. "The clock is ticking." She set down her cup. "Captain Rizzi visited us earlier to remind us that his report is due in three days. Three!" She rolled her eyes to the ceiling as if seeking heavenly corroboration, then added piously, "Moral turpitude is the term he wished *not* to use—but he will use worse if that emerald pendant is not found. Of course I told him you were a creature fully redeemed—"

"I have nothing from which to be redeemed," Venetia cut in, heat burning her cheeks. "We all know these charges are completely false."

"Oh, yes, yes, I have done my utmost to ensure that dear Count di Montefiore and Captain Rizzi understand as much," Miss Bentley said hurriedly. "I was chosen to report on what I witnessed at the masquerade because I am well known for my discernment, and I have discerned you to be a highly virtuous young lady. I told Captain Rizzi so."

"I am sure that was most helpful," Venetia murmured, "after what you told him before." She reached for a biscuit, her excitement almost at fever pitch, fizzing beneath her skin, but she could not afford to let Miss Bentley scent it.

Carefully, she said, "I rather fancy a very energetic walk along the canal. Would either of you ladies care to accompany me?"

Miss Bentley, who considered a promenade only tolerable if it were conducted at a dignified crawl and preferably in a sedan chair, visibly recoiled at the word *energetic*. Venetia's heart lifted when only Lady Townsend answered.

"I should be delighted to take the air," she said at once, putting down her cup. "Give me a few minutes to change."

As Venetia was already attired in a neat walking gown and half boots, the intervening time had to be spent listening to Miss Bentley.

Sadly.

The older woman launched into a ponderous recitation of every dire possibility that might befall Venetia should there be no complete vindication—preferably via a full confession from Sofia or "that wicked Griselda," who in Catherine's opinion "ought to be languishing in a prison rather than skulking about Venice like a sewer rat."

"But what chance of that when the lovely Signorina Sofia is clearly wild with jealousy and bent only upon her own gratification?" Miss Bentley continued, shaking her head until her cap ribbons fluttered. "Why can the sisterhood not be as supportive as, for example, you, Lady Townsend, and myself have been? There is nothing—*nothing*—I would not do on your behalf, Miss Playford, to ensure you the successful future you deserve. Oh, how often I have said this to Captain Rizzi and Count di Montefiore."

Apart from the sentiment being blatantly untrue, Venetia was struck by something else.

Just how often *did* Miss Bentley find herself alone in the company of Captain Rizzi and Count di Montefiore?

More often than any of them suspected, perhaps.

She was saved from dwelling on that uncomfortable thought by Lady Townsend's returning in a very fetching soft dove-gray pelisse trimmed with black braid, her bonnet set at a jaunty angle that made her eyes sparkle. There was an eager glint in those eyes now that made Venetia's heart leap.

"Tell me everything you were not prepared to tell Miss Bentley," Lady Townsend said as soon as they were outside, hooking her arm through Venetia's. The two of them set off along the *fondamenta*, the air smelling of brine and sun-warmed stone, gondolas rocking gently against their moorings. "Something has happened, I can tell. Good news? Signorina Sofia is going to confess? Or you have discovered the whereabouts of the marchese…?"

Venetia could barely keep her feet from skipping. "Both!"

For once, Lady Townsend was struck quite dumb. She blinked, then let out a little laugh that held the edge of disbelief. "This all happened in the church after we left you for some moments of solitude? My dear girl… then by tomorrow you and Edward will have your happy ending."

"Not quite," Venetia said, sobering. "I had to strike something of a bargain with the young lady. One that involves, perhaps, enabling her to find her own happy ending with Paolo. She will not confess anything unless that is promised."

Concern—and confusion—clouded Lady Townsend's features. "How are you to unite a pair of star-crossed lovers like Count Morosini's granddaughter and her... unsuitable paramour?"

"To begin with, he is not entirely unsuitable," Venetia replied. They stood aside for a fishmonger's barrow to rattle past, the sharp scent momentarily overwhelming. "Paolo is the second son of a noble family. At present, that is enough for Count Morosini to refuse him. But Paolo's elder brother is much older and has been childless for the duration of his ten-year marriage. It will not be too long before Paolo is considered the heir apparent. It is a fair assumption to make."

She glanced up at her friend, urgency making her heart race. "So in uniting them, I do not think we are scandalizing Venetian society beyond repair. And as for *how* I mean to accomplish it—well, it all hinges upon the balloon ascension."

"Dear Lord, no." Lady Townsend stopped dead, clasping her gloved hands together and lifting her eyes to the bright strip of sky between the houses. "Not another balloon ascension requiring luck and timing and a guardian angel. Are you truly prepared to risk such danger again, Venetia, when we know it was only by a hair's breadth of good fortune that Mr. Rothbury galloped in to save the day? Who will gallop in on a black stallion so that Signorina Sofia and her worthy groom enjoy similar providence? For I take it that is the condition upon which she will confess. Though I cannot begin to understand why she would so readily reveal her own moral deficiencies."

"She believes that doing so publicly will shame Count Bembo who will want to wash his hands of her," Venetia explained. The thought of Bembo's wounded dignity gave her a wicked twinge of satisfaction. "If she admits everything before all Venice, she becomes undesirable to him—while at the same time clearing my name."

She squeezed Lady Townsend's arm. "So, will you help me unite these two worthy lovers? You have made something of a career of such things, after all. And I am sure Lord Thornton will help you once you have persuaded him—as you always manage to do."

They resumed walking, their reflections wavering together in the canal. Venetia dropped her voice. "As for running the marchese to ground, Signorina Sofia has given me all the information we require for a beginning. Our only difficulty is that he is notoriously hermit-like and does not receive visitors."

"A reluctant gentleman with a love of books and little inclination for society who has perhaps never received visitors?" Lady Townsend's mouth curved into a delighted smile. "My dear, I am quite certain we shan't let such small difficulties stand in our way."

Chapter Forty

SINCE IT HAD become well established that the best place for intelligence gathering was La Serafina's salon, it was there that Venetia and Lady Townsend presented themselves yet again the following morning.

It had been mutually decided that they would not tell Lord Thornton of their visit.

"He is such a darling, helpful man," Lady Townsend said as their gondola nosed through the green water, "but in this instance I do think we shall move faster—and more efficiently—if the fact-gathering is left to the ladies."

"Is this based on his skepticism and the fear he might throw cold water on our enthusiasm?" Venetia asked.

Lady Townsend merely patted her arm.

Now, seated opposite La Serafina at a small table set with thin porcelain cups and a dish of tiny sugar-dusted biscuits, Lady Townsend got straight to the point.

"We are hoping, madam," she said, lifting her teacup, "you might advise us how a reception with the Marchese Valenti might be arranged."

"The Marchese Valenti?" La Serafina, lounging opposite in a robe of white, sat abruptly straighter. "Marchese Alessandro Valenti? Why would you wish to see *him*?" Her dark brows arched. "I am astonished you even know of his existence. Oh yes, I told you he was the widower of the great Isabella Monteverdi, but that was many years ago. For the past twenty years he has moldered away in his old castello on the Isola di San—" she flicked her fingers "—a little scrap of stone in the lagoon. He comes into Venice only when he grows impatient with the progress Count Morosini reports to him about his other passion. The passion second only to the love he had for Isabella."

Venetia's fingers tightened around her cup. "He is involved in the project to translate Sir Walter Scott?" she whispered. "*Ivanhoe*?"

"And all the other great works the Scottish master has sent into the world since he began publishing his romances five years ago," La Serafina agreed. "Barely are they printed in English before the marchese demands them in Italian. It is a torment and a blessing for your Mr. Rothbury, I suspect."

Venetia opened her mouth, but no sound came. The marchese was involved in the *Ivanhoe* translation? "So he is a great scholar, then," she managed. Her mouth felt suddenly as dry as a desert. She turned a wide-eyed look on Lady Townsend, who was watching La Serafina with a look of stupefaction.

"You mean," Lady Townsend said carefully, "that Count Morosini and the marchese are both bibliophiles with a particular passion for Sir Walter Scott?"

"Bibliophiles?" La Serafina gave a little laugh. "They are fanatics. Two old men behaving like love-sick boys over tournaments and doomed maidens."

Venetia could scarcely take it in. The room seemed to narrow around the three of them: the crimson walls, the glittering chandelier, the faint clink of glass as a servant picked up a tray of glasses—all of it receded behind the pounding in her ears.

"Does he... does the marchese know the man who translates these masterpieces?" she asked, trying to sound casual, as if so much didn't hang upon her answer.

La Serafina's smile turned sly. "Oh, signorina, I am told the translator is worth his weight in gold. In fact, I have it on excellent authority that when Count Morosini mentioned his young Englishman was in love with a lady who might lure him away from his desk—nay, Venice—the marchese was so desperate to keep such talent at work that he insisted my dear count enter into what you might call a devil's bargain to keep the poor fellow beholden."

"A devil's bargain?" Venetia's heart gave a painful leap. Edward. Shackled not by one powerful old man, but by two... promising to protect Venetia provided their translator remained on a tight leash so he could do their bidding.

La Serafina tilted her head, studying her. "Is it that you share this passion for Sir Walter's romances, perhaps? That might be the only means of persuading the marchese to receive you. And even then, I promise nothing. He is a recluse and a curmudgeon. Books and ghosts are his preferred company."

Venetia glanced at Lady Townsend, silently asking how much they ought to reveal. Their true purpose—to prove Edward's birth and restore him to a father who did not even know he had a living son—seemed far too fragile to expose to daylight, let alone to a woman who traded in secrets.

No. Not yet. Their hunch might be entirely misplaced, and gossip multiplied like pigeons in Venice.

"We are... great admirers of Mr. Scott," Lady Townsend said smoothly. "And naturally curious about any gentleman who shares such taste. But you have already been more than generous with your information, La Serafina."

Venetia sipped her cooling tea, trying to quiet the tremor in her hands.

On a lonely island in the lagoon, this widowed marchese pored over the same stories that filled Edward's days. He wore the same crest on his finger that Isabella had worn in her portrait—and that Edward wore now.

If she and Lady Townsend were wrong, this was nothing but a series of coincidences.

But if they were right...

Then the translator Count Morosini kept on a scholar's chain was the son of the Marchese Alessandro Valenti. And every step Venetia took from this moment on would bring them closer to a truth that could either set them all free—or burst their careful plans apart like an overfilled balloon exploding above the piazza.

Chapter Forty-One

IN TWO DAYS all Venice would be held in thrall to Count Morosini's extravaganza—Sofia's betrothal celebration, crowned by the much-anticipated balloon ascent over the lagoon.

In two days, Captain Rizzi's superior would return to the city and Rizzi's report on the jewel thefts would be due. He needed to put a neat line under the unsolved scandals that had cast a shadow over *La Serenissima*—the Most Serene Republic as it had been until Napoleon had conquered the city a little more than twenty years before. So much civic pride rested upon it.

If Venetia was not completely cleared by then, Edward feared for her future.

But, oh, how difficult it was to attend to tales of love and valor when one's own heart felt like a battlefield. The words of *Ivanhoe* blurred before his eyes; noble vows and shining deeds mocked him from the page.

He tried to accept that he and Venetia could not be together. No, he *had* accepted it. But he agonized daily over how much to tell her the whole truth—that his true barrier was not *just* poverty nor lack of position, but the shame of his birth.

Her kind heart would leap to reassure him; she would insist it did not matter.

But it did. For any children they might have, it would. Miss

Playford, the great English heiress, inveigled into marriage with the illegitimate son of an Italian opera singer and her mysterious lover. It was bad enough that he would already be regarded as a fortune hunter. Let gossipers sniff out the full extent of his unworthiness and they would feast on it for years.

That was if—*if*—Venetia's own reputation survived. If she fulfilled the three-year moral provision in her uncle's will. If she retained her fortune at all.

The very least he could do for her, as a man who loved her and could not wed her, was ensure she emerged untarnished.

But how?

For much of the afternoon, that question teased him far more cruelly than any dilemma Sir Walter had set for his noble knight. His quill scratched, stalled, scratched again; blots gathered accusingly on the page.

When the count breezed into the library late in the day, the air shifted. Morosini brought with him a heady whiff of expensive cologne and impatience.

"You are not on track to finish *Ivanhoe* by the agreed date," he said sharply, surveying the scattered pages. "Your pace has declined greatly. What is it you need? How shall we increase your speed? It is that young lady, is it not? I told you to have nothing more to do with her."

Edward's temper, frayed thin by worry and sleepless nights, snapped. "I have not sought her out," he said, more roughly than was wise. "I am here at my desk from dawn until dusk and often beyond. But I am plagued by fears that Captain Rizzi's report will damn her—that the trustees in England will hear only that she has failed to maintain the spotless conduct required before the three-year deadline falls."

His hand throbbed from hours of cramped writing. His shoulders ached. His heart felt heavy as lead. How much longer could he pour other men's passion into Italian while an outlet for his own passion was so utterly stifled?

"I have promised her my protection," the count replied with a frown, "so long as you do what I contracted you to do. What does it matter? She will leave Venice soon enough to make a brilliant marriage with a man her equal."

Anger flared hot and sudden. Edward curled his fists beneath the table so the count would not see them shake. "All Venice knows those emeralds were found in your granddaughter's tiara," he muttered before he could stop himself.

Morosini's eyes flared. "Are you accusing Sofia?" The words were soft; the tone was not.

"What good would such a dangerous allegation do me?" Edward shot back, then forced himself to lower his voice. "Unless I wished to be rid of this perpetual grinding work entirely." He gestured helplessly at the piles of paper. "All I do is translate the adventures and emotions of imagined lovers. I am choking on them."

Suddenly he felt utterly drained. He rubbed a weary hand across his forehead, resisting the urge to slump over his desk like a schoolboy.

For a heartbeat he thought he had gone too far, that dismissal was imminent. Count Morosini did not tolerate intransigence. And what then? The post in Constantinople was still open. Another letter had arrived only last week, politely inquiring whether he had reconsidered. He could be gone within a fortnight.

He would not be marrying Venetia in any case. There seemed little he could truly do for her from here. Perhaps he was merely a millstone about everyone's neck. Perhaps he ought simply to leave and be done.

Morosini opened his mouth, his expression thunderous—and then, unexpectedly, paused. He drew in a breath, narrowed his eyes, and something like calculation replaced anger.

"You are right, Rothbury," he said at last. "I have kept you chained to this desk without proper regard to the fact that creativity must be fed as well as driven. Gather your things. I shall send a note ahead to my dear friend La Serafina to ensure you are properly entertained this evening. Every man needs comfort in a woman's arms from time to time."

"That is not the kind of comfort I crave, with all due respect—"

"But it is what I insist upon." The count sliced a hand through the air. "You will not argue, Signor Rothbury. You will go to La Serafina's tonight as my honored guest. In the meantime, I shall do what I can to see that Miss Playford is reported on favorably, so that she may leave Venice unblemished and I may count on your continued service."

Edward's breath lodged in his chest. "So... you do know the truth, then, of who stole the emeralds?" he asked. "You know it was—"

"I do not need to know who it was," Morosini snapped. The answer came too quickly; Edward heard the lie in it, or at least the evasion. Whether the count either suspected—or knew—his chief concern was keeping his translator working, pliable, and indebted.

"So you are *ordering* me to visit La Serafina?" Edward said bluntly. "Now?"

"You will go home, change, and for once not bury yourself in manuscripts. You will not speak to that young woman. You will find yourself a pair of accommodating arms at the salon of Venice's premier woman of letters and... pleasure." Morosini's mouth twitched. "And tomorrow your pen will fly."

Edward was in no position to refuse, and truthfully, too exhausted to mount a serious resistance. His hand ached, his head was stuffed with gloom, and a perverse part of him wondered if a few hours away from the inkpot might let him think more clearly.

Perhaps he might even find some thread of hope to tug at La Serafina's.

Chapter Forty-Two

Two and a half hours later he was stepping once more through the doors of her elegant palazzo, the sounds of laughter and music rolling out to meet him.

"*Lo mio caro!*" La Serafina herself swept forward, every inch the queen of this peculiar kingdom. Tonight she wore deep violet, her silver-threaded hair piled artfully beneath a spray of jeweled pins. "Count Morosini wishes me to convey his admiration for your tireless work, Signor Rothbury. He has charged me to ensure your evening is as pleasant as possible. Alessia—!"

She lifted a hand to summon one of her girls.

Edward hastily shook his head. "I am not in need of... that kind of companionship," he said, coloring. "But an evening of good wine and conversation would be a welcome change from the silent company of Sir Walter Scott."

"Then conversation you shall have." Her eyes twinkled. "Alessia is well versed in the Greek tales and philosophy. If you wish to discourse on heroes and fate, you could not ask for a better partner. She appears to have disappeared for the moment, but I shall bring her to you."

He had hardly time to murmur his thanks before a familiar, unwelcome presence descended.

"I did not think you would dare show your face anywhere

you might encounter me, Rothbury," snarled Count di Montefiore.

Edward turned. The man's once-handsome nose was decidedly crooked, the bruising livid beneath powder. Edward supposed he ought to feel some remorse. He did not.

"You have a nerve," the count continued. "In fact, if you do not get out now, I shall make a spectacle of you."

"And what appears to be the problem, Count di Montefiore?" La Serafina's voice floated between them. She had reappeared, her smile serene, her gaze sharp.

di Montefiore touched his swelling nose with an injured air. "This Englishman assaulted me without provocation."

"I merely objected to the count manhandling a lady who is dear to me—Miss Playford," Edward said evenly. "I stepped in to uphold her honor."

"Honor? Pah." The count sneered. "Miss Playford is a thief. When Captain Rizzi's report is delivered, I shall see to it that her trustees in England are informed of her true character. She will lose the fortune she does not deserve." His lip curled. "In three days' time, Rothbury, she will have only you. Nothing else."

Rage clawed at Edward's throat, but before he could respond, La Serafina slid a hand onto the count's arm.

"Gentlemen," she said smoothly, "my salon is devoted to the finer arts, not the airing of personal grievances. Conte, Alessia has been speaking of your admiration for French verse. Perhaps you would favor her with your opinions?"

She signaled to a dark-haired young woman behind her. At once the girl glided forward, murmured something charming, and gently but firmly steered the count away.

La Serafina watched him go, then gave Edward a wry look. "Bad blood, Signor Rothbury?"

"I think you understand why," Edward growled.

La Serafina nodded. "He is not a man I would trust."

Edward raked a hand through his hair and shook his head. "If I could only reveal the depth of his villainy."

"And his connection with the Englishman, Greene?"

Edward blinked. "You know?"

She nodded. "I have learned something of the plot to discredit the young lady, Miss Playford."

Edward exhaled. "She was wrongly accused of theft, yes! And it has been confessed to me that the contessa's maid, Griselda, was prevailed upon to steal the pendant. She is terrified, and with reason. But if I could only find her, offer her some hope of safety, perhaps she might agree to testify and clear Miss Playford's name. But in this city…" He spread his hands. "I do not know that any promise I make would be worth the breath."

"Miss Playford," La Serafina repeated thoughtfully, "has been here several times."

Edward frowned. "She returned here after… she was followed by Count di Montefiore?"

La Serafina studied him, head tilted, then changed the subject. "You are a recent visitor to Venice, Signor Rothbury, yet already much cherished by Count Morosini, as evidenced by his letter this afternoon and his concern that you be 'kept happy.'" Her smile thinned. "Your Italian is exquisite. Yet you are English. Perhaps you grew up in Italy?"

He shook his head. "I grew up in a small town in England. My father—" He stopped, then forced himself on. "My father was an English bailiff. In fact, steward to Miss Playford's late parents. That is how we knew one another. Meeting her here was… coincidence."

"And what brought you to Venice?" she asked softly.

"My mother was from here," he said after a moment. "From Venice." The words tasted strange on his tongue in this room where so much of her youth had echoed. "She died when I was twelve."

"And who was your mother?" asked La Serafina.

"It was a long time ago," he evaded gently. "And I am very tired. I think I shall take my wine and a seat by the window, if I may. The count drives me hard; he wishes Sir Walter Scott rendered into Italian almost before the ink is dry on the English editions. It is… difficult to concentrate when my entire mind is fixed on finding this Griselda and sparing Miss Playford any further pain."

La Serafina's expression softened. "It sounds as though the young lady holds your heart—as Rowena held Ivanhoe's." She gave him a teasing smile. "I am sure there will be the same happy ending for you both, considering your chivalry to date."

He attempted a smile of his own, but it felt thin. "There can be no happy ending for us," he said quietly. "As the count has reminded me many times, Ivanhoe only won his Rowena after his lands and title were restored."

La Serafina made a small moue and, impulsively, touched his cheek with the back of her hand. "What can I do to help you, *caro*? There is nothing so moving—as profitable, in my line—as a man in love."

He sighed, accepting a glass of wine from another young woman who had drifted to his side at Serafina's gesture. "Alas, I have no lands or title to restore."

"No," La Serafina said slowly, "but perhaps I can offer you something better than consolation."

She turned to the girl at Edward's elbow. The young woman was perhaps a year or two older than Venetia's maid, her dark hair smoothed neatly beneath a modest cap, her gown simple but of good cloth. Her face was pale and serene.

"This is Griselda," La Serafina said. "Formerly maid to the contessa you mentioned. I make it my business to give protection, when I can, to those in need."

Edward's brain spun. "Good Lord." He looked the girl over with fresh attention. Dressed in clean homespun, her dark hair partly covered by a pristine linen cap, she looked neat and wholesome.

"But surely your salon is frequented by the very men who might wish her harm," Edward protested.

"Count di Montefiore?" La Serafina shrugged. "He has never

met her. And the Contessa Barbarigo would never cross my threshold. Griselda reads aloud beautifully and keeps accounts better than most bankers. I believe," said La Serafina, "that the safest place for those who most want to find her, apart from yourself and Miss Playford—"

"You mean, Count di Montefiore?"

"Exactly," agreed La Serafina. "As I was saying, the safest place for Griselda is right under their noses."

"Good heavens!" Edward's heart was thudding. "How did she come to be here?"

"I think Griselda is best placed to answer that question." La Serafina nodded to the girl to speak.

Twisting her hands together, Griselda raised her eyes to Edward's face. "It was the young gentleman Paolo, signore," she said. "That is the name he gave me, and he said it was best I knew no other. He told me his beloved Sofia insisted I must be brought somewhere safe—somewhere Captain Rizzi would never think to look."

Chapter Forty-Three

EUGENIA FIDDLED WITH the tassel of the cushion as she waited for Venetia to come downstairs.

Normally she found the sound of water slapping gently against the stone soothing; today it set her nerves jangling.

The girl was taking longer than expected to get ready for the gondola ride to the marchese's island, and Eugenia was growing restless.

No—anxious.

At any moment Catherine might sweep in and begin asking all manner of incisive—no, simply sharp and intrusive—questions, and Eugenia doubted she'd do a very good job of offering the vague, harmless replies required. The last thing she and Venetia needed was Catherine's well-intentioned interference now, when finally, after three days of waiting, a note had arrived from the marchese. As a "special indulgence to two English ladies," he had granted them permission to visit his library—though he added that it was unlikely he would be there to receive them.

Eugenia suspected the man would sooner receive a troop of invading Turks than two curious foreigners. Still, the permission was something.

She must have looked as restless as she felt, for at the sound of Thornton's voice she jerked her head up with a little gasp.

"My dear Eugenia, such agitation is unlike you." He came into the room, tall and broad shouldered in his dark coat, eyes twinkling. "I am almost tempted to believe you are up to something."

For one breathless moment she thought he was about to take her hands—ridiculous, at her age—but instead he sank into the chair opposite and stretched out his long legs.

"Out with it," he said. "You are scheming."

"Good heavens, Thornton—what on earth would make you think such a thing? Of course I am not."

"You have been scheming for three days." His smile was gentle, but his gaze keen. "Do not imagine I have not noticed your distraction. And not all of it, I think, is on account of your concern for what will happen tomorrow regarding Miss Playford's future. Oh no, Eugenia—I miss nothing. So, out with it."

With a sigh of capitulation, she began, "It was as a result of a visit to La Serafina's that we—"

"Dear Lord, Eugenia, do not tell me you have been to that woman's den of iniquity!" cried Catherine, choosing that unfortunate moment to sweep into the room in a rustle of black silk and disapproval. "Surely you are as horrified as I am, Thornton. Whatever can Eugenia have been thinking?"

Her eyes gleamed with curiosity. "And what was it La Serafina told you that has you confessing all to our dear friend Thornton? What could you possibly have been asking such a woman?"

Eugenia, quite unable to frame a reply that would not worsen matters, sent a helpless look toward Thornton.

"Perhaps," he said calmly, "Eugenia does not feel comfortable sharing every detail of her conversation with La Serafina."

"Well, she was comfortable enough to tell *you*," Catherine grumbled, planting a hand on the back of the sofa, clearly not prepared to let the matter go.

"I doubt you would be willing to reveal all matters of the

heart to a public audience either, Catherine," Thornton returned mildly.

"Matters of the heart?" Catherine's head snapped round, eyes wide. "You speak of Count di Montefiore? Or perhaps Captain Rizzi? Why, they are both regulars at La Serafina's."

Eugenia and Thornton exchanged a look of sharp comprehension before Thornton said, still in that deceptively mild tone, "I wonder that you should know this, Catherine, unless you yourself have ventured over the threshold of La Serafina's salon."

"Indeed I have not!" Catherine colored. "I have merely visited the captain to apprise him of further particulars in Venetia's pending case, knowing how important it is that the right impression is given when he presents his report tomorrow."

"You did not, perhaps, consider that Eugenia—or even I—might wish to present a united front with you?" Thornton asked. "Though I suppose it may not be entirely united."

"How can you possibly accuse me of disloyalty, Thornton?" Catherine cried. "If you have nothing useful to say to Eugenia that might temper her propensity to take bolder steps than are wise, then I have nothing more to say to you. Good evening!"

She spun toward the door and almost collided with Venetia, who was entering, dressed for the outdoors in a peach pelisse and matching bonnet, cheeks faintly flushed with excitement.

Venetia stepped aside to let Catherine pass, then looked between the older pair in bewilderment. "Why is Miss Bentley so upset?"

"I suspect," Thornton said dryly, "that our Miss Bentley has formed an attachment that is perhaps somewhat inappropriate—and she is embarrassed to find herself questioned."

Eugenia pressed a hand to her chest. "That is very blunt of you, Thornton," she said, unable to keep the admiration from her tone. "And very perceptive."

"Ah, but I am becoming more perceptive by the day," he replied, smiling at her. "Living with two—no, three—ladies who have secrets of their own, a man must keep his wits about him.

Out with it, Eugenia. Where are you and Venetia going now? If it is to La Serafina's again, I question the wisdom of venturing without a male escort."

Eugenia hesitated, then decided on the truth. In quick, low sentences she told him of their suspicions regarding Mr. Rothbury's paternity and how this had led them to petition the marchese for access to his island library.

"You mean the marchese's library," Thornton said, brows rising. "For it still sounds unlikely that he will see you. Just as I think it highly unlikely your suspicions are correct." His smile was sympathetic rather than mocking. "However, I shall not stand in your way—or pour cold water on your hopes. I understand very well how dearly you wish Mr. Rothbury to be Venetia's equal—"

"He is every bit my equal!" Venetia burst out, eyes bright. "More than my equal, in fact! It is he who refuses to see it, for he only anticipates the opprobrium that will be heaped upon him as a supposed fortune hunter—even if that accusation exists only in his own mind."

"My dear sweet girl, if only that were entirely untrue," Thornton said gently. "Society would judge him harshly; there are no two ways about it. And his pride will not bear it. But go to the island, by all means. You need to feel that you have done everything in your power." He gave her arm a paternal pat. "I have no doubt Mr. Rothbury is, at this very moment, doing all he can to secure a favorable outcome tomorrow. I understand he has spoken to Count Morosini."

"Even if the emerald pendant is not recovered," Eugenia added softly, "there is still hope."

"Indeed." Thornton inclined his head. "Now—off with you. I believe I hear your gondolier calling. I shall not stand in the way of two ladies in arms venturing forth with hopes I fear are hopeless, but whose nobility I fully applaud."

Venetia gave him a tremulous smile and hurried from the room.

Eugenia followed at a more measured pace, heart thumping. As she drew level with him, Thornton rose. For once, he did not content himself with a teasing remark from a safe distance. Instead, he lifted a hand and very lightly cupped her cheek, his palm warm against her skin.

"Take care, my dearest general," he murmured, his voice pitched for her ears alone. "Do not stay away too long. I find I have grown quite used to plotting mischief at your side."

Her breath caught. For a foolish, glorious moment she allowed herself to lean ever so slightly into his touch. Then she gathered her composure, smiled up at him, and swept after Venetia, the imprint of his hand lingering against her cheek.

Chapter Forty-Four

THE GONDOLA BUMPED lightly against the weed-slick landing steps and the gondolier steadied the craft with his pole. Venetia rose, placing her gloved hand in his as she stepped out onto the slimy stone. Lady Townsend followed, gathering her cloak away from the puddles as the gondola rocked and fell back into the water with a soft slap.

Before them, the marchese's palazzo reared out of the lagoon like something half drowned and reluctant to return to life. One tower leaned at a perilous angle, and a jagged crack zigzagged down its side.

Venetia's heart, which had been beating high with hope all the way across the lagoon, gave an uncomfortable lurch.

If this was Edward's father's domain, then perhaps the rumors were right and the Marchese Alessandro Valenti was nothing more than a ruined recluse, an eccentric relic of an old nobility. Poverty she could have borne—Edward's worth had never rested on his pocketbook—but what if the old man's wits were gone? What use would it be to discover he was Edward's father if he had no memory left, no capacity to recognize the significance of the signet ring Isabella had left to her son?

The great door creaked open before she could lose her nerve. An elderly servant, stooped and stiff jointed, regarded them from beneath heavy brows.

"Il Marchese is not receiving visitors," he said in heavily accented English, giving only the barest inclination of his head. "But he welcomes the signora to look at his library."

Venetia's fragile optimism dipped further. So they might admire the marchese's dusty volumes, but not the man himself—the very reason for their pilgrimage—when time was running out and tomorrow would see her fate decided.

If Captain Rizzi's report went against her, if she lost her fortune, what future could there be for herself and Edward? He was chained to his employer for an unknown span of years. She would have to find some means of supporting herself alone. Edward had not spoken of any alternative to her exoneration. Did he know something she did not? Or was he simply trying to spare her despair?

No. For now she must focus on what she could do: search for any clue that strengthened the connection she believed existed between Edward and the owner of this decrepit stronghold. A noble father—with or without money—would change everything.

In silence she and Lady Townsend followed the stooped retainer through a warren of narrow, chill corridors, their footsteps echoing.

At last the servant halted before a heavy door, produced a large iron key and turned it with an effort. The hinges groaned.

"See." He pushed the door wide and stepped aside. "I wait here." Folding his hands over his livery, he took up a post by the door, clearly intending to keep watch.

The sight that met them stole Venetia's breath.

The library was vast: a high, vaulted chamber where the walls were lined from floor to ceiling with books, their leather spines in rich shades of brown and red and gold. A narrow gallery ran around the upper level, reached by two elegant spiral staircases. Light filtered in through tall, arched windows and mingled with the glow of wall sconces, picking out the gleam of gilt lettering and the drifting dust motes.

"Oh my goodness," Venetia whispered, stepping forward as if drawn. She made straight for a section where familiar names leaped out at her. "Lady Townsend, look—Sir Walter Scott! *Waverley, Guy Mannering, The Bride of Lammermoor*...here in English—and here in Italian." She touched the bindings reverently. "Do you suppose Edward translated all these? You have been in Italy longer than I; was he already translating for Count Morosini when you arrived in Venice?"

"I believe he came almost immediately after my comet-viewing gala," Lady Townsend replied, moving beside her. "It is possible."

"Really?" Venetia's heart gave a small, foolish leap. How had she never known the exact moment he had gone from her life? But everything had been so full of commotion then, with the surprise of her inheritance, the excitement, the flurry of congratulations. She had wanted Edward to be part of it. Instead, he had vanished to Italy without a word.

Well, she had found him now, she thought fiercely. She did not intend to lose him again.

She drew out the English copy of *The Bride of Lammermoor* and opened it with care. Dense type marched down the page. "Look, Lady Townsend." She reached for the corresponding Italian volume and opened the first page. "Here it is—*La Sposa di Lammermoor.*" In slow, halting Italian she began the opening lines, her voice echoing faintly beneath the vaulted ceiling, until emotion constricted her throat and she broke off on a shaky breath. "To think of Edward spending all his days rendering such beauty into another tongue. Does the world even understand how adored Scott is here?"

She hugged the book to her chest. "It is so beautiful—and so tragic. It seems cruel that we will not meet the marchese to speak with him of his treasures. Edward would wish to know what manner of library belongs to the man who so devours his work."

She rounded a towering bookshelf—and stopped dead.

"Oh," she breathed, all thought of books forgotten. "Lady Townsend...look."

Her friend joined her, then gave a low exclamation.

Dominating one wall, flanked by candle sconces positioned to cast a flattering glow, hung an enormous portrait of Isabella Monteverdi. This likeness was finer even than the one at La Serafina's: the colors richer, the brushwork more delicate. Isabella's dark hair was swept up to display the graceful line of her neck; her eyes, luminous and alive, seemed to follow them. Her hands were folded at her waist, fingertips just touching.

"It is magnificent," Lady Townsend murmured, stepping back to take in the full effect. "An even better likeness than La Serafina's."

The sconces threw a halo of light about the singer's face and picked out the gleam of a ring upon her middle finger. Venetia's breath caught.

"She is so very beautiful," she said. "And—look at her eyes. Edward has her eyes, Lady Townsend. He does." Giddiness swept over her. She darted closer, pointing. "And her ring—it is painted in such detail. The same signet, except for that tiny extra star. Oh, Lady Townsend, I am right, am I not—?"

A movement to their right made both women turn sharply.

An old man stood there, half emerging from the shadows between two towering bookcases. He wore an old-fashioned velvet coat, the color dulled with age, and his gray hair hung to his shoulders; his beard, equally gray, was worn long. The light from the sconces fell across a face lined by time and grief. His eyes, dark and wary, regarded them with such suspicion that Venetia instinctively took a step back.

These were not Edward's eyes. There was no physical resemblance that she could see between the proud-featured young man she loved and this gaunt, haunted nobleman. In a single, dispiriting rush, she felt her carefully built edifice of hopes topple like the leaning tower outside.

Of course. She had been inventing fairy tales, trying to fashion a happy ending out of scraps.

On the heels of that disappointment came another chill thought: Tomorrow's grand spectacle would likely bring more disillusionment. The men of power in Venice were not motivated by truth. Captain Rizzi knew enough of it to clear her name, yet he had far more reason to write a damning report to her English trustees and claim whatever reward Mr. Greene, through Count di Montefiore, had promised him.

And now here stood this old man, seeming as distant from their troubles as the moon over the lagoon.

"You speak as if you knew Isabella," he said abruptly, his voice harsh with feeling. He addressed Lady Townsend, for Venetia was plainly too young to have known a woman who had died around the time of her birth. "You are English. Did you know her in your country?"

Lady Townsend cast Venetia a quick glance before she replied. "I did not have the honor, my lord. It is only in Venice that I have learned from so many of her talent, her beauty…and how beloved she was."

"Indeed, she was beloved," the marchese murmured, his gaze shifting to the portrait. "All Venice worshipped at her altar."

"Including you, my lord?" Lady Townsend said gently, looking between him and the painting. "Is that why she has pride of place in your library?"

He had not yet introduced himself, but it hardly seemed necessary. His assumption that they must know who he was suggested he had at least been told of "two English ladies" who would visit his books.

"She was the light of my life," he said quietly. "My reason for drawing breath." As he spoke, he turned slightly. The firelight winked on the signet at his hand.

The tiny flash of gold seemed to strike Venetia like a spark. Her hopes, so recently doused, flared again. If that ring connected him to Isabella, then perhaps—

"She wears your ring," she heard herself say, barely recognizing her own voice. She looked from his hand to the painted one in the portrait. "There. It is almost the same."

His gaze came back to her, sharper now. "Your observation does you credit, signorina, though you have missed the detail that matters. Her ring bears two stars." He extended his hand, palm down, for them to see. "Mine has only one."

Venetia's pulse thundered. She forced herself to sound merely curious. "Why does she wear your ring, my lord? Were you related?"

"She was my wife," he said, without flourish. His eyes had already strayed back to the canvas. "The worthiest woman who ever lived, though my family would not sanction the match. We were forced to marry in secret."

"Yet if your family would not sanction it, all Venice revered her," Lady Townsend ventured, her tone gently probing. Venetia sensed that her friend was trying to coax from him what he might not otherwise divulge.

"She was magnificent," he said simply. "Her voice—" His own cracked. "She sang to me every day. She sang to our child—"

"You had a child?" Venetia could not stop herself. She prayed he would not notice the urgency in her voice. The story she'd heard said Isabella had a young child when his ship was lost.

The Marchese nodded slowly. "A fine boy. Lusty lungs—his mother's—and her eyes." A faint smile touched his lips. "Eduardo, we named him."

Venetia's knees felt weak.

"Where are they now?" she asked, scarcely above a whisper.

The marchese turned fully toward them at last. "Both are gone," he said. "Long gone. Lost to me." A single tear gathered at the corner of his eye but did not fall. "That portrait is all I have of my Isabella. She died in a far country."

"In my country," Lady Townsend said softly. "In England."

"You heard her sing there?" he asked quickly, hope flaring for an instant—but Lady Townsend shook her head.

"She never sang in England," she said, taking a delicate risk.

"She was too broken-hearted. She had lost her true love. She and her son left Venice when her protector's ship was lost." She hesitated, then went on, "Two years passed without word. An Englishman—a good man—offered his protection to her and her child, and brought them to a land that was…"

"Gray and cold…Ah, so you know the story," the marchese finished hoarsely, staring at some point far beyond them. "A prison compared with her beautiful Venice." His hands clenched at his sides. "I tried to come back to her. When the *Santa Lucia* went down, I alone survived. For two years I wandered half mad, fighting to return to what I loved. When at last I reached home, three years had gone. Isabella Monteverdi had left Venice. England, they said. Taken by a man bewitched—as I was—by her beauty and her voice."

He gave a broken laugh. "I thought that with a voice like hers she would be easy to find. A nightingale like that? I asked about her everywhere. I begged for news of the great Monteverdi. I gave every name, every description that might stir a memory." He shook his head. "Nothing. She had vanished. She no longer sang. By the time I learned she was dead, so was the Englishman who had stolen her. A bailiff, they told me. A clerk of estates. Of my son, there was no word. Perhaps he died of the same fever that took his mother."

His shoulders sagged. "I was defeated. By grief, by time. I returned here, to the house of my fathers. My own father was gone. I had nothing."

Venetia met Lady Townsend's gaze. Her friend's eyes were bright, her expression intent. *Now*, Venetia thought wildly. *Now, you must tell him. Tell him his son lives. Tell him his son is—*

But Lady Townsend only lowered her voice and said gently, "Not quite nothing, my lord. You had your stories. Your novels. Perhaps…because they were a pleasure you once shared with your Isabella, they became your refuge?"

The marchese drew in a sharply audible breath and stepped toward her. "Yes," he said. "Exactly." His hand lifted as if to touch a nearby shelf. "She was enamored of your Mrs. Ann Radcliffe. I have all her books, even if I read English badly. And then, when Sir Walter Scott burst upon the scene with his tales of knightly valor, it was as if my blood stirred again. My old friend Morosini had *La Sposa di Lammermoor* translated into Italian. I felt life return to me."

He gave a strained smile. "Now Scott's *Ivanhoe* mirrors everything I have lost. Each week new chapters are delivered, and I grow feverish for the next. It is a sickness, almost. Rowena is my Isabella; Ivanhoe the man who is finally reunited with her. They tell me this is the ending in the English. I will read it in the Italian." His eyes gleamed with a sudden, almost boyish mischief. "And if the ending displeases me, I shall have my translator change it—for me alone."

Venetia's heart hammered against her stays. "Your translator, my lord," she said, her voice trembling despite her efforts. "Who is he?"

The marchese looked at her as though only now recalling her presence. For a long moment he studied her face, then spoke slowly, the words seeming to surprise even himself.

"He is," he said, "the man who makes my dreams come true."

Chapter Forty-Five

THE DAY OF Sofia's betrothal dawned bright and deceptively beautiful, Venice glittering as if nothing truly dreadful could ever happen beneath such a sky.

Feverishly, Venetia submitted to Mollie's ministrations as her maid helped her into a gown of palest-blue silk.

How would today unfold?

Seeing the marchese the previous afternoon had imbued her with fresh hope after her earlier despair, but still the old man remained in ignorance of Edward's true identity. Would he even attend? He had been so adamant that he would not leave his island; yet he had clearly been moved by the service his mysterious translator had rendered him.

Edward, however, was not to be there. He had said as much several days earlier, the last time she and her elderly friends had managed to corner him with questions.

"Apparently Morosini is dissatisfied with my progress," he'd said with a wry twist of his mouth. "He wishes the next chapter finished by the end of the week, which means I must work like a galley slave. There is no opportunity to enjoy the frivolity of his granddaughter's betrothal festivities. Besides, I am merely a servant."

He had looked so downcast Venetia had almost thrown her

arms about him on the spot. But a distance had crept up between them over the last few days. She had barely seen him, and when she had, he'd seemed far away, as if his mind lived entirely in the pages he translated.

A tap sounded at the door, and Lady Townsend swept in.

"Oh, my dear, you look quite ravishing," she declared, taking in Venetia's gown, and the soft curls Mollie was arranging about her face. The affectionate admiration in her eyes was so warm that Venetia felt, as she often did, like the most cherished creature in existence.

How could such a woman still be unwed? Venetia wondered not for the first time. Truly, if she were to pair two of the dearest people to her, it would be Lady Townsend and Lord Thornton. Why they had never thought of it themselves was one of life's great mysteries.

But she had no leisure to matchmake for others. Today she must contrive her own salvation—and, if Heaven was kind, Edward's.

"I wonder if my dress ought to have been a touch more modest," she murmured, studying her reflection as Mollie set the last curl. "In view of how Captain Rizzi may choose to render me in his report." She clasped her hands together, briefly closing her eyes as she made a quick appeal to any celestial power within hearing. "Oh, how I wish Edward were to be there. I cannot believe Count Morosini thinks so little of him that he would be left off the guest list."

"It is because the count thinks so very highly of him that he has done so," Lady Townsend replied, coming to stand behind her. "But I heard a little rumor that may lift your spirits." She dipped her head closer to Venetia's, her eyes twinkling. "Count Morosini intends that Edward shall read a passage of *Ivanhoe*—in Italian and in English—for the entertainment of his guests. Who knows? It may even tempt our marchese from his lair, given the great rivalry between the two men, for all that they are united by their love of literature."

Venetia's heart gave a hopeful little leap. "Edward might be there? And the marchese too?"

Lady Townsend nodded, satisfied by the effect of her news. "I know you thought I did not go far enough yesterday in revealing our suspicions regarding Edward's... connections." Her lips curved. "But, my dear, sometimes less is more. The marchese will be far more receptive to a connection he deduces for himself than to one thrust upon him by two English ladies armed with wild theories."

"But when you asked him about today, he said he was not going to attend at all," Venetia protested. "That was why I was so disappointed, Lady Townsend. I do agree that subtlety is required, but I feared you had not told him sufficiently what he needed to hear to have his interest piqued about his translator enough to even attend Signorina Sofia's betrothal."

"Ah, my love, you have much to learn about men." Lady Townsend brushed her fingertips briefly over Venetia's cheek, a touch that was half caress, half conspiratorial signal. "They must believe themselves in charge. They like to imagine that any brilliant notion, any wondrous event, is all their own doing. I said as much to Lord Thornton last night, and he was in full agreement—after a little grumbling." Her smile grew fond. "On the strength of our conversation he sought out our host and, I understand, contrived matters so that what we learned on the island was couched as a challenge and an enticement to the marchese. Clearly, upon reflection, the old gentleman decided he could not resist hearing the voice of the translator upon whom his happiness now rests."

Venetia gazed at her with frank admiration. "I hope one day I am as wise as you."

"Patience is all that is required," Lady Townsend said lightly. "Just another thirty years and you will be brimming with such wisdom. Now, my dear girl, not another alteration to your appearance is needed. You look precisely as you ought: innocent enough to soften Captain Rizzi's report, and desirable enough to make Edward cast every other consideration to the wind—the marchese and Morosini be hanged—in order to pledge you his troth. That is, after all, your greatest desire, is it not?"

Venetia's throat tightened. "Yes," she whispered. "It is."

"Well then," Lady Townsend said briskly, squeezing her hand. "Let us go and meet our fate—with good posture and our chins held high."

Chapter Forty-Six

EDWARD FLEXED HIS cramped hand, causing a fresh scatter of ink across the already-blotted page, and forced his attention back to Ivanhoe's latest declaration of noble self-sacrifice. Count Morosini had decreed that this chapter must be finished before week's end, and it was barely half done.

Outside, Venice was making merry over Sofia's fate.

From the open casement, the sounds floated up in bright, taunting snatches: the clatter of hammers as temporary stands were raised on the *piazzetta*, the sing-song cries of hawkers, the excited babble of children. Church bells rang across the water. Once, when Edward rose to stretch, he glimpsed the pale bulge of silk above the rooftops—the balloon, half inflated, swaying like some monstrous sea creature straining at its tether.

Restless delight for everyone else. A sense of mounting judgment for him.

For Sofia, too. He had not seen the girl in days, save for that one brief, wretched encounter when her sobs had echoed faintly down from the upper gallery of the library. He had been angry with her—justly so—for setting in motion the chain of events that had placed Venetia's liberty in jeopardy. Yet the memory of those choked entreaties to a higher being, her shoulders shaking beneath the lace veil, would not quite let him condemn her entirely.

She was so very young. So very trapped.

Like me, he thought grimly, bending again over his desk. Chained to a paper gallows.

He tried to lose himself in Sir Walter Scott's rhythms, but the lines blurred. His gaze drifted to the folded note lying beside the inkwell.

Rizzi's hand. Rizzi's threat.

The captain's superior returned to Venice on the morrow. With him must go a report that "brought the matter of the jewel thefts to a satisfactory conclusion." Without new evidence, Rizzi had said with bureaucratic regret, he would be obliged to describe Miss Venetia Playford as morally compromised and "possibly complicit"—a phrase that, in the mouths of English trustees, would be quite sufficient to pry her inheritance from her grasp.

Edward's jaw tightened.

He knew the truth. Griselda's confession at La Serafina's had been halting but clear enough: the contessa's maid, bribed and bullied by Paolo and Sofia into slipping the emeralds into Venetia's tiara. No malice toward Venetia herself. Merely a reckless gamble to fund an elopement.

Merely.

He had tried that same night to persuade Griselda to repeat her story where it mattered—in front of Rizzi. The girl had shaken her head until her cap slipped sideways, her dark eyes rolling in terror at the thought of dungeons and the contessa's vengeance. Even La Serafina's assurances of protection had not moved her.

And time was running out.

His quill hovered impotently over the page. Ivanhoe, blast him, could afford to ride into battle with clear purpose. Edward had nothing but a guilty maid, a venal policeman, and a city that preferred appearances to truth.

"How," he murmured to the empty room, "in God's name am I to make you listen, Captain Rizzi?"

"Il conte wishes to see you, Signor Rothbury."

Edward started. The footman in the doorway looked faintly apologetic, as if aware that no summons from Count Morosini ever boded well for a man's peace of mind.

"Very well," Edward said, laying down his pen. "Tell him I am coming."

Morosini's private salon had been transformed from the half-dusty retreat of a scholar into the command post of a general on the eve of a campaign. Papers littered every surface—lists of guests, lists of suppliers, lists of expenses that would have made a lesser man blanch. Bolts of colored bunting lay tumbled on a chair. A footman was fussing with a tray of crystal flutes; another stood ready with a silver inkstand.

At the center of the chaos, in a coat of dark-blue velvet, stood the count.

"Ah, Rothbury." He turned. "You look as if you have spent the night in a crypt."

Edward bowed. "You sent for me, sir?"

"I did." Morosini waved a hand, encompassing the room, the palazzo, Venice entire. "As if arranging my granddaughter's betrothal were not enough—fireworks, music, that infernal balloon—I must also contend with the caprices of poets and policemen."

He began to pace.

"Captain Rizzi will bring his superior—arrived a day early—to my *festa*," he grumbled. He ventured a glance at Edward, as if uncertain whether to voice the threat that lay between them. *Sofia is not to be drawn into any of this.* "He says it will show Venice that the law is diligent. Bah. The law is always diligent when there is an English fortune involved. And, the Marchese Valenti has condescended to leave his moldering island with demands of his own."

"Indeed, sir?"

"He has been enticed—" Morosini stopped pacing and speared Edward with a look. "By the promise of hearing with his own ears the man who translates his beloved Scott. He demands that you read from *Ivanhoe*. In English—so he may remember the cadence—and in your Italian prose, so that he may judge whether you have captured the soul of the thing—though he is more than happy when he sees it on the page."

"I am honored," Edward managed.

"You ought to be." Morosini's tone softened slightly "Between you and me, Rothbury, the old fool is half in love with you. Or with your pen, which in his case is the same thing. I have spent a year of my life enduring his complaints that your progress is too slow, his paeans of ecstasy when a new chapter arrives. Now he wishes to see the magician."

He clapped his hands together as if the matter were settled. "So. You will attend the betrothal. You will read one passage in English, then the same in Italian. Briefly, you understand. We must not bore them. We are promised a display of fireworks over the lagoon, and Sofia is to shriek in terror when the balloon lifts. This will amuse Bembo, who has all the sensibilities of a codfish. After that, you may slink back to your desk and drown yourself in ink to make up for the lost hours."

Edward inclined his head. "Very well, sir. I shall do my best to excite the crowds—or rather, the marchese—and return quietly to my desk, as you say."

Morosini gave a satisfied nod. "Excellent. Wear something respectable. And if I catch you making calf's eyes at the English heiress when you ought to be thinking of knights and tournaments, I shall have you locked in the library with nothing but your work for company."

A faint smile tugged at Edward's mouth despite the knot in his chest. "Then I shall be very careful where I direct my gaze."

"See that you do." The count dismissed him with a wave of his hand and turned back to his papers, already barking orders about torches and musicians.

Venetia arrived at the piazza in company with her two English friends.

The day had blossomed into one of those crystalline Venetian mornings when every dome and campanile stood etched against an impossible blue. Ahead, the great square and the adjoining piazzetta were thronged. Silks and satins and bright parasols appeared like a glitter of jewels, and the hum of excited voices rose and fell like the lap of the lagoon.

And in the near distance, tethered above a wooden dais like some captive moon, floated the balloon.

Its vast silk envelope—striped in cream and faded blue—heaved and shivered with each breath of wind. Ropes creaked. The wicker car swayed a little, making Venetia's own stomach pitch as she imagined what it would feel like to be lifted high above the glittering water with all of Venice watching.

She'd been spared the sensation of lifting off, suspended in a basket, by Edward's timely intervention at Lady Townsend's Comet Viewing Gala.

The last preparations were in full swing. Liveried servants wove through the crowd with silver trays, the delicate chime of glass punctuating the babble of Italian and French. Musicians tuned their instruments near the steps while children craned on tiptoe to see the progress.

"There is Signorina Sofia with her grandfather," Lady Townsend murmured, squeezing Venetia's arm. "My, but she is a very beautiful girl—though she has not your presence, my dear."

Sophia, in palest pink, stood flanked by maids and footmen, her face composed, her mouth just tight enough to betray the strain. Beside her, Count Morosini swelled with satisfaction, and bearing down upon them with the air of a man approaching a newly purchased prize was Count Bembo.

"What with that long face?" Lord Thornton said, leaning

closer so his words would be swallowed by the noise around them. "Enjoy today's festivities, my dear. Tomorrow will be soon enough to worry about Captain Rizzi and his report when you meet his superior and plead your case. For now, take comfort in the fact that you are not the one destined to marry Bembo."

Venetia managed a smile for his sake. She had not confided in him about the wild scheme she and Sofia had spun in the dim quiet of the church. In the clear light of day it seemed outlandish—reckless to the point of madness. Two helpless young women plotting escape while surrounded by men who commanded the law, the courts, and the sky itself.

From this distance, with Morosini's discreet guard of servants and retainers forming an almost invisible ring around his granddaughter, the idea of spiriting Sofia away in a balloon with a different bridegroom felt like something out of one of Scott's more improbable romances.

Sophia was as much a victim of her circumstances as Venetia. Grandly conceived plans, born of fear and desperation, seldom survived when confronted with reality.

"Come now, Venetia, it is not all so very bad," Lady Townsend said, giving her arm another reassuring pat, only to break off with a little gasp. "Oh my. I think I see the marchese. Yes—there, by the fountain. No one else would dare appear in such an unmodish suit of velvet. He is very easy to pick out."

A tiny flame of hope flared in Venetia's breast. It faltered almost at once. What use was the marchese's presence if Edward was not to be here? The old man might listen; he might even begin to suspect the truth. But without Edward...

For a while they mingled dutifully, responding in halting Italian and better French when approached by Morosini's guests. Venetia felt as if she were moving through a dream—nodding, smiling, exchanging pleasantries—while all the while her gaze slid back, again and again, to the dais, the balloon, and the cluster of important men near the front.

There was Rizzi, in full uniform, his expression bland as he conversed with a grave-faced gentleman. She felt herself blanche. Not far from them stood Count di Montefiore, his once-fine nose still a little crooked.

Both of them desiring to strip her of her liberty, fortune, and good name—with a few strokes of a pen.

Then, with a great flapping and fluttering, the balloon gave a majestic lurch, rising fully above the platform. A cheer went up from the crowd. The silk canopy glowed like a strange new sun against the sky.

Count Morosini stepped forward, clapping his hands for attention. His voice rolled over the assembled company, hearty and expansive.

"*Signore e signori!* It gives me the greatest pleasure to welcome you all to this magnificent celebration—" his hand swept toward Sofia and the dour-faced groom at her side "—to unite my beloved granddaughter, Sofia Morosini, with a husband worthy of her, the highly esteemed Count Bembo!"

Enthusiastic clapping erupted. Venetia joined in, though her hands felt stiff. Count Bembo bowed repeatedly, his fleshy lips stretched in a smug smile, his waistcoat straining over his stomach. He looked, Venetia thought with a shudder, precisely like a prosperous fishmonger dressed up in borrowed brocade.

Morosini raised his hand again for silence.

"As many of you know," he went on, "I am a great admirer of the English author Sir Walter Scott. His works are as yet unknown to many in our beloved Italy, but soon you shall read them in our own tongue and be transported to worlds of chivalry and romance!" He thumped his chest with theatrical fervor. "At the request of my dear friend and my granddaughter's godfather, *il Marchese Valenti*, I have commanded my translator to read a passage for your entertainment."

"Well, well, my dear, this is excellent," Lady Townsend breathed in Venetia's ear, her voice alight with excitement. "Edward is here. Look—there, mounting the steps. And there is the marchese just behind Count Morosini. Was it he who requested the reading? At Thornton's suggestion? Perhaps last night was not in vain, after all."

Venetia's heart gave such a leap she thought she might be ill. But it was true. Edward had stepped up onto the dais, looking rather as if he would prefer to face a firing squad than an audience. Yet even as the crowd swallowed her, even as Morosini reached out to draw him forward, he seemed to know precisely where she stood.

His gaze swept the piazza and found her. For a fleeting heartbeat the world narrowed to the space between them: his dark eyes locking with hers, the quick flare of feeling he could not quite disguise, the slight inclination of his head that acknowledged her. Then he turned to his patron and bent respectfully.

He took the proffered book—an English edition of *Ivanhoe*—and another slim volume bound in Italian calf. The murmur of the crowd faded into an expectant hush.

"*Signore e signori*," Edward said, his voice carrying clear and steady. "By the count's command, I shall read first in the English, and then in our Italian, from the moment when the disinherited knight is at last acknowledged for who he truly is."

A little shiver ran down Venetia's spine.

He opened the English book, and began:

"Then threw the stranger from him his casque and plume, and the face of Wilfred of Ivanhoe looked forth, pale with wounds, yet bright with that high courage which no reverse could quell..."

Venetia shot a glance toward the marchese.

Sunlight slanted across his lined face, carving his features into planes of gold and shadow so that it was impossible to read his expression. Did the words Edward had just spoken touch any buried memory? Would he notice the elegant hands turning the pages—Isabella's fingers. And the ring he had gifted her?

Her heart thundered. From this distance, there was no way of knowing. All she could do was hope and pray, while an unhelpful little voice in her head murmured that hope was a foolish thing for a woman in her position.

Not a romantic heroine, Venetia. Merely a girl one step away from ruin.

She barely had time to quell that thought before Count Bembo, pink and perspiring, lumbered to the front of the dais. His stout form dwarfed the slim figure of Sofia at his side.

"My friends!" he boomed, spreading his arms. "My deepest gratitude for your presence in making me the happiest of men, united with such a paragon of virtue—"

"Paragon of virtue?"

The words spoken in a clear male voice dripping with disdain sliced through the applause. The crowd gasped and turned as one. Bembo's mouth snapped shut; he took a threatening step to the edge of the dais, searching for the speaker.

"She is a jewel thief!" the voice called again, louder. "She stole the emerald parure of the contessa. It is she who has kept all Venice awake at night, fearing the same will happen to them!"

"Arrest that man!" Count Morosini thundered, clapping his hands to summon the guards stationed below.

"He speaks the truth!"

This time the exclamation rang out even more clearly—and the shock that rolled through the piazza was almost tangible, for it was Sofia's voice.

All heads swiveled. Sofia had broken from Bembo's side. Color burned in her cheeks, but her chin was high, her pink gown fluttering in the breeze.

"It is true," she cried, and when Bembo lunged toward her, hand outstretched as if to clap over her mouth, she ducked away. "I am the thief. I had the emeralds taken and hidden because it was the only way to escape my fate!"

A collective shiver of outrage and morbid delight ran through the crowd as her words were feverishly conveyed to those who had not heard. Venetia felt it as a physical thing, like the ground tremoring beneath her slippers. This, then, was the confession Sofia had promised—spoken not in some quiet corner, but here, in front of half of Venice.

Guards jostled the onlookers as they hurried toward the first speaker: a fair-haired young man with the look of an Adonis, fleet of foot and laughing even now. Venetia saw him weave away from reaching hands, dodge a soldier's grasp and, in three astonishing bounds, leap onto the dais.

Paolo.

Before anyone could stop him he had swept Sofia bodily into his arms, vaulted across the planking, and deposited her into the wicker car of the balloon. He jumped in after her, landing beside the startled French aeronaut.

"Stop them!" Morosini roared, voice breaking with fury. "No one shall speak ill of my granddaughter, the paragon of virtue who is to wed Count Bembo!"

"I will not be so humiliated!" Bembo bellowed, purple with rage. "Better she hang for theft than carry my name to shame!"

"Good Lord!" Miss Bentley squeaked somewhere behind Venetia. "What on earth is Mr. Rothbury doing? He has a knife! Dear heaven, he is not going to attack Count Bembo, is he? I always knew he was not to be trusted."

"Good heavens, Catherine," Lord Thornton murmured, "I think you attribute altogether too much bloodthirstiness to those who capture your interest—in this case, our very self-contained translator."

Venetia's heart lurched painfully. Knife? Edward? She craned to see.

There he was, moving with swift, purposeful steps along the edge of the platform, the small blade glinting in his hand. For one terrifying instant, she, too, imagined carnage.

Then, quickly, Edward stooped and slashed through the thick rope tethering the balloon to its stake.

The great silk envelope surged upward with a mighty heave. The car rocked; Sofia gave a breathless laugh that carried faintly on the wind. Morosini leaped to seize the trailing rope, only to let it go at once as his feet left the ground. His weight was no match for the balloon's soaring power. It wrenched free and climbed higher, the shouts of the crowd fading into a roar of astonishment.

Just as his power, Venetia thought, had proved no match for the combined determination of Sofia and Paolo.

"Oh my goodness," she whispered, hands clapping together of their own accord. "Did you see? Edward must have colluded with them—and now he has given them their hearts' desire. He has done this for them. No, for me," she finished in astonishment as she realized the implications. "Oh, but what will it cost him—?"

Her question died as she saw Morosini wheel upon his translator like a striking hawk. He seized Edward by the lapels, dragging him close, his face contorted with rage.

"You will pay for what you have done!" the count snarled. "Captain Rizzi! Arrest this man at once!"

Rizzi stepped forward, hand going to his sword, eyes flickering between his employer, his superior, and the English guests. Count di Montefiore watched on with fascination. Miss Bentley clutched at her reticule, looking as if she were torn between horror and unseemly fascination. The marchese, Venetia saw, had gone quite rigid.

Then he moved.

With a speed that belied his age, the Marchese Valenti strode across the open space, shoving through the frozen ring of onlookers. He shouldered Morosini aside so forcefully the other man staggered.

A stream of rapid Italian poured from the marchese—his anger needed no translation. Rizzi hesitated, caught between two great houses. The crowd fell into an awed silence, watching the two old lions snarl and snap at one another while, far above, the balloon drifted over the lagoon, Sofia and Paolo silhouetted against the pale sky, their heads bent close in a kiss that even at this distance was unmistakable.

At last, Morosini's bluster faltered. Whether it was the presence of Rizzi's superior, the excited murmur of his guests, or the iron fury in the marchese's eyes, something made him fall back a pace.

The marchese stepped into the space he left. In one decisive movement, he caught Edward by the wrist and thrust his arm up for all to see.

"Behold," the marchese cried, his voice ringing over the square, "the Valenti signet upon the hand of my long-lost son, Eduardo—prince of his craft, given back to me by divine Providence—nay, by Sir Walter Scott himself. Behold my son and heir, the next Marchese Valenti!"

Chapter Forty-Seven

Fire was still coursing through his veins as Edward straightened from the severed rope.

He had meant only to give two desperate young lovers a chance at freedom. That the plan had actually worked—that the balloon now drifted, astonishingly, over the lagoon—felt like something from the pages he translated rather than real life.

Then rough fingers closed about his wrist and yanked his arm high.

Edward braced for a blow, for Rizzi's shackles, for Morosini's roar of triumph.

Instead, the old man in the velvet coat—Marchese Valenti—was staring at him, not with fury, but with eyes luminous with something so fierce that Edward scarcely recognized it as joy.

"*Guardate!*" the marchese cried to the crowd before dropping into English, his voice shaking. "Here it is. The ring. My ring. And on the hand of—" His gaze searched Edward's face, traveling from brow to jaw, lingering on his eyes. "You are Isabella's son. I see her in you. And I see the child I held before I was swept from your lives." His breath hitched. "My son."

The words fell slowly into Edward's mind like stones into deep water, sending out widening rings of disbelief.

My son?

He had spent so long flinching from that question. Whose son? Whose shame? Now, under the pitiless Venetian sun, the answer was being shouted in front of half the city.

The marchese's arms closed around him in a fierce, shaking embrace. Edward stood rigid for a heartbeat, then something inside him simply... gave. His own hands lifted—awkward, astonished—and gripped the old man's shoulders.

Over the marchese's velvet-clad shoulder he saw Venetia pushing through the ring of onlookers, her face alight. No trace of doubt, no caution. Only radiant certainty.

"It's true, Edward," she said breathlessly, coming to his side as the marchese released him. "I saw the ring on Isabella Monteverdi's hand in the portrait at La Serafina's. And when we visited the marchese's island last night, I saw it again. The same crest, the same design—only hers with the extra star."

The Marchese turned to her, blinking as if remembering his surroundings. "You," he said slowly. "The little English signorina in my library. Yes. You came with the other lady. You spoke of Isabella as if you... knew her. And you know this young man?" His gaze darted between them, wonder softening the harsh lines of his face. "You suspected? You knew he was my son?"

Venetia blushed as she lifted her chin. "I suspected," she admitted. "When I heard the Venice gossip and remembered what Mr. Rothbury had told me—of his mother, and why he had come here. It seemed... more than chance."

"Why did you say nothing last night?" the marchese demanded.

"Because why should you have believed me?" Venetia replied. "A stranger with a fanciful tale in your library? That would never have done. It had to be your own heart that recognized him."

Edward caught her hand, almost without knowing he'd moved. He brought her fingers to his lips, needing the anchor of her touch. "You did this," he said hoarsely, "for me?"

"And for me," she said, her eyes bright with unshed tears and triumph. She curled her fingers firmly about his. "You insisted you were not worthy of me—that you were the bastard son of some nameless Italian. But I knew your worth, even if your name and estate were never restored. You are my Ivanhoe in spirit and in truth, Edward. No ring could change that. It only... makes the rest of the world see what I already knew."

Something hot and fierce rose in his chest—joy, sharp as pain. For so long he had carried his birth as a brand of shame, the secret that barred him from the future he most desired. Now the weight of it slid away so that he almost staggered.

Illegitimate. Unworthy. Fortune hunter.

All the ugly words seemed to shrivel in the light of the marchese's open pride, and Venetia's unwavering gaze.

Around them, the crowd murmured, shocked and avid. Morosini glowered. Miss Bentley fluttered her handkerchief as if she might faint from sheer romance. Thornton and Eugenia stood side by side, faces alight with a satisfaction they were doing a valiant job of concealing.

Edward no longer cared who watched.

With no thought for propriety, he drew Venetia into his arms and kissed her—deeply, gratefully, as a man who had finally, unexpectedly, been handed back his future.

Chapter Forty-Eight

EUGENIA GAZED AT the gentle motion of the canal through the tall windows of the water salon, the light shivering across the ceiling in wavering bands. A faint breeze slipped in, bringing with it the cool, damp tang of autumn on the water, and she drew her shawl a little closer about her shoulders.

"Time to return to England, my dear Eugenia?"

She turned, her heart warming at the sight of Thornton framed in the doorway. His coat sat a little more loosely than it had when they'd first arrived in Venice, his hair threaded with more silver, but his eyes were as kind and shrewd as ever. He leaned on the lintel with deceptive casualness, as if he had merely chanced by and was not, in fact, watching her very closely.

"And why would you say that?" she asked.

He crossed the room and held out a hand to her. "Come here."

She rose and let him lead her to the window. "Look there," he said, nodding toward the bustle outside.

Across the canal, a laundry line snapped in the breeze. A gondola slid past, its prow garlanded with late roses; the gondolier began to hum a tune that had been played at the betrothal celebrations.

"Do you remember," Thornton went on softly, "the first time

we saw Venetia and Edward together on that very step? We thought ourselves such wise observers as we plotted their future."

Eugenia's lips curved. "We were very foolish," she said. "And very smug."

"Exactly so. And now our lovebirds have flown the coop, leaving us with nothing to supervise but our dreary selves." He glanced sideways at her. "Our work is done. What, then, keeps us in this city of crumbling splendor?"

Eugenia let her gaze rest on the familiar scene a moment longer. It had been tugging at her for days—that sense of completion and, beneath it, an unexpected hollowness.

"Perhaps you are right," she said at last. "Since that glorious day at the balloon betrothal, everything has changed. Venetia and Edward's hearts joined as one, Sofia and her Paolo vanished into the clouds, like two characters from Sir Walter Scott himself. And the following day, Venetia exonerated. What else is there for us to do?"

She spoke lightly, but something in her chest pinched.

"Exonerated?" Thornton repeated. "My dear, she was not merely exonerated. She was triumphantly vindicated." He ticked the points off on his fingers. "Sofia's public confession, Captain Rizzi forced to admit that appearances can deceive, Griselda stepping forward with the missing emerald pendant and swearing—under Edward's protection—to the truth of the matching emeralds in the secret compartment of the tiara worn by Venetia and loaned to her by Sofia... and let us not forget Count di Montefiore slinking away like a whipped cur once Greene's letters were produced to prove that he had engineered the destruction of her reputation."

Eugenia shuddered delicately. "Yes, well. I shall be perfectly happy never to hear either of those names again."

"Quite so. And now Edward's word is as good as any nobleman's," Thornton added. "The marchese's heir, no less." Thornton's voice gentled. "And yet here you are, responsible for the restoration of Edward's birthright and uniting him with his true love."

Eugenia felt a glow at being so honored. But then, toying with the fringe of her shawl, she sighed. "I suppose my work is done," she said. "To what worthy cause do I now turn my attention? I am in danger of becoming idle. Or worse, redundant."

Thornton's brows drew together as he assumed an expression of exaggerated gravity. "We cannot have that. Let me think." He tapped his chin. "Catherine and Count di Montefiore, perhaps? I begin to suspect they deserve one another."

A laugh burst from her, quite against her will. "A union made in purgatory," she said. "How could I be so cruel? Though Heaven knows both of them displayed a callous disregard for the feelings of others when it suited them." She considered. "Still, perhaps that is reason enough to leave them here to torment one another. Catherine di Montefiore?" She practiced the title with a frown.

"Quite so," Thornton said mildly. "But if you mean to remain here in order to supervise Miss Bentley's moral reform, I must protest. I cannot be banished back to England alone."

"Alone?" Eugenia replied. "You would never be alone when you have your club and your... horses."

"All very worthy companions," he allowed. "But none of them to tell me when I am sorely in need of the truth. None of them to talk me into some absurd wager. And none of them, Eugenia, to laugh with me quite so charmingly as you do."

She felt a ridiculous sting behind her eyes. "Thornton," she said, striving for levity, "are you flirting with me?"

"Good heavens, no," he replied. "I am proposing a joint venture."

She blinked. "A joint venture?"

"In matchmaking," he said. "We have between us quite a record. First there were Sir Frederick and Miss Fairchild. Then Caroline and Henry. Now, Venetia and Edward." He listed off on his fingers their successes over the past three years. "And we can absolutely count Sofia and her Paolo as a bonus."

"You would make a profession of it?" she teased. "Advertise in the news sheets, perhaps? A joint venture—"

She stopped, fearing from the look on his face that she had taken levity too far.

Thornton stepped closer, so close she could see the tiny lines fanning from the corners of his eyes.

"You said the words, and I fully concur, Eugenia. A joint venture sounds just the ticket. I am weary of Venice," he said quietly. "But I am not weary of you. I do not think I ever could be. If you are resolved to return to England, then I shall be at your side. If you wish to haunt Venetian salons for another year and terrify wayward noblemen, I shall happily play the Greek chorus. Only—" His voice roughened. "Do not speak of our 'work' as if it were finished and you and I were to go our separate ways. I find I have grown rather attached to my partner in crime."

Her throat tightened. "Partner in crime?" she repeated.

He took her hand very gently and pressed it to his lips. "And that is only the start of how to describe what you are to me."

She couldn't seem to breathe. "What... else?"

"Everything," he said simply. "Friend. Confidante. Coconspirator. And, if you can find it in that formidable heart of yours to accept me—with my creaking joints and my tendency to lecture—the woman I call my wife."

For a moment, the room blurred. The sensible reply—to tease him, to demand details, to ensure he understood exactly what he was asking—deserted her.

Instead she lifted her free hand and cupped his cheek, feeling the rasp of his evening stubble against her palm. "You foolish, wonderful man," she whispered. "I have been your wife in all but name for years. It will be a relief to at last have the matter settled."

He laughed then, a sound of pure, startled joy, and bent his head.

The kiss was not the headlong, desperate fusion of youth, but something slower and deeper, shaped by shared years and battles fought side by side.

When at last they parted, she rested her forehead against his. "Very well," she said. "We shall return to England together. We will brave the gray skies. And we shall continue our matchmaking—though I warn you, I mean to be very particular about our subjects."

"I should expect nothing less," Thornton replied. "We have a reputation to uphold."

Eugenia slipped her arm through his as they turned back to the canal. Outside, a gondola glided past, its prow lifting over the wake.

"Our lovebirds have flown," she said softly.

"Yes," he agreed, giving her arm a tender squeeze. "But there are still two old birds left to tend the nest."

Side by side, minds spinning with the excitement of future adventures, they watched the Venetian light fade.

THE END

About the Author

Beverley Oakley is an Australian author of more than 30 Regency romps, and Victorian and Georgian-set romances laced with mystery and intrigue.

Under her other pen names—Beverley Eikli and B.G. Nettelton—she writes Africa-set romantic suspense and Women's Fiction.

Born in the African mountain kingdom of Lesotho, Beverley married the handsome Norwegian bush pilot she met in Botswana's beautiful Okavango Delta while managing a safari lodge.

She began her writing career as a journalist, but it was during long aerial survey contracts around the world—typically as the sole woman among the crew—that she in effect launched her romance novels, finding in them an escape from the isolation.

Beverley also adores making historical costumes, knitting, and travelling, usually to Norway to visit her older daughter.

She lives just north of Melbourne with the same wonderful husband she whisked away from Botswana thirty years ago, together with their youngest daughter, and a gorgeous, dopey Rhodesian Ridgeback who weighs more than she does.

When she's not writing, she runs a bed & breakfast & Farm-stay business (called *Wuthering Heights*) in South Australia's beautiful wine growing Clare Valley with her two sisters.

You can visit her websites at:
www.beverleyoakley.com or www.beverleysbooks.com

You can also find her at:
facebook.com/AuthorBeverleyOakley
instagram.com/Beverley.Oakley
TikTok: @beverleyoakley

www.ingramcontent.com/pod-product-compliance
Lightning Source LLC
LaVergne TN
LVHW011928070526
838202LV00054B/4537